MW00616787

CELTIC HEAT

LOVER'S DAWN, MIDNIGHT SINS, RITES OF PASSION

KRISTINA COOK
WRITING AS KRISTI ASTOR

GROSVENOR
STREET PRESS

Copyright © 2009, 2011, 2012, 2020 by Kristina Cook

All rights reserved.

No part of this book may be reproduced in any form or by any electronic or mechanical means, including information storage and retrieval systems, without written permission from the author, except for the use of brief quotations in a book review.

Cover Design by James, GoOnWrite.com

www.grosvenorstreetpress.com

GROSVENOR
STREET PRESS

FOREWORD

Winter's Desire (2009), containing my novella "Lover's Dawn," was the first of three anthologies published by Harlequin Spice that were conceived by and written by me and my dear friends and co-collaborators, Amanda McIntyre and Charlotte Featherstone.

In 2011, we continued the series with the *The Pleasure Garden,* including my novella "Rites of Passion," followed by *Dark Pleasures* in 2012, with my novella "Midnight Sins." All three anthologies were based on Celtic legends tied to the Winter Solstice, Beltane, and Samhain, respectively. Amanda, being the talented poet among us, wrote lovely poems for each volume, and her poems are included in my novellas with her permission.

In this collection, I have republished my three novellas (in a slightly different order) along with bonus new epilogues for each.

I hope you enjoy them!

LOVER'S DAWN

CELTIC HEAT VOL. 1

Copyright © 2009, 2020 by Kristina Cook

All rights reserved.

No part of this book may be reproduced in any form or by any electronic or mechanical means, including information storage and retrieval systems, without written permission from the author, except for the use of brief quotations in a book review.

"Winter's Desire" poem Copyright © 2009 by Amanda McIntyre, used with the author's permission

Cover Design by James, GoOnWrite.com

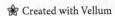 Created with Vellum

CHAPTER 1

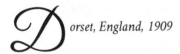 *orset, England, 1909*

"Here," Aisling said, shoving a stack of papers onto Jack's lap as she perched on the sofa's rolled arm beside him.

Pushing his wire-rimmed spectacles up the bridge of his nose, he pulled out a page at random and began to read aloud.

His lips, warm and moist, traveled from the swell of her creamy, rose-tipped breasts down to her stomach. Onward they moved to her navel and then below, tracing slow, wet circles upon her goose-fleshed skin. Her back arched off the settee in wicked anticipation, her entire body quivering with need. At last she felt the tip of his tongue part her, circling the nub of sensitive flesh till she cried out in pleasure...

. . .

"Good God, Aisling! This is positively scandalous! We'll make a fortune with this one."

Aisling arched one brow as she reached for her cigarette case. "Do you really think so? It's not a bit over the top, is it?"

"Of course it is. That's what makes it bloody brilliant." Jack's cheeks reddened. "I'll read the rest later."

"Of course." Aisling fiddled with the jeweled case, deciding that she didn't really want a cigarette, after all.

Jack removed his spectacles and laid them down atop the manuscript. "I don't even want to know where you get your inspiration, Ash," he said, shaking his head. "Honestly, if Mother knew—"

"It's called 'using one's imagination,' dear brother. You should try it sometime. And Mother is never going to know. Unless you tell her, of course."

Jack looked positively outraged. "And why would I do that? Devil take it, Aisling, you're my cash cow."

"I should probably box your ears for such a sexist remark as that." She rolled her eyes heavenward as she stood, smoothing her hands down the front of her skirts. "Anyway, the usual plan. You'll take it to *The Boudoir* when you're in London this week, collect the fee, and deposit half into my account." She sighed loudly, trailing her fingertips over the couch's plush, plum-colored upholstery. "Honestly, I don't know why I give you half. They're *my* stories, after all."

"Yes, but without me, you'd have nothing." He rose, unfolding his impossibly long legs and striding over to his desk where he deposited the manuscript with a *thunk*. "It's not as if you could peddle your stories yourself—they wouldn't let you past the front door of *The Boudoir*'s office. Anyway, just promise me that it *is* your imagination fueling these stories, and nothing more. I'd hate to be forced to defend your honor. You know what a terrible shot I am," he said with a grin.

"Of course it is," Aisling murmured. She wasn't a virgin, not that she'd ever admit that to Jack. But her one sexual experience had been lackluster at best—rushed and hurried, with no attempt made at pleasuring *her* at all. Aisling grimaced, remembering Thomas Esterbrooke's wet, sloppy kisses; his damp palms and unimpressive member as he'd writhed and grunted atop her. She couldn't help but shudder at the memory.

No, her stories were nothing like that. Instead they were full of passion and longing, of expert lovemaking and deeply felt emotions—all things twenty-three-year-old Aisling Wainscott had never once experienced in all her life.

God, but she was bored. Sick of Dorset, sick of Bedlington and everyone who lived there. Sometimes Aisling thought she'd go mad with boredom, if not for her pen and the escape her imagination provided.

"I suppose I should get back to the books," Jack said, a tinge of regret in his voice. "Don't forget that I've invited guests to join us tonight for dinner."

"Oh?"

"Yes, some friends of mine are in the area, visiting family. Roger and Edmund Dalton, you remember them? We went up to Eton together."

"Vaguely," Aisling said with a shrug.

"I thought we'd play cards later," he continued, "so I've invited Will Cooper—you know, to even out the numbers. He's in Bedlington for a fortnight, spending Christmas with his mum."

Aisling couldn't help but groan. "Not Will Cooper!"

Jack's blond brows drew together. "What do you have against Will, the poor chap? It's not his fault that his mother is a washerwoman. Besides, everyone knows his father was a gentleman."

"Yes, but *which* gentleman?" She shook her head. "Anyway,

something about the way Will looks at me makes me uncomfortable."

"But you haven't seen him in years, not since he went up to Cambridge."

"It was all well and good to be friends with him when we were children, but now? Educated or not, he's still, well...not exactly our sort, is he?"

"Why, you little hypocrite," Jack accused, though he smiled delightedly. "Who would have thought that you, of all people, would be such a snob? All for the voting rights of women, even common women, yet you think the son of a washerwoman isn't 'our sort'."

Aisling scowled at her brother. "He watches me when he thinks I'm not looking, and he's far too full of himself, besides."

"It's true, then," Jack crowed. "You *are* a snob."

"Do shut up." She headed for the door. One hand on the brass handle, she turned back toward her brother. "Better a snob than a pompous ass like you."

"You shouldn't swear, Ash. It isn't at all becoming."

"Oh, go fuck yourself," she called out, tossing her hair over her shoulder as she let herself out.

She could still hear him sputtering in indignation as the door swung shut. As she headed toward the stairs, she passed a long, gilt-framed mirror and winked at her reflection in smug satisfaction. It was far too easy to one-up her brother.

Minutes later, she'd retrieved her gloves and coat and hurried through the foyer, past the enormous Christmas tree that was decorated with red bows and colorful blown glass, its small electric lights just waiting to be lit. Mother loved Christmastime and left no hall undecked, no mantel undecorated.

But for Aisling, Christmas simply marked another year's passing, each one no different from the one before it. There'd been no Eton for Aisling, no years at university like Jack had enjoyed. Just season after season, year after year there in Dorset, with only brief jaunts to London to relieve the monotony. Brief because Father had Mrs. Gaylord in London, of course, and how he hated his wife and family intruding on his time with his mistress.

Aisling let herself out the back door and skimmed down the stairs, buttoning up her coat. It had grown colder, and her breath made puffs of smoke in the wintry air as she hurried away from the house, toward the graveled path that led toward the now-frozen swimming pond and beyond.

I'll never be like Mother, she silently vowed. Someday, Aisling would be free. Exactly what that meant, she wasn't certain. Just that she wouldn't necessarily be dependent on a man, particularly one who didn't put her needs equal to his own; who would leave his wife and children rotting away in the country while he lived it up in town.

Shaking her head in frustration, she picked up her pace, veering off the path and through the copse of trees, toward the circle of standing stones in the distance. It was her favorite spot, just beyond the eastern border of Wainscott House's property, in a shady little clearing. In the summer months, she would sit with her back against the largest of the stones and write. The almost-mystical atmosphere seemed to fuel her creativity, and she'd written some of her best work there. She liked to think of the stone circle as hers—her own private retreat, her refuge.

But now, as Aisling stepped out of the tree's shadows and into the clearing, she saw a lone figure in a cloak standing there, watching her approach. The hood's folds shadowed the intruder's face, concealing the features, yet Aisling felt sure that the figure was a woman's. Dark, unbound hair escaped the stranger's hood, dancing on the breeze that caused the heavy woolen folds of Aisling's coat to flap noisily against her limbs. Icy snow began to swirl about, stinging Aisling's face.

At once the sun began to dip beneath the horizon, casting an eerie red glow on the tallest stone. In the blink of an eye, the blood-red light moved across the stones like a serpent, undulating around the circle once before melting away on the snow-dusted ground, leaving nothing but a grayish-lavender twilight behind.

It's the winter solstice, Aisling realized with a start, a shiver working its way down her spine.

Her eyes scanned the circle—once, twice, searching for the strange, cloaked woman. Nothing. "Miss?" she called out, then tried again, louder this time. "Miss? Are you there?"

The woman was gone. Vanished, in what had been no more than a heartbeat's time. Aisling dashed into the center of the circle, noticing that the wind had grown quiet—in fact, everything was quiet now, as silent as a tomb. Snow continued to fall softly, silently, making the ground at Aisling's feet look as if a carpet of glittering crystals covered it.

A queer feeling rushed over her, raising gooseflesh on her skin. It seemed as if the stones themselves were holding their breath, watching, waiting...

And then she saw it, there atop the tallest of the stones. Something that wasn't there before—something that didn't belong. A box. Aisling's feet seemed to move involuntarily, taking her closer. Before she knew it, the box was in her hands and she was staring down at it, her heart thumping noisily against her ribs.

Swallowing hard, she ran her fingertips over the lid, brushing away the dusting of snow to reveal an unfamiliar symbol—Celtic, perhaps—etched into the wood. She took a deep, fortifying breath, allowing the cold air to fill her lungs as she summoned the courage to lift the lid and see what lay inside.

A bone-and-leather fastening held it closed, and it took a bit of work to unfasten it, especially with fingers that trembled as hers did. She had to remove one glove, exposing her fingers to the chilled air. At last she accomplished the task and slowly raised the lid, holding her breath in anticipation.

Don't be so dramatic, she chastised herself as she peered inside. *It's only a box, for God's sake, with nothing inside but a folded slip of paper.* She almost laughed aloud at her own ridiculousness as she set the box on the ground by her feet and unfolded the page. On what appeared to be a very old piece of parchment—fragile and worn with age—were lines of neat, precise script, looking much like a poem.

HOPE REBORN, come with the sun
dispel the chill of darkness
bright fire of dawn
reach to our hearts
burn bright of winter's desire

ENCHANTED stream of brilliant light
amid the crystal ground
dark traverse blending of the night
bring sweet lover's kiss
burn bright of winter's desire.

NO WANDERER'S curse
be he thus beckoned
a slave to passion's fire
return his head, upon my breast

burn bright of winter's desire.

AISLING HADN'T REALIZED she'd read it aloud until the last word spoken echoed off the stones, reverberating back to where she stood. Such beautiful words! *Winter's desire.* But whatever did it mean?

And then her heart swelled with it—her *own* winter's desire, a wish held so close to her heart that she'd never before acknowledged its existence.

I wish for someone to awaken my cold, frozen heart; to make me feel things I've never felt before, to make me experience longing and desire, passion and love, hurt and hate, all at once. I wish for a man who appreciates words as I do, an educated man—an artist, perhaps—whose hands are strong and rough and calloused; a man who will worship me, yet treat me as an equal.

A painful lump formed in her throat as she realized exactly what she'd wished for—the impossible. A man who did not exist. What a fool she was, hoping for things she could never have, feelings she'd never experience. All these years she'd convinced herself she was satisfied with her choices, trapped as she was between her own ideals and society's dictates. But now she'd allowed doubts to creep into her consciousness, upsetting her entire sense of self, and all because of a silly, ridiculous poem.

Stuff and nonsense, she told herself as she briskly refolded the slip of paper and shoved it back inside the box, then refastened the lid. Tucking the box beneath her arm, she headed toward Wainscott House without a backward glance, refusing to let herself think about what had just happened there in the circle of stones.

Instead she concentrated on getting home before darkness fell.

CHAPTER 2

For perhaps the tenth time in so many minutes, Aisling furtively glanced at the man seated across the table from her, and then dropped her gaze as quickly as she'd raised it. Heat flooded her cheeks, no doubt staining them red as she twisted the napkin in her lap. Whatever was the matter with her?

It's just Will Cooper, she told herself angrily. And yet it wasn't Will; at least, not the Will she remembered. No, the Will Cooper she remembered was slight, not much taller than she was. His face was pale, rather unremarkable, his eyes a shade she could not recall.

Whereas this Will was tall—not quite six feet, she'd guess, but close to it. His shoulders were broad, his skin browned, his eyes a startling shade of blue. She watched as he lifted his glass to his lips, her gaze inexplicably drawn to his hand, a hand that appeared strong, calloused, and entirely masculine. Just imagining those hands on her body made her tremble, made her thighs clench together.

"So, Mr. Cooper," she heard her mother ask, "when must you return to Cambridge?"

"Just after the New Year, ma'am," he answered.

Cambridge? What was he doing at Cambridge? By her own calculation, he should have left university long ago. He was a year her senior—the same age as Jack.

Jack turned toward the elder Dalton brother—Edmund, perhaps?—who was seated to his right. "Cooper here has a position at the Botanic Garden at Cambridge," he clarified.

"Of course, a botanist." Aisling hadn't realized she'd spoken the words aloud till all eyes turned toward her. "I...that is to say, you *did* study botany at university, didn't you?"

Will's gaze met hers. "Indeed. I was lucky to find a post there once I finished my studies. Have you seen the Botanic Garden's new glasshouse?"

Aisling shook her head, feeling slightly breathless. "No, I...I don't believe I've been to Cambridge in quite some time."

"Well, we must rectify that at once, mustn't we? Jack, surely you can spare the time to accompany Aisling and Mrs. Wainscott up to Cambridge, can't you? The winter gardens are spectacular."

Jack grunted noncommittally as he took a sip of sweet, mulled wine.

Mother folded her napkin and set it on the table beside her plate of uneaten sweets. "So, Mr. Cooper, what exactly is it that you do there at the Garden?" she asked.

"I mostly catalog the species. Draw them, label them." He shrugged, an easy smile on his lips. "Though I don't mind getting my hands dirty now and then, either."

"Why, that sounds like fascinating work," Mother replied. "Your mother is so proud, you know. It's lovely to hear her speak of you. I saw her just yesterday, you know, when I picked up some mending." She then turned her attention back to the Dalton brothers. "So, Mr. Dalton—Roger, is it?

Do you spend all your time in London, or have you taken a property in the country, too?"

As the topic of conversation shifted, Aisling continued to stare across the width of the table, wondering how Will had grown so handsome without her noticing it. Perhaps it was the lines around his eyes that crinkled when he smiled that made his face so intriguing. Or was it the hint of a beard that shadowed his face, making his jaw appear so strong, so defined?

She shook her head, hoping to clear it, hoping to distract herself from such troubling thoughts so that she could concentrate on their other guests, instead.

As the dinner conversation buzzed on around him, Will continued to watch Aisling, wondering, as he always did, just what was going on in her mind. It was a sharp mind; of that he was certain. But beyond that, she was mostly a mystery to him. They'd been playmates as children—friends, even. But as they'd grown older, she'd become cold, distant. An ice queen, if ever there was one. The last time he'd seen her, she'd mostly just ignored him.

And yet, inexplicably, she was not ignoring him tonight. In fact, he'd felt her eyes on him since the moment they'd sat down to dinner. Aisling had breezed in, smelling of violets, wearing a wispy, pale rose-colored gown that fluttered behind her like gossamer wings. She'd kissed her mother on the cheek while apologizing for her tardiness, and then taken her seat at the long table, directly across from him.

It was only when she'd raised her goblet to her lips that she'd seemed to notice his presence. She'd looked startled, almost astonished, and he could not credit why. Surely Jack had told her he was joining them tonight. Hell, even if Jack hadn't, his appearance there at the Wainscott's dining table was a common enough occurrence. Yet Aisling's apparent discomfiture hadn't lessened throughout the interminable meal—five full courses in all.

In all the years he'd known her, he'd never seen her so discomposed. It was disconcerting, and yet somehow arousing if his cockstand was any indication. It would prove embarrassing as hell if he couldn't rein it in before they finished with dessert.

"I say, Cooper, you've not listened to a word I've said, have you?" Jack asked, shaking his head.

"I'm sorry?" he asked distractedly. Aisling had taken a bite of pastry and a dollop of chocolate cream remained on the plump center of her lower lip. His pulse began to race as her tongue darted out, licking it away. Good God, that mouth of hers...a perfect, pink bow, just begging to be kissed. And that tongue...just imagining how she could use it, how—

"Bloody hell, Cooper, snap out of it." Jack tossed his napkin to his lap. "If you'll pardon my language, Mother."

"Might I remind you that there's another lady present besides Mother," Aisling said sweetly. "Honestly, Jack, have you no manners at all?"

Mrs. Wainscott arched a brow in censure, though the woman could not entirely conceal her smile. "Indeed," she murmured.

"Indeed?" Jack sputtered. "Why, Aisling curses more than I do, the hoyden."

"Fascinating," the elder Dalton said with a leer that made Will's skin crawl. "A gently bred lady who curses?"

Aisling just shrugged. "I only do it to get under my dear brother's skin. He's just ill-tempered because my curses are far more original than his own. I'd be happy to demonstrate—"

"You most certainly will not," Mrs. Wainscott interjected, shaking her head. "Honestly, it's as if I've raised a pair of hunting hounds."

The younger Dalton grinned. "I beg to differ, ma'am. Your daughter is quite the original. A breath of fresh air, if I might venture to say so."

Which meant he wanted to fuck her, Will realized, balling his hands into fists.

Jack looked entirely unruffled. "Suffice it to say that my sister has no equal."

"I'll take that as a compliment, thank you very much." Smiling brightly, Aisling rose from her seat and moved to stand behind Mrs. Wainscott. "I think I'll leave you gentlemen to your after-dinner smoke. Mother?"

The woman nodded. "Of course, dear."

"Sure you won't join us, Miss Wainscott?" one of the Daltons called out, sounding slightly drunk.

"Quite," came Aisling's reply. Her skirt's lace-trimmed hem had caught on a chair's leg, exposing a good four inches of her stocking-clad ankle. And what a well-turned ankle it was, Will realized with a start. Delicate. Gently curved.

Slowly he slid his admiring gaze up her body, to her face, and he could have sworn he saw her shiver in response, as if she'd physically felt his appraisal. Their eyes met, her hazel ones blinking rapidly, her blond brows knitted in what look like confusion.

With a silent curse of frustration, he pushed aside his napkin and rose. For the briefest of moments, he considered offering to escort her out, but decided it best to ignore whatever impulse was tempting him to do so. After all, no good would come of it.

For what felt like an hour but was likely only a fraction of a minute, they both stood, watching one another in silence. And then, just like that, the spell was broken. She shook her head, reaching a hand to her temple, her fingers trembling.

"Aisling? Dear?" Mrs. Wainscott reached for her daughter's arm.

Aisling threaded her arm through Mrs. Wainscott's. "If you'll excuse us," she said with a nod. Moving in perfect unison, the pair made their way out.

Will held his breath, mentally willing Aisling to turn around, to glance back just once before departing. Why, he could not say. But when she did just that, glancing back over one finely shaped shoulder, his breath caught in his throat and he stood there gaping like a stupid ox. *She's beautiful*, he realized. How had he never before noticed it? He'd always thought her looks to be rather ordinary, her features too sharp, perhaps. But now...now he realized just how extraordinary her hazel eyes were, how her wheat-colored hair was threaded with pale gold strands that sparkled under the electric lights. The urge to follow her out was overwhelming, and he literally had to grip the back of the chair to keep himself from doing exactly that.

Jack tossed his cigarette case to the table. "Good God, Cooper, you look like the devil. Whatever's the matter with you?"

"I'm not entirely sure," he answered, slumping back in his seat. Exhaling slowly, he raked a hand through his hair. "Perhaps I'm taking a fever." *Or a complete leave of my senses.* What the hell had come over him?

"Well, you can't go now, old boy. You'll leave us one hand short, and then what'll we do?" Jack frowned, tapping the end of one cigarette against his palm. "Though I suppose I could ask Mother to join us. God knows she loves to play. Go on, then, if you must."

"I think I will." He stood, nodding toward the two Dalton brothers. "If you'll excuse me, gentleman. It was a pleasure."

"Yes, likewise," they muttered in unison.

"Wait, Cooper," Jack called out. "Before you leave, I've got that novel you insisted I read in my office. Take it home with you, if you like. I vow, I couldn't get through the damn thing. You really like that rubbish?"

"Very much," he bit out.

"Well, to each his own, I say. Anyway, it's on my desk somewhere. Dig around and I'm sure you'll find it." He dismissed him with a wave of one hand toward the door.

"What about your sister? Won't she play?" one of the Daltons asked as Will made his hasty retreat, not awaiting Jack's reply.

Not if I find her first.

He entered Jack's study and headed for the desk, his mind awhirl in thought. He had to see her again. Tonight. But how? She'd likely retired to her own room, and it wasn't as if he could just saunter up to the family's private quarters and knock on doors till he found her.

He grunted in frustration; Jack's desk was a mess, books piled high on the blotter, papers scattered everywhere. Where was the frigging book? He needed to find it, and fast.

In his haste, he knocked a stack of papers to the floor. He bent down to pick them up, cursing as he did so. They were handwritten, numbered pages, and scattered all out of order, damn it. He reached for a page, his brows knitting in surprise as the words written in flowing script swam into focus.

What the hell was this? Overwhelmed with curiosity, he squinted, attempting to make out the words in the dim light.

"On your knees," he commanded, and she obeyed, sinking to the floor, her fingers wrapped around the length of him. Her shell-pink tongue darted out, skating across the sensitive tip. "Touch yourself,"

came his next command, his voice hoarse now. "Pleasure yourself
while you pleasure me."

GOOD GOD! It was some sort of erotica. Handwritten, which
was all the more puzzling. What the devil was this doing on
Jack's desk, right out in the open for anyone to find? And
more importantly, who had written it? He would almost
swear that the writing looked like...like a woman's hand.

"What are you doing with my manuscript?" came a voice
beside him, startling him so badly that he dropped what
papers he'd already retrieved back to the floor at his feet.

Aisling. Looking both fierce and terrified all at once.

"Your *what*?" he asked, his voice rising as her words began
to register in his muddled brain.

HER HEART THUMPING MADLY against her ribs, Aisling
snatched the pages from Will's hands. How could Jack have
been so careless? "Stupid fool," she muttered, "leaving them
lying around like this. I swear I'm going to throttle him." She
hurried to the door and pushed it closed, turning the key in
the lock before striding purposefully back toward the desk
where Will stood as still as a statue, looking as if he'd just
received a terrible shock.

"You...you wrote this?" he sputtered.

"No, of course not," she lied. "How much did you read?"

He shook his head. "Only a few lines. But...but you *did*
write it, didn't you? You called it *your* manuscript."

"Well, what if I did?" she snapped, stooping down to
retrieve the rest. "You needn't look so shocked." Good heavens, what now? What if he told her mother? If word got out,
she'd be ruined. Her mind cast about frantically, searching

for a solution, searching for something she could say to protect her secret—to protect *herself.*

"Here, let me help you," Will said, stooping down beside her.

"I'll thank you not to make more of a mess than you already have, you clumsy oaf," she snapped, then instantly regretted it. It wasn't Will she was furious with, it was Jack. Stupid, stupid Jack.

"Hand me those and I'll attempt to put them back in order," Will offered, mercifully ignoring her insult. Their eyes met, and he smiled—a warm, reassuring smile. Something passed unspoken between them, and Aisling nodded in reply, relief flooding her veins.

She stood with a sigh, pressing a messy sheaf into his hands. "Thank you. Truly, I'm going to kill my brother. He's so damnably careless. What if Mother had found it instead of you? Or one of the housemaids? I must have your promise—"

"You have my word, Aisling." His gaze traveled back to the stack of papers in his hands, and he began to flip through them, putting them back in order. "But devil take it, there's so many pages here. What were you planning to do with it?"

"Jack sells them in London—my stories. Have you heard of the publication *The Boudoir*?"

"Of course," he said with a shrug. "What red-blooded male hasn't?"

Aisling couldn't help but smile at his candor. "They've published five of my stories so far. Serialized them. They fetch a fair price, too."

"Surely not under your own name—"

"Bloody hell, of course not. Here, give me that." She snatched the stack of pages from his hands and hugged them protectively to her breast. "They wouldn't even consider them if they knew they were written by a woman. I use a pen name."

"But, good God, how do you even know—" He stopped short. "Never mind. It's not my business."

She realized at once the direction his thoughts had taken. "Are you asking me if I'm a virgin, Will Cooper? I should order you out of my house for such impertinence." She tossed the stack of papers to Jack's desk.

"I apologize," was all he said in reply. Shoving his hands into his pockets, he continued to watch her with that same curious stare—the one that, in the past, had made her so uncomfortable.

Only now...now it made her pulse leap, made her skin warm, made gooseflesh rise on her skin. There was something so open, so honest, so entirely lacking of artifice in his countenance. Her chest rose and fell several times as she stared back, finding herself lost in his heated gaze, wanting to tell him the truth—wanting *someone* to know the real Aisling Wainscott.

"I'm not a virgin," she said at last, tipping her chin in the air defiantly. "What do you say to that?"

"I say that you are perhaps the most perplexing woman I've ever known," he said simply. "And also the most fascinating."

Aisling shook her head, her breath coming far too fast. "I suppose I've been called worse."

He ran a hand through his hair, further mussing the deep brown waves that fell carelessly over his forehead. "It was meant to be a compliment. I've more, if you'd like to hear them."

All rational thought flew out of her mind. She wanted him; there was no point in denying it. Her brother and his friends were in the parlor, playing cards. Mother had joined them. It would be hours before they quit their game, before anyone came looking for her.

She took two steps toward him, wanting more than

anything to give in to this unfamiliar longing, this newfound hunger running through her, drawing her toward this man like nothing had ever drawn her before.

"Kiss me, Will Cooper," she said, before she had a chance to reconsider.

CHAPTER 3

*W*ill wasted no time in complying. In three strides he had her in his arms, his mouth crushing hers. Aisling's hands slid up Will's back to his neck, her fingers tangling in his hair as she drew him closer, her breasts pressed flat against his coat.

With a low moan of satisfaction, she opened her mouth against his. His tongue, warm and alive, skated along her lower lip, sending a ripple of shivers down her spine. He tasted of wine, smelled of soap, a hint of tobacco. Heat coiled in her belly, radiating down toward her thighs, dampening them with need.

"I shouldn't," Will murmured, his mouth retreating from hers.

"Nor I," Aisling answered, but her lips sought his once more, her hands now clasping the lapels of his coat, dragging his mouth back to her hungry one.

She gasped as he lifted her off her feet, carrying her back toward the desk, his mouth never once leaving hers as he deposited her onto the desk's smooth edge, knocking piles of books and papers to the floor in the process.

Their hands were seemingly everywhere at once—frantic hands, unbuttoning his coat, tugging at her bodice's neckline, pulling his shirttails from the band of his trousers. A button fell to the carpet, but Aisling couldn't say whose it was, or where it had come from.

She struggled to keep her balance on the edge of the desk while attempting to raise her skirts, to free her limbs so that she could spread her knees, allowing him to press himself between her thighs.

As if Will sensed her intention, he lifted her, scooping up her skirts and gathering them about her waist as he set her back down on the hard, cool surface with nothing between her bottom and the desk's surface but her thin cotton drawers.

Tugging on his shirttails, Aisling drew him back toward her till she felt the firm pressure of his erection pressed against her drawers, teasing the sensitive nub of flesh between her slick, wet folds.

Her entire body trembling with desire, she looked over Will's shoulder and eyed the closed door, knowing that, at any moment, someone could try to open it. That thought alone should have deterred her, should have forced her to flee. Instead, her pulse quickened, her heart thumping against her ribs in rhythm to Will's, their breath mingling.

Quickly, her mind screamed, urging her on. Without another thought, Aisling reached for his trousers' fastenings, her fingers clumsy as she hurried to free his cock. In seconds she held him in her bare hand, running the pads of her fingertips over the velvety-smooth surface. Wrapping her fingers around the shaft, she stroked the length of him, up and down, marveling at the contradictory sensations— smooth yet hard, soft yet corded. As she continued to explore every inch of him, she felt him grow harder, heard his breath come faster, his eyes growing heavy-lidded.

With a low groan, he reached for her delicate, lace-trimmed drawers, very nearly tearing them as he roughly shoved them down. Aisling wriggled her hips, pushing them lower, past her knees, till they dropped to the floor beside her slippers.

"Now," she whispered, unable to stand the ache, the need, that grew and intensified with every breath she took. "Hurry."

Will met her gaze and nodded, his pale, piercing eyes never straying from her face as the tip of his cock prodded her entrance. In one sharp motion, he buried his entire length inside her.

Aisling gasped with pleasure, wrapping her legs around his waist. Slowly, sensuously, he withdrew, then thrust back inside her, his eyes still holding hers captive, his hands on both sides of her face. His thumbs stroked her cheeks as they found a rhythm, their bodies moving in perfect unison.

His movements were slow, determined, almost willful. She bit her lip, trying not to cry out, trying not to beg him to go faster, harder. Aisling felt herself grow wetter, slicker with each thrust, her hips bucking to meet his, her need growing more and more persistent, more tightly coiled by the second.

And then with one last thrust, she found the release she sought. Her quim tightened, pulsing against his deeply buried cock just as she felt his hot seed pump into her. For a moment her mind emptied of everything but the exquisite sensation, the oblivion she felt as wave after wave of sweet pleasure washed over her.

Neither spoke for a full minute as they fought to catch their breath. Aisling buried her face in his neck, breathing in his scent as her racing heart finally slowed its frenetic pace. At last she sat upright, taking two deep, calming breaths.

"You're bleeding," Will said, reaching up to brush her lower lip with the pad of his thumb. Aisling glanced down, surprised to see the crimson-red smudge there, marring his skin.

She shook her head, hoping to clear it. "I bit my lip." It hurt now, a vague, throbbing pain.

He bent toward her, his lips finding hers, his tongue gently sweeping across the tender spot. "There," he said, his voice soft. "Is that better?"

She could only nod in reply.

He smiled then, a slow, lazy smile that only made her heart accelerate again.

"What have we done?" she asked, shivering as his cock slipped from inside her, leaving her damp, cold—empty.

He reached down to pull up his trousers, fastening them with precise, confident motions. "Do you regret it? Here," he said, plucking her drawers from the carpet at his feet.

Aisling slid off the edge of the desk, her legs unsteady and weak as her feet found the ground. She took her drawers and wadded them into a ball, still considering his question.

Did she regret it? This...this wonderful feeling she now felt in her heart, the way her blood raced through her veins, warming her skin?

It had been lovely. Wondrous and entirely pleasurable. Nothing like her ill-considered coupling with Esterbrooke—nothing at all. That had been about satisfying her curiosity, nothing more. This had been about satisfying *her*. And it had. Entirely.

"No," she said decisively. "I don't regret it. Not a bit. Do you?"

He shook his head. "I've never wanted anything more in my life. I cannot explain it, but from the moment I saw you tonight, I could think of nothing else."

"I...I felt the same," Aisling agreed with a nod. "From the moment I sat down and saw you there. It's like...like I was seeing you with entirely new eyes."

"Almost like a spell, isn't it?" Will said with a chuckle.

And then it hit her, like a dousing of cold water. The poem! *Her winter's desire.* She'd read the poem, there in the circle of stones, and made that ridiculous wish. And now...now...

But that's nonsense. There's no such thing as spells, she told herself.

"When can I see you again?"

Drawn from her musings, Aisling looked up at Will, surprised by the earnest expression she saw there on his face. "See me again? But how? I mean, what will we tell everyone?"

"We needn't tell anyone anything. Jack said he's leaving for London tomorrow. There must be some way—"

"Of course! Tomorrow my mother has an appointment at the draper's in the village. She always pays a call on Mrs. Brandon afterward, and usually ends up staying for tea. She'll be gone by half past eleven, I'd say, and won't return till sundown."

"Yes, but the servants," he said, straightening his necktie. "It's not as if I can simply waltz in and—"

"Of course not. Damnation!" Aisling shook her head. "What I wouldn't give to have the freedoms a man has."

"There must be somewhere here on the grounds, somewhere we can—"

"The old gatekeeper's lodge," she interrupted. "It's not the finest of places, but it's furnished, and there's a small stove for heat. We keep it clean and the linens fresh for guests' servants, just in case. I think Mrs. Weston's son stays there from time to time. Anyway, it's empty now."

"Are you sure?" Will asked, reaching for her hand and clasping it tightly in his. She felt the calluses that marked his hands as working hands—and yet, strangely enough, she didn't care, didn't care that Will's mother was a washerwoman, that no one knew exactly who his father was. All those things were suddenly inconsequential.

She nodded. "Yes, I'm sure. At noon, then? I'll bring us a picnic lunch, if you'll bring a scuttle of coal."

"Very well. Noon, then. I'm already counting down the minutes."

"Who knew you were such a romantic?" she said with a laugh.

"I could say the same of you."

"Oh, I'm not a romantic. Not in the least." At least, she never had been before.

"We'll see about that," he said, sounding like the cocky, self-assured Will she remembered.

"See if you can melt the Ice Queen, is that it, then?" she teased.

His face reddened like a schoolboy's. "How did you—"

"Oh, I won't hold it against you," she teased. Jack had told her, of course. "But you should go. Truly, before we're caught."

He nodded, running his fingers through his hair. "Do I look at least moderately presentable?"

Aisling grinned. "No, you look as if you've just had quite the tumble."

"Well, they're much more likely to assume it was one of your maids I was tumbling than you."

"I suppose I can take comfort in that. Now go." She tipped her head toward the door.

He nodded, then leaned in to press his lips to hers once more. "Till tomorrow," he whispered against her mouth, drawing gooseflesh across her skin.

"Tomorrow, then," she murmured.

An hour later, Aisling sat at her typewriter, her hand-written manuscript beside it on the desk. She preferred to write in longhand, but the story had to be typed for submission and Jack was leaving for London on the morn. She took a deep breath, willing herself to concentrate, but her focus was drawn instead to the strange wooden box with the Celtic symbol sitting there on her desk beside the typewriter.

Warily, she reached for the box and removed the folded slip of parchment and smoothed it straight, her hands trembling ever-so-slightly as she did so. Wherever had it come from? And how did it find its way to the circle of standing stones?

She read the poem once more, silently this time, her lips moving as her eyes skimmed the words. What exactly had she wished for when she'd read it aloud, there in the circle? She forced herself to remember her exact thoughts, to examine them thoroughly.

A man who would make her feel things she'd never before felt. Like she had just now, with Will. *An educated man, an artist, perhaps*—and wasn't Will both? A botanist, with a university education. He catalogued plant species, drew them, he'd said. *Rough, calloused hands*—just like the hands that had held her face captive while Will had made love to her in her brother's study. *A man who would worship her, yet treat her as his equal.* Would he? Only time would tell. Whatever fire had been stoked between them today would not be doused so easily.

But the poem...her wish. She shook her head. It was a coincidence, she told herself as she folded the age-worn page and placed it back inside the box. It had to be a coincidence. There was no other reasonable explanation, and Aisling was nothing if not a woman of reason.

She could have sworn she felt a tear slip from the corner of one eye, which was nonsense, of course. Aisling never cried. *Never.* And yet, when she reached up to brush her cheek with the back of one hand, she found it strangely wet.

With a small groan of frustration, she set the wooden box on the floor at her feet, out of her sight. She turned up the lamp and settled back against her chair's plump cushion, wondering if, perhaps, she was on the verge of a crying jag. She'd always thought she might enjoy one. Still, no matter how hard she'd tried in the past, she'd never been able to summon even a single tear.

Perhaps it was just the solstice, working some strange magic on her mind. Or perhaps she was just exhausted. Either way, everything felt somehow different, as if she'd stepped into someone else's skin and was now seeing the world through their eyes instead of her own. And yet, oddly enough, it was a pleasurable sensation.

Indeed, she could not deny the frisson of excitement that shot through her veins when she thought about meeting Will tomorrow at the gatekeeper's cottage. Will Cooper, of all people!

She shook her head, willing herself to focus on her manuscript, instead—it had to be typed, and tonight, if she wanted another neat little sum deposited into her account by the week's end. Nodding to herself, she began to type, quickly losing herself in the story. Every kiss, every touch she described became Will's, every wicked sensation her own.

CHAPTER 4

*W*ill checked the time once more, then dropped his heavy watch back into his pocket. Five minutes till twelve. He paused, setting down the scuttle of coal as he looked toward the gatekeeper's cottage up ahead. He did not want to appear too eager—or too nonchalant. In fact, he wasn't quite sure how to proceed where Aisling was concerned. He had no experience with women like her, after all.

But then again, Aisling was a thing unto herself, in no way representative of women of her class. The gently bred ladies of his limited acquaintance were not nearly as outspoken, as confident or independent-minded as Aisling was. They neither cursed nor smoked nor secretly published erotic stories, as far as he knew.

And while he had no first-hand experience in such matters, he could only assume that well-bred, unmarried ladies did not generally go around fucking their brother's childhood chum while said brother played cards with his guests a few doors down.

He had no idea what to expect from her today—or, for

that matter, what she expected from him. He'd come prepared, with a packet of French letters in his pocket. He was leaving nothing to chance this time. Last night he'd been caught up in the moment, careless. But today…today would be different.

Feeling restless, he checked his watch once more. Only two minutes had passed, but he could wait no longer. He picked up the coal and made his way across the bare winter-scape to the cottage door. It was unlocked, and several minutes later he had doffed his overcoat and lit the stove, which now belched out sooty heat in the room's far corner. Smiling in satisfaction, he rose, dusting off his hands. As he did so, he heard the door creak open behind him, followed by the faint whistle of the wind, and then the door slammed shut with a bang.

"You're here," she said, sounding surprised.

He turned to find her there by the door, wrapped up in a heavy, woolen cloak, a basket clutched in front of her. Her cheeks were pink, her eyes bright and full of mischief.

"You look like Red Riding Hood," he said with a smile. "Only in black, of course."

"I certainly hope you aren't the Big Bad Wolf," she replied, setting the basket down by her feet and pulling back her cloak's hood.

"Did you know," he began, taking two tentative steps toward her, "that Red Riding Hood has been seen as a parable of sexual awakening?"

"Really? Quite fitting, then, that you made the comparison, all things considered."

"Are you trying to shock me, Miss Wainscott?" he teased, feeling immediately at ease in her presence.

She reached up to untie the cloak's fastenings at her throat. "Perhaps. It *is* what I'm best at. Shocking people, I mean. At least my mother would say so."

"Well, I suppose I'm of a hardier constitution, because it will take more than that to shock me. Much more."

"Well, we've got all day, haven't we?" she asked with a shrug.

All day. Will let that phrase sink in, thinking just what could be accomplished in a single afternoon. First, he would undress her. Slowly, sensuously, revealing her form inch by tantalizing inch. This time he could afford to pay attention to her breasts, to taste her, to savor her. He could picture her now, sprawled naked on the narrow bed there across from the stove, her legs spread while he feasted—

"I see you've got the stove lit," she said, effectively ending his lustful imaginings. She turned in a slow circle, surveying the room they stood in. "It's not so bad, is it? It's clean, and there are blankets in the cupboard." She pointed to a door opposite the stove.

"It's cozy," Will answered with a nod. "I'm glad you came."

She arched one dark, delicate brow. "Why wouldn't I?"

He shook his head. "I don't know. I suppose I figured that once you'd given it more thought, you might reconsider. After all, we've never been what you might call friends, have we? At least, not since we were children."

Aisling smiled as she shrugged out of the cloak, revealing a simple bottle-green skirt and white blouse underneath, a black kidskin belt around her waist. "You always looked at me queerly," she said, hanging her cloak on a hook by the door.

"I was always trying to figure you out," he said, stroking his chin.

She peeled off her gloves and laid them on a spindly wooden chair. "And did you?"

"Not in the least. You're quite the enigma, you know."

"I've brought a luncheon basket," she said, deftly changing the subject. "Are you hungry?"

"A bit. How was your walk over? Pleasant, I hope."

"Quite so. I'm fond of outdoor exercise. I try and take a daily turn about the grounds, regardless of the weather."

"Very good. Would you like to sit?" He gestured toward the wooden trestle table beside the stove.

"Thank you, I would." She bent to retrieve the basket.

"No, let me," Will said, hurrying to take it from her.

"Goodness, Will, how long must this go on? This polite chit-chat, I mean. We've known each other in the most intimate fashion, and yet here we are, acting like complete strangers. I suppose next we'll discuss the weather."

"I can't help but feel that I didn't quite court you before… well, before I took advantage of—"

"You didn't take advantage of me, Will Cooper," she snapped. "I'm perfectly capable of making my own decisions where men are concerned, and I wouldn't have let you in my drawers if I hadn't wanted you there. I told you I wasn't a virgin, and I can only assume that neither were you."

He nodded. "You assume correctly."

"Then what harm is there in two consenting, experienced adults taking pleasure in one another?"

Good God, just how experienced *was* she? For a moment, he wondered if he was simply a pawn in some game she played with men. "Is that all it was to you, Aisling? Because I must confess that I'm finding myself conflicted about it. I'm not certain I feel comfortable considering you nothing but an easy fuck." He wanted to shock *her* this time, but her indifferent expression proved him unsuccessful. "It was more than that, and you know it. But I'd like to get to know you better, before I ravish you again. If you don't mind, that is."

He could have sworn he saw a tear there, fluttering on her lashes, but she quickly blinked it away.

"Do you like ham?" she said, changing the subject once more as she headed toward the table. "I've also brought bread and cheese, some fruit, and a bottle of wine. I had no idea what you might like."

He followed her, setting the basket down in the table's center. "It all sounds delicious. Are you warm enough? I can make the stove hotter, if you'd like."

"I'm perfectly warm, thank you. Here," she removed the cloth from atop the basket, and pulled out two delicate, china plates followed by cut-glass wine goblets. "I had to lure poor Cook out of the kitchen before I packed the basket. I hope I didn't forget anything. Here's a corkscrew."

Will took it and saw to uncorking the wine, a fine bottle of French merlot, then poured a generous amount into each glass as Aisling set out the food on a thick damask cloth.

"Now," she said, taking a knife and slicing the rind off a wedge of cheese. "What would you like to know about me before you can ravish me with a clear conscience?"

"Well, if you insist on putting it that way." Will shook his head, trying not to look as eager as he felt. "Hmm, let's see. Do you read much?"

"Of course," she answered with a shrug. "Do you?"

"Incessantly," he said with a smile, reaching for the long loaf of crusty bread and breaking it in two. "Though it would appear your brother does not approve of my tastes. I lent him a copy of Forster's newest, and he actually had the nerve to call it rubbish."

"Jack wouldn't know fine literature if it whacked him in the head. Anyway, he's not one for novels." Aisling handed him a chunk of cheese. "I'm surprised he even made the effort."

Will frowned. "Truly, I don't think he made much of an effort all, the lazy bastard. If you'll pardon my language."

"Oh, don't worry, I've called him much worse." Aisling took a sip of wine, her eyes meeting his over the rim of her glass. She set the goblet back down with a mischievous smile.

All Will could think about was taking her in his arms, touching her, kissing her. Instead, he remained seated across from her, doing everything in his power to resist his urges, to tamp down the need that seemed to grow and blossom with every moment spent in her company.

"Anything else you'd like to know?" she asked, drawing him from his thoughts. Her thickly lashed hazel eyes were positively glowing now, her cheeks growing pink from the heat of the stove and perhaps the wine. How long could he last, sitting there without touching her, without feeling her smooth, warm skin against his?

Not long, he realized. Despising his own weakness, he reached across the table and took one of her slim hands in his, rubbing slow circles on her palm with the pad of his thumb. Almost as if such an intimacy was foreign to her, she glanced down at their joined hands with wide eyes, her lashes fluttering like butterfly wings.

"Surprise me," he said softly. "What would like me to know about you?"

～

FOR A MOMENT, Aisling couldn't speak as she considered his question. She swallowed hard, her mouth dry and parched despite the wine. "I...I'm not right. My heart, I mean. My feelings," she clarified, knowing she wasn't making a bit of sense. "I don't...don't feel things like other women do."

She expected him to laugh at her, to make a joke of her confession. Instead, the warmth, the understanding there in Will's eyes nearly took her breath away. "How can you be sure what other women feel, Aisling?" he asked, his voice so very gentle, so caring.

It all spilled out in a rush. "Because I know. I listen, I read. Passion and hate and love...all those emotions mean nothing to me. I read about them in books, I even write about them in my own stories. But it's…it's all a sham. I've no firsthand knowledge of any of it."

He spoke slowly, cautiously, as if he were carefully considering each word. "Perhaps it's only that you've never really had the opportunity to live yet. At least, not your own life. You've been stuck up here in Bedlington all this time, living the life your parents have chosen for you. You're Sir Reginald Wainscott's daughter, Jack Wainscott's sister, Lady Wainscott's daughter. Perhaps once you've had the chance to live your life—Aisling's life—things will feel differently."

She shook her head, suddenly overwhelmed with despair. "Don't you see? I haven't a choice. Until I marry and become someone's wife, I'll just remain my parents' daughter. That's all I can ever be, nothing more than that. Just someone's possession."

"Why not? You defy convention in so many ways as it is."

Closing her eyes, she inhaled sharply. "In small ways, that's all. None of it changes anything. This…this feeling between you and me, whatever it is, it's the first thing I've done that feels as if it's truly mine, my own decision." She opened her eyes, focusing on their still-joined hands, refusing to meet his gaze, fearing what she might see there.

"What about your writing? No one knows but Jack, you said. It's your own, isn't it? Something you do for you and you alone."

"And for the money," she murmured.

"What will you do with the money?"

"I've no idea. I always tell myself that the money will someday buy my freedom, but I haven't thought much beyond that."

"Well, then, that's a start, isn't it?"

"Do you know about Mrs. Gaylord?" she blurted out, then immediately wished she could take back the words.

"You mean your father's"—he cleared his throat loudly. "I meant to say, Charles Gaylord's widow? The London socialite?"

Aisling rolled her eyes. "Go on and say it—my father's mistress. Everyone in London knows; you must know, as well."

"I spend very little time in London." He was hedging, she realized.

"Take my word for it, then. Everyone knows."

"And what if they do? Your father is by no means the only man in England to take a mistress. Besides, isn't it almost fashionable with your set to do so?" He took no pains to disguise the disgust in his voice.

"I suppose so, though most men are discreet. It's more common in marriages of convenience, but my mother...well, she loves him. Desperately. I hear her crying at night, you know. He takes no pains to hide his relationship from society, but if my mother were to even mention it, she would be considered vulgar. She would be the outcast, not him. It's so unfair."

He reached across the table and took her chin between his forefinger and thumb, tipping her gaze up to meet his. "And this is why you've remained unmarried, isn't it?"

She shook her head, surprised once more to find her eyes strangely damp. Whatever was the matter with her? "No. Yes, perhaps. Oh, I don't know!" she cried, snatching back her hand.

"Perhaps it's just that you've never met the right sort of man—the sort who would treat you as his partner and not as some possession," he said, hitting so close to the truth that Aisling's breath caught in her throat.

My winter's desire.

She took a deep, fortifying breath, willing her racing

heart to slow. "I think you've been reading too much of Forster's work."

He laughed then, a soft, gentle laugh. "Perhaps. To think, all those years I had no idea what lay under that tough exterior of yours. I'm not sure you knew, either."

Aisling eyed him sharply. "Are you calling me weak? The weaker sex, is that it?"

"There's nothing weak about you, Aisling. Here, would you like some more bread? More wine, perhaps?"

She shook her head. "I'm not very hungry, after all."

He rose, nodding. "Nor I. Aisling, I...damn it, I don't know what to say. Part of me wants to do the gentlemanly thing and walk out of here today without further complicating your life. But the other part, well, suffice it to say that that one inch of bare skin above your collar is just about enough to send me over the edge."

Aisling stood, entirely sure of what she wanted. With fingers that remained mercifully steady, she started unbuttoning the row of tiny buttons that began at her throat.

Will watched her, unmoving, his hands clenched into fists by his sides. She could see the rise and fall of his chest, could see the heat there in his pale, piercing eyes. A muscle in his jaw flexed perceptibly.

"Stop," he called out, and her fingers froze. "Wait. I don't want you to do this just to prove your independence."

"That's not why I'm doing it," Aisling said, shaking her head.

"Then why?" he asked, raking a hand through his hair.

As she considered the question, Aisling's gaze traveled from the top of Will's head, where his mussed brown hair fell in soft waves that brushed the back of his collar, down to his brown coat and striped vest, to his matching brown trousers and scuffed shoes. As she watched, he reached up to straighten his necktie—or to loosen it, perhaps.

She was keenly aware of his situation, far too aware. He was Celia Cooper's son—Celia, with her reddened cheeks and even redder hands, her simple good looks faded with the strain of hard work, of hard living, of disappointment. Somehow she had purchased her own modest cottage in the village, years ago, but still she took in washing and sewing, or hired herself out when needed. No one could keep linens as crisp and white as Mrs. Cooper, rumor had it.

No man had given Will his name, and no one but Celia Cooper knew exactly who had sired him, though there were plenty of rumors. Still, he'd managed to secure a gentleman's education, a respectable position at a prestigious university. Though his hands were as rough as his mother's, his speech was polished and refined. And what's more, her own brother trusted him, respected him, treated him as his equal.

And yet all of that would make no difference at all if anyone were to find out what she and Will had done last night in Jack's office, or what they were about to do now there in the cottage. Everyone would be shocked—horrified, even. Was that why she wanted it so badly? Was it simply yet another form of rebellion? Or was it something else? Something more organic? She took a deep breath, willing her mind to speak the truth.

Suddenly she was sure of her answer, entirely so—more sure of it than anything else in her life. As to the consequences, well...she would not think of that now. She couldn't.

"It's you, Will. *You.* That's why I'm doing it. I cannot say why, cannot explain it, not really. Perhaps in my heart I've always known it, always felt it. And then yesterday..." She trailed off, shaking her head.

"You should know that I feel the same, Aisling. Precisely the same. Most men would take any woman who offered herself willingly, and I cannot pretend to be any different from them. But in this case…it's different. You're different. I hope I've made that clear."

Aisling just nodded.

Will smiled, then hurriedly set about pulling closed the cottage's worn drapes. "Now," he said once he'd finished the task and turned back toward her. "Feel free to continue what you were doing before I so stupidly interrupted you."

Aisling couldn't help but laugh. "You mean…undressing myself?"

"Yes, precisely that." He gestured toward the buttons at her throat, now half-undone. "If you don't mind."

"And you'll….what? Simply watch?" she teased, feeling suddenly bold.

"I thought I might. Simply watch, that is. Unless you'd prefer that I join you."

"I think I'd prefer your full attention, if you don't mind." She reached up and found the remaining buttons on her blouse, her fingers positively flying over them.

"Trust me, I don't mind in the least. You've no idea how little sleep I got last night, trying to imagine you naked. As satisfactory as I found our encounter in Jack's study, I was cheated of seeing what lay beneath that dress of yours. I won't deny myself that pleasure today."

Aisling felt her cheeks warm, felt her pulse leap as Will's gaze swept over her. The raw lust in his admiring gaze made her breath hitch, made her fingers work faster till her blouse fell fully open. She made quick work of her belt, then reached around to unfasten her skirt and untie her petticoat, dropping them both to the floor. In seconds she stood in nothing but her remaining underthings—her combinations, corset, and stockings—her slippers discarded by the puddled folds of her clothing.

"More?" she asked, though she knew full well the answer.

"Definitely more," he answered, closing the distance

between them. He reached out to trail his fingers down her arm, drawing gooseflesh in their wake. His breath was warm against her neck, coming as fast as hers now.

"Then you must do the rest. Go on, Will. Undress me," she whispered, feeling much like a character in one of her naughty stories.

"Oh, I shall take great pleasure in doing exactly that," he answered, reaching around her to find her pale pink corset's lacings and tug hard at them.

Aisling held her breath in anticipation, near desperate to feel his hands against her bare skin.

CHAPTER 5

*I*t only took two tugs on Aisling's corset lacings to loosen them, and a minute later the garment slipped to the floor with a decidedly loud *thump*. Next came some unidentifiable undergarment, a one-piece combination of vest and knickers, ending just above her knees. Damn the layers—he'd never get her naked at this rate.

She tipped her chin in the air, meeting his gaze as he hooked his thumbs beneath the shoulder straps and eased the garment down, inch by inch, first revealing the gentle, creamy white swell of her breasts, followed by dusty-pink nipples that pebbled when the fabric slipped over them. With a groan, he bent to lick one rosy tip, his cock now straining against the flap of his trousers.

She swayed against him, a small moan escaping her lips as he took her entire nipple into his mouth, suckling her now, increasing the pressure as his hands cupped her breasts—firm, round breasts, and surprisingly full. She smelled so sweet, like sugared violets, and tasted even better.

Fearing he might spend himself then and there, he pulled away, continuing to push down the troublesome undergarment—past her waist, her hips, until her dark curls, already damp with need, were exposed. Lower still he tugged the fabric, resisting the urge to bury his face in her curls till he had her fully naked.

At last the garment dropped to the floor, leaving nothing but her stockings to dispense with. Easy, he thought, untying her silk garters and tossing them aside. His fingers brushed her thigh, as smooth as the finest silk, as he reached for one stocking's top. Taking his time, he knelt and pressed his lips to her skin as the stocking bared it, his mouth following the trail down past her knee, to her ankle. With the grace of a dancer, she lifted one foot, her toes pointed toward the ground, and allowed him to slip off the stocking.

One more to go and she'd be entirely bare, he realized, blood thrumming hotly through his veins. The anticipation, the need...it was like nothing he'd ever experienced before, making his breath come fast, his heart thumping noisily against his ribs. *Slowly,* he commanded himself, wanting to savor every moment.

This time he allowed himself to leisurely discover her soft thighs, to part them gently as his mouth explored the skin just above her stocking's top. As he rolled it down and slipped it off her foot, his fingers moved higher, to her sex, searching for the little knot of flesh hidden in her curls.

He knew he'd found it when he heard her gasp, her entire body going rigid beneath his hands. At once his mouth replaced his fingers. The tip of his tongue danced across the hard bud, teasing it until she cried out, clutching fistfuls of his hair.

"Do you like that?" he asked, looking up to see her bite her lower lip, her head thrown back.

"Oh, yes. Yes!" she answered breathlessly. "But you must stop, you must...I mean, not yet. I want you naked, too. Now," she added, tugging him to his feet.

"Very well." He stood, ready to oblige her. He couldn't help but stare at her, transfixed, as he untied his necktie—marveling at her figure, at her posture as she stood there, entirely bared to him. She displayed no maidenly shyness whatsoever, made no effort to cover herself as she watched him unbutton his coat, then his waistcoat, and shrug out of both.

Indeed, she simply watched him as if fascinated, desire heating her eyes as she followed his every movement.

He slipped his braces off his shoulders before unbuttoning his linen and tossing it to the ground in a rumpled heap beside his coat. Moving quickly now, he unfastened his trousers and pushed them down along with his stockings, then stood in nothing save his own drawers, his cock a hard bulge in the flannel. He saw her gaze travel downward, her eyes widening. *Invitation enough.* With no further hesitation, he pushed down his drawers and stepped from them. For a moment, they both stood silently, admiring one another.

"God, you're beautiful," she said at last.

"I was just thinking the same thing. Of you, I meant," he added. "I've never in my life seen anything so lovely. Come here," he commanded, and she readily obeyed, striding proudly into his embrace. Their bodies met—hot, eager, a melding of limbs.

"Your hair," he murmured against her ear. He was suddenly desperate to see it down, unbound.

"Mmmm," was all she responded before pulling away and reaching up toward the elaborate arrangement piled high on her crown. One by one, she removed the pins and dropped them carelessly to the floor. First one wheat-colored lock fell across her shoulder, its shiny end curling across one pale ivory breast, and then another, till at last her entire face was framed in a pale, wavy mass that fell down her back in a glossy ripples.

Will could only stare speechless at the sight. How long had it been since he'd seen her with her hair down? Many, many years, he realized. They'd been children. But now... now she was every inch a grown woman, and never would he have imagined the practical, always-sensible Aisling with such glorious hair.

In one sweep of his arm, he lifted her off her feet and carried her across the cottage's small room to the narrow iron bed in the far corner.

Aisling propped herself up on one elbow, watching him with a mischievous smile. "The bed, Will? But that's so very predictable, so pedestrian, isn't it?"

He shrugged. "Perhaps, but I won't be rushed today, not like last night. You might want to get comfortable," he teased, plumping the pillow behind her. "This might very well take all day."

"As if you could last that long," she challenged, eyes dancing.

He took a step toward the edge of the bed, his cock heavy with need. "Can't I?"

"Let me see," she answered, rising to her hands and knees before him. Before he had a chance to react, she had taken his entire length in her mouth, her tongue stroking the underside of his shaft. His entire body shuddered as he stared down at her in utter surprise.

Slowly, sensuously, she rocked back, releasing him inch by inch till nothing but the head of his cock remained between her lips, her tongue dancing over the sensitive tip. Over and over again, she stroked him with her mouth, taking him more deeply each time. She cupped his ballocks in one hand, squeezing gently, making it impossible for him to pull away.

At last she released him, sitting back on her heels and

looking up at him sweetly, all innocence now. "All day, you say? Are you so sure of that?"

"Never mind," he said, nearly throwing himself to the bed beside her and pulling her atop him. "I must have been mistaken."

AISLING SUCKED in her breath as she climbed atop him, straddling him. Oh, how she wanted to tease him, to make him nearly weep with desperation as she tormented him with her mouth. She had no idea it would be so lovely to pleasure him like that, to taste him and tease him. She'd felt him grow harder, longer with each stroke of her tongue, and a part of her wanted to wield that power more, to see it to its completion. After all, she'd written about it so many times as it seemed something that men particularly enjoyed, if the stories in *The Boudoir* were to be believed.

But she couldn't wait, couldn't restrain herself as she sought to fit her quim over his cock instead. She felt the heat of him, the throbbing hardness as he parted her and then filled her entirely. She was already wet, slippery with need as her body found a rhythm, her hips raising and lowering with a quickening pace.

Will grasped the iron bedstead behind him as he strained against her, raising his head to capture her mouth with his, kissing her roughly and ruthlessly as she rode him—harder, faster, the creaky old bedsprings protesting loudly beneath them.

And then he broke the kiss, falling back upon the pillow. His head tipped back, the cords of his neck standing out hard and taut. "Oh, God, Aisling...now...I can't stop—" A deep groan made the rest of his words unintelligible, but Aisling no longer cared. Their bodies had grown slick, their bodies slapping noisily against one another.

Already she felt her womb begin to clench, her insides quivering, her thighs trembling. Pinpoints of light exploded behind her eyelids as she lowered herself one last time, taking in every inch of him, allowing him to fill her, to stretch her as he spent himself deep, deep inside her.

Their cries of pleasure mingled, hers breathy and high, his low and guttural as they both arched into one another one last time. At last spent, Aisling fell across him, her lips just inches from his throat as she caught her breath. He smelled so clean, slightly salty, and all male—a heady scent, she realized. Nothing at all like Esterbrooke, who'd smelled faintly of onions and smoke when she'd so stupidly allowed him to take her virginity.

"So much for all day," Will said at last, running his fingers through her hair and making her shiver. "And so much for the French letters. Damn."

French letters? *Of course.* She hadn't even thought to reassure him, though she had been keenly aware of the timing herself. "Don't worry," she said, pressing a kiss against the spot where his pulse leapt below his ear. "My monthly courses came only last week. It should be safe enough right now."

She felt his lips against her hair. "And here I'd planned to take my time. It's all your fault, you know."

"Next time, perhaps," she murmured sleepily, suddenly wishing more than anything for a short nap, there in his arms.

"Will there be a next time, Aisling? Truly, how long can this go on?"

She sat up, looking down at him. His brow was furrowed, his jaw tight as he rubbed one temple. He seemed almost...

angry, but Aisling could not fathom why. "As long as we want it, Will," she said, shaking her head in confusion.

"If you say so, then."

"What do you mean, if I say so?" she snapped. "I don't understand you, Will Cooper!"

"I don't quite understand it myself." He ran the pad of his fingertip across her lips. "It's just that I find myself greedy, wanting more, not wanting to let you go. And yet I know that this cannot go on forever."

Aisling felt a lump form in her throat. Why did he have to keep bringing up the end, when they'd only just begun? She didn't want to think of the end, not yet. Yet there was no denying it—time was not their friend. Christmas would come and go, and Will's holiday would end. He'd go back to Cambridge, to his life there, leaving her—

"Do you remember that time when we were children, when I pushed you in the swimming pond?" he asked, drawing slow, lazy circles on her skin with his fingertips. "You were fully clothed, wearing a frilly white frock with pink ribbons. I can still remember the look of fury on your face when you climbed out, dripping wet."

"I can still remember the black eye I gave you not a minute later," she said, smiling in smug satisfaction.

"Jack put me up to it, did you know that? Offered to pay me, even, but I refused his coin."

"Why, that bastard!" she said, shaking her head, knowing it sounded exactly like something her brother would do. "I had to toss that dress in the rubbish bin, you know. It was entirely ruined, and Nurse was furious with me."

"Well, have you any idea what kind of hell I got for having my eye blackened by a girl?" He chuckled softly. "Jack told everyone, as if he were proud of you or something, and I never heard the end of it."

"I'll never understand that brother of mine," she said,

shaking her head. Jack had always been her greatest tormentor, and yet her dearest friend. Perhaps it was because they were so close in age—only thirteen months separating their births. Irish twins, their grandmother liked to call them.

Will reached for her hand, threading his fingers through hers. "Say you'll see me again tomorrow."

"Tomorrow? Yes, yes, of course." But how?

"My mum's house," he said, as if he'd read her mind. "She'll be out tomorrow, in the afternoon, helping Mrs. Brandon prepare for guests. She told me I'd have to get my own tea. Can't you come up with an excuse to spend the day in Bedlington?"

"I might as well be a child, needing permission to go anywhere or do anything on my own." She sighed loudly. "But I can promise that I'll try. Will that do?"

"I suppose it will have to," he answered, his voice tight. "Do you have to return home now?"

"No," she said, snuggling back against his chest and pulling up a rough, woolen blanket to cover them both. "I've got hours till Mother returns. What about you?"

"I'm not expected until teatime. If my mum shows up then, that is. Did you know she's stepping out with Mr. Beeton these days?"

Aisling nodded. "I'd heard that from Mother. She gets all the local gossip, you know. Anyway, good for your mum. Mr. Beeton is a decent man. I think he will treat her well."

"I hope so. I hate leaving her all alone in Bedlington. I've tried to get her to come up to Cambridge, but she refuses. She's so damn proud of that shabby little cottage. I just don't understand it."

"Because it's hers. I...I almost envy her that. Her own home, her own livelihood, difficult as it might be," she added.

"She could get on well enough with what I send her each month," he said, sounding defensive. "But she refuses to give up her work, hiring herself out like she does. It's almost as if she wants to demean herself."

Aisling could hear the frustration in his voice, could feel his body tense beside hers. "You're being much too hard on her, Will. She's proud of the work she does, and rightly so. It can't have been easy for her, all these years, raising you all alone amidst the whispers, the innuendo."

"How can you touch me, knowing I'm someone's bastard?" he said, his voice catching. "Someone's by-blow, nothing but a cast-off? You, of all people? The daughter of a baronet, for fuck's sake."

The pain, the self-loathing she heard in his voice tore at her heart. A tear gathered in the corner of Aisling's eye, and she wiped it away quickly, before it fell, giving her away. "I don't care about that, Will. Perhaps I did...before. Perhaps I thought myself better than you, superior in some way, simply because of my birth. But now that I know...now that"—she swallowed hard, willing the tears to remain at bay, damn it —"I'm ashamed for feeling as I did before. Jack called me a snob, and he was right. I was a terrible snob, and I'll never forgive myself."

"There's nothing to forgive, Aisling. But you have no idea what it was like, growing up as I did, never quite fitting in anywhere. The working-class boys picked on me for my education, and my schoolmates picked on me for my working-class background. I was damned either way."

Aisling nodded, having heard such tales from Jack through the years. "I can't even imagine. But then, I've never felt as if I fit into my world quite right, either. I never could do what they asked of me—smile prettily, hold my tongue, act as if I hadn't the brains God gave a goat. I let a gentleman take my virtue, and then do you know what I did when he offered marriage? I laughed. The very idea of being married to him, of feeling his damp, slippery hands all over me every night…" She trailed off, her stomach pitching uncomfortably. "I couldn't do it. I knew my secret was safe. After all, it wouldn't reflect well on his masculine pride if everyone knew I'd refused him after giving him a tumble, would it?"

"Most definitely not," Will agreed.

"Anyway," she said, waving one hand in dismissal, "enough about that." Propping herself up on one elbow, she gazed down at him admiringly. Though the mischievous glint in his eyes was the same, everything else about him was so very different from the boy she remembered. Gone were the bony shoulders and skinny chest, replaced now with a well-sculpted torso with a dusting of dark hair that narrowed into a fine line, bisecting his taut, rippled abdomen.

"By the looks of you, I'd say you've broken your own fair share of hearts," she said, feeling strangely possessive now.

He shrugged, drawing her closer as he did so. "Perhaps," he answered noncommittally, then immediately changed the subject. "Tell me about your stories. Whatever made you start writing them?"

"I found a copy of *The Boudoir* in Jack's office a couple years ago, and, being the wicked girl I am, read it from cover to cover that very night. Suddenly I had this idea that I could do that, write stories like that. I wrote the first one in a matter of days, and showed it to Jack. Once he got over the initial shock, he agreed to take it to London. I suppose I have some talent, because *The Boudoir* snapped it right up and asked for more."

"You've no idea how impressed I am. And these things you write about, are they fantasies of yours?"

"A lady never tells," she answered coyly.

"You must let me read some, then. The curiosity is near enough killing me, especially after the tease of reading that one little bit in Jack's study."

She snuggled against him, rubbing her nose against his neck. "Would you like that? Reading my stories?"

"You've no idea," he said, cupping her bottom.

"Very well." Aisling sat up and looked longingly at the discarded food on the table, her stomach grumbling. "Is there any way you could bring the basket of food over here? And the wine, perhaps? I took it from Father's personal wine collection, after all, and I wouldn't want it to go to waste. I think it's a rare vintage."

"You *are* a naughty girl," Will teased. Disentangling himself from her limbs, he stood and wrapped the blanket around his waist. "Sir Reginald will be most displeased."

"Sir Reginald is a son-of-a-bitch, and he can go to the devil for all I care." And take his Mrs. Gaylord with him, she added silently. "But right now, I think I would very much enjoy a picnic in bed."

"If a picnic in bed will make you happy, then that's what you'll have, Miss Wainscott," he said with a mock bow, looking slightly ridiculous with his tousled hair and near nakedness. "After all, I aim to please."

Aisling only smiled, thinking just how well he *did* please her. Perhaps the picnic could wait a bit longer, after all.

CHAPTER 6

S miling happily to herself, Aisling guided her little
motorcar down Bedlington's dusty main thoroughfare, the engine a noisy hum. She pulled up in front of the
haberdasher's shop and cut the engine, supposing this was as
good a place as any. She had a few errands to run—a ruse,
mostly, though she'd buy some hat trimmings and pick up a
pair of shoes she'd brought in last week to be re-heeled.
She'd make her presence known in town, however briefly,
and then duck inside the Cooper's cottage at the top of the
road.

Anyone who saw her in town would assume that, after
her errands, she'd stop in to take tea with Louisa Abbott, the
shopkeeper's daughter, as she always did. Or that perhaps
she'd take a basket of fruit and some of Cook's muffins and
breads to the old Misses Simmons or to the poor Barrett
brood. Either way, no one would find it odd to see her little
Renault roadster left outside the shops for a couple of hours,
even if they didn't see her out and about.

Reaching over the door, she secured the brake, then
removed her goggles and gloves and placed them inside the

drawer on the dash. How she loved her shiny red motorcar, and what pride she took in mastering it! It had been Jack's before he'd grown tired of it and decided he needed a larger, more powerful one, one with seating for four rather than two. Aisling had managed to convince her reluctant brother to let her have it, if she learned to drive it. It hadn't taken her more than a couple afternoons to do so, and she'd been racing around the countryside ever since.

Of course, that had given the wagging tongues of Bedlington yet another reason to consider her 'fast'—both literally and figuratively—but Aisling didn't care. Even now, she saw a pair of women come out of the draper's and shake their heads when they saw her sitting there on the tufted red leather seat, unpinning the crepe-de-chine veil from her tweed motoring hat.

Aisling raised one hand and waved, smiling broadly. "Mrs. Roberts, Mrs. Appleton," she called out gaily. "A lovely day, isn't it?"

"Indeed, Miss Wainscott," they replied in unison, then bent their heads together to whisper about her, no doubt.

Still smiling to herself, Aisling opened the door and stepped down to the road where she stood briefly, dusting off her Jaeger-lined cream serge coat and tightening the muffler about her throat, before she set off on her errands. Thankfully, the sky was clear today, a bright blue without a hint of clouds. The air was brisk, but not unpleasantly so. A perfect winter's day.

Not a quarter hour later, she stood in front of Celia Cooper's cottage, looking around furtively before hurrying forward to rap on the door. The door swung open, and without a word of welcome, Will hustled her inside, gathering her into his embrace.

"Do you think anyone saw you?" he asked, his breath warm against her neck.

Aisling shook her head. "I don't think so. Besides, if anyone saw me headed this way, they'd assume I was on my way to the Barretts'. They're only a few doors up the road, after all."

"Ah, yes. The angel of mercy, visiting the poor," he said, sounding vaguely sarcastic.

Aisling bristled at once, pulling away from him. "Don't say it like that, Will. What would you have me do, instead? Ignore them?"

"I was only teasing you, Ash. That's what Jack calls you, isn't it? 'Ash.' It somehow suits you, I think."

"Really? How so, if you don't mind my inquiring?"

He shrugged. "I don't mind at all. It just sounds...I don't know, somehow modern. Like you. A modern woman. I saw you drive up in your jaunty little motorcar, you know. Is this your motoring ensemble?" he asked, gesturing toward her garments.

"Indeed," she said, reaching up to unfasten her coat and remove her muffler. "Along with a veil, goggles, and gloves. You should see me in it all—I'm such a fright! Though not half the fright I would be without such things to protect me from the dust."

"Here, let me take those," he offered, and Aisling handed over her things. "Though perhaps I shouldn't leave them down here, just in case."

"In case of what? Your mother's untimely return?" Aisling couldn't help but laugh. "Pray, what would you have me do in that case, sneak out through your window?"

"Just how nimble are you?" he asked, leading her toward the stairs.

"Nimble enough, I suppose. It sounds as if you've experience in such matters. I'm not certain I approve," she teased, looking around, taking in her surroundings. After all, she'd never been inside the Cooper's cottage before. Not once, in all her life.

It was, first and foremost, clean and tidy. Homely, but decorated in what she'd call comfortable simplicity. The room they stood in boasted a built-in window seat and inglenook, a sofa, and a pair of spindle chairs with embroidered cushions. In the room's far corner stood a small Christmas tree, waist high and simply decorated with red bows, a painted gold star on top.

The floors were maple, with colorful rag rugs scattered about. The hearth was simple brick, the mantel uncrowded, with only a carriage clock and a photograph of Will looking scholarly in his Cambridge robes decorating it, along with a seasonal drape of pine boughs and holly. The walls were stark white, unadorned with paper, but framed botanical drawings were placed at pleasing intervals, and Aisling stepped up to one, a drawing of a multi-fronded fern, for closer inspection.

"Did you draw this?" she asked, noting the fine detail. It looked so very real, almost as if it were a pressed specimen, preserved forever in its most perfect form. Beneath the drawing, the species was labeled in a neat, familiar hand.

"I drew them all," he answered with a shrug. "Specimens native to Bedlington. I've no idea why Mum likes them so much."

"Beautiful," she breathed. "I had no idea you were so gifted."

"Perhaps one day I'll draw you, if you'll allow it."

Aisling nodded. "I'd like that very much."

"With your hair down. I've never seen anything lovelier than you with your hair down," he added.

Aisling couldn't help but laugh. "Funny you say that, as my mother has been lamenting my hair since the day I was born. 'There's nothing more unfortunate than being a born a blonde,' she always says. Between my fair hair and light eyes, I'm about as far from fashionable as they come."

"Fuck fashionable," he said sharply, then, "You must forgive my language. I sometimes forget—"

"What, that I'm a lady? Don't apologize, Will. I think that's why I like you so much—you say exactly what you think. I admire that."

"Can I get you something?" he asked, gesturing toward the kitchen behind them. "I'm capable enough with a teapot. I'm sure there are some cakes around, too, if I look hard enough."

"No, thank you." Aisling headed for the stairs. "May I go up?"

"Of course. Come, I'll finish showing you around. It's not much, I know, especially compared to Wainscott House."

"I think it's charming," she said, following him up the narrow stairs. "What is it they call it, 'cottage quaint'? Wainscott House just seems so cluttered in comparison." It was the truth. With its Elizabethan styling and dark wood trim, heavy furniture crowding every room and knick-knacks on every available surface, Wainscott House often felt crowded and oppressive, despite its cavernous size.

"You realize this entire cottage would fit easily inside your drawing room alone? I used to worry I'd make a wrong turn and get lost there when I was a boy. Here, this is my mum's room." He opened a door to reveal a small, square bedroom with a narrow bed in its center, a tall maple dresser opposite it.

Aisling nodded her approval, then moved on. It somehow seemed wrong to step inside the woman's room in her absence.

Will paused at the next door, and Aisling peered inside. "This is where Mum does her sewing," he said his voice filled with pride. A sewing machine sat on a stand beneath the window, and tables held bolts of fabric, piles of linen, and pieces of clothing. Baskets lined a row of shelves on the wall, filled with ribbons, flowers, and lace. In the room's far corner, a rack held various garments including what looked to be Aisling's mother's lilac watered silk gown. The hem had ripped last week, she remembered. Of course she would have brought it to Mrs. Cooper for repair.

Her cheeks reddening slightly, Aisling followed Will out into the corridor. More than anything, she wished she hadn't seen her mother's gown. It only reminded her of their differing circumstances, something she did not wish to dwell on, not now.

Luckily, Will did not seem to notice her discomfiture. "And this is my bedchamber," he said, opening the opposite door and leading her inside a room that was twice as large as the other two.

"I know, it's ridiculous, isn't it?" He laid her coat and muffler across the back of a chair. "I don't even live here anymore, and still she insists on me having the largest room. As if I were royalty or something."

"Perhaps you are," she said wryly, hoping he would appreciate her humor. "Your father could be a prince, for all you know."

The iron bed was larger than Mrs. Cooper's, and finer, too. There was a saucer of half-drunk tea on the bedside table, a book lying open beside it. A well-worn trunk sat on the floor by the footboard, its contents spilling out rather haphazardly. In the corner, a closet stood ajar, a row of suits hanging inside. Beneath a pair of dormer windows was a roll-top desk, papers scattered across it. A tall stack of books sat on one edge, looking as if they might topple over at any minute.

"One could never accuse you of being neat, could they?" she teased, taking in the clutter, the lived-in feel that her own room back at Wainscott House lacked, despite the fact that she actually *lived* in it. Will was only a visitor here, she reminded herself.

"I won't let my mother come in to clean as if she's my housekeeper. Is it really so bad? Believe it or not, I tried to tidy up a bit, just in case you came by."

She sidled up to him, batting her lashes like a coquette would. "So sure I'd make it up to your bedroom, were you?"

"I'm nothing if not optimistic," he answered with a wicked smile. "I did allow my mum to change the bed linens, however. I shudder to think what she must suppose happened in my bed last night to result in such a request."

Aisling laughed, surprised at how comfortable she felt alone in man's bedroom, discussing bed linens as easily as they'd discuss the weather. Feeling bold, she reached inside her skirt's pocket and withdrew the folded pages she'd tucked inside earlier that day.

"Look what I've brought you," she said, unfolding the pages and smoothing them flat. "It's one of my favorite scenes."

"Indeed?" he asked, reaching for the pages. "One of your own personal fantasies, I hope."

"If I say it is, will you indulge it? No matter how wicked it might be?"

"Good God, Aisling, don't tease me that way. Just how wicked is it?" As he scanned the page he held in his hand, his cock made a visible bulge in his trousers.

Aisling longed to reach out and stroke it, to coax it. But she would wait, patiently, till he finished reading. She sat on the bed, testing its plumpness, running her fingers across the worn coverlet while Will read, standing by the window, his hair falling across his forehead.

At last he looked up at her, his pale eyes piercing hers. "You really wrote this?"

She nodded. "I really wrote it. Are you shocked?"

"In a good way. I just never imagined that women like you...I mean, that a gently bred lady..." He trailed off, shaking his head.

"Say it, Will. That a gently bred lady would wish to be fucked like that? Why not?" she asked with a shrug, hoping she sounded more sure of herself than she felt.

Indeed, a niggling doubt crept into her head—what if it *was* unnatural? What if the very idea repulsed him? After all, her knowledge of sex came almost entirely from reading erotica, not from real-life experience. *I'm a fraud,* she thought miserably.

"I'm only wondering where you've learned such things, that's all," Will said at last, sounding slightly awed.

Aisling shrugged, forcing her voice to sound breezy and light. "I read. Besides, I grew up in the country. Around livestock," she added. "That doesn't leave much to the imagination."

"No, I suppose not. Come here," he said, laying the pages on his desk. Aisling rose on shaking legs and quickly closed the distance between them. He took her hands in his, raising both to his lips. "Have you any idea how badly I want you?" he asked, his gaze burning with an intensity that nearly stole away her breath. "All the time. I can't sleep, I can't eat. You've entirely taken over my mind, my heart, my soul. How can I go back to Cambridge after this? How can I leave you here? It's as if I've been bewitched by you."

Dear God, there it was again—the notion that they were both under some sort of spell, that what they were feeling wasn't real. That poem, that damnable poem and her wish... was it possible? "There's something I should tell you," she murmured, no longer able to keep quiet her fears. "I found a poem, you see. On the solstice. I made a wish," she continued hurriedly, now desperate to get it all out in the open. "I wished for the perfect man, one I knew didn't exist. And yet...and yet you did. That very night, at Wainscott House, it was as if my wish had been granted the moment I laid eyes on you."

His eyes narrowed, his brow furrowed in confusion. "Wait. What does this have to do with a poem?"

She pulled her hands from his grasp and rubbed her temple, aching now. "I don't know. It was almost like a chant. I found it, tucked inside a box, a very old box. I read it aloud, and then I wished for...well, for this. For what we have. It's almost like some sort of white magic."

"But that's ridiculous," he said, shaking his head. "Surely you don't believe that?"

She squeezed her eyes shut and took a deep breath, then opened her eyes once more, gazing up to see the hurt there, etched on Will's face. "One minute we were completely indifferent to one another. And then the next...well, how else can you explain it?"

He raked one hand through his hair. "I think it was always there, a spark of some sort. Perhaps it's why you hated me so. God knows I hated you, hated the way you looked at me, as if I were worthless. I think I always wanted you, deep down. And hated you for not wanting me."

Aisling reached one trembling hand to her temple, feeling suddenly lightheaded. "Perhaps you're right. I...I just don't know. All I *do* know is that I can't help myself, can't stay away from you. It must be the magic."

"Damn you, Aisling. It's convenient timing, isn't it? I bring you here today, show you the home I grew up in, show you firsthand the differences between us, between our families, and suddenly you claim that what we're feeling isn't real? That it's some sort of magic, summoned by some goddamned poem you found? I'm supposed to believe that?"

"I...I don't know, Will. Truly, I don't. I'm so confused,

feeling things I've never before felt. And that's exactly what I wished for, don't you see? I'm not myself, not who I was last year, not even who I was last week."

"Who are you, then?" he challenged, his eyes stormy now. "Tell me, Aisling."

"I don't know!" she cried out, hating herself, hating the hurt she saw there on his face. And the worst part? Even now, all she could think of was the secret fantasy she'd written about in the story he'd just read, the rumpled pages still lying there on his desk.

She wanted him still—oh, how she wanted him! Despite it all, despite her fears, her confusion. He was angry, furious, even—and still she was going to let him take her, just as she'd imagined he would, just as she'd fantasized about all night long, anticipating this day.

Without another thought, she rushed into his arms, rising up on tiptoe to press her lips against his, her hands finding his trousers' fastenings as she did so.

"Damn it, Aisling," he said against her open mouth, his body taut against hers, his fully aroused cock pressing into her belly. "What is it you want from me?"

"Sshhh," she whispered, then moved her mouth to his throat, her tongue lapping against his bounding pulse. "That fantasy, Will," she ordered. "Now."

CHAPTER 7

*F*or a moment Will thought to protest, to refuse to fuck her in her current state of mind. It would be the gentlemanly thing to do, after all—refusing her. But damn it, he was no gentleman, and he was tired of pretending he was. She'd come to him, after all, that erotic clipping in hand, claiming it was her own fantasy—and now she was practically begging him, stroking his cock while she tried to unfasten his trousers.

By God, he would indulge her. What else could he do? He was weak where Aisling was concerned—weak and needy. It was as if his mind had been taken over by his longing, his desire, as if it were utterly beyond his control.

But he would not be fooled by her claims of white magic —of some poem, some wish, that had brought them together. That was rubbish. Perhaps it was her way of justifying what they were doing, what she was doing with a man so far beneath her. But he didn't believe it, wouldn't believe it. He was a modern man, a man of science, for fuck's sake. He acted on his own accord, his own desires. And he wanted her. Damn, how he wanted her.

"Turn around," he growled, disentangling her hands from the front of his trousers. Reaching around her waist, he half-dragged, half-carried her back toward the foot of the bed and deposited her there. A discarded necktie lay on the edge of the bed and he reached for it, snatching it up and quickly looping the soft folds around her wrists.

In seconds, he had her captive wrists pressed against the bedstead, her back toward him. He could hear her breathing grow faster, more ragged as he slipped the cloth through the iron bars and tied a knot, making sure that the bindings were neither too loose nor too tight.

"Are you certain, Aisling?" he asked, once the knot was secured. "I'll stop now, untie you this instant if you're not."

"I'm certain," she answered breathlessly. "I trust you, Will. With all my heart."

Trust. How could she trust him, when he could barely trust himself? When she couldn't even trust her own feelings? Will shook his head, refusing to think about it now. Instead, he grabbed at her skirts and petticoat, raising them, bunching them around her waist. He heard her gasp as he tugged down her drawers, relieved that she seemed to be wearing fewer layers of undergarments than she had the day before. Anticipating *this*, no doubt.

Her hands still restrained, she bent over the bed's low iron footboard, her back arched, her thighs parted invitingly. In seconds he managed to shove down his trousers and free his straining cock, pressing it against her backside as he bent to kiss her neck.

"Like this?" he asked, grinding his hips against her pale-white buttocks. "This is what you've fantasized about?"

"Yes. Oh, yes." Her pulse leapt wildly against his lips as he breathed in her scent—violets, sweet and fragrant, a scent that would forevermore make him think of her.

"Bend over more, then," he whispered, nibbling at her earlobe. "Show me."

She did, arching further. She was already wet for him, glistening with desire. "Good God, Ash," he groaned, taking a deep, steady breath. "You're so very beautiful." He didn't want to spend himself, not yet, but the sight of her like that— her cunny ready for the taking—nearly undid him. Urging himself to slow down, to savor every moment, he reached down, parting her, slipping one finger inside her tight sheath.

"You're so wet," he murmured against her ear. "So ready." He drew his finger out, rubbing her wetness across the tight nub of flesh at her entrance. "It's not magic, Ash. It's desire, don't you see?" Desire that coursed through his veins like fire, that stole away his breath. He'd never felt anything like it before, this possessiveness, this primal need for a woman. And not just any woman—for Aisling.

"Now, Will," she urged breathlessly.

Slowly, carefully, he probed her slick entrance with the tip of his cock, his hands gripping her shoulders, his lips buried in her neck.

With a small cry, Aisling rocked her hips back against him, taking him deep inside her in one single thrust. Knowing full well he wouldn't last long, he found her clit with his fingers and stroked it, hard and fast, making her moan, making her writhe against his hand as he drove into her, again and again.

In seconds her cries became louder, more insistent. God, how he wanted to please her, to satisfy her to the point that she'd never desire another. He wanted her—only her— forever. He dropped his mouth to her shoulder, kissing her through the layers of clothing, wishing he'd taken the time to undress her before he'd tied her to the bedstead.

One more thrust, one more stroke, and together they

climaxed, their bodies shuddering against one another, his heart hammering against her back. Could she feel it? Did she know that he was in love with her, entirely mad with it? *I'm a fool,* he told himself, trying to catch his breath, to slow his racing heart.

"My hands," Aisling murmured, turning her face so that his lips rested against her jaw.

"Of course," he said, hurrying to untie the necktie that bound her. In seconds he freed her, wincing as she rubbed each wrist, her pale skin reddened where the fabric had abraded her.

He dragged up his trousers, fastening them as she pulled up her drawers and shoved down her skirts. Once she was done, he reached for one of her hands, cradling it in his own. "I should never have agreed to this," he murmured, bringing her hand to his lips and feathering kisses across her irritated skin. "I would not hurt you for the world."

She smiled up at him, her hazel eyes aglow. "Of course you wouldn't, Will." He released her hand, and she reached up to stroke his cheek. "I think you could use a shave," she said, rubbing her palm back and forth across the stubble outlining his jaw. Her touch was so familiar, so intimate— like a long-time lover's.

Without saying a word, he captured her hand, laying his overtop her smaller one and holding it there, against his cheek, rubbing his face into her palm. For a moment they stood like that, silent but for the sound of their breathing, slow and easy. *Comfortable.*

Will swallowed a painful lump in his throat, suddenly overwhelmed with emotions that made his chest ache, his eyes burn. If only this moment could go on forever, this tender little tableau. But it couldn't. Of course it couldn't. "Can I get you something?" he said at last, his voice unnaturally gruff. "Some tea, perhaps?"

She nodded, reaching up to tidy her hair as she did so. "That would be lovely, actually. I'm quite parched."

"How do you take it?" he asked, amazed that he didn't know, despite their intimacy.

She smiled at him, a tiny dimple in her left cheek. "Two spoons of sugar and a dash of cream. Should I go down and help?"

"Of course not, you're my guest. Sit"—he gestured toward the chair in the corner—"and I'll be right up with it. I can manage, I swear," he added when he saw her look of surprise.

AISLING NODDED, her legs feeling strangely weak as Will hurried out. She could hear his footsteps on the uncarpeted stairs, fading away, and she sighed heavily. So many emotions flickered across her consciousness, all jockeying for position. Her feelings were such a jumble that she couldn't make out a single one—except perhaps satisfaction. Yes, that was it. Will left her satisfied, entirely sated.

When she was with him, everything felt strangely right. For the first time in all her life, she felt truly alive. Animated. Fulfilled. She shook her head, feeling foolish. *I'm making too much of this.*

She turned toward the desk, thinking to straighten the stack of books and move them safely from the edge. Only she moved too quickly and her elbow caught the edge of the topmost volume, sending it flying to the ground where it lay, open. Stooping down, she retrieved it. As she did so, a folded page fell out, fluttering down to the floorboards where the book had lain only seconds before.

Sighing in exasperation, she bent down and retrieved the letter, noticing Will's name written in a decidedly feminine script at the top of the page. Curious, she unfolded it, smoothing it down with damp hands. It was a recent letter, dated a fortnight ago. Her eyes scanned down to the bottom of the page, seeking a signature. *Entirely Yours, Helena*, it read.

Her stomach pitching, she hastily shoved the letter back inside the book. *I should not have looked,* she told herself. She'd invaded his privacy, and there was no excuse for it. Shame mixed with something else—something unsettling—made her cheeks flush hotly.

For a full minute she stood there, drumming her fingers on the desk, staring down at the edge of paper that stuck out from between the book's gilt-lined pages while she waited for Will to return. And then, as if of their own volition, her fingers moved closer, sliding along the cover's edge, itching to snatch back out the letter. The curiosity was positively eating her up inside. Who was Helena? Were they friends? Lovers?

Aisling looked toward the empty doorway, listening to the sounds of rattling dishes and footfalls below. She tapped one foot impatiently, unable to staunch her growing curiosity. The letter was recent, and Helena had signed her first name—a sure sign of intimacy.

Glancing furtively one last time at the doorway, she made up her mind even as guilt ate away at her conscience. She *had* to know—otherwise she'd go mad, supposing the worst, imagining that Helena meant more to him than she did. For all she knew, they were engaged. The tea kettle downstairs whistled plaintively, and Aisling knew it was now or never.

Taking a deep breath, she reached for the edge of the letter and pulled it out, unfolding it as quickly as possible.

My dearest William,

I hope you will forgive this letter, but I could not let you leave for Dorset without having my say, as you left my flat so hurriedly last night. I did not mean to make you uncomfortable, surely you realize that? But after what we've shared, can you simply throw it all away so easily? So carelessly?

I should never have lied to you—I know that now. Still, it does not lessen what I feel for you. I want you, William. Back in my life. My bed.

Think on it, my sweet William. I will have your answer upon your return to Cambridge. Perhaps then we will have reason to celebrate the New Year.

Entirely Yours,

Helena

SHE HAD HER ANSWER: Helena had been his lover. Was perhaps *still* his lover. How would he answer her when he returned to Cambridge? Would he simply forget Aisling, forget *this*, and return to this woman's bed? That thought alone made bile rise in her throat, made her blood run cold even while her skin flushed hotly.

An uncomfortable knot had formed in Aisling's stomach, making her feel queer, almost queasy, making her chest ache and her breath come fast—far too fast. And then she heard it —footsteps, on the stairs, getting louder.

Moving quickly, she refolded the letter and stuffed it back inside the book it had fallen from, straightening the stack and moving it towards the center of the desk with clumsy, awkward hands.

She turned back toward the doorway just as Will strode in smiling, a tray with two steaming cups of tea and a plate of biscuits in his hands. She could only stare at him as he set the tray on the bed, reached for one of the teacups, and held it out to her.

She took it with visibly trembling hands, feeling like a damned fool.

The smile on his face vanished at once. "Good God, Aisling, what's wrong?"

Dear Lord, was she that transparent? "Nothing at all," she said, cradling the steaming cup in both hands. "I...I'm perfectly fine."

"You're a terrible liar. You're white as a ghost, and positively trembling. I wasn't gone but ten minutes. What can possibly have happened in so short a time? You're not thinking about that poem again, are you? Having regrets?"

"I'm...no." She set the teacup down on the desk behind her, her gaze straying guiltily toward the book with the folded letter inside.

She had to know, had to have answers. Even if it meant exposing her guilt. "Who is Helena?" she asked, refusing to turn and meet his eyes.

"Helena? How did you..." His voice trailed off, and she heard him move closer, toward the desk. "The letter," he said matter-of-factly. "Of course."

Her cheeks burning with shame, she turned to face him. "I was trying to straighten the books, that's all. It fell out. I know I shouldn't have read it."

"No, you shouldn't have," he answered, sounding slightly amused now. "But since you did, I must tell you that she means nothing to me. Helena was...someone with whom to pass the time, nothing more. We had an understanding of sorts. No strings attached, as they say."

"What did she mean about lying to you?"

"She was married. Separated, but married. When I found out, I ended it. And that's all there is to it."

"Not from her point of view. She wants you back, Will. Back in her bed."

"There's no chance of that," he said tersely.

"So she was just...just a casual lover? Had you many of those?"

"I'm not a monk, Aisling," he snapped. "I never claimed to be one."

"And did she…she did she please you? In bed?"

A flush climbed up his neck. "Why are you asking these questions? What does it matter—to you, to us?"

Because she could not stop thinking about it, that's why. Because she couldn't get the image out of her mind—Will, in bed with another woman, kissing her, loving her, touching Helena the way he'd touched her. She rubbed her eyes with her fists, wishing she could stamp out the images, banish them forever.

This was jealousy, she realized. Pure, unadulterated jealousy. And it hurt—oh, how it hurt. She knew it was ridiculous, knew that Will had every right to his past. She hadn't come to him a virgin, and she'd known full well that he was likely far more sexually experienced than she was. It was only natural, after all. And yet…there was something about reading that damned letter, about seeing the woman's hand. And the worst part? She called him *William.*

Her Will. *Hers.*

Hot tears filled her eyes, scalding her eyelids. Aisling spun back toward the desk just as they spilled over, pounding her fists on the blotter in frustration.

"Bloody hell, Aisling. Are you crying? About Helena?" His disbelief was evident in his voice. In seconds he was standing directly behind her, his chest pressed against her back, his arms wrapped protectively about her waist.

"I can't change my past," he murmured against her hair. "I don't know what to say, but please, *please* don't cry."

"I never cry," she blubbered foolishly. "Never. Not once, till these last few days. Not till you and I…" She trailed off, shaking her head. She swallowed hard, trying to rein in the humiliating tears. "It's all too much, these feelings. Too much at once. I…I can't bear it."

She twisted from his arms, still blinded by the tears that refused to stop falling. "I must go."

"Don't go, Aisling. Not like this. Not over Helena, for Christ's sake," he pleaded while she retrieved her coat and muffler.

"I must," she repeated, refusing to look at him.

"But I told you, she means nothing to me. Nothing. Not like you, Aisling. Damnation, I think I'm falling in—"

"Don't say it!" she interrupted, before it was too late, before he said the words he could never take back, forcing her to face them, to face her own feelings. "Please. I can't hear it, not right now. Don't you see? It's just too much, too overwhelming."

"No, I don't see. Not at all. I never took you for a coward," he said coldly, a muscle in his jaw flexing as he stared at her, piercing her with his vivid blue gaze.

"Oh, but I *am* a coward. The worst sort of coward. I'm so sorry, Will. Please forgive me." Without awaiting his reply, she fled from the room, hurrying down the stairs on legs that felt as if they might give out at any moment.

In seconds, she made her way out the front door, nearly bumping into a woman on the walk as she headed toward the shops in the distance, toward her little motorcar.

"Miss Wainscott?" a voice called out, but she dared not turn around.

Instead she simply hurried on, shivering as her boots beat a quick staccato on the cobbled walk, the winter sun blindingly bright to her swollen eyes.

❧

WILL STOOD at the bottom of the stairs for several minutes, debating whether or not he should go after her. Before he'd made up his mind, his mother came in, a puzzled look on her face as she pulled off her gloves and rubbed her hands together.

"Wasn't that Miss Wainscott I just saw leaving here?" she asked with a scowl.

Good God, how to answer that? "What are you doing home so early?" he asked instead. "I thought you'd be at Mrs. Brandon's till well after teatime."

"I thought so, too. Turned out her sick housemaid made a remarkable recovery and she didn't particularly need my help, after all. And don't think I didn't notice that you ignored my question, Will Cooper. Was it or wasn't it Aisling Wainscott that nearly bowled me over on the walk just now?"

"It was," he hedged, casting about desperately for an explanation. "It seems that I...I left something at Wainscott House when I dined there earlier this week. My gloves," he finished lamely.

His mother's faded eyes narrowed as she shrugged out of her coat and hung it on the peg by the door. "So I'm to believe that you left your gloves, and Miss Wainscott delivered them personally? What kind of fool do you think I am?"

He sighed heavily, knowing he'd lost. His mother was far too sharp. "I don't think you're a fool at all, Mum. But that's all I'd like to say on the matter, if you don't mind."

"Oh, Will, darling. Please tell me you're not trifling with Aisling Wainscott. Not with the likes of her. Nothing good will come of it. Surely you must know that."

He held his ground. "As I said, I'd rather not discuss it."

She shook her head, her mouth drawn in a tight, angry line. "I thought you were smarter than that, Will. Smarter than me. Don't you see? People like that—like the Wainscotts —they use people like us. Use us, then cast us aside. Aren't I proof enough of that?"

"You've done well enough for yourself, Mum," was all he said in reply, his windpipe suddenly tight, as if he were strangling. How he hated to be reminded of the cocksucker who'd fathered him, who'd deceived his mother with false promises just to get his rocks off, and then abandoned her. He knew his mother had been the victim, had been cruelly used, and yet sometimes he couldn't help the niggling doubt that she should have fought harder for the man she loved, the father of her child. And how he hated himself for such treacherous thoughts!

"Oh, Will," his mother said on a sigh. "It's too late, isn't it? How could you be so stupid? So foolish?"

He looked toward the window, where the late afternoon sun shone brightly through the glass. "If you don't mind, I think I'll go out for a bit."

"You're stubborn as a mule, aren't you? Always were. Fine, then. Go." She threw her hands in the air in frustration. "Learn the hard way, if you must. But don't say I didn't warn you. Mark my words, she'll use you, then toss you aside like yesterday's rubbish."

Judging by Aisling's hasty exit, perhaps she had already done just that. Clenching his hands into fists by his sides, Will took a deep, calming breath, then reached for his overcoat and gloves. "If you'll excuse me," he said, his voice deceptively calm and collected.

He had no idea where he was going, but he needed to get out, to get some air. Clear his head. Only then could he consider what his next move would be, as far as Aisling was concerned.

The only thing he was certain of was that it wasn't over, not yet. At least, not from his point of view. And if she thought it was, well...

He would fight for his woman.

*I*t was Christmas Eve. The calendar above Aisling's writing desk was insistent upon it, no matter how hard she tried to ignore the holiday, to eschew the good cheer and jollity she knew she was supposed to feel this time of year, but never did. And this year the melancholy was worse than ever.

She laid her head back on the chaise longue's tasseled pillow and stared up at the ceiling, listening to the sounds of bustling activity below. Her father had arrived home that very morning, Jack the day before. The entire household was now in a tizzy, preparing for the Wainscott's annual Christmas Eve open house.

At that very moment, Aisling's mother was downstairs with the housekeeper, making certain that every little light on the Christmas tree was twinkling brightly, that every red velvet bow was straight, that the eggnog was perfect and the wassail just so.

In no time, their guests would begin to arrive. A buffet supper would be served, followed by a pantomime, and then a concert featuring traditional holiday music. The evening's

festivities would conclude at the stroke of midnight when
the musicians played "Silent Night." Each guest would light a
taper and form a processional through the house and out the
front door, where they'd all gather in the drive and stare up
at the night sky for a few moments before blowing out their
candles, gathering their coats, and heading back to their own
homes.

These events had happened in precisely that order as far
back as Aisling could remember. Everyone in Bedlington was
invited, and for weeks afterward the entire village would
discuss the food, the décor, the table linens—every little
aspect of the evening dissected in minute detail. Never in her
presence, of course. In fact, in the weeks following
Christmas it generally seemed that all conversation ground
to a halt whenever she entered a shop. But Louisa, the shopkeepers' daughter, always shared the gossip with her over
tea, embellishing each tale to such grand proportions that
Aisling couldn't help but laugh about it.

The clock downstairs chimed the hour and Aisling
sighed, turning her head to glance over at the amethyst velvet
gown hanging beside her bed, the matching velvet slippers
sitting at the ready beneath it. The ensemble was new,
specially bought in London for this occasion. Her mother
had thought the neckline scandalous, and even more so the
back, which dipped far lower than anything Aisling had ever
worn before. But Madame Aubergine had insisted it was the
height of fashion in Paris, and Lady Wainscott had reluctantly relented.

At the time, Aisling had adored the gown, thinking it
entirely perfect. But now the very idea of putting it on and
going downstairs to greet guests seemed unpalatable at best.
Mostly, of course, because Will would be one of those guests.

What he must think of her!

Two full days had passed since she'd run out of his mother's cottage. She'd spent those days at home, refusing to go out lest she run into him. She'd claimed a stomach malady had incapacitated her, and kept almost entirely to her room. There, away from prying eyes, she'd spent a good portion of the time crying like some sort of silly, lovesick schoolgirl while she examined her situation from every possible angle.

When she'd first let Will make love to her, there in Jack's study, it had been an impulse, nothing more. She'd wanted him, and so she'd had him. She'd acted out of curiosity, a desire for experience beyond what she'd had with Thomas Esterbrooke. It had been as simple as that.

But in the following days, everything had somehow changed. *She* had changed. Feelings beyond lust and curiosity had crept into her consciousness, into her heart, awakening it, awakening her. Before, she'd been an observer of life. Now, she was living life. Experiencing it—painfully so.

If only she'd never found that blasted box, that damned poem! Now she would never know for certain if what they felt was real. If only she could find that mysterious woman in the cloak, the one she'd seen there in the circle of stones on the solstice. Perhaps she had left the box there; perhaps she knew something about the poem. But Aisling hadn't even seen her face—she'd only seen her hair, whipping about in the breeze. And then she'd disappeared, without even—

A sharp knock sounded on the door, startling her. "Aisling, dear? Are you dressed?"

"Not yet, Mother," she called out, rising from the chaise longue and reaching for her hairbrush, trying to appear as if she were at least making an effort to get ready.

Her mother opened the door and peered inside. "Good heavens, dear! Whatever are you waiting for? Our guests should begin to arrive within the hour. I'll send Clarice right in." Her gaze landed on the dress, and she shook her head.

"I'm still not sure about that gown," she said, shaking her head. "It's...it's positively indecent."

"Oh, hush, Mother. I haven't anything else to wear."

"That scarlet-colored watered silk, perhaps? It still fits nicely."

Aisling sighed, fingering the velvet gown. "I wore the red silk last year. You know how everyone would talk if I wore it again."

"I suppose. Still, this one shows far too much of your back. People are bound to talk about that."

"Didn't Madame Aubergine say it was the height of fashion in Paris this year?"

Her mother rolled her eyes heavenward. "It's not as if the folks here in Bedlington know what's fashionable in Paris, dear. Oh, well. I suppose there's nothing to be done about it now. Just...just stand with your back to the wall as much as possible, won't you?"

"I'll try," Aisling answered, though she had no intention of doing so. If she had her way, she'd claim another bout of illness and retire as early as possible—before the pantomime began, if she could manage it.

"Well, hurry, then," her mother said. "You haven't much time, you know." She closed the door, and Aisling heard her call out loudly for Clarice.

Seconds later, the girl burst breathlessly into the room. "I'm so sorry, mum." With a scowl, she snatched the hairbrush from Aisling's hand. "Here, sit and let me dress your hair."

With a nod, Aisling sat at her dressing table, staring at her own reflection while Clarice began to drag the bristles through her tousled hair.

"Oh, I almost forgot!" The brush clattered to the marble-topped table as Clarice dug inside her pocket and dragged out an envelope. "This came for you earlier this afternoon.

Quite mysterious, as it appeared after the regular post had arrived."

Aisling took the envelope with shaking hands. There was nothing on it but her name, typed.

"Who do you think it's from?" Clarice murmured around a mouthful of pins, now gathering Aisling's pale hair up on her crown and securing it.

"I've no idea," she lied.

Will. It had to be from Will. Who else? She took a deep, fortifying breath, willing her racing heart to slow.

"Well, mum, aren't you going to open it and find out?"

Trying her best to look nonchalant, she laid the envelope down on the dressing table. "Not now. It's probably just from Louisa, with some last-minute gossip she felt the need to share before the party. I'll open it later."

"Perhaps it's from a secret admirer," Clarice said with dreamy smile. "And perhaps whomever he is will be in attendance tonight. Here, put on some rouge. You're far too pale."

Aisling twisted off the cap and lightly dabbed a bit of the cream onto her cheekbones as Clarice wrapped her coiffure with an amethyst velvet ribbon, the exact same shade as her gown, and secured it with pins.

"There, mum. Just lovely! Now, let's get you dressed so you'll have time to read that letter before the guests arrive."

WILL STRAIGHTENED his tie as he stepped into the crowded ballroom. Wainscott house was packed, people standing shoulder to shoulder as servants pushed their way through with silver trays filled with savory canapés and flutes of champagne. Long tables lined the far wall with silver chafing dishes, the delicious aromas wafting over the crowd. On the far table sat a decorated wassail bowl, delicate glass cups stacked in front of it.

Boughs of holly and fir were draped across every available surface, mistletoe hanging in each and every doorway. Wainscott House at Christmastime was definitely a sight to behold. Somehow, he'd missed their annual Christmas Eve party the past couple of years—he couldn't even remember why.

Had his mother been ill last year? Yes, that was it. And he'd spent the previous Christmas in Cambridge. His mother had taken the train up on Christmas Day and they'd spent the holiday touring the Botanic Garden's glasshouse—a private tour, as it was closed to the public—and then eaten dinner at the University Arms Hotel. Despite her protestations of it being far too fine, he'd made his mother stay the night there at the stately hotel, and he'd taken great pleasure in seeing that she had one the finest rooms overlooking Parker's Piece.

This year, he would not have missed the Wainscott's open house for the world. His mother had allowed Mr. Beeton to escort her there, leaving him free to search for Aisling among the festive, boisterous crowd. He only hoped she'd received his letter. He'd paid a boy from one of the shops in the village to hand deliver it, and he had no idea if the boy had actually done so, or simply pocketed the money and tossed the letter away.

Either way, he would see her tonight. See her, and speak with her. She could not go on avoiding him. In his letter, he'd asked her to meet him in the library once the pantomime began. They'd have at least a half hour, likely more. Long enough to say what he had to say to her.

He began to elbow his way through the crowd, determined to find her.

"Champagne, sir?"

With a nod, he took a delicate crystal flute and downed its entire contents with one jerk of his wrist. He set the empty flute back on the tray while the serving maid scowled at him, shaking her head in disapproval.

The champagne burned a path down to his stomach, warming him, giving him confidence.

"Cooper, old boy!" someone called out, and Will turned to see Jack Wainscott making his way toward him. "Aisling, come say hello to Will Cooper with me, and try and be jolly, won't you?" he bellowed, obviously already far into his cups.

"Glad you could make it," Jack said once he reached Will's side, clapping him on the back. "Have you had your supper yet?"

"No, I've only just..." Will trailed off as Aisling appeared at Jack's side. She looked positively stunning in a purple velvet gown, her narrow waist accentuated by a wide band of black, the skirt narrow at her hips and only flaring as it reached the floor, trailing out behind her. The deep U-shaped neckline was made modest only by crisscrossing bands of wispy black fabric, exposing a generous amount of skin. Indeed, the gentle swell of her breasts was bared to his hungry gaze.

"Scandalous, isn't it?" Jack asked, following the direction of Will's gaze. "Still, it *is* only Aisling, and let me warn you, she's as waspish as ever tonight. I suggest you take care where she's concerned."

Aisling's gaze met Will's in a heated battle, but she remained entirely mute.

"Miss Wainscott," Will said at last, bowing sharply. "You look lovely tonight."

"Thank you," she murmured, her face as blank as a statue's.

"Do me a favor, eh, Cooper? Keep an eye on her and make sure none of the village swains get any ideas, will you? Especially that Lucas James. Oh, come now, Ash," Jack added, seeing his sister's frown. "Cooper here doesn't bite. Do you, old boy?"

Will shrugged. "Not unless she wants me to."

Jack threw back his head and laughed heartily. "I vow, the pair of you! Do try and be civil, won't you? Ah, look. It's Mrs. Brandon with her niece. An heiress to a small fortune, they say. Best go inspect."

With one last clap on Will's back, Jack left them.

For what felt like a full minute, neither of them said a word. They simply stood, being jostled by the crowd as they stared at one another.

"You look breathtaking," he said at last, leaning toward her to be heard over the din of the crowd.

Her smile positively lit up her face. "Thank you. You look rather dashing yourself. I can't remember the last time I saw you in evening dress. It suits you."

"I'm glad you approve," he teased, bolstered by the direction of the conversation. Perhaps this boded well for later. "You received my letter?"

"Yes," was all she said in reply.

"And dare I hope that—"

"Aisling, darling!" Lady Wainscott appeared from nowhere, favoring Will with a bright smile. "Oh, good evening, Mr. Cooper. How good to see you! Is your mother here?" Without awaiting his response, she turned her attention back to her daughter. "Dear, the Brandons just arrived with their niece, Miss Gilchrist. You must go greet them at once, and see that your brother doesn't make a fool of himself, won't you?"

"Of course, Mother. If...if you'll excuse me, Mr. Cooper," she said, allowing herself to be led away by the arm. Once she'd taken a half-dozen steps, she turned, glancing back over one shoulder, her unreadable gaze meeting his for a fraction of a second before she continued on her way.

Will tamped down his anger, wondering just how calculated Lady Wainscott's interruption had been. He hadn't long to think on it before Louisa Abbott plucked at his sleeve.

"Will! Thank goodness. Come, escort me to the supper table, won't you? I'm positively famished and I can barely make my way through this crush."

"Of course," he said, forcing himself to smile as he offered his arm. He liked Louisa Abbott—always had. They'd grown up in the village together, had been childhood playmates. She'd always been uncomplicated and refreshingly direct.

Why not her? he asked himself, admiring Louisa beside him—her willowy frame, her simple good looks. She was of the right age, after all. Smart. Attractive. But most importantly, she was part of his world. Whereas Aisling...

How much simpler everything would be if it were Louisa who made his blood sing, his heart race, who made his cock stiffen with just a single thought of her.

"It all looks delicious, doesn't it?" Louisa asked as they reached the buffet tables. "I vow, I didn't eat a single bite all day, saving up my appetite. You *are* going to join me, aren't you?" she asked, handing him a plate.

"Of course." He took the plate and began to fill it without really noticing what he was taking.

Minutes later, he followed her into the adjoining room and found seats at an empty round table laid with red and cream brocade linens, a silver candelabra casting warm light that competed with the overhead electric chandeliers. "Shall I get you some wine?" he asked, setting down his plate beside Louisa's.

Louisa nodded as she took her seat. "That would be lovely. Hurry back, won't you? I hate sitting all alone."

Not five minutes later he returned, surprised to see the table now entirely full of diners save his empty seat.

"There he is," Louisa called out. "Look, Aisling has joined us. See, I told you he wouldn't mind," she added.

He forced his face into a mask of ennui. "Of course not. Here"—he placed one wineglass down in front of Louisa before taking his seat between the two women—"I hope you like red."

"Yes, thank you. I was just telling Aisling that this is the largest crowd I remember seeing at Wainscott House on Christmas Eve. Oh, this roast beef is divine!"

Will stared straight ahead, twirling the stem of his wine-glass between his fingers. How long must he remain there, between the two women? On his right, Louisa continued to chatter on brightly between bites, enthusiastically compli-menting the food, the company, the decor. On his left, Aisling seemed to push her food about her plate, saying very little and eating even less. He was painfully aware of her there, her shoulder brushing against his every so often. He could smell her scent—violets, as always—could feel the heat of her, warming his skin.

Every time she leaned forward in her seat, he glimpsed the vast expanse of porcelain skin bared by the low-dipping back of her gown and nearly groaned aloud as his cock twitched in his dress trousers. Bloody hell, he was growing hard, just sitting there beside her, desperate to touch her, to brush his fingertips down her bare back, toward her buttocks.

How he wanted to lift her to the table and hike up her skirts, to spread her legs and flick his tongue across her clit till she cried out, arching off the table, clutching at the brocade table linens, her mouth an 'o' of ecstasy.

"Good God, Will. Has the cat got your tongue? You look as if you're a million miles away!"

He blinked away the vision and turned toward Louisa. "I'm sorry. Just a bit distracted today, that's all." His napkin slid off his lap and he reached to catch it, his hand somehow colliding with Aisling's as he did so.

He heard her breath catch, though her face remained as unreadable as before. And then somehow her hand found his again beneath the table, her skin as hot, as flushed as his own.

As the conversation continued around them, their hands met and retreated, fingers brushing flesh, capturing and releasing. He thought he'd go mad with it, this illicit touch. As he massaged the center of her palm with his thumb, it seemed as if they were the only two people in the room, despite the crowd, the merriment surrounding them.

"Cooper, old boy! There you are."

Aisling's hand slipped away as Jack appeared behind them. "Good, good, keeping an eye on my sister, I see. If you've finished your supper, come and join us for a smoke."

Will flexed his now-empty hand, wishing Jack would go away, that they'd all go away.

"It's all right, go on," Louisa said with a nod. "You're just sitting here like a dumb ox, anyway."

Which left him with no choice but to agree, damn it.

*a*isling glanced back over her shoulder, making sure no one was following her, and hurried toward the library. The pantomime had just begun—she could hear the sounds of laughter, floating down the empty corridor from the ballroom.

It was time.

Her little velvet slippers tapped against the marble floor as she quickened her pace, determined to arrive without discovery. When she'd decided that she would meet Will at the requested time, she could not say. Perhaps she'd always meant to, from the moment she'd read his letter, though she'd told herself then that she could not possibly do so—that being alone with him was dangerous, far too dangerous.

But sitting there beside him at supper, pretending they were no more than casual acquaintances had near enough killed her, and she knew she could not let him leave Wain-scott House tonight without seeing him in private, without speaking her piece.

She had to make him see, make him understand. She had to say goodbye, even if it was the most painful thing she'd ever done. Because she couldn't go on like this, wanting him, loving him, knowing she could never truly have him. For how could she? There were so many reasons why it would never work.

Reaching the library at last, she took a deep, fortifying breath, then opened the door and stepped inside.

Will was standing at the far end of the room, gazing out the window, his hands shoved into his pockets. A light snow had begun to fall, pattering gently against the glass. Though he must have heard her entrance, he didn't move, didn't turn around. He just continued to stand there, staring at the night sky beyond the glass.

Aisling closed the door, turning the key in lock. Moving slowly, silently, she took several steps toward him, wishing beyond measure that he would turn around, that he would speak. When she was no more than an arm's reach away, she paused, reaching out one hand toward him, meaning to pluck at his sleeve. Instead, she dropped her hand back to her side, swallowing hard.

And then, like a statue come to life, he turned to face her. Dear God, but he was handsome in his black trousers and tuxedo coat, his boyish tumble of hair falling across his forehead as it always did.

As his penetrating gaze met hers, his mouth lifted into a smile. "I didn't expect you would come," he said at last.

"I had to come. Had to tell you...well, there's so much to say. But first I must apologize. I had no right to read your letter that day in your room, and even less to hold its contents against you. I should not have run out like I did. It was foolish of me. Foolish, and childish."

"You don't have to apologize to me, Ash," he said, shaking his head, though he made no move toward her, no effort to touch her, to take her in his arms.

And, oh, how she wanted to be in those arms!

"Oh, but I do. My behavior these past few days has been nothing short of erratic, my mood swinging wildly from one extreme to the next. I cannot make heads nor tails of it myself, so I can only imagine how puzzling it must be for you."

He shoved his hands more deeply into his pockets. "But you've always been a puzzle to me, Aisling. This week, last year, a decade ago. I've long since given up trying to figure you out. Besides, this thing between us...I think it took us both by surprise. You cannot apologize for that. You cannot apologize for being yourself."

She shook her head, wrapping her arms about herself, suddenly cold. "But don't you see? I'm not myself, not anymore. I was always so sure of who I was, of what I wanted from life. And now..." she trailed off, shaking her head. "Now I'm not sure of anything."

"I'm sure of what I want," he said softly, and Aisling's breath caught in her throat. "I want you, Aisling. Only you. Always."

Aisling squeezed her eyes shut, taking a deep, rattling breath. Her greatest desire, and her greatest fear—all in one tidy package. However would she bear it?

"I love you, Aisling." His fingers brushed her cheek, softly, gently. He had moved closer, so close that she could feel his warm breath against her neck.

Her eyes still closed, she reached blindly for him, pulling him closer, wanting to feel his lips upon hers. "I love you, too, Will," she choked out as he pressed his lips to her throat, just below her ear. "I do, and I'm so very frightened by it."

"Why?" he murmured against her skin. "I won't hurt you, Aisling. Ever." He trailed featherlight kisses up the column of her neck, back down toward her collarbone, raising goose-flesh on her skin.

"Because, don't you see? We'll always wonder, never quite

sure…" She shook her head, unable to say more, knowing he would think it utter nonsense.

Grasping her chin between his forefinger and his thumb, he forced her to meet his gaze. "Never quite sure of what? You must tell me, so I can give you every assurance imaginable."

She swallowed hard before speaking. "The poem, Will. My wish. There was a woman there in the circle of stones that day, a woman I've never seen before or since. She was there one minute, and then, just before I found the box, she simply disappeared into thin air. Like some sort of spirit."

He released her chin, shaking his head with a low chuckle. "I think you've been reading too much fiction, Aisling. Surely you know that's not possible."

"If you'd asked me a fortnight ago, I would have laughed with you and agreed. But…but I can't explain it, Will. You had to be there. It was just at the moment of the solstice, and it felt odd, almost magical. Even as I made my wish, I knew it was impossible, knew I was wishing for a man who did not exist. And then, there you were, that very night at supper. And you're everything I wished for, everything I hoped for."

"Isn't that enough, Aisling? What more do you want from me? I'm willing to give you everything, don't you see? Everything. I know I can't offer you much. Damn it, it sounds bloody ridiculous even suggesting it. You, growing up here"—he waved his hands toward the door—"and me, the bastard son of a washerwoman. That's it, isn't it? I'm asking far too much of you." He turned away from her, raking a hand through his hair.

"That's not it," she cried, clutching at his sleeve, pulling him back to her. "It's not. I swear to you it isn't."

"It isn't? Then pray, enlighten me. You say you love me, that—"

"I do love you. My heart…it's near to bursting with it. It's not as if one day I looked at you and said, 'Oh, dear me, I think I've fallen in love with Will Cooper, isn't that lovely.' No, it was so much more intense than that, almost violent. And don't you see, I've never before felt anything intensely, much less violently. Never, in all my years. But after reading the poem, and making the wish…" She shook her head. "It's like we're both under a spell. How can I ever be sure of my feelings? How can you?"

"Because I don't believe in spells, Aisling. I simply don't believe that you can read a poem, make a wish, and suddenly find yourself feeling things you weren't meant to feel. And the Aisling I've known all these years is a sensible girl who doesn't believe in such nonsense, either."

"I'm no longer that same girl," she said, shaking her head. "All I used to care about was my writing. I would lose myself in my stories for hours on end. And these past two days, I've tried." She took a deep breath. "God knows I've tried to write, to put my newfound experience to good use. I've sat for hours, pen in hand, staring at the blank page. But you know what? The words won't come. For the first time in years, the words simply won't come."

"Have you considered that you no longer have the need to write your fantasies? That you're living them now, instead? You should try another form of fiction—a novel, perhaps, or poetry. Don't you see, in Cambridge there are people like you, writers and poets. You could join a literary circle. Stay at home and write while I'm off at work. I could buy us a house, something modest, but cozy." He looked so earnest, so eager, so damn adoring that it tore at Aisling's heart.

Tears welled in her eyes. "And what then, Will? How long till the doubts creep in? Till you begin to wonder if my feelings for you are real, till you turn to Helena for comfort? Till the spell wears off and we find ourselves shaking our heads in confusion, wondering just how we found ourselves in such a predicament?"

He grasped her shoulders, shaking them hard, *too* hard. "My feelings for you will never change, Aisling. Never. I promise you that."

"I want to believe that, truly I do. But if they do…don't you see? It'll be too late," she said, tears welling in her eyes. She was a coward, after all. Just as she feared. "If I were to go with you to Cambridge, to…to…" she stuttered.

"To marry me?" he supplied.

"Yes. If I did…my parents, they would never accept it. Society would never accept it."

"Since when have you cared what society thought? Damn it, Aisling, be truthful for once."

"I am being truthful," she said miserably. "But you must see what's at stake here."

He released her shoulders, nearly shoving her away. "You truly are a coward, then. God damn you, Aisling. You stand there, denying what we feel, denying what we have." He began to pace, his hands shoved back in his pockets now, his anger palpable.

A single tear traced a scalding hot path down Aisling's cheek. She couldn't move, couldn't speak. She'd been gone too long—surely the pantomime was over by now. Yes, she could hear the faint lilt of Christmas hymns coming from the far side of the house. Soon it would be midnight, and the guests would be lighting their tapers and heading outdoors.

She took a tentative step toward him, wanting to soothe him, to try once more to make him understand. But he turned on her, grabbing her by the shoulders and pulling her toward his chest.

"Damn you, deny *this*," he said, his voice a low growl. His mouth slanted over hers, hot and demanding.

Aisling could not resist—she had no desire to. She opened

her mouth against his, murmuring his name as her tongue sought entrance to his punishing mouth. Desire coursed through her, warming her skin, making her heart race as her tongue tangled with his, searching, exploring, tasting.

She felt him stiffen, felt him try to pull away. *No.* Her fingers tangled in his hair, drawing him closer, refusing to let his mouth leave hers. She wanted to lose herself in his kiss, wanted him to make her forget her doubts, forget everything but how exquisite it felt there in his strong, comforting arms.

Rising on tiptoe, she deepened the kiss, her fingers moving from his hair to his jawbone, cupping his face, holding on to him for dear life. He tasted of wine, of tobacco —entirely male, utterly intoxicating. Dear God, but she could kiss him like this forever; she could never get enough. *Never.*

She moaned softly when his hands moved down her shoulders, to her back, his fingertips grazing her bare skin, moving toward her backside. And then his hands were between their bodies, cupping her breasts, his fingertips massaging her peaked nipples through the layers of clothing.

The friction made her squirm, made her thighs dampen. Pleasure coiled in her belly, radiating down her limbs, making them weak.

With a low groan, he tore his mouth from hers, trailing hot, wet kisses down her throat, over her collarbone, his tongue finding the valley between her breasts. Lower still his mouth moved, his teeth nipping at her now-puckered nipples through the fabric of her gown. Aisling tipped her head back, holding Will's head to her breast, guiding it, whimpering quietly as he sucked and laved.

"Oh, Will," she said on a sigh. "I do love you. Truly, I do."

His face still pressed to her gown, Will fell to his knees, his arms still wrapped around her, clinging to her as if for dear life. Aisling stood there trembling, listening to the first faraway strains of "Silent Night" growing louder as voices joined in.

They were out of time. The guests would be departing soon. Her mother would come looking for her—for all she knew, she was looking for her now. She looked down at Will, still on his knees, the side of his face pressed against her skirts. He was fumbling in his waistcoat's pocket, reaching for something.

And then he released her, holding something up, something that glinted in the dimmed light, like a jewel, a gem. "Marry me, Aisling," he said, gazing up at her hopefully. "I know it isn't much, isn't nearly what you're worth."

All the breath left Aisling's lungs in a rush. There wasn't time—wasn't time to think it through properly, to think logically and reasonably. She turned her head, unable to look, unable to see his offering, knowing full well that, however simple, however modest it might be, it would be the most beautiful jewel she'd ever seen, the most desirable. "I…I can't, Will. Not now. But that does not mean—"

"Don't," he said, rising to his feet, shoving the ring back inside his pocket. A shadow had dropped over his eyes, dulling them, dimming them. "Don't say another word."

The voice of the carolers grew louder, more insistent. Tears filled Aisling's eyes, making her vision blurry. How she despised herself—her cowardice, her insecurity, her inability to trust her own feelings. And there was nothing—nothing at all—she could do about it.

Unless…unless she took a chance. Unless she changed her answer. Unless she took what Will was offering, something she wanted more than anything in all her life, something that would perhaps make her the happiest woman alive. If only she could believe it, if she could trust in it. If only she had faith.

"Wait," she said, reaching for Will's sleeve as he made to move past her. "It's just...I'm not certain, but perhaps—"

"No," he said firmly, removing her hand from his sleeve, shaking his head. He was smiling now, a sad, rueful smile. He leaned in, kissed her softly on the mouth, then stepped away, straightening his coat as he did so. "Thank you, but no. Happy Christmas, Aisling."

And then he left her there, feeling as if her heart had just been cleaved in two.

From out in the drive, the sound of the carolers' voices rose in unison, then faded into nothingness.

Sleep in Heavenly Peace.

At that moment, Aisling knew she'd never again know peace. Not as long as she lived.

*W*ill sprawled in the chair in the corner of his room, one hand clutching a glass of whisky, the other cupping his throbbing temple. His vision slightly blurred from the drink, he stared at the foot of his bed, trying his damnedest to erase the vision of Aisling there, her wrists tied to the iron bars.

If he inhaled deeply enough, he could almost recall her scent—the scent of violets mixed with desire. The memory of their coupling hung heavily in the air, almost a living, breathing thing. He took another swig of whiskey, hoping to drown out the memories—the feel of her skin, the heat of her body, sheathing him. How would he ever get her out of his head? How would he cure himself of this hopeless infatuation, this ill-fated obsession?

Somehow, he had to. She'd refused him—fucking refused him, and just minutes after telling him that she loved him. He threw back his head and laughed at the irony of it. She loved him, yes. But not enough to marry him, apparently. A sharp, piercing pain tore through his gut.

Well, he was done with her, then. He rose on unsteady

legs, taking one last draught of his drink, then slamming the empty glass down on the desk. He wouldn't think of her. Wouldn't dream about her. And, most importantly, he wouldn't give her the chance to come running back to him with more excuses, more ridiculous nonsense about magic and spells forcing them to feel things that weren't real.

His feelings *were* real, and right now they were ripped to bloody shreds.

He reached for his trunk, throwing open the lid and gathering the stack of books from his desk, tossing them inside without care. Forget staying through the New Year—Christmas had come and gone, and he was ready to go back to Cambridge, back where people respected him, where they didn't give a damn who his father was, or what his mother did to make her living.

He refused to sit around, twiddling his thumbs, waiting for Aisling to see the truth. She'd had her chance, damn it. There was nothing else to keep him in Bedlington. Only memories.

Just walking through the village brought them back, one by one, long-forgotten memories of days gone by. The huge oak at the edge of the village green, the one Aisling had climbed at Jack's dare and then gotten frightened, clutching the tree's trunk for dear life, refusing to come back down. He'd climbed up himself, pretending to be far braver than he was where heights were concerned, and led the trembling girl down by the hand. She couldn't have been more than six or seven at the time, her wheat-blond hair held back by a bow, her white dress ruffled and flounced.

And then there was the grassy field where they'd played cricket as children—him, Jack, Aisling, Louisa, and the Brandon children. So many Sunday afternoons, spent there. Aisling always got to choose her team first, and she always chose Will, claiming he was faster than the rest of them. Which was true, now that he thought about it.

And then there was the circle of standing stones near Wainscott House where Aisling liked to sit and write, nibbling on her pen. How many times had he stopped and stood beneath a tree, secretly watching her, wondering just what kind of words she put to the page? He'd imagined her writing poetry, just because it seemed the kind of thing that a proper young lady like Aisling would do.

He vividly remembered the day that Jack went up to Eton, leaving her behind. It had seemed so unfair—she'd always been the smartest one, smarter than any of them. All her playmates had been sent to school, even Louisa—everyone but Aisling, despite her intelligence, because young ladies of Aisling's station didn't get formally schooled, of course. They were taught to speak French, some German, perhaps. They studied literature and music, learned to sew and to paint. Useless things, all. Aisling had been groomed to be some gentleman's wife and nothing more, despite the fact that she was wickedly clever, that she was far better at sums than her brother was.

He shook his head, forcing away the memories, willing himself to stop thinking about her as he tossed his belongings haphazardly into his trunk. Tomorrow he would get on the morning train and go back to Cambridge, back to his life there.

And Aisling...she would stay in the past, damn it. Buried in memories, where she belonged, before he'd been stupid enough to think otherwise.

Damn it all, what he wouldn't give to take back those words he'd spoken so carelessly on Christmas Eve. He shook his head, glaring at the hateful little box that sat on his dresser holding the ring he'd gone all the way to Dorchester to purchase, so bloody confident that he'd be able to convince her to marry him.

He'd actually gotten down on his knees like a lovesick fool! No doubt she was having a laugh about it now. Crossing the room in three long strides, he took the box and threw it as hard as he could, not giving a damn where it landed. It didn't matter; it was rubbish now, as far as he was concerned.

His anger now spent, he collapsed back in the chair, cradling his head in his hands. A wave of humiliation washed over him as his vision blurred, his eyes suddenly damp.

Damn you, Aisling Wainscott. Yes, he would get on that train tomorrow, and he would never look back.

AISLING FELT a hand on her shoulder and turned to find Jack standing there behind her.

"Good God, Ash, what's the matter with you? You've been sitting here staring out the window for hours now."

Aisling just shrugged in reply, turning back toward the window. The sky was gray and a heavy fog was rolling in, obscuring the trees in the distance now, moving slowly toward the house in dark, curling wisps.

"Actually, you've been moping about since Christmas," he accused. "As if it isn't morose enough around here with Mother upstairs crying all day."

Because Father had left, returning to London—to Mrs. Gaylord, of course—the day after Christmas. The gifts had barely been put away, the fruitcakes and various other seasonal treats not yet entirely consumed. But that hadn't stopped Sir Reginald from fleeing back to his mistress with the barest of excuses, the bastard.

She glanced down at the new ruby and diamond bracelet

she wore on her wrist, her father's gift, and a rather lavish one, at that. *I'll give it to Jack to sell in London,* she thought to herself, fingering the exquisite gems. It would fetch a fair sum, fattening her bank account.

"Aisling?" Jack sat down beside her on the settee and reached for her hand. "You must tell me what's wrong. I can't bear to see you like this."

"What do you mean, 'like this'?" she asked, refusing to look at him, to meet his gaze.

"Why, pale and drawn, your eyes red-rimmed, as if you've been crying. You, crying! God only knows you've never been one for tears."

"My eyes are just…just irritated, that's all. I'm sure I'm coming down with something."

"I'm sure you're lying, Aisling. Come, now, it's me you're talking to. I know you as well as I know myself. There's no fooling me—surely you know that by now."

"I'd rather not talk about it, if you don't mind," she said sharply, pulling her hand from his grasp.

"Oh, no. You're not getting off that easily. You can't simply brush me aside like you do everyone else. I'll hound you till you break—you know that I will," he threatened, his voice light and teasing.

"Oh, bugger off, won't you?" Aisling snapped. In her heart she knew that Jack didn't deserve it, her ill temper. Yet she could not tell him the truth. It didn't matter that Will was Jack's friend, that he was as educated as Jack was. It was well and good for them to be friends, but for Will and Aisling to be lovers? No, Jack would never approve. Worse, he would be furious. There was no telling what he'd do, what he'd say. Besides, it didn't matter. They were done. There was nothing left to discuss.

"Aisling, please," Jack tried once more, his voice so tender that Aisling thought her heart might break. *Again.*

"I can't," she choked out. "I can't tell you what's happened, Jack. I wish I could, but I can't."

For a full minute, Jack simply started at her, not saying a word. And then realization lit his eyes. "It's a man, isn't it? You look heartsick. I hate to say it, but you look just like Mother does right now." He stood, an angry flush stealing up his neck. "Who's done this to you? Tell me, so that I can wring his bloody neck, the bastard."

Aisling inhaled sharply, refusing to give in to the blasted tears yet again. No, she was done crying. Done feeling sorry for herself. It was time to pull herself up by the bootstraps and get on with life, such as it was.

"It's done, Jack. Over. Besides, if anyone's neck should be wrung, it's my own."

He shook his head. "You may be stubborn, tenacious, even. Irritating at times, yes. But deserving of whatever is making you look so damned miserable? No, I don't believe it."

"Then I don't know what else to say, Jack."

"Whoever he is, he's not worth *this*, I can tell you that," he snapped.

"That's just it. He *is* worth it. And I'm the biggest bloody fool in all of England."

Jack paced a circuit back and forth, his hands thrust into his pockets. "I can't even imagine who. It isn't as if there have been any eligible men around here, not lately. The Dalton brothers, I suppose, but you barely glanced at either of them."

Aisling fiddled with the hem of her sleeve. "The Dalton brothers are a pair of boorish pigs."

Jack stopped his pacing and knelt beside her, the color drained from his face. "Dear God, Aisling, please tell me you haven't been dallying with Lucas James!"

"Good God, no!" she answered, taken aback. Lucas James

was the butcher's son, two years her junior, and as thick and dumb as an ox. "Just how desperate do you think I am?"

Jack raked a hand through his hair. "Well, it isn't as if there's been anyone else around these past few weeks. I mean, besides Will Cooper, of course."

Aisling willed her face to remain blank so as not to betray her. "And weren't you chastising me just last week about him, calling me a snob?"

Jack laughed uneasily. "I was, wasn't I?"

Aisling said nothing in reply, hoping that Jack would drop the subject and leave her in peace.

"Though mark my words, you could do far worse than Will Cooper, gentleman or no. Just don't tell Mother I said so. I mean, of course she wouldn't approve, not at first. I imagine she'd come around eventually, though. After all, Will's a good chap."

Jack rubbed his chin thoughtfully. "Now that I think about it, you two are as well suited as any two people I've ever met. You're so much alike, the pair of you. And truthfully, I've always thought that perhaps he secretly fancied you, though he'd never in a million years admit to it." Jack sighed loudly. "If only you weren't such a blasted snob. Ah, well. I suppose if you won't tell me..."

Aisling shook her head, trying her best to appear calm when beneath the surface she was anything but. He'd come too close to the truth—far too close.

"Will you at least promise me, then, that you'll stop moping around? Go write one of your scandalous stories or something. The editor at *The Boudoir* is positively begging for more of your work—I can't get it to him fast enough. If you can't be happy, at least make us some money while you're busy being miserable."

"You'd like that, wouldn't you?" she asked with a wry smile. "Money for nothing."

"I'd like for you to be happy, Ash," he said, all serious now.

She swallowed a lump in her throat, thinking just how much she loved her brother. "I know, Jack. Please...just give me time."

"Very well." He leaned down and kissed her on one cheek. "Carry on, then."

She just nodded, unable to say a single word in reply.

Several hours later, Aisling sat in bed, propped up with feather pillows behind her back, the heavy eiderdown quilt pulled up to her chin. The little wooden box with the poem inside sat there in her lap, though she resisted the urge to open it and examine the old parchment yet again. Instead, Jack's words were playing over and over again in her mind.

He'd thought Will had fancied her all along. Was it possible? Hadn't Will himself said something to the same effect? If only she could remember his exact words.

Something about a spark that had always been there, about wanting her, and hating her for not wanting him. But what if she *had* wanted him? What if she'd been angry—with him, with herself—all these years because she had realized they were perfectly suited, but assumed that she could never have him?

Hope flamed brightly in her breast. Perhaps these feelings they had for one another weren't so new, after all. Perhaps they'd been there, taking root, blossoming all these years, until they were both ready to recognize them, until Aisling was brave enough to defy her parents—because that's what it would require for her to cast her lot with Will. She knew it to be true, despite Jack's approval, his optimism.

Her mother was not nearly as liberal-minded as her brother was, no doubt about that. The bastard son of a washerwoman would never be good enough for Lady Wainscott's daughter, no matter his education, no matter who his father might be. Perhaps Aisling could only recognize her feelings for Will once she was old enough, strong enough, to go against the opposition she was sure to face in the form of her mother.

And if that were true, then it had nothing to do with the poem, nothing to do with the wish she'd made on the solstice. Or perhaps the poem only made her realize her true feelings, made her subconsciously wish for someone exactly like Will, so that she could finally acknowledge that *he* was her winter's desire. Her summer's desire, her autumn's desire, her spring's desire.

He was her *every* desire.

Throwing back the bed linens, Aisling swung her legs over the side of the mattress and reached for her dressing gown, standing as she belted it tightly around her waist. She retrieved the little wooden box from the bed and placed it on her desk, beside her typewriter, and sat, reaching for a pen and piece of paper.

She would write Will a letter; she would tell him what was in her heart, what had always been in her heart. She would tell him that she'd been mistaken. And then she would beg him for another chance, another opportunity to prove herself worthy of his love, his ring. They could start over, lovers *and* friends this time.

First thing tomorrow morning, she would drive to the village and deliver the letter herself. She only hoped it wasn't too late.

*A*isling swallowed hard before reaching up to rap on the door. Clasping the letter in front of her, she took a step back and waited, listening as the sound of footsteps grew louder.

Please let it be Will, and not his mother.

The door swung open. "Miss Wainscott," Mrs. Cooper said, her brow furrowed as she stared down at her.

Aisling cleared her throat, her resolve wavering. "Good day, Mrs. Cooper. I…um, I do hope you're well."

Mrs. Cooper's eyes narrowed a fraction. "I'm very well, thank you. Have you come to fetch your mother's gown? I'm not quite done with it, I'm afraid."

"No. I came…that is to say…" she trailed off miserably. Now what? *The truth.* There was no other way. "I was hoping to have a word with Will."

She wiped her hands on her apron. "You've come to see Will?"

"Yes, I….ahem, you see, I need to speak with him. I know this is a bit irregular, but—"

"Well, miss, I'm afraid you're too late for that," she interrupted. "He's gone back to Cambridge, left this morning on the early train. Judging by your appearance here today, I suppose I have *you* to thank for his sudden departure."

"I'm sorry, Mrs. Cooper. I don't know what he's told you—"

"He's told me nothing," she snapped. "Not a single word of it, though I've got two eyes and ears. I know my own son, and I know when he's hurting. Hasn't he had a hard enough time of it, all these years, without you toying with him?"

Aisling didn't know what to say. She'd never felt so small, so ashamed as she did at that very moment. She'd driven him away—and not just from her, but from his mother, too. All because she'd been too afraid to listen to her own heart.

"I...I came here today to try and make it right," she stuttered, her cheeks burning uncomfortably under the woman's scrutinizing stare.

"Well, as I said, it's too late for that. Now, if you'll excuse me, I have work to do." She pulled the door shut with a *thump*, leaving Aisling standing there on the front step, her legs suddenly weak and wobbly.

She hadn't counted on this. He'd said he was staying till after the New Year. As she'd lain in bed waiting for the sun to rise, she'd pictured several different scenarios in her mind, imagining exactly what she'd say to make things right. But this? Never. In each of her imagined scenarios, she'd had the chance to speak with him, to give him her letter.

Turning away from the door, she shoved the letter inside her coat's pocket and began to walk through the thick fog, back toward her motorcar. What now? She hadn't any idea how to proceed, short of taking the train to Cambridge herself, and she was lucid enough to realize that she needed to think it through more carefully before she did something like that, showing up unannounced on his doorstep.

First of all, her mother would never allow it. Secondly,

she had no idea where, precisely, he lived in Cambridge. *Perhaps Jack would agree to accompany me,* she thought as she reached her motorcar. But that would require telling him everything, confessing her sins, she realized.

No. She couldn't tell Jack, not yet. Damn Will for taking the coward's way out, for fleeing Bedlington like he had! What was she to do now? Simply post her letter and sit patiently awaiting his reply? For all she knew, he might reconcile with this Helena woman before her letter even arrived.

With a huff, she opened the car's door and scooted inside.

A telegraph, perhaps? No, she could never say the things she needed to say in a telegraph. *It's hopeless,* she realized. Entirely so. She'd lost her chance, just as she feared.

Reaching into the compartment on the dash, she retrieved her veil and goggles, putting the silly looking glasses on before pinning the veil to her hat and pulling it down around her face. Feeling almost numb, she went through the motions of starting the car, pushing the plunger on the dash, then hopping out to turn the crank. The engine roared to life, and she returned to her seat, gripping the wheel tightly as she forced herself to concentrate on the fog-obscured road as she motored through the village toward home.

I should have walked, she told herself as she guided the car off the village's main thoroughfare and onto the wider, tree-lined road that led to Wainscott House. The dense fog made it near enough impossible to see, even with headlamps lighting the way. It was just after noon, and it was already as dark as dusk. Somewhat eerie, she thought, tightening her grip on the wheel.

At least the fog had brought with it warmer air. It almost felt balmy compared to last week's frigid chill. Still, the dreary gray skies did nothing for her mood, nothing to calm—

"Damnation!" she cried out, slamming on the brake, the force of the sudden stop slinging her so far forward that she nearly cracked her forehead on the wheel. A figure had appeared in the road directly in front of her, seeming to materialize out of thin air.

Aisling blinked several times, trying to focus her vision on the woman who stood there, not five feet in front of the car, wrapped in a black woolen cloak. Dark, curly hair peeked out from the hood's folds, the woman's face cast entirely in shadows.

"Pardon me," Aisling called out loudly over the motor's hum. "I'm so sorry, I didn't see you there. Can I offer you a ride?"

The woman shook her head, then lifted one arm and pointed toward the woods to her right.

Whatever did she mean by that? There was nothing over that way, no houses. Nothing but the circle of stones, off in the distance... Of course! It was the woman she'd seen on the solstice—she was strangely sure of it.

"I must speak with you," Aisling called out, her heart pounding in her breast. "Just let me cut the motor." She glanced down at the dash for a single second, then looked up again, gasping in surprise. The woman was gone. Vanished, just like that, in the blink of an eye.

All the breath left her lungs in a rush. No, it couldn't be. She reached over the door to pull the hand brake, then stood, looking in every direction, searching wildly for the woman through the thick curtain of fog.

"Miss?" she cried out. "Please, come back!."

Nothing. She'd simply disappeared. Good God, but she was losing her mind. Reaching back over the door, she released the brake and continued on. She was overwrought, that was all. It was the fog, making her see things that weren't there. That had to be it.

A quarter hour later she reached Wainscott House, pulling up into the drive and cutting the motor. She unpinned her veil and hurried inside, listening carefully to see if anyone was about. The house was quiet as a tomb. Peering down the corridor, she saw a light shining from her brother's study. He must have heard her car motoring up the drive, but mercifully he did not open the door and call out to her, so she continued on, up the wide staircase toward her room.

She knew what she had to do, and quickly, before anyone waylaid her. She would put an end to this nonsense —and now.

Not five minutes later she stepped out the back door, the little wooden box clutched in her hands. The poem was folded up inside, just as she'd found it. She moved silently across the park, past the swimming pond and off toward the copse of trees in the distance.

Ducking through the bare, spindly branches, she hurried on, easily finding her way despite the limited visibility. After all, her feet knew this path well. Finally, the stones came into view, wispy fog seeming to cling to them.

Taking a deep, fortifying breath, she continued on to the center of the circle and placed the box at her feet. Kneeling down beside it, she removed her gloves and opened the box's fastening, just as she'd done on the solstice. She took out the parchment and unfolded it with shaking hands, her anger mounting, gathering strength, burning like fire through her veins.

It had to be done. The poem had brought her to this—this deep despair, this dark melancholy. All because she'd allowed herself to believe in it, however briefly, however reluctantly.

But now…now she knew better.

"Take it back," she cried out, her voice echoing off the stones. "I don't want it. I don't believe in your magic. Do you hear me?"

With that, she ripped the old parchment into tiny little bits and tossed them into the air, watching as the torn pieces rained back down to the damp earth, littering the center of the circle around her.

And then she heaved a sigh, her shoulders sagging. Never again would she allow herself to feel those things—love and longing, passion and desire. She couldn't. Her heart felt as ripped to shreds as the poem, and nothing could put it back together again, no more than she could reassemble the scattered pieces of parchment.

Stooping down, she retrieved her gloves from the ground and shoved her hands inside them, flexing her fingers as she rose and turned to leave, to head home. But a figure standing there, off in the distance, stilled her feet. She couldn't see properly—the blasted fog made it impossible. But it looked like... Dear God, but it looked like Will!

No, I'm imagining it. She shook her head, hoping to clear it, to make the vision disappear. *Just like the woman in the road.*

But the figure didn't disappear. Instead, it started moving toward her, moving out of the fog, becoming less specter-like and more solid with each passing second. She could've sworn it was a man—a man, wearing a dark coat and bowler hat. He stepped into the circle, entirely revealed now.

It *was* Will. She didn't know how or why—didn't care, really. All that mattered was that he was there, not a dozen feet away now. One hand rose to her throat as she swallowed hard, unable to speak, unable to move a single muscle, afraid he would disappear if she did so.

At last he stood directly before her, close enough to touch. His mouth lifted into a smile, his bright blue eyes the only spot of color in the otherwise bleak, gray surroundings.

"This isn't real," she murmured. "I'm imagining it. You can't be real. You went back to Cambridge on the morning train."

He nodded, removing his hat and holding it against one hip. "I made it as far as London. Changed for Cambridge, and as I sat there waiting for the train to depart, they called another leaving for Dorset. The return train. Something told me I had to get on that train, had to come back to you. I couldn't do it, couldn't leave you."

"I'm so glad," she breathed. "So very glad, Will."

His gaze met hers, held it for heartbeat's second before he turned away from her, looking around the circle as if he were seeing it for the first time. "I had a feeling I'd find you here."

"You were right," she said hurriedly, before he could silence her. "Entirely right, about everything. It wasn't the poem, wasn't the magic. I think whatever it is we're feeling was always there, just waiting for us discover it. I should never have doubted it, doubted *you*. Will you ever forgive me?"

"There's nothing to forgive, Ash," he said with a shrug. "How many times must I say that to you?"

"I should have been more sure of my own heart, more sure of yours. But now…"

"Now, what?" he prodded. "Will you let me kiss you, make love to you, and then change your mind again? Decide it *is* the magic, after all? Back and forth, all over again?"

"I won't," she answered, entirely sure of it. "Never again. I know I have no right to ask you to trust me, to believe me. I would not fault you if you didn't, if you turned around and left right now. But please, hear me out first. It's all I ask of you."

He nodded, looking exhausted, she realized, his face drawn, his eyes shadowed. "I'm listening, Aisling."

"You're my perfect match in every way, Will Cooper. My

heart's desire, everything I've ever wanted in a man. All these years, I've resisted my mother's efforts, refused to have a Season, refused to marry Thomas Esterbrooke, because I knew—deep in my heart—that I wasn't meant to be some fancy gentleman's wife, the mere possession of some man who would never consider me his equal, his partner. I think deep down I always knew I was meant to be yours—a botanist's wife, an artist's lover."

Will's mouth twitched, as if he were suppressing a smile. "Just so you know, I'll never be able to afford a country house, an estate like the one you grew up in. I don't go to London unless I have to, and I employ no servants. My life is simple, modest—nothing like yours and Jack's. I'm not certain it's fair to ask you to give up the things you're accustomed to, the privilege you were born to."

Aisling shook her head, desperate to make him see, to make him understand. "But without you, those things mean nothing to me, Will. I know it sounds trite, melodramatic, even. But it's the truth. I've never been more sure of anything in all my life."

"Your parents will never approve. They'll likely disown you, you know."

"That's their misfortune, then. Besides, Jack will be on our side."

He cocked one brow. "What makes you say that?"

"A conversation we had just yesterday. He doesn't know, was only speaking hypothetically. But he made his approval perfectly clear."

"You really think we can do this?" Will asked, dropping his hat to the ground and reaching for her hand.

"Well, just so *you* know, I won't be anything near an obedient wife, and I throw things when I get angry. I can't cook, so you'll have to do more than just get your own tea. Oh, and I don't care how fashionable it is to take a mistress.

I'll require full fidelity, utter devotion—otherwise, I'll castrate you myself," she teased, her racing heart slowing at last.

"I have no doubt that you would," he said with a laugh. "Anything else I should be aware of?"

"I think that's everything. For now, at least. I'm sure I can come up with more later."

"So, it was Esterbrooke then, was it?" Will asked with a mischievous glint in his eyes. "Gad, I almost wish I didn't know that. Now every time I see the man, I'll be tempted to knock his bloody teeth down his throat."

She couldn't help but smile, strangely pleased by his show of jealousy. "Trust me, Will, he's no competition, none at all. When I compare...well, never mind that."

Will removed his gloves, shoving them into his pockets, and then he pulled her up against his chest, his lips just inches from hers. "So, what do we do now?"

"I can think of several things. Several naughty things, in fact."

"You *do* realize you're still wearing your driving goggles, don't you?" he asked, grinning down at her.

"Hell and damnation!" She reached up to her face, surprised to find that she *was* still wearing them. With a wince, she removed them, shoving them into her coat's pocket. "How foolish I must have looked! Why on earth didn't you tell me before now?"

He shrugged, pulling her back against his chest, stroking the sides of her face with his calloused thumbs. "You looked so charming, having your say while wearing them. You can't even imagine...threatening to cut off my ballocks while you glared at me, looking almost cross-eyed. It was adorable, really."

Slowly, his mouth moved toward hers, his eyes never leaving

her face. Aisling thought she'd go mad, waiting for his kiss, wanting him, needing him. When their lips touched at last, she moaned, barely able to stand the very exquisiteness of it. Gently, tenderly, he captured her lower lip, suckled it, his hands sliding down her back, cupping her bottom as he drew her closer still.

Tipping her head back, she opened her mouth against his —inviting him, near enough begging him. He answered her silent plea, taking her mouth harder this time, tasting and retreating till Aisling flung her arms around his neck and refused to let him go, kissing him deeply, thoroughly, till they were both breathless.

"Have you any idea how badly I want you, Aisling?" he asked, his voice rough and ragged.

"Right here? In the circle of stones?" she teased, trying to catch her breath.

"Why not? I'm sure this place has seen such things before, back in ancient times. Some Druid ritual, perhaps." He dragged her back toward the tallest of stones, pressing her back against it, caging her in with both hands on either side of her head.

She ducked under his arms. "Yes, but afterwards you'd probably be expected to sacrifice me." When he turned to face her, she leaned into him, pressing herself against his erection while she nipped at his neck.

"Do you have a problem with that?" he asked, smiling wickedly. "Me, sacrificing you to the gods?"

In reply, she moved her hand to his cock, grasping it tightly through his wool trousers.

"Yes? Well, then, we'll do it differently. Start a new tradition." He captured her around the waist and lifted her, pushing her back against the stone. Bending down, he reached under the hem of her coat, under her skirt and petticoat, trailing his hands up her limbs, to her hips, bunching her skirts up at her waist. "Are you cold?" he asked, reaching for the tapes that held up her drawers.

"Warm me," she answered with a shrug. Reaching for his coat, she began to unbutton it, one by one. "Take me—right here, right now."

"Trying to shock me again, I see," he murmured, slipping a finger inside her, making her gasp with pleasure. "And here I thought you were a proper young lady. A baronet's daughter."

"Didn't you know?" she said breathlessly as he began to stroke her. "I'm to be married to a botanist—a very wicked one. Now unfasten your trousers."

"Bossy, too," he said, pushing open the front of her coat, exposing her throat, pressing his lips against her lace collar, his breath warm and moist against her skin. "But I suppose one of us will have to be obedient."

She felt him fumble with his trousers and sighed with relief when she felt the tip of him pressing against her sex, searching for entrance. Raising one leg, she hitched it around his hip.

"This botanist," he said, his voice gruff. "Do you love him?"

"Oh!" she cried out as he thrust into her, pinning her against the stone. "Yes. Yes, I love him."

Again, he thrust into her—harder, more insistent this time. "Then he's the luckiest man alive." Faster, harder he began to drive into her. Aisling met his every thrust, tilting her hips toward his, her breathing growing more ragged as the now-familiar coil of pleasure made her begin to tremble, made her limbs go weak, made her sex weep with desire.

With one last thrust, Will pushed her over the edge, her insides pulsating against the length of him as his hot seed pumped into her, warming her.

"Dear God, Aisling," he groaned, collapsing against her. "My love," he whispered. "My life."

Aisling's heart swelled, a quiet sob torn from her throat as tears burned behind her eyelids. Only this time they were happy tears, she realized. Good tears. Tears of joy. One slipped down her cheek, but Will's thumb wiped it away before it reached her chin.

"You," he said, his gaze meeting hers, their bodies still joined, "are the most exquisite creature I've ever known."

Return his head, upon my breast, burn bright of winter's desire. The words slipped into her mind, uninvited. A line from the poem, the one she'd just torn into a million little bits. And yet…it was fitting, wasn't it?

Thank you, she thought, *for returning him to me.* Whatever the cause, whatever the reason…it didn't matter. She had her winter's desire, and she was never letting him go.

Kissing her softly on the forehead, Will withdrew from her, reaching down to fasten his trousers. With gentle hands, he pulled up her drawers, retying the tapes before smoothing back down her skirts. "I do hope you're not freezing," he murmured against her temple.

"No," she said, finding her voice at last. "It's so warm today. Perfect, really, for such outdoor pursuits as this."

"Come with me, back to my mother's cottage. I've got something for you there. If I can find it again, that is. It would seem that I throw things when I'm angry, too." He retrieved his hat and tipped it back on his head, then held out his hand to her.

Aisling just nodded, linking her fingers with his.

"So, what do you think of our new tradition? Here in the circle, I mean?" he asked, smiling down at her with that lazy, cocky grin she loved so well.

She gave his hand a squeeze. "I think we should return

here each year and repeat it. On the winter's solstice, perhaps."

"Didn't it snow this year on the solstice?"

Aisling shrugged. "We'll just be quick about it, that's all."

Suddenly Will stopped and turned back toward the stones. "Wait, what about that box? The little wooden one with the strange symbol on it. You left it in the circle."

"Oh, I don't need it anymore," she said without glancing back. "Besides, I think it belongs there." She tugged on Will's hand, and with a nod he matched his step to hers.

A wind picked up as the lovers continued on, their heads bent together in quiet conversation, their laughter echoing through the copse of trees. Back in the circle of stones, the little pieces of parchment lifted off the ground, swirling briefly around the circle like snow, and then scattered on the breeze, disappearing into the mist.

Hope reborn, come with the sun
  dispel the chill of darkness
  bright fire of dawn
  reach to our hearts
  burn bright of winter's desire

EPILOGUE

*S*ix months later...

"I still can't believe it," Jack said, shaking his head. "You, a mother?"

Aisling rolled her eyes heavenward. "Is it really so hard to believe? And stop laughing. Anyway, we've been married nearly six months now."

"Here's your tea, Ash," Will said, reaching over his wife's gently rounded belly to hand her a cup and saucer. "How do you take yours, Jack?"

"One lump of sugar and a dash of cream," Jack answered with a wry smile. "So very domestic of you, old boy."

"I won't let Aisling lift a finger, not till this baby is born. The doctor says she's not to overtax herself."

"By pouring tea?" Aisling set her cup on the side table. "Really, Will, I promise you I'm not as delicate as that."

Will leaned over and planted a kiss on the top of her head. "I'm not taking any chances, if you don't mind. Besides, I rather like pouring the tea."

"Do you?" Jack stroked his chin thoughtfully. "I vow, this

is a side of you I've never seen. What has my sister done to you?"

"Shouldn't you be asking what he's done to your sister? Look at me." Aisling spread her arms wide. "I'm already as big as a house, with four months more to go."

"I've never seen you so radiant," Jack answered with a smile. "Or so happy. It suits you, Aisling."

Tears sprung to Aisling's eyes, forcing her to blink them away. "I've never been happier. It seems I was just waiting for this—for Will, for our own home, a baby on the way. And I'm writing again, Jack. A novel this time—a serious one. I'm so content, so very pleased with my life. Who would have ever thought it so?"

Jack shook his head. "I'm glad. Truly, I am." He appeared to sober. "I've brought a letter from Mum."

Aisling's mood soured at once. "Oh, lovely. I'm sure you've read it—what does it say?"

Jack didn't even bother to look apologetic. "She wants to come to Cambridge. To pay you a visit. To apologize, I believe. Will you let her?"

"I'll consider it," she said shortly.

"She knows she was wrong—about Will, about your marriage. I do think she's sorry, Ash. Give her a chance."

Aisling plucked absently at the hem of her sleeve. "Does she know about the baby?"

"Of course not. It's not my place to tell her. But you must know she'll be thrilled. Once she gets over the initial shock, that is. Certainly no one thought you had it in you. You've never had a nurturing bone in your body, have you? You despised our little cousins, thought they were noisy and dirty and—"

"Yes, I think we get the picture," Aisling said with a silencing wave. "Just so you know, dear brother, this was a choice we made, Will and I, and not a careless accident.

Besides, our cousins were little brats." She reached down to rub her belly affectionately. "My baby—*our* baby—will be lovely. Won't he, Will?"

Will nodded as he moved to stand behind Aisling, his hands on her shoulders. "Or she. But yes. Absolutely." He bent and placed a kiss on her neck. "As lovely and clever as her mother," he murmured.

Aisling's head fell to the side with a sigh, a dreamy smile on her face. "Or as handsome and talented as his father."

"Good God, are the two of you always this revolting? Here, the letter." Jack pulled the folded page from his breast pocket, the wax seal visibly broken, and slapped it down on the table. "Ill take that tea now."

While Will poured for Jack, Aisling quickly scanned the letter, which her brother had summarized well. It was short and to the point. Her mother was sorry; she wished to reconcile. She was lonely, no doubt, Aisling realized. How quiet the house must seem now, with her husband in town, entertaining his mistress, and Aisling settled in Cambridge. She had no one but Jack to keep her company, and Jack had his own affairs to attend to.

It was also possible that she'd heard about the baby from Will's mother, though they'd asked her to keep the news quiet for now. Mrs. Cooper had softened toward Aisling once she'd realized that she was serious about her son—that she planned to marry him. And now that she *had* married him, what more could she hold against her? It was clear to anyone who bothered to look that they were madly in love—dizzyingly so.

Aisling glanced around the room, so cozy and attractive with its hand-carved furniture and inviting fabrics, the walls decorated with several of Will's botanical sketches. Aisling had taken great pride in furnishing the small house just so, never before realizing she had such an eye for decor. It had given her great pleasure, something she had not expected. After all, she'd simply taken everything in Wainscott House—the art, the fine furnishings—for granted.

Her new maple writing desk sat in the room's far corner, overlooking the garden that was carefully and meticulously tended by Will. The house was always filled with fragrant blooms and cuttings, their table with fresh herbs and fruits and vegetables. Indeed, theirs was a lovely home, a happy home. Her life was nearly perfect, except for the inevitable rift with her parents.

She would accept her mother's apology, of course. Aisling had never been one to hold grudges. And besides, why should her little one have just one besotted grandmama when she could have two? Yes, she would invite her mother to Cambridge at once, and make peace with her.

With a satisfied smile, she reached for her tea, her gaze meeting her husband's over the rim of her cup as she brought it to her lips. His blue eyes lit with a smile, a twinkle of mischief, before he winked and turned his attention back to Jack. Even now, her skin warmed and her heart fluttered when her husband so much as glanced her way. It was all she could do not to send Jack on his way so that she could have her way with Will—right then, right there. He was, indeed, her *every* desire.

At last, Aisling was finally free.

MIDNIGHT SINS

CELTIC HEAT VOL. 2

Copyright © 2012, 2020 by Kristina Cook

All rights reserved.

No part of this book may be reproduced in any form or by any electronic or mechanical means, including information storage and retrieval systems, without written permission from the author, except for the use of brief quotations in a book review.

"Beware the Dark Lords" poem Copyright © 2012 by Amanda McIntyre, used with the author's permission

Cover Design by James, GoOnWrite.com

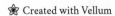 Created with Vellum

CHAPTER 1

Lake District, England, 1914

By Madeline's estimation, the best part of traveling by motorcar was that it rendered conversation impossible—or nearly so, at least. She glanced over at Francis sitting beside her on the black tufted seat, the bracing autumn chill reddening his cheeks. The wind whipped the ginger hair that peeked out from his tweed motoring cap.

As if sensing her gaze, he turned toward her, his pale blue eyes narrowing a fraction. "Don't scowl," he shouted over the motorcar's engine. "It isn't at all attractive."

She flicked her gaze back to the passing scenery, a blur of burnished reds and golds as they motored through the Cumberland countryside. The Lake District was beautiful this time of year, though that was little consolation as she faced the prospect of spending the next several days in her husband's company.

For the most part, she and Francis led separate lives. She preferred their country estate in Herefordshire, while he preferred London and all its trappings. Francis was far too busy spending the fortune she'd brought to the marriage to care what anyone thought about their arrangement, least of all Madeline. But the truth was, Madeline was satisfied.

She appreciated the quiet solitude of the countryside, enjoyed the nearby village of Aylestone Hill and its people. After all, she'd grown up in Plymouth, the youngest of six. Her father had been a wealthy merchant, and their household had been a loud, raucous one. Though it had not been of her own choosing, marrying Francis and taking the title of Lady Briarton had decided advantages to the life she'd left behind, and she would not allow herself to regret it.

Hers was a leisurely life, one that left plenty of time for the things Madeline loved most—reading, drawing, playing her cello. Briarton Hall was peaceful and pleasant, and even more so whilst her husband remained in town.

Seldom was she called on to join Francis socially, but Lord and Lady Hartsdale's annual autumn house party was one such exception. Lord Hartsdale had been Francis's late father's closest friend, and when the elder Briarton passed away, Hartsdale had taken Francis under his wing.

The Hartsdales' party was always a pleasant enough affair, five nights rather than the usual two-night "Saturday to Monday" that was so popular with their peers. They were charming hosts with a spectacular home—a castle, no less. And then there were the owls, a variety of species populating the grounds. Madeline particularly loved the owls.

And so, each year she forced a smile and put on a show of marital bliss. Unfortunately, that meant that she and Francis were forced to share a room—a bed, even. And as he did every year, Francis would use it as an opportunity to try to conceive an heir.

A shiver worked its way down her spine at the thought. It wasn't that she didn't want children—she did, in theory. But the very idea of subjecting a poor, innocent child to Francis's cruelty...well, she could hardly bear the thought.

Indeed, there was no denying that her husband was a cruel, hard man. She'd suspected as much when she'd married him, though he hid it well beneath a veneer of good breeding and false charm.

When sober, he was merely unpleasant. But when drunk —and he was often drunk—he became coarse and mean and sometimes violent. No woman was safe from Francis in one of his drunken rages. Everyone, from the elderly housekeeper down to the youngest, most timid housemaid, took care in such circumstances. On more than one occasion, Madeline herself had received a blackened eye or bruised skin at his hands. Why, he'd sprained her wrist just a week after their wedding, a result of twisting her arm behind her back as he'd punished her for some inconsequential infraction.

I'd mentioned one of his mistresses, she remembered suddenly, one who had dared to pull him aside and whisper in his ear at their wedding reception. How foolish she'd been then. How naive. She'd had no idea that the vows they'd spoken so solemnly before the vicar had been meaningless, nothing but empty words as far as Francis was concerned.

"We're almost there," Francis shouted, drawing Madeline from her dour thoughts. "Try and look pleasant, if it's not too much trouble."

Madeline clenched her hands into fists as they turned off the main road and began the uphill climb toward the Hartsdales' estate. She held her breath as the magnificent house came into view, simply stunning this time of year. The late morning sun cast a glow against the gray stones, bathing them in soft yellow light. The grounds surrounding the house were a patchwork quilt of color—green lawn edged by the gold and ruby leaves of oak, birch, and larch. The heavily wooded fells rising behind the manicured grounds were velvety blankets of red, colored by the lush heather, bracken, and bilberry brush. Madeline sucked in her breath in admiration as the car motored around a still, dark lake that mirrored the kaleidoscope of color. Hartsdale Castle always managed to awe her with its savage grace and beauty.

She would make the best of the visit, she resolved, straightening her spine with determination. What choice had she, after all?

Ten minutes later, they'd pulled up under the port cochere and stood idly by as a team of servants rushed out to retrieve their luggage and escort them inside the massive, marble-floored front hall.

"Welcome to Hartsdale Castle," trilled the housekeeper, her steel-gray hair pulled into a neat bun beneath her lace cap. "I'm afraid Lady Hartsdale has been briefly detained, but if you'll let me take your coats, you may wait in the front parlor. Edgar will be happy to pour you a drink, sir."

Madeline handed over her coat to the housekeeper as Francis continued on to the parlor, no doubt eager for the offered drink.

"Francis, darling!" pealed a feminine voice. "I'm so glad you've come."

"Ah, Lydia," came Francis' booming voice. "As lovely as a rose, as always. Have you met my wife?"

Somewhat perplexed by the familiar nature of the greeting, Madeline stepped into the parlor just in time to see the unfamiliar woman's smile disappear from her face, wiped entirely clean as her dark eyes widened with obvious surprise.

Surprise that Francis had a wife, or that he'd brought her to the Hartsdales' party? Madeline wasn't sure.

Whoever she was, she was lovely. Of course she was. All of Francis's paramours were. There was no doubt in Madeline's mind that this woman was one of her husband's lovers.

The woman shook her head. "I'm not...no, I don't believe

I've had the pleasure," she stammered. Her hands were visibly trembling as she held them out to Madeline. "I'm Mrs. Lydia Dawes, from Surrey. Oliver and I spent the summer in town, you see, and were lucky enough to make Lord Briarton's acquaintance."

"How lovely," Madeline murmured. So *this* was the infamous Mrs. Dawes. Madeline had heard of her—everyone had. When she'd married old Mr. Dawes five, maybe six years ago, the gossip had traveled all the way out to Hereford's best parlors. Rumor had it that she had been a prostitute, working in an upscale brothel that served London's most esteemed gentlemen until Dawes, not a day under eighty, had plucked her out and married her. His grown children had vehemently opposed the marriage, calling the new Mrs. Dawes a gold-digger, among other unfavorable names. But Oliver Dawes had married her anyway, then cut off all relations with his distraught children and grandchildren.

"And has Mr. Dawes joined you here at Hartsdale Castle?" Madeline asked, her gaze pointed and direct.

Mrs. Dawes' smile was brittle and false. "No, I'm afraid Oliver is at home nursing the rheumatism in his back, the poor dear. But he did not want me to miss out on the fun."

Madeline shrugged. "Of course not."

"Lord and Lady Briarton!" called Lady Hartsdale as she hurried into the room. "How good to see you both. I'm so sorry I wasn't here to properly greet you. Some trouble belowstairs—you know how that goes." She waved one hand dismissively. "Shall I show you to your room so you can freshen up for tea?"

"That would be lovely," Madeline said with a nod. "It was so good to meet you, Mrs. Dawes."

"Indeed," the woman replied, but her gaze was fixed on Francis, one delicate brow raised questioningly.

The corner of Francis' lips twitched with a smile. "Yes, you go on up, dear. I'll be there directly."

Madeline felt suddenly ill.

~

TEA HAD BEEN AN INTERMINABLE AFFAIR. Now, the guests sat around the Hartsdales' drawing room waiting for the evening's entertainment to begin. On the far side of the room, a string trio tuned their instruments. Beside her, Francis sat fidgeting in his seat. Madeline was keenly aware of Mrs. Dawes' presence, directly behind her. She could feel the woman's gaze boring into the back of her head.

However had she secured an invitation to the Hartsdales' house party? Madeline supposed it was possible that Francis had had something to do with it, though he usually kept his mistresses tucked safely away in London. Whatever the case, none of the ladies present seemed acquainted with her, nor appeared to have any inclination to become so. Madeline almost felt...*sorry* for her.

"What a lovely gown!" came a voice beside her. Madeline turned to smile at Miss Eloise Portnoy, Lady Hartsdale's youngest sister. "The lace is simply exquisite," the girl continued on breathlessly. "Spanish?"

Madeline shook her head. "Portuguese, I believe." She smoothed her hands down the folds of her peacock-blue skirts. She'd purchased an entire new wardrobe just last month, and this gown was her particular favorite, trimmed with rich, cream lace and cinched with a kidskin belt at the waist. The dressmaker claimed the rich hue brought out her eyes. Idle flattery, of course, but she *had* bought the gown, and several more.

"And you look lovely as always," she directed toward Miss Portnoy, a wisp of a girl with dark, doe eyes and chestnut hair piled atop her head. She was the very epitome of beauty and grace, and yet there was a hint of sadness about her features. Of course, rumor had it that Miss Portnoy's parents had shuttled her off to live with her sister and brother-in-law last fall following a scandal involving a stable boy, so perhaps that explained it.

Madeline was pleased to see that the Hartsdales' guests included several young, eligible bachelors of good breeding, most of whom sat goggling at Miss Portnoy throughout tea. Even now, young Lord Dunham sat staring at her, nervously fiddling with his watch chain.

Miss Portnoy glanced over at him and blushed, dropping her gaze back to her lap.

Madeline leaned closer to her. "Perhaps you should ask him for the time," she whispered into her ear. "Put the poor boy out of his misery."

"My sister would consider that forward," she whispered back. "In case you have not heard, I have a reputation to overcome." She smiled mischievously, her cheeks dimpling with the effort.

"Nonsense, you're only asking for the time, not his hand in marriage. I vow, he's going to sit there staring at you with calf eyes all evening long. He's clearly smitten, yet terrified to approach you."

Miss Portnoy stifled a giggle. "I like you," she said. "Very much."

"The feeling is mutual," Madeline answered, reaching for the girl's hand and giving it a squeeze. She admired Miss Portnoy's frank nature. It was refreshing, really, to hear someone so young speak so plainly.

"Champagne?"

Madeline glanced up at the servant bearing a tray of flutes. "Thank you," she said, taking the proffered glass and passing it to Miss Portnoy, then taking another for herself.

Miss Portnoy glanced over one shoulder, then leaned toward Madeline's ear. "Have you any idea why *she's* here?" she whispered. "I vow, her reputation's worse than mine."

She was referring to Mrs. Dawes, of course. "I've no idea. But apparently she is"—how to put this delicately?—"*acquainted* with my husband."

Above the rim of her flute, Miss Portnoy's eyes went wide. "Oh, dear," she murmured, lowering the glass.

Madeline nodded. "Precisely."

She wanted Miss Portnoy to know—wanted them *all* to know—that she was no fool, that she was well aware of her husband's activities, and not the least bit bothered by them. If only he didn't have to make an embarrassing spectacle of them both.

Across the room, Lord Dunham rose, his gaze fixed determinedly on Miss Portnoy. He clenched his hands into fists as he made his way to where she sat, only to be foiled by the musicians, who began playing with gusto at precisely the moment he reached her side.

Madeline bit her lower lip, trying not to smile as the poor red-faced man silently took a seat beside Miss Portnoy.

She'd all but forgotten her husband's presence by her side until he bumped her knee with his own. She turned toward him just in time to see him glance over his shoulder toward where Mrs. Dawes sat, and wink.

Please, let the musicians play on forever, she silently prayed. Because the very thought of joining him afterward in their bedchamber made bile rise in her throat.

Her only saving grace was the thought that perhaps he'd choose Mrs. Dawes's bedchamber, instead.

*M*adeline had delayed her return to her bedchamber as long as possible, happily engaging Miss Portnoy and the rather tongue-tied Lord Dunham in conversation until the room began to empty. She and Miss Portnoy were the last to leave, promising to meet up for a brisk morning walk before breakfast.

Francis had retired a good half-hour before, and Madeline could only hope that she would find him in bed snoring softly when she headed up the long, curving stairs to their room.

Instead, she found him standing bare-chested by the window. "It's about time," he said with a sneer.

Madeline sighed heavily. It was going to be a *long* night, if his mood was any indication.

"I'm sorry, I was so caught up with—" She stopped short, her mouth forming an 'O' of surprise as Mrs. Dawes sauntered in from the washroom, wearing her dressing gown.

"What is *she* doing here?" Madeline asked, her mouth suddenly dry.

"Lydia has graciously agreed to join us in our amorous activities tonight, my dear wife. Doesn't that sound positively delightful?"

"Wha—whatever do you mean?" Madeline stammered, sure she had misheard him. There was no way he was suggesting that Mrs. Dawes join them in...in...*that*.

Was he?

Francis shrugged. "I meant just what I said. Surely you're not so naive as that, Madeline? Come, it will be fun." He gestured her to his side. "I've promised Lydia that you'll help take care of her...ahem...*needs*." He stroked his whiskers thoughtfully. "It occurred to me that perhaps you prefer women to men. That would explain your frigidity, now, wouldn't it? Lydia, dearest, don't be shy. Show her your assets, ample as they are." He made a flicking motion with one wrist.

Compliantly, Mrs. Dawes opened her dressing gown and dropped it to the floor, where it formed a puddle of gold silk around her ankles.

Madeline could only gape in horror. Mrs. Dawes straightened her spine, her head held high as her dusty-pink nipples tightened with the cold. Involuntarily, Madeline's gaze traveled downward, over the woman's stomach to the dark triangle between her thighs.

"Go on, spread your legs for her," Francis prodded, motioning toward the bed.

Mrs. Dawes obeyed, scurrying to the bed and lying down, her legs splayed, a wicked grin on her lips.

"Let's see what you can do with your tongue, my dear," he directed at Madeline.

Her cheeks flaming, Madeline dropped her gaze. Without a word, she strode toward the door, her hands clutching her skirts.

Francis hurried to intercept her, his fingers closing

painfully around one wrist as she reached for the door. "Where do you think you're going?" he asked.

"Out." She shook her head, hoping to clear it. "Anywhere but here."

His eyes were glittering and hard. "You'll go where I say you go, wife."

"Unhand me this minute," Madeline said through gritted teeth, "or I shall scream."

Her gaze met his challengingly. She would not hesitate to do exactly as she threatened.

She could see the uncertainty in his features as he stared down at her. If she screamed and caused a scene, however would he explain the extraneous naked woman in their bedchamber?

With a low growl at the back of his throat, he released her. "Go, then. Get out of my sight."

"With pleasure." Madeline swept out of the room without a backward glance. She hadn't any idea where she'd go—her hosts were already abed, as were the other guests—but it didn't matter overmuch. She'd sleep in the stables before she'd spend another moment in her husband's company.

Silently, she made her way to the cloakroom, where she located her velvet traveling coat. Mercifully, someone had taken it outside and beaten the dust from it before hanging it up. Madeline slipped into its warm folds as she hurried toward the front door.

A housemaid carrying a lamp blocked her path. "Wherever are ye off to at this hour, Lady Briarton?"

"Just out for a walk. I find a bit of fresh air helps me sleep, that's all." She made to brush by the woman.

The maid clutched at her sleeve, her brow creased. "Ye mustn't, not tonight," she said. "It isn't safe to go near the woods."

"I won't venture beyond the gardens." Madeline forced a smile, desperate to flee before Francis came looking for her.

The maid shook her head. "No, ye don't understand. 'Tis the eve of Samhain. Ye canna go near the woods, or the Dark Lords will take ye for sure. 'Tis the one night they can!"

Good heavens! Whatever is she going on about? Madeline's frustration rose a notch as she took two steps toward the door. "I assure you I will be *most* cautious. Now, if you'll excuse me." She reached for the knob and heaved open the heavy door.

"Don't say I didn't warn ye," came the maid's voice just before the door slammed shut.

Hurrying out into the night, Madeline let out a sigh of relief as the crisp air cooled her skin. She walked briskly, purposefully, headed toward the glasshouse at the far side of the lawn. Above her, a full, silvery moon lit her path, casting shadows across the rolling grounds that spread out before her.

She wouldn't think of Francis, wouldn't even consider what was happening back in their room at present. Had he lost his mind? He must have, if he thought there was any chance she might join him and his lover—

An odd, rustling sound off to her left made her pause, one hand clutching at her throat. She stood stock-still on the path, listening. Waiting.

Hoo, hoo...

She let out her breath in a rush. *Just an owl,* she thought, smiling ruefully to herself. *Of course.*

If only the housemaid hadn't spooked her with her superstitious chatter. Dark lords? Such stuff and nonsense. There were owls in the wooded expanse that surrounded the castle's grounds—nothing more sinister than that.

Her gaze traveled the line of trees off in the distance,

marking the edge of the wood. She almost swore she saw something deep within the darkness—a glimmer of light piercing the trees' shadows. A shiver raced down her spine. *I'm imagining it*, she thought, pulling her coat more tightly about herself.

She hurried her step, imagining herself enveloped by the glasshouse's warm, scented air. She could sit inside for a spell and gather her thoughts. At some point, she'd have to return to her room—but not yet. Not for a while. A *long* while.

And there it was again—the eerie, flickering light. Whatever was it? There were no other homes, not for miles about. She took two steps off the path, then two more, craning her neck for a better view.

The housemaid's warning rang in her ears, but she could not lend credence to such superstitions. Perhaps it was only a groundskeeper with a lantern, she reasoned, though why he'd be out walking through the woods so late at night, she could not fathom.

Pushing it from her mind, she turned back and continued on toward her destination. Only, somehow she'd lost sight of it. Hadn't it been just off the path, to her left? She was sure it had been there, set away from the heavy copse of trees at the edge of the woods.

She shook her head in frustration. She hadn't veered so very far off the path; she was sure of it. It must be the moon, playing tricks with her eyes, she decided. *If I can't find it, I'll just head back to the house.*

A quarter hour later, she could find neither the glasshouse nor the main house. Somehow, she'd gotten lost in the castle's vast grounds, with no idea which way to turn. However had she gotten herself so turned around? Particularly puzzling was the fact that the woods were still off to her left, cloaked in darkness.

And yet...there was the light again. More steady now, she decided, taking several steps toward the edge of the trees. It almost looked like...like a window. Like a light flickering against panes of glass.

She moved closer, willing her hands to stop trembling. But she was cold, so very cold. What had seemed a bracing autumn chill during daylight hours now felt almost wintry cold. She was wearing nothing save her silk evening gown and traveling coat—she hadn't taken the time to find her gloves before storming out of her bedchamber, and she wasn't even wearing a hat.

She would have been perfectly comfortable inside the heated glasshouse, but instead she'd been wandering aimlessly for an interminable time.

Her breath made puffs of white in the air as she moved closer to the edge of the woods, squinting now. A vague outline took shape in the shadows, perhaps a hundred yards in. It was some sort of stone structure—a cottage, she guessed. How very odd. She could see the roof now, dark gray slate. Smoke billowed from a chimney in one corner, and lamplight illuminated a window.

Someone was there. Someone with a fire, who might be able to help her find her way back to the castle. The cottage was clearly within Hartsdale Castle's grounds, so it might very well house a land steward or gamekeeper. A tenant, perhaps.

For a moment, she weighed her options. Continue walking aimlessly, growing numb with cold, or risk knocking on a stranger's door and asking for assistance. She took a dozen steps more, into the woods now. Twigs snapped beneath her shoes as she ducked beneath branches. Closer and closer she crept, still unsure of her decision. She only needed a better look...

Hoo, hoo.

Wings flapped loudly, startling Madeline so badly that she jumped as an owl dove past her head. Her heart thrumming against her ribs, she made up her mind in an instant. She would take her chances, and continue on.

Out of these deep, dark woods.

"Are you lost?" came a deep, masculine voice.

"Oh!" Madeline cried, her heart nearly leaping from her chest as a man—a gentleman, from his dress—moved out of the shadows and into her path. "Sir, you startled me."

"I thought I heard footsteps," he said, moving closer. A shaft of moonlight pierced the darkness above his head, illuminating his fair hair while his face remained in shadows. "Whatever are you doing so far from the house?"

Though his tone was friendly enough, a cold knot of fear lodged in the pit of Madeline's stomach. "I was just out... walking. I'm sorry, but have we been introduced?"

He shook his head. "No. I assume you are one of Lady Hartsdale's house guests?"

"I...yes." Shivering, Madeline shoved her hands into her coat's pockets.

"You must be freezing. Come, I've got a fire." He gestured over one shoulder, toward the cottage behind him.

"I—I really should be going," she stammered.

"It's a long walk back to Hartsdale Castle. Come, warm yourself by the fire first. I was just about to put on a kettle for tea." He took several steps toward her, his face emerging from the shadows at last.

Madeline gasped at the sight of him.

Tousled blond hair fell nearly to his shoulders, framing an elegantly sculpted face. His pale eyes seemed to glitter; his lips were full, his chin strong. Even his attire was handsome, his tweed suit fitted perfectly to his tall, muscular form.

In the silvery light of the moon, he looked as if he were carved from marble. He was...*breathtaking*.

Madeline dropped her gaze, her cheeks burning as she silently chastised herself. He was handsome, yes, but that did not mean he wasn't dangerous. He was a stranger, and she was alone with him in a darkened wood past midnight.

If she were to cry for help, would anyone hear her?

"I can assure you that you are perfectly safe with me," he said, almost as if he had read her mind.

Swallowing hard, she raised her gaze to meet his. "Who are you?"

"Simon McKenzie, at your service, madam." He bowed stiffly.

"I am Madeline, Lady Briarton," she offered. "From Aylestone Hill in Herefordshire."

He strode toward her and offered an arm. "Now that the formalities are out of the way, let's get you inside and warmed up."

Her teeth chattering, Madeline nodded. She laid her hand in the crook of his elbow and fell into step beside him, as if these were perfectly normal circumstances.

"Watch the roots there—"

It was too late. Madeline lost her footing and pitched forward.

Mr. McKenzie's arms circled her waist, drawing her close as he righted her. Ever nerve in her body seemed to come alive at once, her skin tingling at the contact.

"I'm so clumsy," she murmured, her heart thumping painfully against her ribs.

He laughed, a low, deep sound that was somehow soothing and seductive, at all once. "You can't very well be expected to see in the dark, Lady Briarton."

"And yet *you* can," she argued.

"I know these woods well" was all he said in reply. He held her more firmly now as he led the way, lifting low branches as they passed under them.

At last they came to a clearing, the stone cottage just ahead. "You live here?" she asked.

"Just…visiting. My…er, father is the land steward. When I come to stay, I'm given use of the cottage. It used to be the gamekeeper's residence, before they built the newer cottages on the far side of the property. Here, this way." He led her around to the far side of the house. Opening the front door, he gestured her inside.

"Let me take your coat," he offered, stepping in behind her and closing the door.

For a moment, Madeline hesitated. She still wore her peacock-blue evening gown beneath her coat. Somehow she felt silly, overdressed for a midnight stroll. If only she'd changed into something more sensible before charging out of the house.

And yet the cottage was toasty, far too warm for a coat. With a nod, she undid the buttons and shrugged out of it, handing over the pile of fur-trimmed velvet with a weak smile.

Mr. McKenzie took the coat but stood unmoving, his gaze sweeping from the top of her head to the tips of her shoes, then back up again. His eyes—which she now saw were a mossy greenish-gray—appeared to darken a hue. For what felt like a full minute, he continued to stare, his gaze warming her skin and making butterflies flutter inside her stomach.

Feeling somehow emboldened, Madeline stood straighter, her chin tipped proudly. She was vaguely aware that her posture mimicked Mrs. Dawes', yet she couldn't help herself.

He made her feel...attractive, she realized. Appreciated.

"You must excuse me," he said at last, shaking his head. "I'm afraid you've temporarily taken my breath away. Along with my senses, it would appear," he added, turning toward the small closet behind him. "Just let me hang this up."

Madeline took a deep breath, willing her racing heart to slow.

"Now," he said, turning back toward her with a heart-stopping smile, "come and sit by the fire. I'll put a kettle on for tea."

"Thank you, Mr. McKenzie," she murmured, following him across the small space to an upholstered sofa with a curved back and arms. "That sounds lovely."

She let out a sigh as she sat and held out her nearly numb hands to the fire. Closing her eyes, she allowed the heat of the flames to warm her skin.

"There must be a kettle here somewhere," came Mr. McKenzie's voice, accompanied by the banging of pots and pans and cupboard doors slamming. "Aha! Now, where did I see that tin of tea?"

"Shall I help you?" Madeline called out, surprised that he was so unfamiliar with the kitchen's contents. Even a bachelor could generally manage a pot of tea.

"No, no, I've got this," he called out. "Just sit. There are some biscuits here, though I cannot speak to their freshness. Shall we give them a try?"

"No, thank you. Just tea will suffice." She was still full

from the evening's refreshments—cakes and tarts and pastries of all shapes and sizes.

A few minutes later he was back, stoking the fire. The logs crackled and spit, sputtering up red and orange sparks that fell back to the hearth with a hiss.

While in the kitchen he'd discarded his coat and rolled up his sleeves, and Madeline watched in fascination as the muscles in his forearms bunched and shifted with his movements.

He was tall, she realized. At least six feet, probably more, with broad shoulders and a narrow waist. Physically, he was near enough perfect, almost unnervingly so. He moved with surprising grace for someone so large.

As to his age...well, he could be anywhere from twenty to thirty-five, she guessed, unable to narrow it any more precisely than that. He looked young, and yet he moved with an assurance, a self-possession, that she didn't usually see in men under thirty.

"Twenty-eight," he said abruptly, turning to face her.

Madeline felt the blood drain from her face. "Wh—what?"

"I...forgive me." He set the poker back against the wall. "Let me get the tea."

He strode off toward the kitchen just as the kettle began to whistle plaintively.

Madeline swallowed hard. Twenty-eight? His age, perhaps? Had she somehow spoken her question aloud and not realized it?

I must have. There was no other logical explanation, she reasoned.

Except that she was sure she hadn't.

"I just realized I haven't any cream," he called out.

"Just sugar will do, then. Two spoons."

He came back into the room bearing a chipped cup set atop a saucer. "Here you are. Careful, it's hot."

She took it with trembling hands. Setting aside the saucer, she cupped the delicate china between her hands, allowing the warmth to seep into her skin. "Thank you, Mr. McKenzie," she murmured, eyeing him sharply as he took a seat by the fire facing her, his long legs stretched out before him.

"Please, call me Simon," he said, resting an elbow on the chair's arm, his chin cupped in one hand.

"You're not having tea?" she asked, meeting his gaze.

He shook his head. "No, I...prefer coffee."

Madeline took a sip of the steaming tea. It was weak, but warm. Soothing.

"Has Lord Briarton traveled with you here to Hartsdale Castle?" he asked, his voice smooth.

"He has," she answered. She had no desire to speak of Francis—not now, not with this man.

Mr. McKenzie—Simon—raised one brow. "But he does not share your enthusiasm for late-night strolls?"

"Not in the least," she said, her voice clipped. She was trying her best *not* to think of Mrs. Dawes, there in their bedchamber. *Naked.* "I'm afraid his enthusiasm lies...elsewhere."

"I see."

Was she imagining it, or had his eyes darkened, his jaw flexing perceptibly? He looked almost...angry.

He straightened in his seat, his hands gripping the chair's arms so tightly that his knuckles turned white. "And do you find this acceptable, Lady Briarton?"

"Call me Madeline," she hedged. "Maddy, perhaps."

Wherever had that come from? No one had called her Maddy in ages, not since she was a girl. Certainly not someone she'd just met, a man she barely knew. And yet it seemed somehow...right.

"You didn't answer my question, Maddy," he said softly, leaning toward her.

She let out her breath in a huff. "Usually I do. Find it acceptable, I mean. But now?" She shook her head. "Not here, not like this. I don't care to be publicly humiliated in front of my peers." The words spilled out, unbidden.

"Nor should you." He rose, stalking toward the fireplace. He rested one arm on the mantel, fiddling with the handle of a decorative pitcher.

Her gaze traveled appreciatively down his backside, then back up again. The firelight turned his pale hair golden, almost reddish. She longed to run her fingers through it, to tangle her hands at the nape of his neck.

Madeline shook her head, confused. "Have we met?" she asked. "You seem so very familiar."

He turned back toward her, the harsh lines of his face softened a bit. "I don't believe so. I spend most of my time in London and Edinburgh. Rarely do I venture out to the country."

"That's too bad. It's beautiful here, especially this time of year." She took a sip of her now-tepid tea.

"Let me put the kettle back on," he said, moving to stand beside her. "I wish I could offer you cream."

"That's quite all right. I should probably be heading back to the house soon, anyway." She drained the cup, then set it back on the saucer. "Thank you for your kind hospitality, Mr. McKenzie."

He reached for the cup and saucer, his fingers brushing hers as he did so. They were cold, so very cold. Gooseflesh rose on her skin, and she shivered violently.

"Let me just get your coat," he said, setting aside the china on the narrow sideboard against the wall. "It's a long walk back, you know. I'm still not certain how you strayed so far from the path. Here you are." He held out the coat, and Madeline rose on trembling legs.

She was sleepy—exhausted, really. How much time had passed since she left the house? She wasn't sure. She only hoped that Mrs. Dawes had returned to her own chamber by now, and that she'd find Francis sated, fast asleep.

Mr. McKenzie held out her coat as she slipped her arms inside and drew it closed, her fingers fumbling clumsily with the buttons.

"Here, let me," he said, brushing her hands aside and fastening the buttons himself. Once he finished, he leaned down, his lips so close to her ear that she could feel his breath, a warm caress against her skin. "Don't worry," he whispered, "they're all asleep." He cocked his head to one side, looking thoughtful. "And in their proper places."

Madeline just nodded. It was only an hour later, as she lay awake in bed with Francis snuffling softly beside her, that she wondered how Mr. McKenzie knew.

CHAPTER 4

*S*imon stood by the edge of woods, his gaze directed toward Hartsdale Castle. He couldn't see the house —he was too far away for that—but he didn't need to. He could hear every word spoken in the grand ballroom, could hear the thoughts of every guest present. Silk rustled, slippers scuffed as Lady Hartsdale's guests swayed and dipped while the orchestra performed, each melody played more enthusiastically than the one before.

Now and again, champagne glasses clinked as toasts were made. Servants passed silver trays filled with delicious culinary enticements. There was laughter, gaiety.

And in the midst of it all was Madeline. Simon inhaled slowly, savoring her scent even across the distance that separated them. He closed his eyes, narrowing his focus like a spyglass in his mind. Every extraneous sound, every sensation faded away till he was left with only Madeline.

There it was, the sound of her breathing, of her heart beating rhythmically against her ribs, of her blood pulsing through her veins.

Her blood. It called to him, a siren's song meant only for him. If he spoke to her—no more than a whisper in her mind —would she heed his summons?

No. He wanted her to come to him of her own accord. He would not manipulate her, no matter the temptation, damn it.

Just what was it that made him desire her so? He wasn't certain. And yet he felt somehow…*protective* of her, which was ironic, given the circumstances. After all, he could end her life in an instant, if he chose to.

But he wouldn't. He had no wish to. Last night was an anomaly for him. Yes, he'd lured her to the woods. Once he'd sensed her presence, realized she was out walking the grounds past midnight alone, entirely vulnerable, he'd played tricks on her feeble mortal mind, confusing her, drawing her toward his lair.

But then…he'd laid eyes on her, and at once everything changed. He could not explain it—didn't want to, really—but as they sat there together before the fire, he'd felt almost human for the first time in more than a century. He was no longer a predator in search of prey, but a man bent on courtship.

He'd seen the images in her mind, felt the brunt of the humiliation she'd experienced at her husband's hands, and he'd felt murderous. Not toward the lovely woman sitting before him, completely unafraid in his presence, but toward the man who had made her feel such shame, such sadness.

No, there was no explanation for it. And yet he knew that he would do everything in his power to have her—to possess her, body and soul; to protect her from threats far greater than him.

If only she would let him.

With a sigh, he leaned back against the rough bark of an enormous old oak, settling in to wait.

She *would* come—he was sure of it.

Readjusting her elaborate mask, Madeline forced a smile as she watched Lord Dunham lead Miss Portnoy out to the dance floor. Truly, she was delighted for the girl. The pair had been nearly inseparable all day, and it was clear they were both smitten. It would seem that Lady Hartsdale had quite the skill as a matchmaker.

Still, her happiness for Miss Portnoy could not cure the sick feeling in her gut as she watched her husband claim Mrs. Dawes for yet another dance, far more than propriety allowed.

It was impossible to miss the curious glances cast their way, or the pitying looks directed at her as her husband held the gaudily dressed woman far too closely, their bodies pressed together, their lips almost touching as they glided about the floor.

Across the ballroom, Lady Hartsdale watched Francis and Mrs. Dawes with a scowl. Madeline saw her shake her head, then lean toward Lord Hartsdale, whispering in his ear.

About me, no doubt.

Lord Hartsdale nodded, his gaze scouring the space till he spotted Madeline. It was painfully obvious that Lady Hartsdale had asked her husband to rescue her—to ask her to dance.

She watched as he made his way toward her, waylaid now and again by guests eager to express their delight at the night's entertainment. It was quite a crush, the ballroom teeming with ladies and gentlemen wearing their finest, smelling of expensive perfume and hair pomade.

It appeared that a healthy percentage of the Lake District's residents were in attendance tonight, mixing and mingling with the Hartsdale's houseguests. After all, the castle's ballroom was enormous, and everyone loved a masqued ball—everyone but Madeline, that is. The mask made her feel claustrophobic, the tightly knotted ribbon giving her a dull, throbbing headache.

Feeling cornered, like a fox in the crosshairs, her gaze darted around, looking for an escape. *The terrace.* There was a pair of French doors leading outside, there on the far side of the room. If she could just make it to the terrace before Lord Hartsdale reached her.

Without another thought, she darted off, making her way around the dancing couples. She didn't dare turn around to see Lord Hartsdale's expression, knowing full well that she was being rude to her host.

It couldn't be helped. She couldn't bear it another minute, couldn't stand the pitying looks, the hushed conjecture. She hurried her step, keeping her gaze trained on the French doors as she made her way through the crowd.

A minute later she was outside, untying her mask as she skimmed down the terrace's stairs toward the lawn. She hadn't any idea where she was going—except that she did.

Simon McKenzie.

She hadn't been able to stop thinking about him all day. Somehow, she would find his little cottage in the woods, and when she did, she would demand answers. *Truthful* answers. Because she'd learned that the Hartsdales' land steward didn't have a son. It hadn't been too difficult—a question here, a query there.

He wasn't who he'd claimed to be. So who was he, really? All she knew for certain was that she *had* to find out. The rational part of her mind warned her against seeking him out, insisting that he could be a dangerous sort.

Only, he'd been nothing but a gentleman the night before. She didn't fear him, not in the least. She only wanted answers. How had he seemingly read her mind, answered her unspoken questions? No matter how hard she tried, she could not come up with a satisfactory explanation, except that maybe she'd dreamed it all.

It was time to find out, once and for all. Glancing around to make sure no one was watching, she set off toward the glasshouse, hoping that somewhere along the path, she'd see the light in the woods that had drawn her before.

She shivered, realizing that this time she hadn't even a coat to keep her warm. Her gown—black lace over a beige shift—gave her very little protection from the elements.

Hurry, hurry. Her kidskin pumps thumped against the cobbled path in perfect rhythm with her heart. How much farther? She hadn't any idea—had no real recollection of their walk back toward the house after she'd finished her tea. She shook her head, feeling foolish. This was madness.

And yet...there it was—the flickering light, off in the woods. Somewhere up ahead and to her left. How was it that no one else noticed it? It was like a beacon, guiding her, drawing her farther and farther from the house, deeper into the night's shadows.

And then, there he was—at the edge of the woods, leaning against the trunk of a tree, his hands thrust into his trousers' pockets. "You've come," he said simply, pushing off the tree and quickly closing the distance between them.

Madeline nodded. "I need answers."

He stopped an arm's length away, his gaze boring into hers. For a moment, neither said a word. Madeline struggled to catch her breath, to slow her racing heart.

In the distance, an owl hooted. The breeze stirred, rustling the branches above their heads, flapping the hem of Madeline's skirts against her calves.

And then at once everything seemed to go silent and still. Somehow, Madeline was in his embrace.

"You'll get your answers," he said just before his mouth came down on hers.

His lips were hard, demanding. Madeline couldn't help but yield, opening her mouth against his with a gasp. Her hands flexed by her sides, the mask dropping to the ground at her feet. Standing on tiptoe, she reached around his neck, drawing him closer as she tangled her fingers in the hair at the nape of his neck.

Soft, silky. The sensations overwhelmed her—the feel of his body, pressed against hers; the woodsy, entirely male scent of him; the taste of his mouth, like the headiest of wines.

Her knees felt suddenly weak, unable to bear her weight a minute longer.

Reaching down, Simon swept her off her feet, cradling her against the hard muscles of his chest as he carried her off into the woods, toward the cottage.

Several minutes later he managed to muscle her through the front door, kicking it closed behind him. The cottage was warm; Madeline noticed a coal stove in the main room's far corner as he carried her into what must be the cottage's sole bedroom. Gently, he deposited her on the bed atop a downy coverlet. Snatching several blankets from a shelf above the bed, he shook them out, then tucked them around her like a nursemaid might.

"Just let me light the stove," he said, moving toward the iron contraption across from the foot of the bed. Madeline was shivering now, snuggling into the blankets that smelled faintly of cedar.

Several minutes later, the stove was hissing and belching, and Madeline let out a sigh of relief. She was chilled to the bone. Whatever had she been thinking, running out into the night without a coat? She would surely take ill. Another shiver took hold of her, racking her spine and making her teeth chatter noisily.

Simon sat down on the edge of the bed beside her, gazing

down at her with drawn brows. He'd doffed his coast and waistcoat, discarded his necktie and opened the top button of his fine linen shirt. His hair looked as if he'd recently run his fingers through it, and there was a smudge of coal dust on one sculpted cheek.

And yet even is his disheveled state, he was perhaps the most handsome man she'd ever seen, which went against her usual preference for men with dark hair and eyes. Never before had she found herself attracted to a blond, but this one looked like...an angel. A warrior angel, she amended, noting the breadth of his shoulders. He looked powerful. Rugged. *Dangerous.*

"I could get you a warm brick wrapped in flannel," he offered, his voice tender and soft, in direct opposition to her current train of thought.

A lump formed in Madeline's throat, her vision swimming with unshed tears. In all their years of marriage, Francis had never looked at her with such warmth, never spoken to her with such tenderness. How she'd craved it, she realized with a start. She'd never had a man fuss over her, put her needs before his own.

"No," she said at last, her voice thick. "Just...*you* warm me." She wanted nothing more than his body pressed against hers, warming her skin with his touch.

He swallowed hard, his irises dilating, the mossy green suddenly replaced with a fathomless dark depth. "I...can't," he said, his voice seeming to break. "I'd only chill you more."

Madeline laid a hand on his cheek. It was cold, but not uncomfortably so. "Nonsense. Simon, I...I want this. I want you," she added.

"I thought you wanted answers," he hedged, the barest hint of a smile dancing on his lips.

She bit her lower lip. "That, too. They aren't mutually exclusive, are they?"

He reached a hand up to her hair and began pulling out the pins one by one, releasing the elaborate up-do that had taken her lady's maid more than a half-hour to accomplish. Soon her hair lay fanned out around her face while Simon combed his fingers through the length of it.

Madeline closed her eyes, giving herself up to his ministrations.

"Are you warm now?" Simon asked, his lips brushing her ear.

"Mmm," she murmured in reply. Her entire body felt warm and heavy. Comfortable. Relaxed. Even her eyelids felt heavy.

"I won't hurt you, Madeline," came Simon's soothing voice. "You have no reason to fear me."

She could only nod, smiling happily as the room's warmth settled into her bones.

He laid his hand on her wrist. "Look at me, Maddy. Open your eyes and see the truth."

Slowly, her lids fluttered open. Her heart leapt against her breast, her breath catching noisily in her throat.

Simon's eyes were rimmed in red, his canine teeth elongated. He was the same, and yet he was altered somehow. He was beautiful, and yet terrifying.

Whatever he was, he wasn't human.

CHAPTER 5

"*T*rust me, Maddy. Please," Simon pleaded. "Accept me as I am, and let me make love to you."

"Wh—what *are* you?" she stammered, her tongue suddenly thick in her mouth, coated with the metallic tang of fear.

Pale, cold skin. Teeth that looked remarkably like fangs. He'd read her mind, more than once.

"If you can accept me, if you just say the words, you'll be safe from me forever. I swear it, Maddy. Believe me. Believe *in* me."

"Say the words? I don't"—she shook her head wildly—"I don't understand. Am I to believe you're a…a…" She trailed off, unable to say it. She'd heard the stories, read Mr. Stoker's *Dracula*. But it was fiction—myth and legend, nothing more.

"I won't hurt you," he repeated. "You have my word." His face was taut, solemn, his skin as pale and perfect as polished marble. She searched his features, looking for something, some small clue as to whether or not she should trust him.

Inexplicably, Madeline nodded. Her fear seemed to recede. A strange sense of calm washed over her. "I…I trust you," she stammered. What were the words? "I accept you, Simon McKenzie, just as you are."

Simon nodded, the harsh lines of his face seeming to melt away. His mouth found hers once more, claiming it with an almost inhuman growl.

Grasping at his shirt's open collar, Madeline arched off the bed, opening her mouth against his. He kissed her hungrily, thoroughly, leaving her breathless with desire.

With a groan, he drew away from her at last, rising to stand by the side of the bed. Madeline sat up, watching in utter fascination as his fingers worked the buttons of his shirt. He tugged the garment free from the waistband of his trousers and dropped it carelessly to the floor, his gaze never once leaving hers.

Her heart accelerated as he reached down to unfasten his trousers. Dear God, it had been so long—so *very* long—since she'd seen a man naked. Besides, Francis wasn't much to look at, with or without his clothes, whereas Simon...

Her mouth went dry as he slid the fabric down and stepped out. His drawers followed, and then he stood before her, entirely bare, his cock erect and ready.

Her thighs suddenly damp with need, she threw off the blankets and rose to stand before him, kicking off her shoes as she did so. Turning, she offered him her back, waiting for him to undo the row of tiny buttons than ran from her neck to her waist.

He lifted her hair over one shoulder, pressing his lips against the back of her ear as his fingers flew over the buttons. Her gown parted, falling to her feet with a *swish*. His lips moved down the column of her neck, drawing goose-flesh in their wake as he hooked his thumbs under her shift's thin straps. In one quick movement, he pushed it down, past her hips.

Clad only in her undergarments and stockings now,

Madeline turned to face him. She took three steps back, giving him full view of her figure as she removed the last of her clothing, piece by piece.

His eyes seemed to darken a hue as he watched her, a muscle in his jaw flexing. His cock grew larger, thicker, as each successive undergarment joined the growing pile on the floor. His breath came faster, his perfectly sculpted chest rising and falling with the effort.

The moment her second stocking dropped from her fingertips, he was beside her, tracing a finger across her jawbone, down her throat, across her breasts.

Her breath caught as he knelt before her, capturing the tip of one breast with his mouth. She tangled her fingers in his hair as he suckled her till she cried out with need, her head thrown back, her cunny wet, throbbing. She needed to feel him inside her. *Now.*

In an instant, she was on the bed beneath him, with no idea how she got there. The tip of his cock was pressed against her entrance—testing, teasing.

"What do you want?" he asked hoarsely, nudging her neck with his nose. "You must say it aloud. Ask for it, Maddy. Beg me."

For a moment, she allowed herself to wonder if this was some rule his kind was forced to follow where women were concerned. It didn't matter, she realized. She wanted this. Needed this. Deserved this, damn it.

"Make love to me, Simon McKenzie," she said breathlessly, meeting his gaze with her own, her voice sure and steady. "Please."

～

SIMON NEARLY WEPT WITH RELIEF. Consent had been given, and voluntarily. He hadn't manipulated her mind, hadn't influenced her in any way. She was *his* now, and he would give her everything—anything she wanted, everything she desired.

He gazed down at her with pride as he reined in the beast inside him, forcing himself to go slowly, to savor the moment. She was the most beautiful creature he'd ever seen, lovely and soft and sweet smelling. She set his blood afire like no mortal had ever done, not in all the years he'd walked this earth.

"Simon?" she murmured, gazing up at him with clear, hazel eyes full of unconcealed desire. "Now. Please."

How he wanted to take his time exploring her body, licking and tasting, stroking her. He wanted to bury his mouth between her legs, to flick her clit with his tongue till she bucked beneath him.

But oh, how tempting she was, hot and wet and ready for him, her trembling thighs wrapped around his hips. No, he couldn't wait another second to claim her.

In one, short motion, he lifted his hips and sheathed his cock fully inside her. He heard her gasp, her mouth forming an 'O' as her nails dug into his back.

"Dear God, Madeline," he groaned. She was tight, so very tight. He could hear her heart beating, quick as a rabbit's, could smell her blood, racing through her veins. A primal need blossomed inside him—the need to taste that blood, to drink it.

He gritted his teeth, fighting against the bloodlust. Oh, he'd taste her blood before the night gave way to dawn, but not yet. *Not yet.* Forcing his focus to return, he withdrew his cock, slowly, inch by inch, then plunged back inside.

Maddy gasped. For one horrible second, he was afraid he'd hurt her. But then she started moving beneath him, rocking her hips as they found a rhythm together.

Her cries grew louder as she moved toward release.

Faster, faster he drove into her, his pelvis rubbing against her swollen clit with every stroke, his own muscles tensing and bunching as he held himself back, waiting, waiting...

At last she cried out his name, her head tipped back, exposing her pale throat as her channel pulsed against his shaft. In response, his eyes began to dilate, his canines elongating as his gaze fixed on the spot where her pulse leapt against her fragile skin, blood coursing freely just beneath the surface.

Now, his instinct commanded. His cock still buried deep inside her, he bent his head toward her throat, his lips pulled back to expose his fangs.

"This won't hurt," he whispered just before he pierced the skin below her delicate, shell-shaped ear.

Ignoring her surprised cry, he took a long draught, her blood warming his tongue as he came, hard. She whimpered softly as his saliva entered her bloodstream, sending her into waves of orgasms, one after another.

They were one, their bodies in perfect synch. He'd never before experienced the likes of it, never felt anything so wondrously *right* as this.

And yet he knew he couldn't continue to drink from her, couldn't risk taking too much and leaving her weak. Gathering every ounce of strength he possessed, he withdrew his fangs from her throat, running his tongue over the spot where he'd pierced her flesh to cauterize the wound.

"Dear God, Simon," she murmured breathlessly. "That was...I don't know *what* that was, but it was incredible."

"*You're* incredible," he countered, rolling off her and reaching down to pull the blankets over them.

He stroked her hair while she nuzzled his neck, fitting her body tightly against his. Focusing his mind on the lamp beside the bed, he extinguished the flame. Only the light of the moon streaming in the window illuminated the space now, and yet Simon could see just as clearly as before.

The pitch black of night did not deter a vampire—it only served to heighten his senses, allowing him to watch the rise and fall of her shoulders, to hear her breathing began to slow, to feel her limbs grow heavy against his.

In the darkness, he smiled to himself, thinking that, at last, this fragile mortal had given him purpose. *Protect her*, his instincts screamed. *Keep her safe, make her happy*. What better purpose was there?

"Simon?" she murmured sleepily, her breath warm against his neck.

"Yes, love?"

"Thank you."

"Sleep, my sweet," he said, pressing his lips against her temple. "I'll have you back in your bed by dawn."

CHAPTER 6

*M*adeline awoke with a start. She sat up, clutching the covers against her breasts as she glanced about, surprised to find herself back in her own bed in Hartsdale Castle. Francis's side of the bed was empty, thank God. The late morning sun cast long, golden stripes across the tousled linens where he had lain.

Had she slept through breakfast?

She shook her head, hoping to clear it. She felt groggy, a bit disoriented. The last thing she remembered was drifting off to sleep in Simon's arms, naked and entirely sated.

She had no recollection of traveling back to the house, of putting on her nightgown or climbing into bed.

Had she dreamed it all? She reached down between her thighs, realizing she was sore in places that weren't usually sore. The delicate flesh was tender, abraded. Evidence that she hadn't dreamed it, unless Francis...

No. She shook her head. She would certainly remember *that.*

She tossed back the covers and rose, reaching up toward the ceiling as she stretched. Goodness, but she was tired.

Padding barefoot across the plush carpeting, she sat down at the vanity and reached for her hairbrush, smiling happily to herself as she pulled the bristles through her tangled locks. Soon her hair was crackling, falling about her shoulders in soft, shining waves.

The memories were flooding back now, pleasant memories. Her *first* pleasant memories, where sex was concerned. She pulled her hair back to secure it with a ribbon and froze, her eyes growing wide at the sight of her reflection in the mirror. Panic rising, she leaned forward for a closer look.

What in heaven's name?

There were two red puncture marks, there on her neck. At once, another hazy memory came flooding back. *This won't hurt*, he'd said. It hadn't—at least, not after the initial pinch. She must have known that he'd bitten her, and yet she'd somehow blocked it from her mind.

Good God. She'd been bitten by a vampire. And worse? She'd enjoyed it. Oh, how she'd enjoyed it!

Her hands trembling, she reached up and ran the pad of one finger across the wound, expecting to find it tender. It wasn't. The skin surrounding the two red marks felt remarkably soft, and not at all disturbed. *Interesting.*

Just how much blood had he taken from her? She searched the reflection of her face, examining it for signs of pallor. Somehow, her cheeks looked rosy, her skin aglow.

Other than the marks on her neck, there were no signs of ill effects from his bite.

She glanced over at the wardrobe that held her clothing, grateful that most of her blouses had high, lace collars. Because however would she explain it?

Reaching for her watch pendant, she checked the time, startled to find it nearly time for luncheon. Hastily, she slipped the chain over her head and rose, hurrying into the washroom to begin her toilette.

Nearly a half hour later, she dismissed her lady's maid and emerged from her room, making her way down to the drawing room just in time to join her fellow female guests as they followed their hostess into the sunroom for the midday meal.

Apparently, the men had left at dawn to fish and shoot. Madeline was glad for the reprieve, reluctant to face her husband after spending the night in another man's arms.

Unlike her adulterous husband, she'd always expected to honor her wedding vows. After all, with no experience to guide her save the unpleasant encounters with Francis, she'd always thought sex was something she could easily live without. Now she knew better.

"There you are!" Miss Portnoy hurried to Madeline's side, claiming the seat next to her. "I vow, I was beginning to worry about you."

"Oh, I just had a bit of a headache, that's all." Madeline pulled out her chair and slid into it. "I'm feeling much better now."

"How lucky for us all!" trilled a feminine voice from across the table. Madeline looked up to find Mrs. Dawes seated directly across from her, smiling sweetly.

The room seemed to suddenly go silent as all eyes turned toward Madeline, awaiting her response with bated breath.

She would not disappoint them. Schooling her features into a mask of complacency, she forced a smile. "Why, thank you, Mrs. Dawes. And I should also thank you for entertaining my husband so well during our stay here. It's given me so much free time to pursue my own interests. You've no idea how grateful I am."

There were audible gasps around the table.

Ignoring them, Madeline reached for her napkin with steady hands and placed it on her lap. "The ham looks lovely, Lady Hartsdale," she said brightly, turning her attention to her hostess. "Sleeping through breakfast has left me positively famished."

Miss Portnoy reached for her hand beneath the table and gave it a squeeze. Madeline returned it, trying her best not to laugh aloud as the rest of table sat goggling, Mrs. Dawes included.

Mercifully, Lady Hartsdale broke the uncomfortable silence, redirecting the conversation as the footmen began serving lunch. "I thought we'd play some lawn games this afternoon, as it's unseasonably warm out. Tennis, perhaps?" she offered.

Conversation returned to a full buzz, Madeline's egregious social error temporarily forgotten. Of course, a lady never acknowledged her husband's infidelity in public, no matter how brazen he might be. No doubt, Lady Hartsdale would "inadvertently" forget to invite Lord and Lady Briarton to next year's house party, but Madeline didn't care a whit.

She was done being pitied.

She took a deep breath, pushing aside the unpleasant thoughts. "How is your tennis game, Miss Portnoy?" she directed toward the girl.

"Dreadful," Miss Portnoy replied with a grin, her dark eyes dancing with mischief. "And yours?"

"Equally so. What fun we shall have."

And she meant it. Mrs. Dawes could go to the devil, and take Francis with her.

She was going to enjoy her afternoon. And her night? She remembered the intoxicating pleasure she'd found in Simon's arms; mentally compared it to Francis's incompetent fumbling.

Yes, she thought with a smile of satisfaction. She would certainly enjoy her night more than poor Mrs. Dawes would.

~

MADELINE STIFLED a yawn as she followed Francis up the stairs toward their room, calling goodnight left and right as other couples reached their own rooms and disappeared inside.

As always, Lady Hartsdale had arranged her guests by marital status and gender. Married couples were here, on the second floor of the west wing, while unmarried ladies found themselves on the second floor's east wing, at the far end of the main hall. Single gentlemen, however, were relegated to the third floor of the west wing, far enough from the maidens to keep temptation at bay, she supposed.

As a matron, Mrs. Dawes had been situated with the married couples, just three doors down from Madeline and Francis. Convenient, she realized. She hoped he would be on his way there as soon as the corridor emptied. Her muscles were sore from playing tennis all afternoon, and she hoped to soak in a hot bath before setting off to find Simon. Thank goodness she'd gotten a brief nap in before dinner.

The meal had been pleasant enough, eight courses in all. As luck would have it, Miss Portnoy's beau, Lord Dunham, had been her dinner companion, and Mrs. Dawes had been seated as far from her as possible—likely a last-minute change, she realized. She'd enjoyed her conversation with the young viscount. Mostly, they'd discussed music, debating the merits of Rachmaninoff's *Piano Concerto No. 3.*

Every now and then, he'd steal a glance at Miss Portnoy, who was happily engaged in conversing with a portly married gentleman from Surrey throughout the meal. Sensing Lord Dunham's gaze, the girl's cheeks would pinken, her gestures becoming deliberate and self-conscious.

Truly, it was a delight to watch—two young people falling in love. The cynic in Madeline was happy to be proved wrong, to see that perhaps there *was* such a thing as love at first sight. She would be willing to wager that the pair would come to an understanding before the end of the house party, that they'd be happily married by this time next year.

Her own unhappy fate might be sealed, but that did not mean that she could not take pleasure in the good fortune of others, particularly a girl like Miss Portnoy. She had suffered enough this year, the subject of cruel gossip and familial shame.

Miss Portnoy had confided in Madeline just that afternoon—told her the entire tale from beginning to end. Which, it turned out, was far less sordid than the gossipmongers had led her to believe.

The young man in question—indeed, a stable boy—had been Miss Portnoy's friend, and nothing more. He'd been in her family's employ since the age of fourteen—the same age as Miss Portnoy at the time. The last of six siblings, she'd been lonely, desperate for companionship.

An avid horsewoman, she'd enjoyed spending time in the stables. Realizing the boy could not read, she'd made him her own personal project, teaching him whenever they could steal away from prying eyes.

Of course, everyone who worked in the stables knew of the pair's odd friendship—it became a closely guarded secret belowstairs. Her family would never have permitted it, and would have been horrified to learn that everyone, from the housekeeper on down to the lowliest groom, had aided and abetted the pair as they passed books back and forth, meeting covertly to discuss them at length.

When they'd been caught together in the hayloft—simply reading a book of poetry together, Miss Portnoy claimed— her parents had naturally assumed the worst. Despite Miss Portnoy's vehement denial that anything untoward had occurred, her parents had hastily dismissed the boy without a reference, threatening him with bodily harm should he ever get near their daughter again.

To make matters worse, before they'd sent the disgraced girl off to live with Lord and Lady Hartsdale, they'd called in the family physician to have Miss Portnoy examined, to make certain that she wasn't with child. Adding to the poor girl's humiliation, the physician had called into question her virginity.

Madeline let out a sigh as she entered her room and closed the door behind her. Yes, she was pleased to see the girl find such happiness at last. After all, she herself was no stranger to humiliation, to betrayal by those closest to you. She understood the pain, the frustration.

She glanced over at her husband, who stood by the tall dresser in the room's corner, removing his necktie. His discarded coat and waistcoat lay on the bed in a heap. She shook her head, confused. Why was he disrobing now? She'd assumed he was meeting Mrs. Dawes in her room—had counted on it, really.

Apparently, he had other ideas. He turned toward her with a predatory look in his eyes. "Why aren't you undressing for bed?"

"I was thinking I'd take a bath first," she hedged.

He took a step toward her. "Very well. Perhaps I'll join you."

His speech was slurred, she realized with a sinking feeling. He was drunk. "I think I can manage alone, thank you," she snapped, taking a step back. "Just how much did you drink tonight?"

"Enough to make fucking my frigid wife a palatable endeavor. I want an heir. It's time you did your duty."

She shook her head, tired of this game. "I'm exhausted, Francis. Why don't you pay your mistress a visit, instead."

Before she realized what was happening, he advanced on

her, backing her up against the vanity. She reached behind herself, gripping the edge of the marble tabletop that pressed into her lower back.

He loomed over her now, and it was all Madeline could do not to cower. "Exhausted, are you? What a shame." He made a clucking noise with his mouth. "Where were you last night, Madeline? Or the night before?"

She said nothing, tipping her chin defiantly in the air.

"Do you think I don't know that you've been sneaking off somewhere?" he continued. "Coming back at dawn, with mud on your shoes? Have you been out sniffing around a stable hand? Or is it a gardener, perhaps? Well?" He reached for her shoulders, his fingers digging into her flesh. "Answer me, damn it!"

"It's none of your concern where I go or what I do, not while you're off making a fool of yourself with Mrs. Dawes," she snapped.

"Is that so?" His face twisted into a mask of rage. "Listen to me, you little slut. Bear as many bastards as you like—it makes no difference to me. Feel free to fuck every stable boy, every gardener in all of Herefordshire, if it pleases you. Hell, maybe you'll learn an interesting trick or two. But"—he reached for her wrist, gripping it tightly—"not until you give me an heir. Until then, you'd better learn to keep your legs closed, my dear. Do you understand me?" He twisted her wrist painfully for emphasis.

Madeline glared at her husband, her breath coming fast now, fear racing through her veins. "Turn me loose."

He shook his head, a malicious gleam in his eyes. "I don't think so. I'm not yet done with you."

He shoved her against the wall, pinning her there with his knee while he fumbled with his trousers. As soon as he'd freed his cock, he wrapped one hand around her throat while he bunched her skirts up around her waist.

She heard a rip, felt cool air against her thighs as her delicate, lace-trimmed drawers dropped to the floor.

"Let's get on with this, shall we?" Using one knee, he forced apart her thighs.

"Do it quickly, then, and get out of my sight," Madeline bit out.

In response, he tightened his grip on her throat. He was choking her, cutting off her air. Madeline sputtered, and he loosened his grip. And then she felt it, his flaccid cock pressing futilely against her entrance. Madeline nearly gagged as he rubbed himself against her like some sort of animal.

"Spread your legs, damn it!" he grunted.

Hatred replaced her fear, making her skin flush hotly. "As if that will help any. It's hard to fuck your wife when your cock is nothing but a limp noodle, isn't it?"

Madeline took great pleasure in the stunned expression that crossed his face, but it was short-lived.

He drew back one hand and slapped her across the cheek. Her head flew back and struck the wall so hard that she saw spots at the edge of her vision.

Her fear returned with a vengeance. He was going to hurt her, she realized, and take great pleasure in doing so.

"You little bitch," he said with a spray of spittle. "Someone needs to teach you a lesson."

She closed her eyes, bracing herself for the attack, but it didn't come. She felt a rush of cool air, and then...

Chaos.

*S*he opened her eyes to find Simon there, lifting Francis off his feet and pinning him to the wall.

She had no idea where he'd come from. It was almost as if he'd materialized out of thin air. But there he was, his face a mask of pure, undiluted rage.

"I'll kill you, you bastard," he snarled, slamming Francis against the wall so hard that plaster fell loose.

She blinked rapidly as she took in the scene before her. Simon's eyes were an unholy red, his fangs elongated. He *would* kill him, she realized.

Instantly, she sprang to life, reaching for his arm. "Simon, no. Look at me," she pleaded, but he ignored her, his murderous gaze locked on Francis's terrified one. "He's not worth it," she pressed on, tears blurring her vision now. "Think…think of the questions! However will we explain it? The scandal…it will ruin me."

He acknowledged her words with a slight nod, and Madeline nearly crumpled in relief.

Moving so quickly that Madeline could barely make out what was happening, Simon grabbed one of Francis's wrists and sunk his teeth into the flesh, eliciting a squeal from the smaller man.

And then Simon spat Francis's blood and torn flesh into his face, releasing him to the floor in a crumpled heap.

Francis scrabbled back into the corner, clutching his injured wrist with a look of pure terror on his face. The front of his gaping trousers was wet, and Madeline realized with a start that he'd pissed himself.

This quivering heap of a man was her husband, and yet… she felt nothing. No pity, no remorse.

She watched in silence as Simon knelt down beside him, speaking so softly that Madeline had to strain to hear his words. "You will never again lay a hand on her in anger. You will not touch her without her permission. You will not speak to her disrespectfully. You will not harm her, humiliate her, or debase her in any way. If you do any of these things, you have my word that I will come back and rip out your throat. Do you understand me, you cowardly piece of shite?"

Francis just nodded, his eyes wide, his bottom lip trembling.

"I said, do you understand me?" Simon repeated, more loudly this time.

"I—I understand you," Francis stammered.

Simon rose to his feet. "Very good. You won't speak a word of this, by the way. Make up some excuse for your wrist, an injury of some sort. But one word from you to anyone, and I will take great pleasure in ripping you from limb to limb and leaving what's left of you for wild animals to fight over. I hope I've made myself clear."

Francis was sobbing quietly now.

Simon turned toward her, reaching out a hand. "Madeline?"

Unable to speak, she simply nodded her assent.

In one fluid motion, he swept her off her feet, cradling her in his arms. "Close your eyes, love."

What seemed a split-second later, they were somehow in his cottage. Gently, he set her down in front of the sofa.

With a cry, Madeline collapsed to the upholstered cushions, entirely drained.

"He won't hurt you again," Simon murmured, leaning over her, his lips in her hair.

Squeezing her eyes shut, she nodded. "I know. He was going to...he would have raped me. Thank you."

"Just let me light the fire," he said, moving toward the hearth.

A minute or two later, the fire crackled to life, and Simon sat down beside her. "Are you ready for some answers now?" he offered, taking her trembling hands in his.

"Yes," she said, meeting his gaze. Mercifully, the red was gone from his eyes, replaced with the familiar mossy greenish-gray.

"Ask me anything, then. Anything at all."

"You're a...a...*vampire?*" Madeline felt foolish, just saying the word. Before now, she hadn't believed such a creature existed.

"Yes, a vampire. Creature of the night. The walking undead." He shrugged. "Whatever you prefer to call it. Semantics, really."

She nodded. Somehow, putting words to her fears made them seem less terrifying. "And...how long have you been alive?"

His mouth twisted into a wry grin. "A *very* long time."

That wasn't quite the answer she was looking for. "What year were you born?"

"I was born in 1718. Near Inverness, in the Scottish Highlands. The youngest of five boys."

She tipped her head to one side, eyeing him closely. "You

don't look like a Scot, or sound like one, either. A High-lander, at that."

"I've spent most of my years in London. I find it far easier to…to *blend* in there. I suppose I've lost my brogue, though I imagine I could turn it on, should the need arise. Wouldna it please ye, wee lassie?"

She couldn't help but smile, realizing she felt calm now. Safe. "That's the best you can do?"

He shrugged, his mouth widening into a grin. "I'm a bit rusty, I see. Ah, well."

"Go on with your story, then," she prompted, eager to hear the rest.

"Very well. There's not much to say. I grew up, became a blacksmith, took a wife. She died two years later, in child-birth. I went on with my life, joining in the Jacobite cause, as any good Highlander did. My mortal life ended in 1746, two days after the Battle of Culloden. I was mortally wounded in battle, and left on the field for dead. My maker found me there, and gave me immortality. I suppose, given the alterna-tive, I should be grateful."

"I suppose so." She tried to picture it, to imagine Simon lying there, dying, and then somehow saved. "And you were just twenty-eight?" He'd said as much the first night they'd met, answering her unspoken question.

He nodded, rubbing slow circles on the inside of her palm with his thumb. "I'd celebrated my birthday just a week before the battle with a tankard of ale. Anything else you'd like to know?"

"A million things more," she said.

"Go on, then," he prodded. "We've got all night."

"Let's see." She tapped her chin thoughtfully. "The first night we met, you told me you were the land steward's son. Why did you lie? Surely you must have known that I'd learn the truth."

His face hardened, all traces of joviality gone in an instant. He swallowed hard, his jaw flexing. A moment passed before he spoke. "It didn't matter what I answer I gave you. At the time, I didn't expect you'd live to learn the truth."

She sucked in her breath, taken aback. "Whatever do you mean by that?"

He reached for her chin, tipping her face upward to meet his gaze. "Just know this—generally, when I lure prey to my lair, they don't leave alive."

All the air left Madeline's lungs in a *whoosh*. "But then what—why?"

"What happened? Why did I change my mind?" he supplied.

Madeline just nodded.

"I wish I knew. This is completely uncharted territory for me. All I know is that I looked into your eyes—into your soul —and felt stirrings of my humanity, the first I'd felt in a very long time. It was almost as if you'd awakened me from a deep, dark sleep. I knew then that you were meant to be my mortal mate."

Madeline shook her head in confusion. "Your mortal mate? What does that mean?"

Simon rose, crossing to the fireplace to prod the logs with a poker. "All these years I've heard the term bandied about, but never truly believed in the concept, till now."

"Explain it to me," she demanded, still shaken by the very idea of how close she'd come to death.

Setting aside the poker, he returned to his seat beside her. "It's quite simple, really. A vampire crosses paths with a mortal, and realizes that he wants more than just her life's blood. Instead, he wants her entirely—body, soul, and mind. If she'll accept him, come to him willingly and of her own free will, then a bond is forged, a bond that lasts till the mortal draws her final breath. They become lovers, companions. For his part, the vampire vows to protect her at all costs. Furthermore, his protection will extend to each of her children—"

"Wait," she interrupted, laying a hand on his sleeve. "Do you mean that I can bear your children?"

"Unfortunately, no."

Unexpected disappointment shot through her.

"But were you to bear your husband's children," he continued, "my protection would extend to them, and their children, and so on and so forth. As you can see, it's a serious commitment, not one to be taken lightly. By the way, I'm using the terms 'he' and 'she' specific to our situation. The same holds true with a female vampire and her male mortal mate, only in reverse, if you will."

Madeline swallowed hard. "And we've entered into such a bond?"

He nodded gravely. "On my part, yes. You, of course, are free to renounce the bond and go your own way. Or"—he reached for her hand again, clasping it in his—"you can accept me as your mate."

"So you're saying that…that you'd remain by my side, even as I age? That this bond between us will still exist when I'm an old woman, while you remain twenty-eight in perpetuity?"

The corners of his mouth twitched with a smile. "I'm not *really* twenty-eight, Maddy."

She shook her head, flummoxed by the concept. "I…I don't know what to say."

"You don't have to give me your answer now. Take some time to consider it. Allow me the opportunity to persuade you." He leaned toward her, pressing his lips against her throat. "Trust me, I can be *very* persuasive."

Madeline felt her heart skip a beat. Fear? Or longing? She wasn't certain.

"When do you leave for Herefordshire?" he asked.

"Monday morning." *Two more nights.*

"Well, then, I suppose you have till dawn on Monday to make your decision."

It wasn't enough time. "Perhaps we could spend tomorrow afternoon together. I could claim a headache and —" She cut herself off, realizing what she was asking. He was a vampire, after all. "We can't, can we?"

"I'm afraid not. I must sleep when the sun rises, and remain abed till nightfall."

"However do you ensure that someone doesn't stumble upon you while you're sleeping?" she asked, morbidly curious now. "Do you sleep in a...a...coffin?"

He looked amused by that. "No, I sleep in a bed. But I'm able to protect my environment. A sort of cloaking maneuver, if you will. Which, by the way, is why no one else has found their way to this cottage since I've been in residence here."

Her mouth felt suddenly dry. "But then...how did I?"

He shrugged. "A fine question, indeed. I can only assume it's because you were meant to find me."

"Your mortal mate," Madeline murmured, still a bit stunned by the revelation.

"Perhaps. It's ironic, really." He rubbed one cheek with the palm of his hand. "All these years, I've jeered at others who took human mates. I've teased them mercilessly, accused them of keeping pets. And now? I would give anything—give up *everything*—for you to be mine."

"Your pet?"

"Your lover," he corrected. "Your friend. Your protector."

Two nights.

"Anything else you'd like to know?" He leaned back against the sofa's cushions, watching her, waiting, and all she could think was that he was the most beautiful man she'd ever seen—the face of an angel, the body of a Greek god.

Dear Lord, how she wanted to wrap her legs around his hips and ride him hard, wanted his teeth buried in her neck as she came, over and over again.

Her mind was spinning, her skin flushing hotly. He'd freely admitted to taking lives, had almost taken Francis's just now, yet all she could think of was making love to him.

What kind of woman did that make her?

She took a deep, steadying breath. "Just answer me this, Simon McKenzie. Say I do accept you as my mate. Will you continue to…to stalk prey, as you so charmingly put it? To take lives?"

"No." He shook his head. "I vow, as long as you live, I will neither hunt nor kill. The only blood I'll taste is yours."

A shudder snaked down her spine at the thought.

He stood, reaching for her hand to pull her to her feet beside him. "But not tonight, Maddy," he said softly, drawing her into his arms. "Tonight, I'll simply hold you while you sleep."

Madeline pressed her cheek against his chest, nodding sleepily.

He kissed the top of her head. "You're safe, my love. Always."

CHAPTER 8

"Where are we going, again?" Madeline asked Miss Portnoy, shouting to be heard over the motorcar's engine.

"To the village, to see a play of some sort. There's a traveling troupe in town, Lady Hartsdale said. Something about the Celtic festival of Samhain."

"Yes, of course," Madeline said, though this was the first she'd heard of it. She'd been distracted all morning, her mind occupied.

The gentleman had gone off to shoot again, leaving the ladies to a leisurely morning spent playing cards. Lady Hartsdale had brought out her exquisite Faro set, and they'd sat gathered around several green baize-covered tables for hours.

Madeline wondered how Francis was managing a gun with his injured wrist—and what he'd said to explain how he'd come by such an injury. She hoped he'd allowed the housekeeper to bandage it, else an infection might set in. *Good God.*

But how could she possibly concentrate on the cards in

her hands, when she had such an important decision to make? She weighed her options in her mind, over and over again.

Walk away from Simon, and everything he offered her. Which left her with nothing save her unhappy marriage and her quiet, uneventful life at Briarton Hall. Before now, it had been enough.

Or accept Simon's offer—accept this mystifying bond, and take a vampire as a lover. Her days would remain the same, but her nights...

Oh, how lovely her nights would be. For once in her life, she'd feel adored, appreciated. She could have children without the fear of them suffering mistreatment at the hands of a cruel father. With Simon in her life to keep Francis in check, she had nothing to fear. It seemed the perfect solution.

Too perfect.

She would age, and Simon would not. How would she feel twenty years from now? Thirty? She would look in the mirror and see a young, beautiful man with a woman old enough to be his grandmother. She shuddered at the very thought.

And then there was the fact that he was a vampire. He would drink her blood, just as he'd done before. How could any rational person accept something so unnatural, so macabre?

She reached up to her throat, running her fingers over the spot where his fangs had punctured her skin. The marks had healed quickly—unnaturally so—leaving not the faintest trace of a blemish. Truth be told, his bite hadn't been unpleasant, not in the least. Still, to accept it so blithely seemed foolish at best.

And yet...she wanted him. That was the simple truth, and there was no denying it. It almost seemed as if her decision would be any easy one.

Madeline looked up as the enormous motorcar made a turn, her attention diverted back to the present. Soon they were motoring down the village's main thoroughfare where buildings clustered together beneath bright awnings. Pedestrians bustled down the sidewalk, calling out to one another in greeting.

They slowed as they passed a church, its steeple casting a long shadow on the adjacent town green. Just beyond, the motorcar turned off the main road and pulled up to a white stone building, the word 'playhouse' spelled out in black letters across the front.

"It's not exactly London's East End," Miss Portnoy whispered as they waited for the driver to hand them down.

Minutes later, Madeline settled herself in her seat, Miss Portnoy on her right, and the aisle on her left. Absently, she tucked the playbill into her purse, not even bothering to glance at it.

"What *is* the Samhain Festival?" Miss Portnoy asked, tipping her head toward Madeline's.

"I'm not entirely certain." Madeline shook her head. "Perhaps it marks the end of the harvest?"

"Perhaps," Miss Portnoy agreed. "But look at the play's title." She waved the playbill. "*The Night Woods*. That sounds rather ominous, doesn't it?"

"Indeed," Madeline said with a laugh, just as the house lights dimmed.

A hush fell over the audience as the heavy red curtain slid open, revealing what looked like a bonfire in the center of the stage.

Around it, women wearing masks danced gaily, holding up wine goblets as they did so. On one side of the stage stood three women dressed as peasants. Behind them, painted scenery depicted a deep, dark wood.

At once, the scene around the bonfire froze, the actors motionless and silent as a spotlight illuminated the peasants.

They spoke in unison, their voices raised in a singsong chant:

BEWARE THE DARK Lords who come in the night, to ravish and whisper every woman's delight.

Beware the Dark Lords who come to your bed, for they and their beauty are to be dread.

Beware the Dark Lords who come in the night, for they will steal your soul upon their murmured goodnight.

Beware the Dark Lords who love and leave, taking with them a part of thee.

A SHIVER WORKED its way down Madeline's spine. There was something eerily familiar about the words, the warning. She shifted uncomfortably in her seat, feeling a vague sense of dread.

The play continued on, depicting several vignettes in which innocent young maidens strayed too close to enchanted forests during the Festival of Samhain. The three peasants—the chorus—warned them each away, entreating them to guard well their secret desires, lest the Dark Lords entice them, drawn to their sweet fragrance, driven to appease.

In each and every instance, the silly young girls ignored the warnings, drawn helplessly into the night woods where they were ravished by the Dark Lords, never to be seen again.

As the play went on, Madeline's unease continued to grow. Where had she heard that phrase before, *Dark Lords*?

She searched her memory, coming up maddeningly blank.

At last the final curtain fell, the house lights rising as the players came out to take their bows.

"That was odd," Miss Portnoy whispered, and Madeline nodded her agreement. "Whatever did they mean about the veil growing transparent during Samhain? I vow, I couldn't make heads or tails out of it."

"Nor could I," Madeline whispered back.

And then she remembered—the housemaid, her first night at Hartsdale Castle. That's where she'd heard the phrase. Just as she tried to escape out into the night, the housemaid had stopped her, warning her to stay away from the woods. "The Dark Lords will get you for sure," she'd said. It had been the eve of the Samhain Festival, according to the woman.

Silly superstitions, she assured herself. The housemaid had a Scottish accent—it was likely a story she'd heard as a girl, a cautionary tale, much like the Grimm Brothers' stories.

Madeline had ignored the woman's warnings, as any sane person would do. She'd set out into the night, and found herself drawn toward the light in the woods, where she'd met Simon, a man who seemed to know her most secret desires, who had…had…*appeased* them, hadn't he?

Good God! She felt the blood drain from her face, the room suddenly titling at an awkward angle.

"Lady Briarton!" Miss Portnoy called out, reaching for her arm.

The ground beneath her feet began to sway, and suddenly everything went black.

∾

MADELINE'S EYELIDS FLUTTERED OPEN, and she blinked in confusion. *Where am I?*

"Good heavens, Lady Briarton!" came Lady Hartsdale's voice beside her. "You gave us all such a fright."

She shook her head, hoping to clear the cobwebs. "I... what happened?"

"You fainted dead away," said Miss Portnoy, leaning over her with drawn brows. "I think you might have hit your head on the edge of the seat."

Madeline reached a hand up to her head, just above her right ear. It was throbbing painfully.

"Can you sit?" asked Lady Hartsdale.

She was laid out in the aisle, she realized, her cheeks flushing with embarrassment. Miss Portnoy offered her hand, helping her to a seated position.

"The physician is on his way," cried a male voice, and Madeline turned to see a young man in spectacles rushing toward her. "Don't try to stand, ma'am. Dr. Prescott will be here any moment now."

Madeline took a deep, steadying breath. "Really, I'm fine. I was a bit warm, that's all. Perhaps I stood up too quickly."

"Perhaps it's that handsome husband of hers' fault," came a voice behind her.

"Hush now, Lady Berkley," hissed Lady Hartsdale. "There are unmarried ladies present."

"Oh, pish, posh," the woman answered. "They're unmarried, not addle-brained. Tell me, Lady Briarton, have you been feeling ill in the morning?"

Madeline shook her head, wincing at the pain. "No, I... I'm perfectly well in the morning."

Lady Berkley looked unconvinced. "Are you certain? Because—"

"Enough!" Lady Hartsdale interrupted. "Come now, everyone move away and let her get some air." She shooed everyone back, though the loyal Miss Portnoy remained at Madeline's side.

"I really don't need a doctor," Madeline told her.

"Well, it can't hurt to let him have a look now, can it? Besides, you're creating a drama far more entertaining than the one we just sat through. You should have seen Mrs. Dawes' face when Lady Berkley made her shocking comment. I vow, I thought her eyes were going to pop right out of her head, and I'm fairly certain her skin turned green."

Madeline laughed weakly. For good measure, she reached down and patted her stomach, sending Miss Portnoy into gales of laughter.

"Perhaps a Dark Lord will do us all a favor, and come for her tonight," Miss Portnoy suggested with a wicked grin.

Madeline's breath caught in her throat.

"Though I'm not certain that her fragrance is sweet enough to entice one," Miss Portnoy continued on, mercifully unaware of Madeline's sudden discomfort. "Such a shame. I hope—oh, look, here comes the doctor!"

Madeline let out her breath in a rush, grateful for the man's timely appearance. Any more talk of Dark Lords, and she thought she might very well lose her mind.

Or perhaps she already had.

"Is there anything I can get you before I go down to dinner?" Francis offered, one hand on the door-knob, eager to flee. His left wrist was still wrapped in a bandage, and there were noticeable dark circles beneath his eyes. He looked tired, skittish. *Terrified.*

Madeline shook her head. "No, I'm perfectly fine. Thank you," she added, just for good measure.

"Very well." He couldn't even meet her eyes. "I'll just be going, then."

Leaning back against the pillows, she let out a sigh of relief when the door shut behind him. The housekeeper had already sent up her dinner tray, which sat untouched on a tray beside her.

She'd been in bed since she'd returned from the theatre, just as the doctor had ordered. Though she felt perfectly well save for the bump on her head, she was glad for the reprieve. She wanted to be alone with her thoughts—needed time to sort them out before she saw Simon again.

She was a sensible woman, she told herself. Sensible

women didn't believe in enchanted woods cloaked in magic or dark lords who lured maidens to their doom.

Of course, sensible women didn't believe in vampires, either. If one were to throw common sense to the wind and believe that such a creature *did* exist, then why not believe that they should be the monsters of legend, capable of trickery and deceit in order to get what they wanted? She was easy prey, after all.

Had she been tricked by a silver-tongued monster? It suddenly seemed entirely possible, and far more likely, really, than the whole "mortal mate" nonsense that she'd accepted so readily.

What a fool she'd been to believe his lies.

"I never once lied to you, Maddy," came a familiar voice, startling her so badly that she almost screamed.

She turned to find him there, leaning against the far wall, watching her.

"Good God, Simon! You scared me half to death." Her heart was pounding against her ribs so hard that she feared it might burst.

"I never lied to you," he repeated, moving toward her on silent feet. "This whole Dark Lords nonsense..." He trailed off, shaking his head. "I suppose there's a kernel of truth to it. Perhaps in less civilized times it helped explain the unex-plainable. I haven't any idea. But how could you possibly believe that I'm some sort of devil, tricking you into...what? Giving up your soul? I'm not even certain I understand what you're accusing me of." He sounded hurt. Betrayed, even.

Of course he would. He was toying with her, like a cat with a mouse. He sat on the edge of the bed, so close now that he could strike without warning. She found herself recoiling slightly, leaning into the pillows behind her back.

"Do you really believe that of me?" he asked, his voice laced with disbelief. "Haven't I had plenty of opportunity to hurt you before now, had I wanted to? Bloody hell, Maddy, you've slept in my arms the past two nights. In the woods, I might add. According to your legend, I shouldn't have ever let you out again. And yet, here you are."

She shook her head, her certainty flagging. "I...I don't know what to believe anymore. This is all too unreal. Sometimes I think I must be dreaming."

"I've had the exact same thought. Only vampires do not dream."

"No?" she asked, her voice unnaturally high.

He shook his head. "No."

For a moment, they sat in silence. Madeline examined him closely, not quite sure what she was looking for.

"You wear your hair long," she said at last.

"As did most men in Scotland in 1745. It's not quite so fashionable now, I'm afraid."

"Why don't you cut it, then?" she asked, her traitorous fingers itching to comb through his silky locks.

He shrugged. "It would just be a wasted effort. The next time I slept, it would return to this exact same length."

"Really? How very odd."

"Isn't it? It's the same with my fingernails." He glanced down at his hands, examining his nails. "It's impossible to alter my physical form in any way. If only I'd known ahead of time, perhaps I might have prepared better." The barest hint of smile danced on his lips.

"How do you do it, Simon? Kill people, I mean. You seem so...unapologetic about it."

He recoiled slightly, as if she'd slapped him. "Do you think I have a choice in the matter? Have you any idea what the bloodlust is like? It's all consuming, a need as primal as your need to breathe air."

She digested that in silence, trying to imagine how it would feel to ignore the need to take a breath—to refuse to do so. It wasn't possible, she realized. Self-preservation instincts didn't allow it.

"I'm drawn to darkness, Maddy. Lost souls. Evil souls. Those who are filled with hate or despair. Once I catch their scent, instinct takes over. I do my best to make it swift, painless."

"I suppose that's something," she said softly.

Tentatively, he reached for her hand. "Don't you see? You're the first light I've had in my life in so very long. I'd almost forgotten what it was like. I realize it's selfish, what I'm asking of you. But with your blood running through my veins, I'll be able to step outside the darkness for the first time in all of my God-forsaken existence."

She clasped his hand firmly in hers. "I'm not quite ready to say yes yet, Simon. I still need more time."

"Of course. You've still got till Monday, just as before."

"Thank you." She sighed heavily. "I'm afraid that whenever I'm with you, I cannot think clearly."

"Are you saying I should leave you now?"

She winced at the disappointment in his voice. "Probably so. I need a clear head to make my decision. Besides, in case you did not hear, I managed to knock myself senseless today at the theatre. The doctor ordered bed rest. I'm not to exert myself, you see."

"I understand," he said, leaning toward her. His lips brushed her, featherlight and teasing. "What if," he said between kisses, "I exert myself a bit before I leave you to your rest."

"Whatever do you mean?" she asked, breathlessly.

His lips trailed down her throat, moving lower, toward her décolletage. "Just that you allow me a chance to persuade you further. Here, on your terms."

She sucked in her breath, her thighs dampening as his

mouth pushed aside the collar of her dressing gown, his tongue dragging across one nipple. "My terms?"

"Yes, anything you want. And no fangs this time. No biting, no feeding."

"You can do that? It isn't necessary?" She squirmed against the mattress as his mouth moved to her other breast, his tongue flicking against the hardened peak. "Oh!" she cried out in pleasure.

"Oh, it's quite necessary for my release, I'm afraid. But not yours."

It took a moment for his meaning to sink in. In the meantime, he'd untied her dressing gown's sash, slipping the silk from her shoulders as he bared her.

"God, you're beautiful," he said, trailing a cold finger from her chin down to her navel, drawing gooseflesh in his wake. Sliding down on the bed, he fitted himself between her thighs, pushing them apart as his head dipped lower.

She was momentarily confused. "What are you—Oh, dear God in heaven!" His tongue found her opening, sliding up and across her swollen clit, causing her to clutch at the bedsheets beneath her hips. Involuntarily, her hips rose up, meeting his tongue with every stroke.

"So sweet," he murmured. One finger slid inside her, then two. His tongue continued to flick across her sensitive flesh while his fingers worked magic, pressing against a spot inside her that made her cry out with pleasure.

Releasing the sheets, she clutched at the back of his head, instead, her breath coming faster now as she ground herself against his face, moving closer and closer to release.

"Simon, I—Oh, God, now. Now!" She had no idea what she was asking of him. She wanted his cock inside her, but knew he couldn't. Or wouldn't.

One more flick of his tongue, two…she could barely hang on another moment. And then at last she fell over the precipice, her entire body humming as wave after wave of pleasure washed over, centered at her very core.

As soon as she caught her breath, she raised up on her elbows, glancing down at Simon. She gasped, surprised to find his eyes glowing red, his fangs elongated. His jaw was clenched in what looked like agony, his hands clutching the sheets as if his life depended on it.

"Just...give me a moment," he ground out, sounding much like a dying man.

She watched helplessly as he fought it. Slowly, the red receded, the fangs retracted. Two, perhaps three minutes later, he released his breath in a rush. "See?" he said with a grin. "I told you it was possible."

"And quite persuasive," she said with a nod. "Very much so, to tell you the truth."

He laughed at that. "I'm glad to hear it. Here, I hope I didn't tear your dressing gown." He dropped the garment in question into her lap. "If I did, I'll buy you a new one. A dozen new ones."

There was a sharp knock on the door. "Lady Briarton? Are you done with your tray?"

She swung her legs over the side of the bed, hurriedly shrugging into the dressing gown. "Just one moment," she called out, rising to tie the sash about her waist. She glanced over one shoulder to the spot where Simon had sat just moments before. "Simon, you should—"

She stopped mid-sentence. It was no use; he was gone. Just like that, in the blink of an eye.

"*I* swear, you're positively glowing," Madeline said to Miss Portnoy as they left the breakfast table the next morning. "Have you something to tell me?"

Miss Portnoy smiled, her dark eyes dancing. "Come, let's take a turn about the garden."

Madeline nodded. "I'd like that. Come," she whispered, tugging on her hand, "let's hurry before someone decides to join us."

Minutes later, they found themselves out in the bright autumn sunshine, hurrying across the lawn toward a shady pergola. "Tell me," Madeline urged, as soon as they reached their destination and took a seat on a wrought-iron bench.

"Lord Dunham and I—oh, Lady Briarton, I can barely believe it, but he's asked me to marry him!"

Smiling broadly, Madeline reached for her hand. "Oh, Miss Portnoy—"

"Please, call me Eloise. I feel that we're such friends now, I can't bear the formalities."

"And you must call me Madeline."

"I'd like that," the girl said, tears filling her eyes.

"I'm so pleased for you! Assuming you said yes, of course. You did say yes, didn't you?"

"Of course I said yes. I admit, I wasn't at all expecting it. I was hoping for an understanding, perhaps, but I never dreamed…" She trailed off, shaking her head. "He wants to get married next summer."

"Before then, you must promise to come to Briarton Hall for a visit. I'll invite Lord Dunham, too."

"I'd love to. Actually, there's something I hoped to ask you, though I'm afraid it will sound too presumptuous."

"Nonsense, Eloise. You can ask me anything at all."

She ducked her head shyly. "It's just that…well, I feel that we get on so well, and I've never felt comfortable here with my sister, to tell you the truth. She looks at me as if I'm some sort of stain on the fabric of her life. I know it's rude to ask, but if you would consider having me as your guest for an extended period…I mean, I remembered you saying that Lord Briarton spends most of his time in London, and I… well, I so enjoy your company." Eloise looked up at her expectantly, awaiting her reply.

"What a lovely idea!" Madeline exclaimed. "I'd be delighted to have—" She stopped short, remembering Simon. How would this affect her decision, where he was concerned?

"Oh, please don't feel obliged," Eloise said, her smile faltering. "I realize it's far too much to ask, and—"

"Not at all. And as I was saying, I'd be delighted to have you. There's just…a detail that I must work out first."

However would she explain him? 'Oh, ignore the man who appears and disappears in the blink of an eye, the man you only see between the hours of dusk and dawn. He won't bother you; he's just my vampire mate.' However would she explain the sudden appearance of puncture marks on her neck, and their equally puzzling disappearance? After all, she couldn't wear high-necked blouses *all* the time.

She shook her head, torn.

"Does this have something to do with your lover?" Eloise asked quietly. "Because you must know I won't judge you. I'm just glad to see that you've found such happiness."

"How did—" She caught herself before it was too late. "I have no idea what you mean."

Smiling mischievously, Eloise shook her head. "Dearest Madeline, I know you've been sneaking off with someone at night. In fact, you've done so every single night since your arrival." She paused, pursing her lips thoughtfully. "Except perhaps last night, though I'm not entirely certain he didn't find his way to you somehow when you were supposed to be resting. I also know that whoever he is came to blows with Francis on Friday night, and from the looks of it, I'd say that he got the best of him, too. What I *can't* figure out is who the man is. It's driving me mad, trying to puzzle it out."

"Goodness, Eloise, whatever are you? Some sort of spy for the crown? How can you possibly know these things?"

"I've a good deal of experience in sneaking about, remember? I've long since perfected the craft, and I recognize the signs when I see them. Please don't imagine that I think any less of you. I'm greatly impressed, to tell you the truth."

Madeline laughed at that. "I suppose I'm glad."

"If you let me come to Briarton Hall, I won't ask any questions. I certainly won't interfere, or betray your confidence."

If only it were that simple. But the situation was complicated, far too complicated to contemplate at present.

"Let me think about it," she said, and Eloise nodded.

IT SEEMED as if night would never fall. Madeline stood by the window, gazing out as the orange sun made its slow descent toward the horizon, painting colorful swaths of pink and red across the sky.

How long after the sun finally set till he rose from his sleep, she wondered? There was still so much she didn't know, didn't fully understand.

What kind of fool went into something so blindly, especially when the stakes were so high? Again, her resolve wavered. It was so easy when she was in his presence, so simple to believe that everything he said was true.

But as the day wore on and the previous night's encounter faded into what seemed a dream, her doubts came rushing back in a torrent.

The housemaid's warning, the play's message, the timing of her first encounter with Simon, right on the eve of Samhain...

She wasn't particularly good with figures, yet she was fairly certain that two plus two added up to four—even if someone insisted that it didn't.

Madeline turned away from the window, taking in the scene before her. Francis sat directly across a felt-covered card table from Lord Hartsdale, two gentlemen on either side of them, playing cards. Lord Dunham and Miss Portnoy sat side-by-side on a low velvet bench by the door, their heads bent in quiet conversation.

Lady Hartsdale was pouring tea, a group of ladies gathered about her chattering loudly as they waited for the dinner bell.

She had no idea where Mrs. Dawes was—didn't care, really. The truth was, her presence didn't bother Madeline nearly as much as it had earlier in the week.

In many ways, Madeline felt like a changed woman since her arrival at Hartsdale Castle such a short time ago. She couldn't explain it, not really, but she felt stronger somehow. More confident.

All because of Simon, she realized with a start.

How could something so positive, so empowering, possibly be based in dark magic? On trickery and deceit?

With a sigh, she turned back toward the window just in time to see the bottom edge of the sun touch the edge of the horizon.

At last.

Forget dinner—she needed some air. Luckily, yesterday's fainting spell provided the perfect excuse to bow out of dinner. Hastily, she made her excuses to her hostess, and went upstairs to retrieve her coat and gloves.

As Madeline hurried across the estate's vast lawn, the last remnants of the sun melted quietly into the hazy lavender of twilight.

~

Simon awoke with a start, sitting up sharply. His senses were on high alert, even though his cloaking mechanism protected his lair. He prodded it with his mind, testing the invisible boundaries. It was intact.

He swung his legs over the side of the bed, glancing over at the shuttered window. Deep, orange-red light tipped the edges of the wooden slats, meaning that he'd awoken early.

How very odd.

Curious, he rose, striding over to the window and folding back one sash.

With a cry, he staggered back, holding up one hand to protect his face from the sun's dying rays.

Bloody hell!

Whatever had he been thinking? He collapsed back to the bed, cradling his hand to his body as the smell of singed flesh reached his nostrils. He turned over the hand, staring down at his palm with shock. The skin was blistered, raw and bubbling.

Fuck.

For several minutes, he sat there silently, waiting. He didn't dare risk standing up again and exposing himself to the dangerous rays, not until the orange gave way to pink, then gray.

Only then did he stand up and close the shutters. He glanced back down at his hand, glad to see that it had already begun to heal, the once red, angry flesh now a puckered pink.

What the hell had awakened him so early? This hadn't happened before, not once, in all his years.

He focused his senses on the environment surrounding the cottage, honing in on the sound of footsteps, perhaps two, three hundred yards away. Not from the direction of the castle's grounds, but from the other side—the woods. The footsteps seemed...erratic, he decided. Going in circles, searching. Someone was lost.

An equally erratic heartbeat accompanied the footsteps. He inhaled deeply, searching for a scent, then froze, his eyes widening with fear.

Maddy.

Whatever was she doing out there, wandering aimlessly? The woods weren't safe for a lady alone, particularly now that night had fallen.

Something was not right. She should be safely inside the castle's dining room right now, enjoying dinner with the other guests.

He dressed quickly, trying to ignore the pain in his hand. Damn it all, he couldn't believe he'd actually allowed himself to get burnt by the sun, like some reckless newly turned fool. After all, he hadn't burnt himself in more than a century. What the hell had come over him?

I'm not the same man, he realized with a start. Where he'd once been careful, cautious, he was now reckless. He'd flown into a rage and appeared there in Madeline's bedchamber to attack her husband without giving it a second thought, without even considering the possibility of discovery. He was lucky that no one had burst in, hearing the commotion.

What if they had? What if a maid had rushed in, followed by a gaggle of servants or houseguests? What would he have done? Threatened them all? Killed them all to silence them?

A shudder snaked down his spine. A century ago, he *would* have killed them all, and not thought twice about it. He could not help it—he came from a more violent time, an era where life was not treated with the same respect as it was now.

Though it seemed contrary to logic, he'd grown *more* civilized over the years, not less.

And now...the very idea of losing Madeline, of something happening to her, sent him into a panic. Panic made one careless. Reckless. A danger to oneself and others.

He leaned down, pulling on his boots. What if she rejected him? What if she denied their bond and refused his protection?

How could he continue on, if that were the case? She'd irrevocably changed him, and now he couldn't go back to the man he was before—the mostly solitary creature who was content to stay in the shadows, courting darkness.

He wanted to step out into the light.

CHAPTER 11

"*M*addy?"

Madeline spun toward the voice, relief coursing through her when she spied Simon standing there, not five feet away.

"Oh, Simon!" she cried. "Thank God you've found me. I've been walking in circles, hopelessly lost."

"How long have you been out here?"

"Not long. Since just before the sun set, that's all."

Precisely the moment he'd awakened, he realized.

"What happened to your hand?" she asked, her brows drawn, mouth pursed.

"What? Oh, nothing." He flexed the hand in question. "It's fine."

"You were stroking your palm with your thumb. Does it hurt?"

"Not really. It was just a minor burn. Look"—he held it up, palm out—"it's almost healed now."

She reached for it, cupping it in her own hand while she examined it. "It looks a bit irritated still." Glancing up, she saw that he was grinning like a schoolboy. "What?"

He shrugged. "I suppose it's nice to be fussed over, that's all. Anyway, come," he said, clasping her hand in his. "I have something to show you. I promise you it's well worth the effort," he added when she hesitated.

His enthusiasm made her smile. "If you say so."

"I'll need to carry you," he warned, lifting her off her feet and cradling her body against his. "This will take a bit longer than the trip from Hartsdale Castle to the cottage. Can you wrap your arms around my neck? Make sure you hold on tight."

"Goodness, Simon, wherever are we going?"

"You'll see. Can you trust me, Maddy? Just this once."

"I never said I didn't trust you," she replied, snaking her arms around his neck.

"Then prove it," he countered. "Ready?"

"Ready." Taking a deep breath, she squeezed her eyes shut and waited.

Immediately, she was assaulted by the sensation of speed. Of height. The night air rushed past her, a low roar in her ears. And then, just as quickly, the odd sensations dissipated. Everything was at once still and quiet.

"You can open your eyes now, love, but do me a favor and remain still if you can. Here"—he shifted her in his lap —"move your arms around my waist, instead."

She complied, wrapping her arms around his middle and then opening her eyes. Blinking rapidly, she looked around, seeing nothing but blackness in all directions. How had the sky darkened so quickly? "Where are we?" she asked.

"Shhh," he cautioned, his voice a whisper beside her ear. "We're still in the woods adjacent to Hartsdale Castle, only far deeper in than most people dare to venture, on the far side of the kells. Just give your eyes a moment to adjust."

She blinked again—once, twice. The shadows began to

shift, the deep black giving way to shades of gray. Objects began to take shape, slowly coming into focus.

Branches. Leaves. Beyond them, the inky canvas of the sky was dotted with twinkling stars. Wispy clouds, their edges glowing with silvery light, shrouded the moon.

And then she made the mistake of looking down. With a cry, she tightened her grip around Simon's waist.

Dear God, they were up in a tree—sitting in the crook of a wide limb, with Simon's feet dangling below them. He had one arm wrapped around her waist, the other reaching up to hold the limb above his head.

"Don't worry," he said, kissing her head just above her ear. "We're secure. I won't let you fall. Now look, off to your right, just at eye level."

Cautiously, she swiveled her head in the direction indicated. At first, she saw nothing. A branch, perhaps, long and slim.

And then she became aware of a pair of wide, golden-yellow eyes, watching them.

There was a rustling sound, some movement.

Hee, hee.

A form took shape around the eyes. Brown feathers, a round, flat face. Long, slender ear tufts forming a 'V' in the middle of the creature's head. It appeared slim and slouched forward.

"An owl," she whispered in amazement. Not more than an arm's length away.

"A Long-Eared Owl, to be precise," he said. "Quite rare in these parts, as there are so many Tawnies about."

She sucked in her breath, awed by the sight. "He's beautiful."

"She," he corrected. "*She's* beautiful."

"Why isn't she flying off? Is she injured or something?"

"She's fine. I've just set her mind at ease, that's all. I let her know that we aren't a threat."

She tilted her head, glancing up at him. "You can do that?"

"I can do many things. Vampires are given a wide range of unfair advantages in order to keep us at the top of the food chain."

"But—but you wouldn't hurt the owl," she stammered. "Would you?"

"Of course not. I'm merely watching it. Observing. It's something I like to do."

She stifled a laugh. "Sit perched in trees? Watching birds?"

"Why not?" he asked, sounding indignant. "There are far worse ways to spend one's time."

Hee, hee.

She loved owls; had always loved owls. "How did you know?" she asked, returning her gaze to the magnificent creature before them.

"About you and the owls?" He shrugged. "Just another of my advantages over mere mortal folk. You see, knowing what people care for gives one power over them."

He paused, as if gauging her reaction.

She shook her head. "I'm not frightened of you, Simon McKenzie."

"Yes, my love, you are. I can sense it—smell it, even—though you hide it well. Five days isn't enough. You need more time."

Only time had run out. Dawn was mere hours away, growing closer with each passing moment. After breakfast, she would return to Herefordshire, to her life there at Briarton Hall.

She needed to make her decision, and fast.

Simon's hand moved up to cup her chin. "That's why I brought you here tonight, Maddy."

"It's just that I'm just not certain, Simon," she said quickly. "I mean, I think I am, whenever I'm with you, and then—"

He kissed her on the lips, effectively silencing her. "You didn't let me finish what I've come to say."

Whek, whek, whek, whek.

Just then, the owl lifted off the branch, its wings flapping furiously. For a moment, it seemed to hover there above the branch, fluttering like a giant moth, before it flew off, swallowed up into the night.

Madeline let out her breath in a rush.

"I'm setting you free, Maddy, as free as that beautiful creature you just observed. Forget the bond—I release you. Someday, I hope you'll find your way back to me, once you've found your *own* wings. Until then, I'll wait—forever, if need be. You see, love, I have nothing *but* time."

THEY NEVER MADE it to the bedroom. As soon as they arrived back at the cottage, Simon pulled her into his embrace, his mouth coming down on hers hard, feverishly. Their hands were everywhere at once—hers, unbuttoning his shirt, tugging on his necktie; his, unfastening her blouse's tiny pearl buttons, bunching up her skirt around her waist.

There was no time to remove everything, their urgency driving them into a frenzy. Before she knew what was happening, Simon had her bent over the sofa's arm, her legs spread, while he pressed against her back, fumbling with his trousers.

"Simon," she begged, unable to wait another moment, desperate to feel him moving inside her. "Hurry!"

Tears sprung to her eyes—they had so little time left. What if…if the magic was broken the moment she left this place? Could they ever recapture it? Or was it true that these woods were enchanted, compelling Simon to appease her needs?

His head dipped down, his lips pressing against the nape of her neck. She heard him groan, felt his swollen cock press against her bottom. And then his fingers were prodding her folds, slipping inside her, readying her. She arched her back, moaning softly as he stroked her.

Soon she was wet, so very wet. Her clit was swollen, her pelvis beginning to tingle.

Hurry, hurry. Her heart seemed to beat the words in quick staccato.

She cried out when he entered her, rising up on tiptoe to meet his thrusts. One hand clutching her bare breasts, the other holding up her skirt, he drove into her hard, stretching her, filling her.

And then without warning, another need took over her senses. As she moved toward climax, her focus shifted away from her sex to her neck. Dear God, but she wanted his mouth against her throat, needed his teeth scraping against her skin.

Without breaking their rhythm, she reached up to move aside the wispy locks that had fallen from her hair's careful arrangement. "Now, Simon," she urged, turning her head, offering her throat.

Even so, she did not expect the quick pinch of his fangs, piercing her skin. She sucked in her breath, then released it with a sigh as the sting was replaced with warmth, with indescribable pleasure that washed over her in waves, sending her off into a powerful orgasm.

His fangs still buried in her neck, he groaned, his entire body going taut and rigid behind her. And then he almost seemed to roar, his entire body vibrating against hers as they both came, over and over again.

When Madeline's legs at last threatened to buckle

beneath her, his mouth moved away from her neck. She was dizzy, breathless, gasping for air as he picked her up and sat on the sofa, holding her in his lap as he sought to catch his own breath.

"Did I hurt you?" he asked, brushing aside her hair to expose the marks on her neck.

"You didn't hurt me, Simon," she sputtered.

"Thank God." He buried his face in her neck, his breath warm against her skin.

Madeline sighed contentedly. They sat like that for a very long time, till Madeline's eyelids began to droop sleepily.

"I should take you back," he said at last.

"But it's still early."

"You should get some sleep, Maddy."

"I'll sleep here," she insisted. "Just take me back before dawn."

"You're sure?" he asked, scooping her up and carrying her toward the bedroom.

She nodded. "I'm sure."

There was still plenty of time to consider her decision—though she was fairly sure she knew the answer already. He'd said he'd wait, but he didn't need to.

She would give him her answer at dawn. She would say yes.

CHAPTER 12

*S*omeone was calling her name. Madeline rolled over, burying her face in the pillow. She was tired, so very tired.

"Madeline," came the voice again, more insistent now. "Get up."

She cracked open one eye, just a narrow slit, and saw Francis there, looking down at her.

Francis? She sat up with a start, glancing about the room. The white walls were bathed in a bright yellow light, their bags stacked near the door.

"What time is it?" she asked.

"Almost half past eight. You're going to miss breakfast."

Breakfast?

"I'd like to be on the road by ten, if it won't trouble you too much. I'm going to continue on to London after I drop you at Briarton Hall. I've got…business…to attend to early tomorrow morning."

She shook her head, confused. Why hadn't Simon woken her up? Dawn had come and go—he was asleep now, impossible to rouse. How would she give him her answer?

Tears flooded her eyes.

Francis visibly flinched. "Dear lord, don't cry. I suppose if you'd like me to stay in Herefordshire for a bit, I could rearrange—"

"No!" Good God, no. "That's not why...never mind. You go on down to breakfast. I'll be there directly. And don't trouble yourself—I'm perfectly satisfied for you to go to London as soon as possible."

"Are you sure?" he asked, his voice a low whisper now. "Because I say, Madeline, I'd really rather not have any trouble."

She let out her breath in a huff. "I'm sure, Francis. Now please, go. I need to get dressed."

With a nod, he obeyed. As soon as the door swung shut, Madeline leapt from the bed and rang for her maid to help her dress. She had to find him, somehow—find the cottage. He'd be sleeping, but perhaps she could leave him a letter. They hadn't made any other arrangements, after all. She hadn't given him her direction in Herefordshire, and she hadn't any idea where he resided when he wasn't at the stone cottage.

He'd said he spent most of his time in London, but London was enormous. She'd never find him, particularly since he only moved about after night fell. It would be like looking for the proverbial needle in the haystack, only in the dark.

Hurrying over to the desk in the corner, she hastily scribbled out a note, simply saying that her answer was yes, and giving him her direction. They'd just had a telephone installed, so he could ring her as soon as he received the letter, she wrote.

After all, she'd be home at Briarton Hall by the time he awakened tonight. She folded the letter and stuffed it inside her coat pocket just as the maid came in, ready to begin her toilette.

And yet nothing went as planned. By the time she came downstairs an hour later in search of breakfast, Francis was already loading his bags into the motorcar. He was eager to get on the road.

Miss Portnoy pulled her aside for a drawn-out and tearful goodbye, promising to make arrangements to travel to Briarton Hall as soon as possible. Lady Hartsdale wanted to discuss her sister's plans with Madeline, and to express her gratitude for her offer of hospitality. After all, Hereford's society was far superior to Cumberland's, she claimed, better suited for someone like Eloise, who was soon to become a viscountess.

By the time Madeline got away from Lady Hartsdale, the car was fully loaded, their driver standing by the door, waiting.

Panicked, she glanced around wildly, finding no means of escape. Why had Simon done this? Had he expected that she would say no? Was he trying to avoid saying goodbye? Or… or had he decided that he didn't want her as his mortal mate, after all?

Her heart contracted painfully at the thought.

"Madeline?" Francis strode over to where she stood under the port cochere. "Are you ready? Everything's loaded."

She glanced back at the door that led into the house, where several maids bustled about, helping guests with luggage, and she was struck with an idea—one last desperate idea.

"Just…give me one moment, Francis. I believe I've forgotten something back in the room." Without waiting for his reply, she dashed off, trying to remember what the housemaid from that first night looked like, the one who'd warned her away from the woods.

Her face had been round, she remembered, her eyes a

clear blue. She'd been in her late thirties, perhaps. She hadn't any idea what color her hair had been beneath her cap.

Moving quickly, she made her way through the drawing room, toward the sunroom. There were two maids there, replacing table linens.

"Well, Mary, ye canna expect me—oh, sorry, mum." The shorter of the two tipped her head in Madeline's direction.

That accent! The maid had spoken with a Scottish accent, she remembered, her heart accelerating. She took a hard look at her face, recognizing the woman at once.

"Might I have a word with you?" Madeline directed at her, gesturing for her join her there in the doorway.

The woman eyed her suspiciously. "Of course, mum. If ye are havin' any problems, though, ye should speak to the housekeeper."

"No, there's no problem. It's just…remember that first night, when you tried to stop me from going out?" She swallowed hard, lowering her voice to a whisper. "Do you know anything about the stone cottage out in the woods? Or about the…the gentleman who sometimes stays there. Very tall," she said, gesturing to a spot well above her head. "Blond hair?"

The woman's pale eyes narrowed. "I dinna know what ye mean. That cottage is empty, m'lady. 'Tis always empty these days."

Madeline let out her breath in a rush. "Are you certain?"

The woman just nodded.

Madeline reached into her purse, digging around inside and drawing out several gold coins and a thick ivory card. She pressed them both into the woman's hands. "If you don't mind, if you could just take this—it's my calling card—to the cottage. Just leave it on the door, or inside in plain sight. I would be most grateful."

"Verra well, m'lady." She tucked the card and money into her apron pocket.

She hurried back out again, finding Francis leaning against the car, checking his pocket watch. He glanced up as she approached. "I was about to come looking for you. Did you find what you needed?"

"I did," she answered brightly, forcing a smile.

"WHAT DID the lady want with you?" the housemaid named Mary asked, her brows drawn.

Bernadette shook her head. "She was talking nonsense, that one. Something about the old gamekeeper's cottage. She asked about the blond gentleman livin' there."

"There ain't no blond gentleman living there!"

"'Tis what I told her, Mary. Do ye think I'm daft?"

"Well, what did she give you, then?"

Bernadette reached into her pocket and emptied the contents. "A few coins, is all."

Mary pointed to the ivory card. "And what's that?"

"Eh, just rubbish." Bernadette crumpled it in her hand.

Mary clucked her tongue against her teeth. "Huh. What a strange one that one was. Per'aps she's not right in the head, if you know what I mean."

Bernadette glanced over one shoulder. "Hush, now. Here comes Lady Hartsdale. We'd best stop flappin' our gums."

With that, she tossed the crumpled card it into the rubbish bin with the breakfast scraps, and went back to work.

HEREFORDSHIRE, England

. . .

SITTING at her desk in her upstairs sitting room, Madeline glanced out the window, watching the sunset. She'd been home a full fortnight now, and every sunset made her think of Simon. Somewhere, he would be rising now, preparing to go about his business while everyone else prepared for bed.

With a sigh, she closed her eyes, trying to picture him in her mind. But the edges of her memories were growing fuzzy now, and sometimes she wondered if it had all been a dream.

She pushed aside her stack of thick, heavy stationery. She didn't feel like writing letters, though she owed Miss Portnoy a reply. The girl had written her just three days after Madeline had left Hartsdale Castle to tell her that she wouldn't be coming to Briarton Hall for an extended visit, after all. She and Lord Dunham had eloped.

Madeline bit back her loneliness, amazed at how empty her life seemed now, when before she'd been perfectly satisfied. Yet now it seemed as if one day stretched seamlessly into the next, creating an uninterrupted stretch of nothingness.

Tapping her pen against the desk, she watched the sky grow darker and darker, casting the room into shadows. *I really should get up and light the lamps*, she thought, but dismissed the idea. After all, at some point the housekeeper would bustle in and light them for her.

And then something caught her eye—what looked like a flickering light, off in the distance. It was coming from the woods behind the orangerie, she realized with a start.

She stood, placing her palms against the cool glass as she stared out into the twilight, her gaze scanning the grounds that spread out beneath her. Except for the stables, everything was dark, cloaked in varying shades of gray—the manicured gardens; the fountain; the hedgerow-lined path that led to the gazebo, the orangerie, and the tennis lawn.

There it was again, the light. *Curious.* Because unlike Hartsdale Castle, there was no stone cottage out in the woods at Briarton Hall, no outbuildings tucked into clearings. She knew every inch of the property, and there was nothing but woods out behind the orangerie—dense woods that stretched all the way to the edge of Aylestone Hill.

She hurried downstairs, taking her coat from the hook by door and slipping it on before stepping outside onto the stone terrace that ran the length of the house. She took off at a brisk walk; the moon illuminated the path, guiding her as she made her way past the gardens, the gazebo, to the orangerie, and then around it, toward the spot where she'd seen the light. She stopped when she reached the edge of the woods, scanning the dark depths for something, anything.

This is foolish, she told herself. She'd imagined it.

Except there it was again, off to her left and rather high, as if it were up in the trees. She took two steps forward, glancing back at the house behind her, looming in the distance. She realized now that she should have told someone where she was going—the housekeeper, Mrs. Potter, or her lady's maid, Sally, perhaps. But she hadn't thought to tell a soul, and now if she didn't make it out again, no one would even know where to look for her.

Oh, stuff and nonsense!

She quickly set off, before she lost her courage, hurrying through the trees and over the downed limbs in her path, her shoes crunching the leaves beneath her feet. On and on she walked, finding nothing out of the ordinary. Perhaps ten minutes later, she came to a clearing, and stopped to catch her breath.

If only she'd remembered her gloves. Now that the sun had set, the temperature had dropped dramatically. She shoved her hands into her coat's pockets, where her right hand encountered resistance. Puzzled, she pulled out a folded piece of paper.

Her heart began to race. It was her letter to Simon, the one she'd written just before she'd left Hartsdale Castle, but hadn't been able to deliver.

Her hands trembling, she unfolded the page, reading it by the light of the moon. *My answer is yes,* she'd written in her loopy script. For some reason, she had the urge to read it aloud. "My answer is yes," she said, then repeated it, shouting now. "Do you hear me, Simon McKenzie? Yes!"

Tears sprung to her eyes, and she sunk to her knees in the springy moss, crumpling the page in her hand.

I'm such a fool.

Whatever had she been afraid of? She'd let happiness slip right through her fingers, and for what? For fear of some silly legend? Had she truly believed that Simon was a Night Lord, intent on stealing her soul?

Simon McKenzie, the man who liked to sit in trees and watch birds? The man who made love to her with a tender passion that left her breathless? The man who would give up his own release, so that she could find hers?

Yes, he was a vampire, but that did not make him a liar, a trickster, or a user of women.

Her *husband* was the user of women, damn it all, and Simon had vowed her to protect her from him. Who was going to protect her now? Who would protect her children?

"My answer is yes, Simon McKenzie," she sobbed, her voice breaking pitifully. "Please, please come back to me."

For some inexplicable reason, she chose that moment in her grief to look up.

And there it was, the light. Like a beacon, halfway up the tree that stood directly in front of her.

What in God's name?

There was a loud *whump* behind her, making the earth shake beneath her feet. She whirled around toward the sound, one hand clutching her throat in a pose of terror.

She wasn't certain what she'd expected to find there in the clearing behind her—a wild animal; some sort of demon; the devil himself, perhaps. None of those would have surprised her in the least.

But Simon McKenzie?

She swallowed hard, her throat aching. "It's—it's—you," she stammered, barely able to form the words.

He set the lantern he was carrying down on the ground. "My answer is yes, Madeline Briarton," he said, his mouth curving into the most dazzling smile she'd ever seen.

A million questions rushed through her mind at once. But then she realized it didn't matter where he'd been, or how he'd found her, or what in God's name he was doing in the woods outside Briarton Hall, lurking in the shadows.

None of it mattered a bit. All that mattered was that he was there, no more than a few steps away from her—not a figment of her imagination, but real and whole and so very beautiful.

He was not her husband, but he *was* her mate. Her lover. Her companion. Her protector.

"Come," she said, reaching out a hand to him. "Let's go home."

"I thought you'd never invite me in," he answered with a grin, pulling her into his embrace.

EPILOGUE

*M*adeline glanced up at Francis, who smiled down at the swaddled, sleeping babe in her arms.

"He's beautiful, Madeline. Thank you."

"Isn't he?" She reached down to trace a finger across Henry's perfect, petal-pink cheek. "One day you shall be Lord Briarton," she cooed. "A lot of responsibility for such a wee one, isn't it?"

"He'll be brilliant. A far better baron than his father, I'd say."

"Likely so," she murmured, but there was no anger, no recrimination in her voice. It was only the truth—no more, no less.

He patted her fondly on the shoulder, and it was all Madeline could do not to flinch. "Well, I suppose I shall set off, then."

"This late? You're welcome to stay the night, Francis. Your room was made up, in case." He'd arrived early that morning in time for the christening, the first time he'd laid eyes on his son.

Henry *was* indeed Francis's child—even he could not deny the likeness in the child's face, in the dusting of reddish-gold hair that crowned his small head.

Not ten months past, Madeline had decided that she was ready for motherhood—that, in fact, she longed for it. She'd written to Francis and told him so, and he'd come to Herefordshire straightaway. Their coupling had been quick, efficient, and businesslike, timed perfectly to coincide with what the midwife claimed was her most fertile time of the month.

Thankfully, the midwife had been correct. Submitting to her husband once had been enough, and she'd been pleased to write to him in London the following month to tell him that a child had, indeed, been conceived.

He'd written back to express his delight at the news of a possible heir, and then he'd mercifully stayed away until after the birth. While today's visit had been perfectly pleasant and cordial, she was relieved when he demurred, shaking his head.

"I'd like to get back to London tonight, if you don't mind. I planned to take the seven o'clock train. Should get me home by midnight, if I'm lucky."

Madeline nodded. "I'm just glad you were able to come today."

"I would not have missed it for the world," Francis said, and for once, Madeline actually believed him. Francis had stopped drinking entirely—he hadn't had a single drop in more than a year now, he claimed—and it showed in his appearance, his demeanor. This new, improved Francis was a good deal kinder than before, and Madeline was glad for it. It made days like this far more tolerable.

He bent and kissed the child lightly on the forehead. "You're sure he'll be...ahem...*safe* here?" His gaze drifted toward the window, where the purple hues of twilight colored the sky beyond the glass. Night was falling fast these days.

"Absolutely. Henry will be never be in any danger, not as long as he lives. I can promise you that." Madeline knew it was true, with every fiber of her being.

Francis nodded, his Adam's apple bobbing in his throat. "Very well, then. You'll let me know if you need anything?"

"Of course. Safe travels, Francis."

"Goodbye, Madeline." With a curt bow, he was gone.

Madeline gazed back down at her child with wonderment and awe. He was beautiful, no matter that he was Francis's. Perfect in every way. Her heart swelled with an all-encompassing love that she'd never even imagined was possible.

"In two years' time, you'll be wanting a sibling for him," came a voice to her right, and she turned to find Simon there, leaning against the wall, smiling at them both. "A lass this time, one who looks just like her mother."

"Three years, perhaps," Madeline answered with a shrug.

"I thought he'd never leave."

"Nor did I. You make him nervous."

"Good. As I should."

Madeline patted the bed beside her. "Come join us, my love. Help me sing him to sleep with one of your Scottish lullabies."

In an instant, he was beside her, an arm around her shoulders, holding her close as he gazed down at her son with adoration in his mossy green eyes.

"You've no idea how badly I wish he were mine, Maddy. I would give anything..." He trailed off, shaking his head. A shock of golden blond hair fell across his forehead, and Madeline reached up to brush it away, combing her fingers through the silky locks.

"He *is* yours, Simon, just as I am yours. After all, yours

was the first face he saw when he entered this world, the first hands to hold him."

Because it had been Simon who'd delivered the babe when he'd decided to come in the dead of night without much fanfare or warning. By the time the midwife had arrived, Madeline had been sitting up in bed with Henry at her breast, suckling heartily. The birth had been quick and nearly painless—Simon had somehow been able to get inside her mind and absorb the pain, to take it from her.

"You *are* his father. You're the one he will call for when he's frightened, the one who will dine with him each evening meal, who will tuck him into bed at night. He will love you as I do." Madeline sighed happily. "Henry Simon McKenzie Briarton," she murmured. "Such a lovely name for a lovely boy. Would you believe, Francis didn't even blink when I told him?"

Simon's eyes glistened as he reached for one of the baby's tiny fists, gently stroking the pale, nearly translucent skin with his thumb. "Thank you, Maddy," he said hoarsely. "Thank you for this beautiful gift."

Who would have thought that from midnight sins would come such beauty, such light and love and happiness?

With a smile, Madeline leaned over and cupped Simon's cool, smooth cheek in her palm, kissing him reverently on the lips.

"Thank you for this beautiful life," she countered. "My dark, dangerous lord."

RITES OF PASSION

CELTIC HEAT VOL. 3

Copyright © 2011, 2020 by Kristina Cook

All rights reserved.

No part of this book may be reproduced in any form or by any electronic or mechanical means, including information storage and retrieval systems, without written permission from the author, except for the use of brief quotations in a book review.

"*Green Man*" poem Copyright © 2011 by Amanda McIntyre, used with the author's permission

Cover Design by James, GoOnWrite.com

❦ Created with Vellum

CHAPTER 1

April 1919

It's the garden they say is haunted, not the house itself. Those words echoed in Emmaline Gage's mind as she approached the walled garden in question, one trembling hand reaching toward the latch on the wooden gate. Pausing, she glanced over at the copse of trees just beyond the garden gate, toward the woods in the distance.

I can do this, she assured herself. After all, Emmaline was a woman of science; she didn't believe in haunts. Such nonsense didn't frighten her, wouldn't send her scurrying away. Not after everything she'd been through, the horrors she'd witnessed over the past several years.

Festering wounds and rotted, burnt flesh. Amputations performed without adequate anesthesia. The cries of the suffering, followed by the silence of death.

Indeed, what were restless spirits, compared to the horrors of war?

Emmaline pushed away the memories, refusing to walk that path in her mind. Instead, she took a deep breath and forced herself to reach for the latch and slowly, cautiously, ease open the gate and take a step forward.

As soon as the gate closed behind her, a breeze stirred. The hem of her skirt flapped against her calves; a lock of hair blew across one cheek. The leaves rustled noisily while Emmaline scanned the garden, looking for the source of the voice she heard carried on the wind.

Come, sit beside me, it seemed to say. She'd felt the pull toward the garden every day since her arrival at Orchard House a fortnight ago. Until now, she'd ignored it.

Feeling suddenly courageous, she took several steps down the uneven cobbled path that wended through the overgrown shrubs and wild plantings, more brown than green. Hastily, she scanned the rectangular space, but saw no one. *Of course not.* It was only her imagination—there was no voice, no intruder. There was nothing but the wind passing through the crumbling stone walls, through the nearby treetops.

It was an eerie sound, to be sure, but not a supernatural one. She let out her breath in a rush, relief coursing through her veins. And then she allowed herself to look around, walking the full perimeter, her heels clicking against the flagstones beneath her feet.

Despite its current state of neglect, something about the garden filled her with a sense of peace. There was something comforting, almost familiar about the space. Still, the garden needed a skilled hand, and she wasn't certain she was up to the task.

Anticipating this, she'd tried to hire a gardener when she'd first arrived at Orchard House, but everyone in the village of Haverham had sworn that there was no point, that in all the years that Mathilde Collins had lived there, no one had been able to make a go of it. The garden was beyond help, they said, and haunted, besides—which was all stuff and nonsense. Emmaline shook her head in frustration, hurrying toward a stone bench in a shady corner. She slipped to the seat with a sigh, running her fingers along the face of the Green Man etched into the rough, uneven stone on the bench's back.

The garden was spacious, with high stone walls traced in vine uninterrupted on all sides save the one with the green wooden gate from which she'd passed through. Though she could still discern the garden's original design, most everything was overgrown and wilted, with several square-shaped fallow beds scattered about. Near the center of the garden stood a stone well, a tin watering pail perched on the rim.

On the far side of the well, what looked like neat rows of rose bushes stood wilting in the sun, not a bloom in sight, despite the season. *Or was there?* Squinting against the glare, she raised one hand to shield her eyes as she attempted to make out a spot of color there at the end of the second row. Rising, she hurried toward it, taking care as she picked her way across the path.

And there it was—one pale pink bloom nestled between the spindly, thorny branches. Her heart swelled with hope at the sight of it, tears stinging her eyes. She retrieved the pair of shears she'd slipped into her pocket and clipped the bloom, bringing it to her nose to inhale its scent. A single tear slipped down her cheek, and she wiped it away as she made her way back to the bench.

It was a sign. Surely it must be. However else could she explain it? A single bloom, no more, and so very familiar.

Her legs trembling, she sank back onto the bench, holding the delicate rose by its stem. She ran one fingertip along the bloom's velvety petals as she allowed the memories to come flooding back.

Oh, Christopher! Why did you leave me all alone? Come August, he would have been gone a year, killed at Amiens.

Emmaline had been on the front herself at the time, assigned to a casualty clearing station at Allonville. They'd been celebrating the news that the Allied forces had broken through the German lines and advanced nearly twenty kilometers when she'd received word of her husband's death from Christopher's field commander.

Their marriage had been brief, yet glorious. Emmaline had never expected to fall in love, to marry. She'd been twenty-three—a spinster—when she'd enrolled in the nursing program at Pennsylvania Hospital. When the war broke out in 1917, she'd volunteered to go to Europe, to join the Army Nurse Corps. After all, what was there to keep her in Pennsylvania?

Nothing. No one. Her parents had died of Influenza, one right after the other, and her brother—a drunken lout, by all accounts—had long since moved to New York where he was no doubt getting himself into all kinds of mischief. And so she'd gone to Europe. She'd been stationed in Liverpool, working in an Army hospital, when she'd first met Christopher Gage, a dashing young captain in Rawlinson's Fourth Army who was recuperating from a broken femur sustained in battle.

Captain Gage had long since been released from the hospital but remained there at the base on administrative duty while his leg continued to heal. He'd come to her ward one day to visit an old school chum who'd lost an arm to a German grenade, and it was love at first sight as far as Emmaline was concerned. He'd asked her to dinner that very same day and began to court her in earnest.

He'd swept her entirely off her feet—figuratively speaking, of course—and they'd married in a quiet ceremony at the base chapel not two months after they'd met, with her wearing her dark blue serge street uniform in lieu of a wedding gown, and Christopher as dashing as ever in his khaki uniform. She'd carried a bouquet of pink roses identical to the one she now held, and was attended by Christopher's sister Maria, who'd traveled up from London for the wedding.

Soon afterward, they'd each managed to secure a week's furlough—seven glorious days—and enjoyed a brief holiday at a nearby inn before Christopher was sent back to the front, fully healed in both spirit and body. She'd gone back to her nursing duties with a renewed zeal. Despite their separation, she'd been deliriously happy. She had hope. A future. And then, with one telegram, she'd lost everything.

Emmaline blinked away the tears that threatened to blur her vision. The past was immutable, entirely unchangeable. There was no point in dwelling on it, in reopening the wound and poking at it with a stick.

Glancing around the garden, at the house looming off in the distance, she reminded herself that this was her future— the future that Christopher had given her. Orchard House, a grand but somewhat crumbling Cotswold estate, Christopher's sister Maria had called it when she'd written to offer it to Emmaline. Apparently, Christopher's great-aunt Mathilde had lived there most of her life and had left it to him—her favorite nephew—upon her death. Which meant it was Emmaline's now, and Maria had insisted that she should have it.

Had she any other alternative, she might have refused to take ownership. But she had no family save her wastrel of a brother, no home, and she could not bear to go back to nursing. Not now. She had some money saved—all of her earnings, tucked safely away—but even living frugally in London, she was sure to run through it far too quickly, and then where would she be? Back on the wards, she guessed, as she had no other skills and no prospects.

No, Orchard House was home now. Only, when Maria

had called it 'crumbling,' she had not been exaggerating. Emmaline had spent her first fortnight there tidying up, and the house still wasn't cleaned to her satisfaction. Perhaps it was a result of all those years living in hospital dormitories, but she could not countenance a spot of dust on any surface, linens that weren't pristine and crisp, or an untidily made bed.

Thank goodness Mrs. Babbitt—Mathilde's long-time housekeeper—had agreed to stay on, if only a few days a week. Beyond that, Emmaline would have to manage on her own. It wasn't that she was incapable of keeping house— Emmaline and her mother had managed well enough during her youth in Pennsylvania. It was just that Orchard House was so very big. At one time, it had been the grandest house in all of Haverham, and would be still, had it been better maintained throughout the years.

Instead, furniture in various states of disrepair had been piled high haphazardly in cobweb-filled rooms, weeds growing up through cracks in the floorboards. In unused wings, exterior walls had begun to crumble. Only the house's main wing remained fully intact and livable. It would be far too costly to restore Orchard House back to its original state. At best, she hoped to simply maintain its current condition.

Luckily, the estate encompassed a great deal of land, most of it parceled out to tenants whose rents would help pay the bulk of Emmaline's expenses. She would keep the books herself; she was clever with sums and enjoyed such work. She would do her own cooking, too. She looked forward to it, really—the busywork. It would keep her mind occupied, help stave off the loneliness that had crept into her heart.

She knew she should be grateful for her current situation. There were so many war widows who were worse off than she was. She had a home, an income. Generous neighbors, she mentally added, remembering the basket of blueberry scones that Mrs. Talbot had brought over that morning. And she would always have her memories, she reminded herself. Nothing, not even the passage of time, could take those beautiful memories away from her. Smiling, she brought the fragrant bloom back to her nose.

If she closed her eyes, she could almost see Christopher's face smiling down at her, his lips curved into a smile. She took a deep breath, remembering his scent—tobacco and soap, purely male—remembering the way the corners of his eyes crinkled when he laughed, his dark eyes filled with merriment.

A shiver worked its way down her spine as she recalled that idyllic week spent tucked away at the inn with her husband. They'd barely left the bed for two full days, and her body had come alive beneath his touch. They'd made love till she ached all over, till she thought she'd die from pure, exquisite pleasure. In one week, she'd learned how to pleasure a man, and how to receive pleasure in return. Of course, she'd thought they'd have a lifetime together.

Instead, she was alone.

She'd had no visitors since her arrival at Orchard House save Mrs. Talbot and her husband. They lived in the vicarage at the bottom of the road—her closest neighbors—and they had been quite welcoming, despite the fact that Emmaline was a Catholic and chose not attend services at the picturesque village church over which Mr. Talbot presided. Besides the Talbots and Mrs. Babbitt, her acquaintance was limited to the various shopkeepers whose establishments she'd patronized for food and sundries, and no one else.

Still, she could not remain a hermit forever. Christopher would want her to get out, to live again. But life would never be the same, now that he'd gone and taken a piece of her heart with him. She'd never feel whole again, like a woman again.

And then, like a whisper on the wind, came the all-too-familiar voice. She'd been hearing it for days now, every time she walked past the garden's walls. Emmaline closed her eyes, knowing full well that her mind was playing tricks on her again, that her self-imposed exile, her loneliness, was making her imagination run wild.

She conjured up Christopher's image in her mind's eye—his rugged face; his muscular body; his cock, hard and ready—and she reached between her legs and touched herself.

Her strokes were gentle at first, almost tentative. But as the vision in her mind grew sharper, clearer, she increased the pressure and tempo. The layers of fabric abraded her tender flesh as she continued to stroke her sex, imagining herself with her legs wrapped around Christopher's waist, riding him hard as he whispered her name against her ear.

Her head tipped back, and she could have sworn she heard his voice, his breath warm against her skin. *Come, Emmaline. Come hard for me.*

With a shudder, she climaxed. It took her nearly a full minute to catch her breath, and she remained there, perched on the edge of the bench, her damp thighs pressed tightly together. Her eyes still closed, she traced the Green Man's face etched into the bench with her fingers. Though she could not explain it, she felt a strange kinship with him. It was as if...as if he'd been waiting for her. Watching her. Enjoying it.

Sighing deeply, she opened her eyes, her gaze drawn immediately back to the rose garden. As soon as her eyes were able to focus, she reached for the edge of the bench to steady herself. Either she was imagining things, or the previously spindly, lifeless bush had suddenly sprung to life, its leaves lush and green, its thorny branches supporting perhaps a half-dozen tightly furled buds.

She blinked hard, willing away the improbable sight, but

there it remained, as plainly visible as it was impossible. Her heart hammered against her breast, her breath coming in short little puffs. Her vision swam, her nails digging painfully into the rough stone seat.

A strangled cry escaped her lips as she rose on trembling legs and made her way toward the gate, wanting to get as far away from the garden as possible.

They were right—the garden was haunted. Either that, or she'd gone stark raving mad.

"*D*on't you look lovely," Mrs. Talbot said, patting Emmaline on the shoulder.

"Thank you," Emmaline responded, smoothing her damp palms down the front of her best dress—a mauve linen drop-waist dress with a wide, sailor collar. Paired with a cream-colored cardigan and knitted cloche hat, it was the most fashionable ensemble she owned, and she was glad that it met with Mrs. Talbot's approval.

Still, she had to force herself to smile, wondering how she'd ever managed to let Mrs. Talbot talk her into this—attending Haverham's annual Beltane festival. Just thinking about the crowds she'd no doubt encounter there on the village green made her stomach churn uncomfortably. She didn't want to leave Orchard House, didn't want to be paraded around and forced into small talk with strangers.

Oh, she appreciated Mrs. Talbot's efforts, truly she did. The woman only wanted to help, to show the village her approval of its newest resident, despite the fact that she was an outsider in every way—an American, a Catholic. She liked them both, found their company pleasant and engaging, even if they *had* been the ones to put the notion in her head that her garden was haunted.

When the roses had seemingly sprung from nowhere, she'd thought perhaps they'd been correct. She'd fled the garden and sworn to never return, to have someone knock down the walls and clear the fields, to remove every last trace of its existence.

And yet the very next day, curiosity had drawn her back again. She hadn't imagined it; the buds remained on the single bush, beginning to unfurl. Only this time she wasn't frightened by them. It was almost as if…as if they were a sign from Christopher.

And so she'd set aside her fears and begun to tend the garden in earnest. She put most of her efforts into the roses, attempting to coax them back to life. And when she wasn't weeding or watering or pruning, she was painting. She'd set up an easel there by the bench, and painted the garden not in its current state, but in full bloom, instead. The garden had become her haven, her secret refuge. She felt safe there between those four walls —protected and secure, and somehow closer to Christopher.

But today she was forced to go out where she felt vulnerable and alone amid a sea of strangers. They would surely want to ask her questions that she wasn't yet comfortable answering—about her wartime experience, about her marriage and Christopher's death.

She took a deep, steadying breath, hoping to calm her racing heart, to tamp down her rising panic. Perhaps she should tell Mrs. Talbot that she'd changed her mind, that she felt unwell. Anything to avoid going.

"Come, now, Emmaline." Mrs. Talbot reached for her arm. "Don't look so terrified. I vow, it cannot be as bad as all that. Just a few hours, and we'll have you safely home again.

The villagers are so eager to meet you, and you can't hide away here forever."

"I know," she murmured, wiping her damp palms on her skirt. "I...I don't know what's come over me."

"There's Mr. Talbot now," the woman said, raising her voice to be heard over the sputtering motorcar that had pulled up beneath the port-cochere. "He hates the festival, you know," she added with a shake of her head. "Calls it pagan foolishness, especially the pantomime. Which I suppose it is, but it's certainly entertaining foolishness."

"Isn't it just some sort of May day celebration?" Emmaline asked, still unsure about the festival's origin—and why they would be celebrating a Celtic one in their little English village, besides.

"Exactly that," Mrs. Talbot answered with a nod. "You see, a few generations back, a viscount of great wealth and influence, Lord Brearleigh, lived here at Orchard House. His wife was Scottish, and she insisted that the village's May day celebration should be a Beltane festival, instead. The young, besotted viscount was happy to humor his wife, and it's been a tradition ever since. Anyway"—she waved one hand in dismissal—"Mr. Talbot only pretends to be scandalized. I've seen him watching the pantomime raptly when he thinks no one is paying him any mind."

Emmaline couldn't help but laugh at that, her fears eased a considerable measure.

Mrs. Talbot rewarded her with a smile, her pale blue eyes full of warmth. "I believe that's the first time I've heard you laugh," she said, then pursed her lips, watching her expectantly. "Dearest Emmaline, the pain will fade eventually. I know it's hard to imagine, but I promise that it will."

"Are you certain?" Emmaline asked, her voice a hoarse whisper.

Mrs. Talbot nodded, her eyes filling with tears. "I'm

certain. Mr. Talbot and I had a son, you see. He was a sickly boy, born with a weak heart. When he passed, well...I thought the pain would eat me up inside. But as time went on, the ache in my heart began to fade, little by little. He's still here"—she tapped the spot above her left breast—"but the hurt is gone."

Emmaline reached for Mrs. Talbot's hand and gave it a squeeze. "I'm so very sorry."

Mrs. Talbot nodded. "Just promise me that you won't shut yourself away from the world. You're far too young for that. Now come, we don't want to keep Mr. Talbot waiting. All that pagan fun, remember?"

Almost an hour later, Emmaline relaxed beside Mrs. Talbot on the village green, watching the young maids twirl brightly colored ribbons around the maypole as the setting sun cast wide orange swaths against the sky. Mrs. Talbot had spread out a blanket on the lawn and unpacked a supper hamper, and Emmaline sat with her legs tucked beneath herself, sipping a glass of cool white wine.

"A pagan ritual, I tell you," Mr. Talbot whispered, leaning across the blanket toward Emmaline. "I don't know why I allow it."

"Oh, pish-posh," Mrs. Talbot replied airily. "Why don't you leave us be, and go throw horseshoes with Mr. Hackley until the fire-lighting ceremony. Though I know you'll hate to miss the pantomime," she added dryly, smiling mischievously at Emmaline.

"Always the same foolish story," he said with a frown before standing and brushing off his trousers. "Perhaps I will go join Mr. Hackley. If you ladies will excuse me." Ever formal, he tipped his hat in their direction before stalking off.

Emmaline reached for a slice of ham and pressed it between two halves of a flaky, golden biscuit. "Thank you so much for bringing supper," she said, deciding between two different types of cheese. She chose a soft, golden one and sliced off a chunk.

"Oh, it was my pleasure," Mrs. Talbot replied, reaching for a plate of tarts. "Here, you must try one of these. Sinfully delicious—it's the sweet cream butter, goes right to the hips. But you could use some fattening up, if you don't mind my saying so."

Not the slightest bit offended, Emmaline took two tarts and placed them on her plate, her mouth watering in anticipation. It was true; she'd grown far too thin. Since arriving at Orchard House she'd had to take in the waists of several of her skirts, and her dresses hung far too loosely on her frame.

She desperately needed to purchase some new clothing, she realized, glancing around at the fashionable ladies and gentleman surrounding her on the lawn. She'd bought most of her wardrobe before the war, and styles had changed so dramatically since—hemlines had risen considerably, and lighter colors and fabrics had come into fashion. Perhaps she could buy some pattern books and try her hand at sewing again. She used to be quite handy with a needle and thread, back in her youth.

At the very least, she could raise some of her skirts' hems, she decided, fingering the edging of mauve silk that reached near enough down to her ankles.

"Ooh, it's time for the pantomime," Mrs. Talbot said with obvious delight, drawing Emmaline from her thoughts as several people in costume took to the makeshift stage before them.

For nearly a half hour, Emmaline watched raptly as villagers recreated the tale of the May Queen, the Winter King, and the Green Man. Love, lust, jealousy, and greed—it all played out on the stage before her, resulting in the May Queen's humiliation and subsequent death, and the Green

Man's imprisonment in the garden cursed by the cruel
Winter King. The drama ended with a poem spoken in
hushed unison...

I am the wind, softly caressing her hair
the breath near her ear
whispering words of passion she yearns
    to hear

I am the hand cradling gently her breast
awakening inside what others cannot,
I not so humbly confess

I am the sigh as she offers me all
and with no reservation,
I answer her call

Reborn in her passion, but faced with
    remorse,
she turns from my arms,
and faces her betrothed

A duel, says he, as I dust off my hands
and comply with his challenge
for her reputation to stand

I am the fire burning bright in my quest
ridding the cold, dark of winter,
winning my May Queen's breast

Yet before Darkness is finished, he utters one
    final warning,
and to his bride now banished

claims her death come the morning

You shall remain imprisoned in this dead
   withered place
as atonement for your sins,
and then to me he did face

No one will admire your seductions,
kept hidden beneath the vines
until thrice over you awaken
stone hearts and cause passion to entwine

WHEN THE LAST word faded away, Emmaline let out her breath in a rush. Was it just a coincidence—the withered garden, the voice whispering on the wind? *Of course it was,* her mind supplied, her reason restored. The story was just that—a legend, told and re-told throughout the years. Still, a shiver raced down her spine. Before, she'd only thought of the Green Man's image as nothing more than a common garden icon—a symbol of sorts—but now, realizing how he fit in with the legend, the fact that his image was scattered about her own garden took on new meaning.

She glanced up at the sky, surprised to see that the sun had dipped below the horizon, the sky now a dusky lavender hue. The temperature had dropped considerably, and she pulled her cardigan more tightly about her shoulders.

Returning her attention to the stage, she watched as Mr. Talbot—acting as the village's spiritual leader—carried up a brightly lit torch. He said a brief prayer, asking the Lord for bountiful crops and robust livestock, before carrying the torch off the stage and lighting a bonfire in the middle of the village green. Everyone stood, and Emmaline followed suit, joining Mrs. Talbot as they gathered around the fire.

Several speeches were made, though Emmaline did not hear the words. Instead she found herself gazing at the fire, watching intently as the logs burned orange and red, sending up spurts of bright, fiery ash into the darkening sky.

When she finally dragged her gaze away from the flames, she noticed a man standing directly across the bonfire from her, watching her intently. She blinked hard, focusing her eyes, trying to decide if she'd already made his acquaintance. She couldn't be sure; after all, she'd met so many people before they'd sat down for supper.

Whoever he was, he was a gentleman. That much was evident by his dress and his manner. He stood proudly yet carelessly, a bowler hat resting on one hip. Tall and slender without being gangly, he towered over the men who stood on either side of him. There was no denying that he was handsome, exceedingly so.

Still, his direct stare made her uncomfortable. She dropped her gaze, pretending to examine her black kidskin pumps as if they were the most fascinating things she'd ever seen. Her stomach did a little flip-flop, and she realized that her hands were trembling. And not because the man was staring at her, she decided, but because she'd thought him handsome. It didn't seem right for her to have such a thought —it was too soon.

Feeling as inconstant as the faithless May Queen, she silently chastised herself. And yet she could not help but abandon the sight of her scuffed shoes in favor of the man who still watched her intently from across the fire.

Her cheeks warmed, a feeling of awareness skittering across her skin. This time, she allowed herself to stare back as the voices around her receded to a faint hum in the background. He was the exact opposite of Christopher, she realized—like the negative of a photograph. Fair, where Christopher had been dark. Thin rather than stocky, blond instead of brunet.

But it was his eyes that she found so unsettling. Even across the distance that separated them, she could see something familiar in them, an expression she recognized far too well. He'd seen horrific things—pain and fear and death—just as she had. She could not say how she knew this, but she did.

Inhaling sharply, she dropped her gaze once more. Who was this man, and why was he watching her? Why was he making her think of things best forgotten?

When she looked up again, he was gone. The two men who had stood on either side of him had closed ranks, filling the space the tall, blond man had occupied only moments before. She turned, searching the crowd for him. But it was no use; he had simply disappeared into the night.

Dear God, I am losing my mind. Panic rose in her breast, and her windpipe felt far too tight, too constricted. She needed to get home, back to Orchard House, before she fell apart entirely. It was the press of the crowd, she assured herself, coupled with the heat of the fire.

"...went to get the car," a voice beside her was saying, and she realized with a start that Mrs. Talbot was speaking to her.

"I'm sorry," she said, turning toward the woman. "You were saying?"

Mrs. Talbot reached for her shoulder, as if to steady her. "I asked if you were ready to go, that's all. You look pale—are you feeling unwell?"

Emmaline swallowed hard before speaking. "I think the heat of the fire has made me a bit lightheaded, that's all."

"Come, then. We'll meet Mr. Talbot by the road."

Emmaline nodded, falling into step beside her. "Did...did

you see that tall, blond gentleman? The one standing directly across from us during the bonfire?"

"The one in the gray sack suit, carrying a bowler?"

Emmaline's gaze snapped up to meet Mrs. Talbot's. "Yes. That's the one. Who was he?"

Mrs. Talbot shook her head. "I haven't any idea. I've never seen him before; he must be a visitor, a tourist, perhaps. Why do you ask?"

"He just...looked familiar, that's all," she said, the lie slipping easily from her tongue.

"Yes, he was looking at you rather queerly, wasn't he? Perhaps you've met before."

"Perhaps," Emmaline agreed. It was entirely possible, after all. Throughout the war, she'd nursed countless men, their faces nothing but a blur to her. They'd been dirty, most of them. Dirty and bloody and bandaged, and generally unrecognizable after months spent in trenches. But perhaps he remembered *her*.

It was an unsettling thought.

"There's Mr. Talbot," Mrs. Talbot said, hurrying toward the enormous black motorcar, its brass fittings glinting in the moonlight. "Come, let's get you home."

Emmaline just nodded as she climbed inside and settled against the tufted leather seat behind Mrs. Talbot. It was early still and the moon was bright; perhaps she'd take a stroll once she was home, check on the roses, and see that she'd latched the gate securely before she turned in.

What she would *not* do, she assured herself, was continue to think about the handsome stranger.

CHAPTER 3

There was an automobile coming up the drive. Emmaline set the teakettle back on the stove and wiped her hands on her apron before hurrying to the front door. She wasn't expecting Mrs. Talbot—she'd said she was going into Chipping Norton to visit a friend today—and Mr. Talbot would have no reason to come without her.

Perhaps it was someone she'd met the at the Beltane festival? Unlikely, she decided, as teatime was not a proper hour for paying calls. She opened the door in time to see a red roadster pull up beneath the port-cochere. The driver cut the engine and stepped out, removing his hat and wiping his brow with the back of one hand.

"May I help you?" Emmaline called out, just before the shock of recognition washed over.

The tall, blond man from the bonfire. Standing right there, in her drive.

He spun toward her. "It's you," he said, his eyes widening with unmasked surprise.

Emmaline shook her head, her mouth suddenly dry. "I'm sorry. Have we met?"

For a moment, he stood there entirely immobile, simply staring at her. "I don't believe so," he said at last, hurrying up the stairs and extending a hand in her direction. "I'm Jack Wainscott."

"Emmaline Gage," she answered, taking his outstretched hand in her own. His felt warm—*too* warm.

He released her hand, reaching up to rub one temple. "You'll have to excuse me," he said. "Perhaps it's the heat, but I'm suddenly feeling a bit odd. Anyway, I hope you'll excuse my intrusion, but Mathilde Collins, the previous owner of Orchard House, was my father's cousin. Or rather, was married to my father's cousin."

"Indeed?" Emmaline was taken aback. She supposed this man must be some sort of relation to her late husband, though Christopher had never mentioned any Wainscotts to her. "But what does this have to do with me?"

"Yes," he continued on, looking suddenly pale, "I'm getting to that. Orchard House should have come to my father upon old Mr. Collins's death. An entailment, you see. The Collinses had no sons, and my father was the closest living male relative. Make no mistake, my father isn't a generous man by any means, but my mother convinced him to let Mrs. Collins live out her days here. But now that she's gone, my father sent me here to check on the property —to claim it, I suppose. It was only when I arrived in Haverham that I learned that someone had taken up residence here."

Emmaline took a step backward, pressing herself against the front door. "But Mathilde Collins left the property to my husband. My late husband," she corrected, her voice barely above a whisper. Was she going to lose Orchard House, so soon after acquiring it? Now that she'd settled in, now that it felt like home?

He nodded, his hazel eyes meeting hers. They looked

feverish, she decided. "I'm afraid the property wasn't legally hers to give," he said, swaying slightly on his feet.

"Would you like to come inside and sit down?" she asked. "I'm a nurse, you see, or *was* a nurse. Army Corps," she added, feeling foolish. She shook her head, hoping to clear it, allowing her nursing instincts—long since abandoned—to return. "Your skin is pale, your face flushed, and I don't like the look in your eyes." She reached for his forehead, wincing when the back of her hand made contact with his skin. "Good heavens, sir, you're burning up!"

Without waiting for his reply, she opened the door and bustled him inside the front parlor, leading him toward the sofa. "What did you say your name was?" she asked.

"Jack," he mumbled. "Major Jack Wainscott, Fifth Army, third division."

Emmaline reached for his arm just as he slumped to the sofa, his eyes rolling up in his head. "Oh, no you don't!" she cried, tapping his cheek several times, trying to rouse him.

His eyes snapped open, entirely unfocused. "Major Jack Wainscott," he repeated, his voice slurring. "Fifth Army, third—"

"Yes, yes, I know, soldier." She reached beneath his arms, tugging him to his feet. "Let's get you to bed, while we still can."

Thankfully, there was a bedroom on the ground floor, near the kitchen. It had likely been a servant's room at some point, but it would do just fine. It had a bed, at least, and its proximity to the kitchen would prove useful. She'd cleaned it and made the bed with fresh linens just last week.

A quarter hour later, she had him settled in bed, his jacket and necktie removed, along with his shoes. He was unconscious, feverish and flushed, his entire body trembling. She unbuttoned his shirt, looking for signs of a rash, or of any sort of wound that might be infected. She saw nothing that would explain his current state.

Reaching for his wrist, she checked his pulse. It was far too rapid and thready. Influenza, perhaps? If so, it seemed a particularly virulent strain, considering how quickly he had deteriorated. After setting a cool cloth on the man's forehead, she hurried back to the front hall to ring up Mrs. Talbot and ask her to send the doctor at once.

JACK STRUGGLED to open his eyes, feeling as if weights were pressing against them. He managed to open them a fraction, and he tried to turn his head. In the dim lighting, he could barely make out the shape of a woman with dark hair standing near the door. Beside her stood a man with gray whiskers and a low, gravelly voice. Their heads were bent together, the two deep in conversation.

No longer able to bear the weight of his eyelids, he allowed them to close, but tried to remain focused on the voices, trying to make out what they were saying. He only caught snippets, a few phrases here and there.

"Influenza...nothing we can do but wait it out... dangerous strain, one we've not seen in these parts...highly contagious...suggest we have him moved."

"I've already been exposed...experienced nurse...he must stay here."

"Quarantine...no visitors at all...at least a fortnight."

"Thank you...yes, on the chest of drawers...will call you if there's any change. Tell Mrs. Talbot..."

Jack swallowed hard, his throat dry and scratchy. He ached all over, and he hadn't any idea how he got into this unfamiliar bed. Where was he? And who were these people?

He was tired, so very tired. He just wanted to sleep. If only someone would bring him a glass of water...

HER PATIENT WAS NOT DOING WELL. Emmaline sat by helplessly, watching him toss and turn, his face a deathly pallor. Every once in a while, his glassy eyes would open, staring unseeing at the ceiling, and she would wipe his forehead with a cool cloth while she whispered soothing words to him.

It didn't matter what she said—he couldn't hear her. He was entirely delirious, his fever raging out of control. More than once his breathing had grown so labored that she'd feared she was losing him.

When that happened, she stripped him down to his drawers and bathed him with rubbing alcohol, cooling his head with ice packs while she said a little prayer.

By the fourth day, he seemed to stabilize a bit, though he remained in a deep sleep. She sat by his side now, working on a needlepoint sampler while he slept on, his limbs occasionally jerking as if he were dreaming.

"Water," he croaked, startling her from her work. She tossed down the sampler and hurried to fill a glass, pressing it to his lips. He tried to drink, but most of the water dribbled down his chin, soaking his thin cotton undershirt.

For the briefest of moments, his eyes fluttered open, fully focused this time. "Emmaline?" he murmured.

"Yes, I'm here," she answered, surprised that he remembered her name. He'd only heard it once, just before he collapsed. She bent over him, examining his pupils. They were almost fully dilated, the hazel ring barely visible now despite the lamp beside his bed.

She reached for his hand and clutched it tightly in her

own, willing him to fight the fever. If only there was something she could do! She hated to watch this strong, handsome
man waste away like this. It didn't seem fair. He'd beaten
death once; he didn't deserve to go like this. No one did.

"Fight, Mr. Wainscott," she urged as his eyes fluttered
shut again. "You must fight this! I can't do it for you. You
mustn't give in. I'm sure there's someone, somewhere, who
needs you. Who loves you. Fight for her, whoever she is."

His legs twitched, and Emmaline dropped her chin to her
chest in despair. His breathing was shallow now, rasping and
dangerously fast. She laid a hand on his burning cheek,
caressing it, willing him once more to fight.

Almost immediately, his breathing improved. "That's it,
Mr. Wainscott," she murmured. He seemed to enjoy her
touch—it appeared to soothe him, somehow. She moved
closer, perching on the side of his bed.

"You just need to know that someone is here, that's all.
I'm not going anywhere," she promised. Smiling down at his
prone form, she ran her fingers through his damp hair,
marveling at its softness as she combed it back from his
forehead.

"See? Just sleep," she whispered as his breathing quieted,
becoming more regular now. "Tomorrow it will be better."

She only hoped she was right.

SHE WAS THERE BESIDE HIM, his angel of mercy. He could hear
her even breathing, somewhere near his left elbow. He hadn't
any idea who she was, but she'd been there beside him all
night. He'd woken several times from a dreamless sleep, and
each and every time she'd wiped his brow with a cool, damp
cloth, and then held a glass of water to his lips, murmuring
encouragement as he drank. He'd wanted to ask her name,

but he hadn't been able to muster the strength to do so. Instead, he'd simply fallen back against the pillows each time, listening as she bustled about the room. Eventually, she'd return to her spot beside the bed—a cot, perhaps? He wasn't sure, but it seemed as if she never left his side.

Just how long had she been tending him? He had no idea; he'd entirely lost his sense of time. He tried to sit, doing his best to remain silent so that he did not wake her. Eventually he managed to pull himself up to a seated position, where he could finally take stock of his surroundings.

It was nearly morning, he realized, the room bathed in the dim, hazy light of dawn. The space was small and sparsely furnished, with only the narrow iron bed he currently occupied, a single chest of drawers, a nightstand, and a small cot pushed against the wall. There wasn't room for much else.

On the cot, the woman lay sleeping on her side facing him, a quilt pulled up to her chin. She looked peaceful, one hand tucked beneath her chin, her rosy lips parted slightly. He watched as her chest rose and fell in perfect rhythm. Her dark hair was fanned out on the pillow, a single stray lock falling across one cheek. His fingers itched to brush back that errant lock, but of course he could not.

Who was she? He vaguely remembered driving over to Orchard House, intent on speaking to the woman who had taken possession of the estate, but beyond that he had no firm memories. Right now, the only thing he could recall was her gentle touch, her soothing voice as she tended him.

Growing tired, he collapsed back against the pillow. He'd shut his eyes for a few moments, perhaps allow himself to doze as he waited for her to awaken.

And then he'd find out who she was and thank her.

～

"You're awake," Emmaline said, watching with surprise as Mr. Wainscott's eyes fluttered open. Wiping her hands on her apron, she hurried over to his side and reached up to feel his forehead. It was cool and slightly clammy, and she let out a sigh of relief. "And your fever has broken. How do you feel?" She reached for his wrist, lifting it off the bed and placing her fingers across his pulse. It was strong and steady, a marked improvement.

"Thirsty," he croaked. "Hungry, too."

Emmaline nodded, smiling down at the man. "That's a good sign. You have *no* idea what a fright you gave me."

"How long have I been here?" he asked, his voice hoarse.

"It's been five days since you took ill. You were lucky you were here when you collapsed. If you'd been out somewhere, alone…" She shook her head. "Anyway, drink this." She held a glass of water to his lips.

"I've got it," he said, taking the glass in one shaky hand.

Her brow knitted. "Are you sure? I vow, you're still as weak as a kitten."

He looked determined—male pride, she supposed. With a nod, Emmaline released the glass and watched as he brought it to his mouth and drank deeply.

"Better?" she asked as she took the empty tumbler and set it down beside the pitcher on the nightstand.

"Much," he said with a nod, then reached for her wrist, startling her. "Thank you."

"It's only water." She glanced down at his fingers, still wrapped around her wrist. They were long and elegant, like an artist's.

"Not for the water," he said, shaking his head. He finally released her wrist. "Though, yes, I suppose I should thank you for that, too. But I meant for everything. I can only imagine the inconvenience I've caused you, the trouble you've gone to. I do hope you've had some help."

She shook her head. "The doctor wanted you quarantined. Since I was already exposed, I did not see the need to have you moved."

"You mean to say that you've been here alone with me, all this time? Five days?" he asked, his voice rising.

"Five days is not so very long, Mr. Wainscott. Besides, I'm a nurse, remember? Or at least I was, before I came here. I'm perfectly equipped to handle situations like this one. I promise you were never in any danger—"

"You misunderstand," he interrupted. "I'm certain I had the best care possible, thanks to you, Miss...." He trailed off. "You'll have to pardon me, but I cannot recall your name."

"Mrs. Gage," she supplied. "Emmaline." She had no idea what had prompted her to provide her given name. She'd certainly never allowed such familiarity with any of her previous patients.

"Emmaline," he repeated. "Of course. And you must call me Jack.

"Very well, Jack." She reached down to straighten the bedcovers—a habit, she supposed.

He looked toward the window. "What time is it?"

Emmaline turned toward the window. "Nearly noon. It looks like rain, doesn't it? Anyway, if you'll excuse me, I'll go prepare you some broth. If that goes well, perhaps you can have some toast later."

"I suppose beggars can't be choosers," he said with a sigh.

A quarter hour later, Emmaline returned with a steaming bowl of broth and set it down beside the bed. "I suppose you're going to insist on doing this yourself, too?"

"You know me too well," he joked.

She set a tray across his lap. "I know your type," she corrected. "After all, bravado was a common war-time trait."

He straightened his spine, readjusting the tray. "Did you serve on the front?"

Emmaline nodded, placing the bowl and spoon on the tray before him. "First at a clearing station at Passchendaele, then Allonville."

His eyes seemed to darken. "When were you at Allonville?"

She swallowed hard before replying. "The last year of the war. Why?"

"I came through that clearing station," he said, his voice suddenly dull. "In 1918. Just after the attack on the twenty-first of March."

"You were at Saint Quentin? In March of 1918? Good God, you were Fifth Army, weren't you?"

His eyes met hers, his gaze unflinching. "Fifth Army, Third Division."

She nodded, sinking to the cot beside his bed. "You said as much the night you arrived here."

How on earth had he survived it? She'd heard that the Fifth Army had been all but decimated. They'd been at the very front and had taken the brunt of the German attack. Trench mortars, mustard gas, chlorine gas, smoke canisters— the casualties had been horrific. There had been very little for them to do at the clearing station afterward—most of the wounded had perished right there in the trenches before Regimental medical officers had even been able to get to them.

She watched as he spooned the broth into his mouth, his hand trembling as he did so. One bite. Two. Tortuously slow. And then he let the spoon clatter back to the tray. Taking a deep breath, he turned toward her. "My entire unit was destroyed that day," he said, his voice entirely flat. "Fathers, brothers, sons—gone, nearly all of them. I've never quite understood why I managed to survive. Me, with no wife, no children. No one back at home who cared whether I lived or died, save my mother and sister."

Emmaline's throat felt tight, her windpipe constricted. She swallowed hard, willing the tears to remain at bay. "I'm sorry" was all she managed in reply.

"So am I," Jack said, sounding utterly defeated.

"I should leave you," Emmaline said, rising from the cot. "Let you finish your broth in peace."

"Please stay." Jack's voice broke ever so slightly. "I...find your company soothing," he added.

Emmaline nodded, rising from the cot and reaching for the spoon on his tray. "But only if you'll let me help you."

CHAPTER 4

*E*mmaline peered at Jack over the top edge of the book she held in her hands. He looked tired, though he'd never admit it, stubborn man. "Shall I stop there for the night?"

"No, keep going," he answered, opening his eyes. "I'm finding this all...quite illuminating."

She was reading aloud from Forster's *A Room With a View*. She'd found it in the library, and Jack had asked her to read it to him. It was clear that the novel wasn't to his taste, and yet he was indulging her, pretending to enjoy the romance between Lucy Honeychurch and George Emerson.

"In fact," he continued, "can you re-read that last bit? You know, the part where she was gazing at him longingly?"

"Oh, do shut up!" she cried, smacking his arm with the book.

"Well, you must admit it's a bit overwrought," he said with a shrug.

She shook her head. "I won't admit to any such thing. It's beautiful and romantic, the writing so very vivid. Why, I can almost see the streets of Florence, just as Mr. Forster has described them."

"I suppose." He sounded unconvinced. "What does Lucy possibly see in George, anyway? He's a rather sullen chap, wouldn't you say?"

"Not at all. His manners are just not as refined, that's all. Anyway, it's all about escaping society's constraints, and George represents that escape, along with an escape from sexual repression. Lucy is a truly brave heroine."

He shook his head. "You've gotten all that from the text? Why, it's just a love story. And a rather dull one, if I might say so."

"Oh, never mind. Perhaps I should find a more titillating passage—would that make you happy?" she teased.

"I should have my sister send over some of her earlier works, and have you read those aloud," he said with a chuckle.

"Is that so?" She'd learned that his sister Aisling was a novelist, married to a botanist and living in Cambridge. Jack spoke fondly of her and her husband, even though their marriage had caused a terrible scandal back home, as the groom's father was unknown, and his mother a washerwoman. Jack loved to talk about Aisling—it was clear that they shared a very close bond.

"Did I ever mention that her first publication credits were short stories in *The Boudoir*? Published under a pen name, of course."

Emmaline just shrugged—she'd never heard of *The Boudoir*, though it *did* sound rather racy.

"Yes, indeed," he continued on. "My sister got her start writing naughty stories. *Very* naughty."

"You're teasing me," she said with a sigh, marking the page in the book with a square of needlepoint. "It isn't nice, you know—teasing one's nurse."

Jack's eyes danced with mischief. "Actually, I'm not teasing at all. They're scandalous stories, I tell you. Trust me, I've read every last one of them. I'm the one who took them to London and sold them to *The Boudoir*."

Emmaline raised one brow. "I presume I'm to find this shocking?"

He shook his head, a shock of blond hair falling carelessly across his forehead. "No? Oh, right. I forgot, you're an American. It's much harder to shock an American, isn't it?"

She resisted the urge to stand and brush back the lock of hair from his forehead. "What, precisely, are you trying to say about Americans, Mr. Wainscott?" she asked instead, allowing herself to enjoy the banter.

"I've no idea, really." He shrugged. "It's all balderdash. But it made you smile, and you've a beautiful smile. Your entire face lights up. And there you have it, my ulterior motive. I've *always* got a motive. Just ask my sister."

Her heart fluttered at the compliment. "I imagine you do," she murmured, her cheeks growing warm. "Always have a motive, that is."

"Speaking of which," he continued on, "do you think we could take a turn outside? In the garden, perhaps? It's far too stuffy in here tonight."

Emmaline shook her head in frustration. "No. No turns outside, no leaving this bed. I let you overtax yourself this afternoon, and you need your rest."

He'd insisted on ambling about the house before tea, and he'd nearly collapsed from exhaustion. She'd let him out of bed against her better judgment, and he'd proven that he wasn't quite ready. The Influenza had taken a far greater toll on his body than he realized. She'd never met such a stubborn man.

"I know what we'll do," she said, suddenly having an idea. "We'll give you a shave. I don't know why I didn't think of it sooner. I found some shaving supplies in one of the wash-rooms when I first arrived. Surely there must be a usable blade among them."

He reached up to rub one heavily whiskered cheek. "I suppose you're right. I would hate to forfeit my claim on being a dandy. I take great pride in it, after all. It's not much, but it's all I've got."

"You're incorrigible," she said with a shake of her head. "I'll be right back. You're *not* to get out of that bed while I'm gone, do you hear me?"

"I wouldn't dream of it," he replied. "You're quite bossy, you know."

Emmaline folded her arms across her chest. "You *do* realize I'm going to be holding a blade to your throat in a few moments, don't you?"

"I like you," he quipped. "Very much, to tell you the truth. Surely you wouldn't harm a man who holds you in such high esteem? Even if I am lying here rather helplessly."

Her pulse leapt. Dear Lord, the man had no idea how his careless words affected her. "You're far too charming for your own good," she said, trying to sound disapproving.

"Perhaps I used to be, before the war. Now I'm just a bore. Like Cecil Vyse," he added, tipping his head toward the book. "The poor bloke."

She rolled her eyes. "Have you been listening to yourself? I vow, you could charm the skin off a snake."

For the briefest of moments, he looked thoughtful, seri-ous, even. "It's been…years since I've laughed the way I have today," he said, somber now.

"I'm glad," she said. "You've made me laugh, too. It's been…" She trailed off, realizing that she'd almost said *fun*— which was ridiculous, really. She was only nursing the man back to health, not enjoying a house party. "I'm enjoying your company," she said instead. "Now if you'll excuse me for one moment, I'll go gather the shaving supplies." She hurried out before the telltale rise of color in her cheeks gave her away.

Not ten minutes later she was back, carrying a bowl, shaving soap, a brush, and a blade. "Here we are," she said, setting it all down on the nightstand.

He'd unbuttoned several buttons on his shirt while she'd been gone, exposing a fair amount of his chest. The skin was smooth, slightly tanned, the muscles sharply defined. Despite his illness, he looked healthy. Virile, even.

She dragged her attention away from his chest and concentrated on the soap instead, mixing it to a thick, rich lather. "Shall I tuck a towel around your neck?" she offered.

He shook his head. "Would you mind if I took off my shirt instead? That way we won't risk soiling this one."

The doctor had retrieved Jack's traveling case from the hotel—it sat on a stand in the room's far corner. Of course, Jack had only meant to stay in Haverham for a night or two, so he'd brought very little. Emmaline had been laundering his clothes with her own—at present, one freshly pressed shirt hung in the kitchen.

"Very well," she relented. "Do you need help?"

He undid the few remaining buttons and began to shrug out of it. "I think I can manage," he said with a wince. "Damn, I hate being an invalid."

Emmaline waited as he finished the task, his face an inscrutable mask. Clearly, he hated displaying any sign of weakness—as if she would hold it against him. "There's nothing to be ashamed of," she said softly. "You were gravely ill. You'll have to be patient, that's all."

"I only wish...well, that we'd met under different circumstances," he said, barely able to meet her gaze. "Do you have any idea how emasculating this is? Being tended to like a child?"

She took a step toward him, dipping the brush into the lather as she did so. "I'm a nurse, Jack. It's what I do."

"And that's how you see me, isn't it? As a patient, and nothing more?"

She met his gaze. "How else should I see you?" she asked, her voice barely above a whisper. *Like a man*, she silently answered. A ridiculously handsome, funny, and altogether irresistible man. A man who had begun to haunt her dreams, to fill her with a sense of longing—of desire—that she hadn't felt since Christopher. She shook her head, as if to clear it. This was madness. It was too soon.

"Never mind," Jack said with a sigh, then lifted his chin. "Go on. Don't worry, I promise to sit very still and behave myself."

"Very well." Emmaline moved closer, leaning over him as she lathered him up. Once she was done, she set aside the brush and reached for the blade. She made one swipe across his left cheek, then another.

"This angle is awkward," she said, shaking her head. "Would you mind if I sat on the edge of bed beside you?"

"Of course not," he answered with a shrug, moving over to make room for her.

She felt his entire body tense as she leaned across him. She tried to ignore the heat that had coiled in her belly, instead focusing on the blade as she dragged it across his skin. *Be professional*, she reminded herself. *He's your patient, nothing more.*

JACK COULD BARELY STAND IT. Damn it, but her breast brushed across his chest with every stroke of the blade. He could have sworn that he felt the hardened peak of one nipple through the fabric of her blouse, pressing up against him. Thank God he was impotent, because otherwise he'd surely be suffering from an embarrassing cockstand that would no doubt send her scurrying from the room.

Because she didn't think of him as a man, but a patient—a weak, helpless patient who could barely wipe his own ass at present, for fuck's sake. He choked back the bitter gall of self-loathing.

The night of the Beltane festival, he'd spied her across the bonfire and had been immediately intrigued. Smitten, even. He wasn't foolish enough to believe in love at first sight, but it had felt like a lighting bolt from the sky, the moment he'd laid eyes on her. She was so very beautiful, fragile-looking and ethereal. He'd been struck with a burning, almost primal desire to protect her, to take care of her.

Instead, he was lying in bed like a weakling, allowing *her* to take care of *him*. When he'd first seen her, he'd only thought how nice it might be to fuck her. In the three days since he'd awakened, he'd come to know her, to admire her strength and humor and kindness. Now, he wanted to fuck her *and* spend the rest of his days by her side, her devoted slave. Pure and utter madness.

"Tip your chin up," she said, moving the blade to his neck. "And do be still. I'm dangerously close to your carotid."

Several moments passed in silence save the sound of the blade scraping against his skin.

"There you are," she said at last, sitting back and wiping his face with a towel. "Now you look more like a baronet's son."

She had shaving soap on her cheek. He wanted to wipe it away but knew that touching her would place him in dangerous territory. "You've got soap—right there," he said, pointing to her face.

"Where?" she asked, reaching up to her chin.

"There." He indicated the general direction with the wave of one hand.

She swiped at her cheek and missed it entirely.

Taking a deep breath, he reached for her. She leaned toward him, and he could smell her now-familiar scent— rosewater and lemon, entirely clean and fresh and sweet. He brushed away the soap, allowing his fingers to linger, to move down toward her mouth, toward her chin. Before he knew what he was doing, he found himself cupping her face, moving his mouth toward hers.

"Emmaline," he groaned just as his mouth came down on hers, hard and hungry.

In a flash, her arms were around his neck, drawing him closer as she rose up on her knees. He heard her whisper his name against his lips, felt her tongue trace his bottom lip.

He reached around her, cupping her ass as he dragged her closer, till she was nearly sitting on his lap. Devil take it, but his cock had stiffened, pressing against his trousers. *What the hell?*

The shock of it made him gasp, and Emmaline pulled away. Her gaze met his, her dark eyes wild.

"Did I hurt you?" she asked.

He just shook his head, unable to utter a single syllable in reply.

"Jack?" she whispered, and it sounded almost like a plea. He wasted no time answering it, dragging her mouth back to his. Her lips were soft and pliant, her breath as sweet as honey. His tongue skated across her teeth, begging for entry.

In the front hall, the telephone rang—once, twice.

"Please don't stop," Emmaline said breathlessly. She was entirely pressed against him now, her mouth opened against his, her tongue touching his, teasing and then retreating, driving him wild. She was like one of his wildest erotic fantasies come true.

God help him, it had been so long…if she kept this up, he was going to come right now. Her bottom was pressing against his hardened cock, providing him proof that he was no longer damaged—that he was a man again.

And she was a woman—a willing woman, in his bed. He'd never wanted anyone like this, with a mind numbing, burning desire that overrode all sensibility and good intentions.

He plucked her blouse from the band of her skirt, pushing up the fabric, trying to free her breasts from whatever undergarment she wore beneath. Sensing his struggle, she pulled away, drawing the blouse over her head in one fluid motion. Seconds later, she'd rid herself of the undergarment, and was entirely bare to the waist, straddling his hips.

Lowering his head, he ran his tongue across one rose-colored nipple. Her head tipped back, a low moan escaping her lips. God, how he needed this—needed her. Taking the now-pebbled peak in his mouth, he suckled gently while his hands reached beneath her skirt, searching for her knickers.

Just as he found them and hooked his fingers inside the waistband, Emmaline moved off him, reaching for his trousers' fastenings. "Are you sure?" he asked her, reaching for her wrists. "Emmaline?" he prodded. "Christ, I want you so badly, but only if you're entirely sure. I haven't anything… no protection with me." Why would he have brought condoms with him to Haverham? He certainly hadn't had any use for them lately. He hadn't been able to get it up since the war—this was a completely unexpected development.

"I'm sure, Jack. Entirely sure," she added, looking him square in the eye. Her pupils were dilated wide, her lids heavy with desire. He nodded, releasing her wrists and pushing down his trousers, freeing his eager cock. Holy hell, but he hoped his erection lasted, hoped he could perform.

Reaching under her skirt, Emmaline slid her knickers

down, removing them before she straddled him again, fitting herself over his tip. Unable to bear it a moment longer, he raised his hips, sheathing himself inside her. She cried out, and he stilled at once, terrified that he'd hurt her.

Bloody hell, what had he done?

But then she began to move, rocking against him, her breath coming faster and faster as she rode him. He wanted to meet her thrusts, but weak that he was, he found he couldn't. He couldn't do anything but lie there, watching her, feeling the pleasure well to a crescendo inside him. Any moment now, any moment and he—

"Jack!" she cried out. "Oh, God, now!"

He felt her come, felt her tighten around him, and it pushed him right over the edge. He cried out her name between clenched teeth, his entire body taut and rigid beneath her as his seed pumped into her. The orgasm seemed endless, their bodies in perfect unison. Finally, she collapsed against his chest.

It took him longer than her to catch his breath. He was still panting when she raised her head and looked at him, her brow knitted with concern. "Oh, Jack, what have I done? I'm such a fool—you're not even well."

"Trust me, darling, I haven't felt this well in ages," he quipped, willing his breathing to slow to normal.

He saw tears gather in the corner of her eyes as she rolled off him. "If I've hurt you, if I've harmed you in any way—"

"Stop," he said, unable to bear it. He reached for her shoulder and drew her back to his chest. "Stay with me tonight. Please?"

Relief washed over him when she nodded. "Let me turn out the lamp, and I'll move to the cot," she said, moving away from him.

"Oh, no, you don't." He held her tight, bending down to

kiss the top of her head. "Though you might consider losing this," he added, tugging on her skirt.

"It goes against all my nursing instincts," she murmured, her breath warm against his neck while she wriggled out of her skirt.

"That was by far the best nursing care I've ever received. Hell, I don't know what I did to deserve it, but you won't hear me complaining."

She sat up and leaned toward the nightstand to turn out the lamp. "Go to sleep, Jack. Nurse's orders."

Lying there in the dark, a naked Emmaline pressed tightly against him now, Jack just smiled. As ill and weak as he was, this might very well have been the best day of his life.

CHAPTER 5

*E*mmaline awakened with a start, confused by the weight across her chest. It was an arm, she realized, blinking at the sight. A man's arm, dusted with fine, dark-blond hair. Confused, she sat up abruptly before she remembered where she was and what she'd done.

Good God, she was in Jack's bed! Her patient, a man she barely knew, a man so weak that he hadn't been able to take more than a dozen steps yesterday. She'd chastised him for pushing himself too hard, and then she'd gone and slept with him? Whatever had she been thinking? Bloody hell, she might very well have killed him.

Panic rising, she looked over at him, watching for the rise and fall of his chest, for some sign of life—anything. She almost wept with relief when he turned on his side, reaching for her.

"Emmaline?" he mumbled sleepily.

She swallowed hard before replying. "I'm here, Jack."

"Thank the devil," he said, opening one eye. "I thought I might have dreamed it."

"Apparently not," she said, reaching for the blanket to cover herself.

Both eyes open now, he dragged himself up to a seated position beside her. "Please don't tell me you regret it, Emmaline. Hell, even if you *do* regret it, do me a favor and lie to me, because that was perhaps the most wonderful night of my entire, pitiful existence. You would not take that from me now, would you?"

What was the point in denying it? "Of course I don't regret it."

His mouth curved into a smile. "Good. Anything else would surely be an act of cruelty. Have you any idea how lovely you are when you first wake up?"

She shook her head. "I'm sure I'm a fright." She reached up to her lips—they felt tender and swollen. Between her legs felt tender, too. It had been so very long since someone had made love to her. Her body was simply not used to it.

And, she realized, it was the first time someone had made love to her without protection. Wartime had not been a time to take chances—not when both she and Christopher had been on their way to the front. They had always used a condom. But this time...this time there had been nothing between her and Jack, no barriers. Just flesh against flesh, and it had been exquisite.

She pushed aside the feeling of disloyalty that was nagging at her heart. Christopher was gone—he was not coming back to her. And Jack, well...Jack was *here*. Now.

"You look so far away," Jack said, brushing the back of one hand across her cheek. His touch was so very soft, so gentle.

"I should get you some breakfast," she said, glancing at the window. The sun was high in sky; it must be close to noon. "Some toast, perhaps, and some tea."

"Not yet," he said, dipping his head toward her neck. His

lips were cool against her skin, drawing gooseflesh in their wake.

"Perhaps it can wait," she murmured.

In the distance, a door slammed. "Yoo-hoo! Emmaline, dear!"

Dear lord, it was Mrs. Talbot! Emmaline's heart began to race as she leapt from bed, frantically searching for her skirt and blouse.

"Emmaline?" Mrs. Talbot shouted once more. "Are you around, dear? I don't want to come any farther than the front hall. The doctor made me swear I'd wait another week, but I just couldn't bear it."

"I'll be right there," she called out, shooting Jack a panicked look. "Just give me a moment." He retrieved her knickers and skirt from the bedclothes and tossed them to her.

Whatever was she going to do? Surely Mrs. Talbot would be suspicious when she saw the rumpled state of her clothing, the tangled mess of her hair. Pulling on her blouse, she hurried to look in the mirror above the chest of drawers. She groaned aloud when she saw the deep purple mark that Jack's mouth had left on her throat. However was she going to hide that?

Moving as quickly as she could, she stepped into her skirt and fastened it, deciding not to worry with her knickers. Instead, she kicked them under the bed.

"Emmaline?" Mrs. Talbot called out again. "Have I come at a bad time? I tried to ring you last night and got no answer."

"I'm...I'm just taking Mr. Wainscott's temperature right now," she lied. It would buy her a minute or two.

"Very well, dear. I'll wait."

Emmaline attempted to tidy her hair, but without a brush, it was no use. It fell past her shoulders in tumbling waves, and for once she wished she'd cut her hair into a more fashionable bob. She tried to arrange it so that it covered the mark on her throat, then smoothed down her clothes as best she could.

She glanced back at Jack, who sat watching her with a boyish smile on his face, clearly enjoying this. "At least put your shirt on," she whispered. "Just in case!"

And then she hurried out, forcing her features into a placid, professional mask. "I'm so sorry to keep you waiting, Mrs. Talbot."

"Good heavens, look at you!" the woman cried out as soon as Emmaline stepped into the front hall. "You're a mess —you look as if you haven't slept in days. I knew this was too much to ask of you. I told Dr. Hayward so, but the man just wouldn't listen."

Emmaline attempted a smile. "Oh, it's nothing, really. You must excuse my appearance. I'm afraid I fell asleep in my clothes last night, and then I overslept. I was just now checking on Mr. Wainscott, but I assure you I'm perfectly well and rested."

Mrs. Talbot's eyes narrowed suspiciously. "Are you certain?"

"Of course. It's all going very well, and my patient is recovering nicely."

Still looking unconvinced, Mrs. Talbot held out a basket. "I brought you some scones and muffins. I was afraid you wouldn't have any time to bake for yourself."

Emmaline took the basket, her heart swelling with gratitude. "That was so kind of you, Mrs. Talbot. They smell delicious. But you really should go—the entire house is supposed to be under quarantine. I'd never forgive myself if you were to take ill."

"Oh, I'll be fine. I'm a tough old bird, as they say. Anyway, I just couldn't bear the thought of you alone all this time with that strange man. Why, you don't know him from Adam!"

"Well, he's one of Mrs. Collins's relations. A cousin of some sort, I think he said."

"Mathilde never mentioned any Wainscotts." She tipped her head to one side, her mouth pursed. "Except maybe an Aisling Wainscott. An authoress of some note, I believe. Some sort of distant relation, she said."

"Yes," Emmaline said, "that's Jack's—Mr. Wainscott's sister."

"Is that so? Well, I still don't understand what he was doing out here when he took ill. He must have known that Mrs. Collins passed."

"Mrs. Gage?" Jack called out, and Emmaline glanced over her shoulder in surprise. "If I might trouble you for some water."

Emmaline bit her lower lip, trying not to smile.

"I should let you get back to your patient," Mrs. Talbot said. "Please don't tell Dr. Hayward that I came by. I vow, I'll never hear the end of it if you do." Her eyes narrowed a fraction. "What's that there on your neck?"

Emmaline reached up to cover it with her palm. "Oh, it's nothing. Just a scrape. I was just…ahem, that is to say—"

"Mrs. Gage?" Jack called out again, clearly trying to sound particularly pathetic.

"I'll be right there, Mr. Wainscott," she called out in reply. "Thank you again, Mrs. Talbot. I'm so grateful for the baked goods. I know Mr. Wainscott will be, too, as soon as he's well enough to enjoy them."

Mrs. Talbot nodded, leaning toward her and whispering conspiratorially. "Just don't let him run you ragged, dear. Let him know who's in charge, that's all."

"Of course." Emmaline walked the woman to the door and saw her out, one hand still covering the mark on her neck. "Good day, Mrs. Talbot!" she called out, then shut the door and turned the key in the lock. If only she'd thought to lock it before now.

Letting her breath out in a rush, she picked up the basket of sweets and hurried back to Jack's side.

"So, this is your garden," Jack said, releasing Emmaline's arm as he sank to the bench. "I must say, from your description, I was expecting far worse."

She shook her head, glancing around the walled space with a look of wonder on her face. "I've totally neglected it since your arrival, and yet it looks much improved. I can't imagine how, as we've had so little rain."

"Curious, isn't it? I say, whoever designed this garden was inordinately fond of the Green Man's image, weren't they? His face is everywhere." An odd sensation prickled his skin. "I almost feel as if we're being watched."

"I feel it, too," Emmaline agreed. "As if this is the garden of legend, the one where the Green Man was imprisoned by the Winter King."

"You saw the pantomime?" Jack asked.

"Yes. I didn't realize *you* did."

Jack shrugged. "I confess I found it a bit melodramatic."

"Of course you would," Emmaline said with a laugh. "Anyway, you sit and rest for a bit. I'm going to pull some weeds and trim the roses."

He nodded gratefully. He'd never admit it, of course, but he was exhausted—the walk from the house to garden had near enough done him in. His traitorous legs felt entirely weak, and his heart was beating like a rabbit's. Blasted Influenza. He wanted to save every last ounce of energy he had for more entertaining forms of physical exertion.

His mouth went dry as he watched Emmaline make her way across the flagstones toward the roses. Devil take it, but she was beautiful. She would never believe it, of course. He'd never met anyone quite like her. He couldn't put his finger on it, but there was something far more natural—more earthy, perhaps—than the ladies with whom he was acquainted.

He watched as she cranked the handle on the well and filled the watering tin, marveling at the grace with which she moved. There was something so very feminine about her, so soft and gentle, despite her waif-like appearance.

She was nothing like Claire—the polar opposite, really. Oh, Claire was beautiful, too, there was no denying that. But there was a hardness to Claire's features, an angularity to her slim, boyish frame. Jack had sometimes thought that everything that Claire said or did was carefully calculated, meant to craft and hone an image rather than express true sentiment. He'd never known exactly what was going on in that sharp mind of hers; never truly understood what she'd felt or cared about. In all the years he'd known her, she'd been mostly a mystery to him—an intriguing puzzle to be solved.

Of course, hadn't he done the same thing? Cultivated the image he wanted to project to the world—that of an uncomplicated, carefree country gentleman. That image was far better than the real Jack, the one who fretted over his future, who hated his father for the callous way he treated his wife, who felt things far too deeply than he ought.

Perhaps he and Claire Lennox were perfectly suited, after all. He'd loved her enough to want to marry her, and *would* have married her if the war hadn't left him impotent, broken in both body and spirit. Breaking off their engagement had seemed the only fair thing to do. She deserved more. She hadn't been happy with his decision, despite the fact that he'd been unable to make love to her—an embarrassing debacle if ever there was one. Twice he'd tried, and twice he'd failed, his cock lying limp despite her valiant efforts to seduce him.

What had happened here at Orchard House to change that? How had Emmaline, a woman he barely knew, managed to cure him? Especially considering his physical state at present? He shook his head in amazement, feeling his cock begin to swell even now as he watched Emmaline bend over the roses, her perfect backside presented to him like a gift. The sun was behind her, and he could clearly make out the shape of her legs beneath her calf-length skirt. God, he wanted her. But he'd wanted Claire, too. Every man had wanted Claire—blond, beautiful Claire with her cornflower blue eyes and perfect little bow of a mouth, a cigarette dangling from her lips while she batted her lashes provocatively.

He had to tell Emmaline about Claire, about his broken engagement. It was only fair. After all, it had only been, what? Three, four weeks since he'd called off the wedding? He wasn't sure. But Emmaline had been entirely forthcoming about her own past, and he knew that he should do the same.

There was no doubt that she had loved Christopher Gage with all her heart. Not that he was surprised. He'd met her late husband on more than one occasion—they were distant relations, some sort of cousins-in-law. Chris had been an attractive man, the kind who turned every woman's head with his dark good looks and easy charm. He was smooth where Jack was awkward, confident where Jack was insecure. There was an intensity about him that women seemed to find irresistible. Of course Emmaline had fallen for him— and why not? As much as Jack hated to admit it, Chris Gage had been a damned good man, generous and intelligent to a fault.

How could anyone live up to that? Why would anyone even try? Gripping the stone bench on which he sat, Jack's fingers traced the outline of the Green's Man's face. Devil take it, but he wanted to try. He couldn't *help* but try. He wanted her that badly.

"What are you thinking about over there?" Emmaline called out, startling him. "You look far too serious."

"Do I?" he asked, struggling to add some jocularity to his voice. "Perhaps you should come over here, and I'll show you exactly what I'm thinking about."

"Should I, now?" Her mouth curved into a smile. "And what about these poor roses? You would have me abandon them in their time of need?"

"What about *my* time of need?" he teased, loving the bloom that had sprung to her cheeks.

She shrugged, setting aside the watering pail. "You look quite well to me. Far better than yesterday. I think the fresh air is doing wonders for your health."

"I think *you're* doing wonders for my health," he corrected. "Come here," he ordered, feeling emboldened. Perhaps he wasn't a confident man, but he could pretend to be one. He'd certainly read enough of Aisling's scandalous stories to know how a sexually assertive male was supposed to act.

Still, he hadn't expected her to obey. And yet she was doing just that, wordlessly crossing the flagstones that separated them, a mysterious smile playing on her lips. As if on cue, his cock sprang to attention.

Yes, Emmaline had cured him. Of that he was certain.

CHAPTER 6

*E*mmaline paused directly in front of Jack, who sat there watching her, open-mouthed, as she begun to unbutton her blouse. She hadn't the slightest idea what had possessed her, what had made her so bold and brassy. She only knew that she wanted him beyond reason.

She wasn't herself, hadn't been for days now. And yet this somehow felt *right*. Perhaps it was just that Jack was nearly a stranger; that he didn't know the sensible, predictable Emmaline, but the impulsive, sensual Emmaline instead. She wanted to be that woman, if only temporarily.

Her trembling fingers fumbled with the final button on her blouse, and then the thin voile fabric parted, revealing the lacy camisole she wore beneath it. She took a deep breath, her gaze locking with Jack's heated one.

"You're sure?" he asked, reaching for her hands and drawing her closer.

She nodded. "Entirely so."

A warm breeze stirred, fluttering the hem of her blouse and raising gooseflesh on her skin. Above them, the leaves rustled. A bird dipped toward them, chattering gaily. The sun warmed her skin as Jack pulled her down onto his lap. The garden seemed somehow...pleased.

Emmaline closed her eyes, inhaling sharply. The air was redolent with the scent of earth, of grass and sunshine—and Jack.

"Your hair," he said, his voice rough. "I want it down."

Emmaline nodded. Only a handful of pins secured the bun at the nape of her neck. One by one she removed them, placing them in her skirt's pocket. Jack loosened the coils with his fingers, gently combing through her hair until the loose waves fell across her shoulders. A shiver worked its way down her spine as his lips replaced his hands on her hair, his mouth moving toward her neck, toward the sensitive skin beneath her ear where her pulse beat like butterfly wings.

A sigh escaped her lips as she melted against him. His erection pressed firmly against her bottom, proof of his desire. She couldn't help but squirm against the length of him, suddenly desperate to feel him inside her again.

"Please," she murmured, unable to stand it a moment longer. "Jack, now—"

He silenced her with his mouth, hot against hers. It was a demanding kiss, and Emmaline relented at once, her lips parting as his tongue sought entry. *Yes,* her mind screamed as he deepened the kiss. *Yes, just like this.* She wanted to be taken hard.

But then his mouth moved away. As if she were as light as a feather, he lifted her from his lap and set her gently on the bench beside him. Again, his mouth slanted toward hers. The kiss seemed to go on forever, their tongues searching, exploring. Finally, his lips moved from hers. Her head tipped back as he trailed hot kisses down her throat, across her collarbone. Roughly pushing down her camisole, his mouth continued lower still. Emmaline felt the delicate fabric give, heard a ripping sound, and then his mouth was on her nipple, his teeth scraping against the puckered skin. All her nerve endings seemed to come alive at once, her skin hot and flushed and seemingly electrified as he flicked his tongue across the sensitive peak, again and again.

Her hands fisted into his hair as she pressed him to her breast, wanting more. When he began to suckle her, she thought she'd go mad with wanting.

"Now, Jack," she tried again, wriggling against him. "Please."

"Now what, Emmaline my sweet? Say it," he ordered hoarsely.

"I want you inside me, Jack. Now."

She heard his sharp intake of breath, saw his pupils dilate, and her heart soared with victory. Next thing she knew, he'd dragged her to her feet and bent her over the bench, her skirt somehow gathered around her waist. Glancing over one shoulder, she watched as he hastily unfastened his trousers and reached inside his drawers to free his erection.

She let out her breath in a rush of anticipation, gripping the back of the bench so tightly that her knuckles turned white. She arched her back, gasping softly when she felt his fingers tug down her knickers, baring her entirely to his sight.

"Dear God, Emmaline," he said on a sigh, his movements slower now. She felt a finger slide down her cleft, parting her. She was already wet and ready for him, aching to feel him inside her.

Instead, he stroked her, teasing her. "You're so very beautiful," he said, his voice thick with desire.

It was as if everything around them ceased to exist—the garden, the cloudless sky, the chirruping birds. It was just the two of them there, in some other plane of existence where nothing mattered but their pleasure. Her legs grew weak, her breath coming far too fast now as he continued to stroke her, pushing her closer and closer to release. Just when she thought she couldn't stand the exquisite sensations another second, he stopped, withdrawing his wicked fingers.

A moment later, she felt the tip of him pressing against her slick entrance. With one thrust, he buried himself fully inside her. Instinctively, she arched further, taking him even more deeply, wanting nothing more than to be filled entirely by him. His fingers dug into her hips as he clutched her to him, her name a whisper on his lips.

In the distance, a motorcar rumbled down the road. A horn sounded, perhaps in greeting. She didn't know, didn't care. All that mattered was Jack pressing against her back-side, pumping into her now with a steady rhythm that made ripples of pleasure begin to radiate from her core.

The force of her orgasm caught her entirely off guard, making her knees buckle slightly as she leaned into the bench for support. Behind her, Jack groaned, finding his own release just in time to make hers even more intense than she thought possible.

His head dropped to her shoulder, his lips pressing against her as he murmured her name, over and over again. It was only when his body began to tremble against hers that she remembered his weakened state. Alarm shot through her at once, and she moved away from him, wincing as he slipped out of her, leaving her cold and empty.

"Good heavens, Jack," she cried, quickly pulling up her knickers and smoothing down her skirt. "You must sit down. Here." She guided him back to the seat, her breath catching as he slumped down with a sigh.

"I'm fine," he said, smiling drowsily as he fastened his trousers. "More than fine, really. Honest to God."

She shook her head. "I think we should get you back inside. You've had enough excitement for one day."

His eyes danced with mischief. "That *was* rather exciting, wasn't it?"

"Perhaps it was," she said, rather annoyed with herself for risking his health yet again. "But now I'm ordering you back to bed."

"Bed, you say? Please tell me you'll be joining me there."

She glanced back at the roses she'd neglected. "I've still some work to do here in the garden. You should get some rest, and I'll wake you in time for tea." She needed to get away from him, to rid herself of the distraction, or she'd never get anything accomplished.

"Oh, very well," he grumbled.

Emmaline couldn't help but smile. It was easy to imagine what he must have been like as a boy. "That's the spirit," she said cheerfully. "Why, we'll have you better in no time."

But as soon as the words left her lips, she wished she could take them back. Her smile disappeared at once. Because as soon as he was well, he'd be leaving her—leaving Orchard House and Haverham altogether. Or, worse still, making *her* leave Orchard House. That was why he'd come there, after all. To put her out.

Reluctantly, she dragged her gaze to meet his. All the mischief and merriment had completely fled his features. Was he thinking the same thing she was? Likely so, she realized. There was no getting around it—they were on borrowed time, and every step he took toward recovery equaled a step away from her.

Tears burned behind her eyelids, but she would not let them fall. Soon enough, she'd be alone again. And then she'd have all the time in the world for tears.

Jack heard a gasp, felt a movement beside him in the dark. In the distance, thunder rumbled. He heard a whimper, realized it was Emmaline. Rubbing the sleep from his eyes, he sat up and reached for her just as a flash of lightning illuminated the room. "Emma?" he whispered, shaking her shoulders. "Emmaline?"

She didn't respond. A crash of thunder rattled the windowpane beside the bed. He heard Emmaline's sharp intake of breath, felt her entire body trembling.

Because of the storm?

It didn't make sense. Emmaline was strong, perhaps the strongest woman he'd ever met. What was a storm, compared to the war and its horrors?

When the next flash of lightning lit the sky, he saw that her hands were pressed against her ears, her eyes squeezed shut. "Emmaline?" he prodded once more, leaning over her prone form.

"Stay down," she murmured. "Trench mortars. Nerve gas…" Her voice trailed off as she rolled to her side, her legs drawn up to her belly.

"No, no, it's just thunder. A storm." He cupped her cheek with his palm, surprised to find it damp. "Emmaline?"

Another crash of thunder shook the glass, and she sat up with a gasp. "What…what happened?" she stammered. "Where am I?"

She'd been sleeping, he realized. Dreaming.

"Home, love. At Orchard House." He drew her against his chest. Her heart was beating wildly.

"Jack?" Her fingers dug into his flesh.

"I'm here," he answered, pressing a kiss against her temple.

She let out her breath in a rush. "Dear God, Jack. I had a dream, a terrible nightmare. I was back at the front, and you were there. You, and Christopher. There were mortars going off everywhere, and I was trying to get to both of you at once, trying to…" She trailed off, shaking her head. "I could not save you, not both of you."

"Shhh," he murmured against her hair. "It was just a dream, probably triggered by the thunder. But you're safe, everyone's safe." Except Chris, of course, who was beyond being saved. He wondered whom she'd chosen in her dream, but didn't dare ask.

She began to cry, hot tears scalding his chest. "I'm so sorry, Jack."

Perhaps that was his answer?

"Don't cry, Emmaline." He couldn't bear to watch a woman cry, particularly if he'd played a part in it. And it seemed he had—at least, in her dream.

At once, rain began to pelt the glass. Lightning flashed, thunder boomed as the storm reached its climax. He held her tight, murmuring soothing words as she continued to sob. By the time the storm subsided, her tears were reduced to sniffles and she lay against his shoulder, spent.

"I hope you'll forgive me," she said at last. "I've no idea what came over me. The dream…it was so very real. I could hear the mortars, smell the smoke in the air, and I was helpless to do anything. It was like losing Christopher all over again. And you"—she shook her head—"I didn't want to lose you, too."

He didn't know what to say in reply; didn't know what she wanted to hear. He'd hoped beyond reason that there was a future for them, but had feared that she wasn't quite ready, that this had only been an interlude of sorts, as far as she was concerned.

"Oh, I know I've no claim on you," she continued on. "It's just that the thought of you leaving, of finding myself all alone again—"

"I'm not going anywhere, Emmaline," he interjected, buying time. "Not just yet. The quarantine, remember?"

"Yes, yes, of course. The quarantine." Raising up on one elbow, she peered down at him sharply. "You must tell me, Jack—is there someone at home, waiting for you? Someone who...well, who would not be happy to know what we've done here?"

He swallowed hard before replying. He had to tell her the truth—there was no other way. "I was engaged until very recently," he said simply.

"What happened?"

He should have known it would not be that easy. "I called off the wedding. Despite my assurances to the contrary, she is not convinced that I won't change my mind, given time."

"Do you love her?" Emmaline asked.

The pain in her voice slashed through his heart. "I did love her once. Perhaps I still do," he answered truthfully. "But whatever I felt with her, it's nothing compared to what I feel with you. I know it sounds trite, but damn it, Emmaline, it's the truth."

She nodded, biting her lower lip. For a moment, she said nothing, and Jack let out a sigh of relief. But then came the question he'd hoped she wouldn't ask. "How long? Since you broke off the engagement, I mean."

This was where it would get dicey. What would she think of him if he told her the truth? That it had only been a matter of weeks? After all, her husband had been dead for nearly a year, and her feelings for him still lingered. Still, he could not possibly lie to her, not if he wanted a future with her. And he *did* want a future with her, God damn it.

"It was recent, wasn't it?" she asked when he remained silent. "I thought as much."

There was nothing to do but say it. "Three, maybe four

weeks." And now she'd think that he'd used her, an easy fuck to help him get past the heartache.

She reached a still-trembling hand up to his cheek. "It's all right, Jack. Perhaps…perhaps we both needed this. To forget the past, to move on with our lives."

No, he wanted to scream. No. It was more than that. He squeezed his eyes shut, resisting the urge to push her on the matter, to try and make her see the truth. Because upon closer inspection, the truth seemed mad—that he'd somehow managed to entirely forget the woman that he'd loved for several years, the woman he'd planned to marry, and fallen in love with *her* instead, in less than a fortnight, and with him barely conscious a good portion of that time.

Why would any sane person believe that? It was far easier to believe that he'd been using her—and worse still, she made it sound as if she'd been using him, too.

"I'll cherish this time we had together," she murmured, her breath warm against his ear. "Always."

Just like that, she'd dismissed him.

Yet when she rolled atop him, he did not push her away. If she wanted to use him yet again, then by God, weak and desperate fool that he was, he would let her.

"What's this?" Emmaline asked, reaching for the ragged leather book that Jack held in his hands. The cover was battered and scarred, some sort of Celtic symbol etched in gold leaf that was crumbling away.

Jack readjusted the wire-rimmed spectacles he wore when reading. "Funny you should ask—it's quite curious, really. I found it tucked in a drawer, over behind the shelves in the back. It appears to be a book of legends, and there was a note card tucked into this spot, here." He held the open book out to her. Around the margins, someone had scribbled notes in red ink.

"Well, what does it say?" she asked, her curiosity piqued.

"It's the same story as the pantomime. You know, the one acted out at the Beltane festival, about the May Queen and her husband, the Winter King. And look"—he flipped the page over—"here's a plate depicting the cuckolding Green Man, just like the etching on the bench in the garden."

She shrugged. "It's a fairly common image, Jack. There's one carved in the gate, too—did you notice? Just above the peephole?"

"Ah, yes, the peephole." He flipped several pages. "There's something here about that, too. According to the legend, that's how the Winter King learned of the May Queen's infidelity. He spied her in the arms of Green Man through the peephole."

Emma couldn't help but smile. "It's not the same peephole, of course. This is just a story, a fancy bit of make-believe. It's not about the garden here at Orchard House."

"Why do you suppose there's a peephole in a garden gate, anyway? What does one do in a garden that would require such a thing?" His hazel eyes were dancing with mischief behind the smudged lenses of his spectacles.

Emmaline felt the heat rise in her cheeks as she remembered just what she and Jack had done in the garden not two days past. "I'm sure it's just for decoration," she murmured. It had never even occurred to her that someone might have spied on them, but now that the idea was planted in her mind, she'd never be able to dismiss the possibility. Good God!

"Anyway, whomever wrote these notes in the margin noted the same similarities as I did. Look, there's even a well mentioned!" He'd become quite animated, Emmaline realized. The color was beginning to return to his cheeks, his jaw suddenly looking less hollow.

She smiled, taking in the length of his legs stretched out from the leather chair in which he sprawled rather inelegantly. "It's just a coincidence, Jack. Surely you realize that."

He tapped the page with his finger. "And here the author talks about how the fruit shriveled up on the trees once the Green Man was banished to the garden. You've an orchard."

"Yes, *outside* the garden walls. Come now, Jack, you're just being silly."

"Haven't you ever felt…I don't know, somewhat lusty out there?" he asked.

"What, in the garden?" she hedged, remembering the times she'd pleasured herself there, before Jack had arrived. She *had* felt somewhat lusty there, though she could not explain why. She'd only thought herself lonely at the time, missing a man's touch.

"I wonder if there are any standing stones nearby," he mused, turning the book sideways to read a note scribbled in the corner of one page.

Emmaline shook her head. "I haven't seen any. I could ask Mrs. Talbot, I suppose."

"We have a circle of standing stones at home," he said distractedly. "My sister used to like to go there to write. She said she felt some sort of energy there, or some nonsense like that."

"Your home is in Dorset?" she asked, curious. He'd mentioned Dorset before, but nothing more specific than that.

"Yes, in Bedlington. A quiet little village if ever there was one. Aisling was always desperate to get away. I quite enjoy it, myself. More so when my father's away," he added cryptically.

"You don't get along with your father?"

Jack's eyes darkened at once. "Oh, we get along well enough, the bloody bastard. It's my mother he torments. Keeps a mistress in London, you see. Which wouldn't be so terrible, I suppose, if my mother didn't love him so desperately." His voice had taken on a hard edge.

"I didn't mean to pry," Emmaline said.

"Don't apologize." He closed the book and set it on the chair's arm. "Anyway, it's not a secret. I suppose I should be grateful that he spends nearly all his time in town. Running the estate keeps me occupied, after all. It's only too bad that Aisling inherited the head for figures instead of me."

"You love your sister very much, don't you?" she asked,

noting the way the tension in his jaw seemed to disappear each time he mentioned her.

His mouth curved into a smile. "She's a bloody brat, but yes. By God, you should hear the way she curses! Always having the last word, and trust me, her words are colorful. Perhaps sometime—never mind." He waved one hand in dismissal.

What had he meant to say?

"Anyway," he continued, "it's a good thing she managed to overcome her snobbery in time to realize what a good chap Will Cooper is. Took a bit of maneuvering on my part, but she played right into my hands," he said with a laugh.

"Was her husband in the war?"

"Yes, and he managed to come through unscathed but for the loss of hearing in one ear. A mortar explosion," he explained. "I lost my hearing entirely for a fortnight after Saint Quentin, but eventually it returned to normal. Seems like a small price to pay, considering the fate of the rest of my unit." His entire face grew taut, his mouth pinched. At once, the appearance of vim and vigor that she'd admired only moments before had abandoned him.

Emmaline lifted the book from the chair's arm and perched there beside him, laying a gentle hand on his shoulder. "If you'd like to talk about it, Jack, go ahead. I know I can't erase the memories, but perhaps I can share the burden. I was there on the front; I know how dreadful it was. And before that, I lost both my parents to Influenza, one right after the other. I'm no stranger to loss."

He reached up to cover her hand with his. "I'm sorry, Emmaline. Listen to me, going on, when your losses were all far more personal than mine. You must think me a terrible coward."

She didn't think anything of the sort. She knew what war did to people, knew the lasting effects of witnessing such horror on a daily basis. "Of course I don't think you a coward," she said, leaning into him.

For several moments they sat like that in silence, their breathing in perfect unison. An energy seemed to course between them, leaching away the sensation of loss and replacing it with a peacefulness that Emmaline hadn't felt in ages. He must have felt it, too, because he seemed to relax against her.

"Go on," she prodded, far too comfortable to move a muscle. "Tell me what else your battered little book says about the garden."

And so he did.

"AMAZING," Dr. Hayward said, removing the stethoscope from his ears and draping it around his neck. "A remarkable recovery." He turned toward Emmaline, smiling broadly. "Perhaps you should consider coming to work for me, Mrs. Gage. I could use a good nurse. Regular office hours, and all that."

Emmaline shook her head. "I'm afraid that managing Orchard House is a full-time occupation at present," she said, then realized her mistake. Jack hadn't yet said what he meant to do with the property. She'd considered asking him if there was any way she could rent the house, but she knew that she could never afford to do so.

She glanced over to where he sat, buttoning up his shirt. His face was an unreadable blank. She wondered at his sudden glumness. They'd had a pleasant morning, after all, poring over old photographs she'd found in the attic. It was only when the doctor had appeared that the smile had seemed to vanish from Jack's face, taking his good mood along with it.

"As for you," the doctor said, turning his attention back to Jack, "I'm afraid you're not quite well enough to risk the drive back to Dorset. Not yet, at least."

"No?" Jack asked. There was something in his voice—disappointment, perhaps? She couldn't be sure.

The doctor shook his head. "No. You're in far better shape than I expected, but still too weak to safely take the wheel, particularly all alone and in a roadster, where you'd be exposed to the elements." He stroked his whiskers, looking pensive. "I suppose you could return to the hotel, but I'm inclined to say that it's not prudent to do so. I'd rather we continued the quarantine till the end of the week, unless Mrs. Gage objects."

Emmaline was caught off guard. "No, I...he can remain here at Orchard House as long as necessary. I've no objection. Unless Mr. Wainscott does, that is."

"Of course not," he said, though he did not meet her gaze.

Dr. Hayward nodded his approval. "Good, good. And what of your health, Mrs. Gage? Have you shown any symptoms since your exposure?"

"No, nothing at all," Emmaline said. "I've been quite well. I must have already been exposed to this particular strain at the hospital in London."

"Likely so," the doctor agreed. "We've had no other cases here in Haverham, so it looks as if we've dodged the proverbial bullet. Well, I suppose I should get back to the office." He busied himself returning his things to his black leather case. "Oh"—he held up an envelope—"I nearly forgot. Mrs. Talbot asked me to give you this—it must have gotten mixed up with her post."

Emmaline took the envelope from him, recognizing the familiar script. "It's from my husband's sister," she said with a smile. It had been ages since she'd received a letter from her. She hoped Maria was well. "Thank you, doctor. Here, let me show you out." She led him out of Jack's room, toward the front hall. Jack remained perched on the edge of the bed where they'd left him.

"I'll stop by again at the end of the week to check on him one last time," Dr. Hayward offered as he tipped his hat onto his head. "He seems a bit distracted. Hope he's not giving you too much trouble. I know this is terribly irregular—Mrs. Talbot is ready to have me drawn and quartered for putting you in this situation. Thank heavens her husband is a man of the cloth!"

"Mr. Wainscott has been a perfect gentleman," Emmaline said, "and an easy patient, doctor. And tending him, well… perhaps it's reminded me why I became a nurse in the first place." She liked to be needed, she realized. Useful.

"Perhaps you'll reconsider my offer, then. Once you're better settled here at Orchard House, that is."

Emmaline just nodded, her entire future far too uncertain to commit to anything at present.

The doctor smiled at her warmly. "Well, good day, then, Mrs. Gage." With a bow, he took his leave.

As soon as Emmaline shut the door, she glanced down at the envelope still clutched in one clammy hand. Maria's letter. She would see that Jack was settled back in bed, and then perhaps she'd go out to the garden to read it. While she was there, she could water the roses and check on the lavender that had begun to bloom behind the bench. Each day seemed to bring something new to the garden, the brown slowly gaining a more verdant hue, spots of color appearing where there had been none. She could not explain it, but since Jack's arrival, life had begun to return to the barren plot.

Much like her own bleak existence, she realized. What would become of them both, once he was gone?

With a shake of her head, she forced away the unpleasant

thought and hurried back to his bedside. She found him reclining back against the pillows, his eyes closed, his chest rising and falling in a slow, steady rhythm.

"Jack?" she whispered, pulling a blanket up to his waist.

"Hmm?" he murmured. He opened his eyes, his gaze at last meeting hers. There was something there that she hadn't seen before, something so raw, so hungry, that Emmaline's breath caught in her throat. For a moment she was rendered entirely mute, her heart thumping against her ribs.

He took a deep breath, a muscle in his jaw twitching as he did so. "Emmaline, I—" He abruptly cut himself off, closing his eyes, shuttering them from her. "Never mind. I'm a bit tired. Would you mind if I rested?"

"Of course not," she murmured, tucking the blanket more tightly about his hips. "I'm going out to the garden for a bit. I'll check on you when I return." She reached for one of his hands as she leaned over to kiss his forehead. *Still cool.* Beneath her fingertips, his pulse felt strong, perhaps a bit fast. She made a mental note to check it again later.

"I won't stay gone long," she promised. Later, she would attempt to lift his spirits. Perhaps they could do a jigsaw puzzle, she decided. She'd seen several in the library.

She glanced back down at the letter, anxious to learn what news it contained.

CHAPTER 8

*E*mmaline was there in the garden, sitting on the stone bench, just as Jack expected. He closed the gate and took several steps toward her, waiting for her to acknowledge his presence. She must have heard the latch open, must have sensed his approach.

And yet she sat unmoving, her head bowed, her hands folded in her lap atop a creamy white envelope. The sky had turned a dusty lavender—teatime had come and gone, and Emmaline had never come to wake him as she'd promised. Instead, he'd awoken on his own, a bit disoriented and groggy after such a long nap.

And then he'd remembered the letter—from her husband's sister, she'd said. It was clear that, in her heart, she and Christopher Gage were still joined. There was no room for him, never would be. He'd realized it the moment the words had left her lips. It had been a sobering thought, an arrow shot through the sail of his confidence. There was no point in declaring his love, not now. At best, he hoped they could part friends.

Still, he grew alarmed when she continued to sit there, as

still as a statue. As he drew closer, he could see that she had been crying. Her nose was red, her eyes wet and swollen. "Did you receive some bad news?" he asked, unable to curb his curiosity.

She started, as if she'd been entirely oblivious to his approach. "What? Oh, no." She swiped at her nose with one wrist.

Her dark eyes looked slightly wild, he realized. Panicked, perhaps. What the bloody hell was in that letter?

"You've been crying," he said, feeling foolish for stating the obvious, but he hadn't any idea what else to say. "You've been sitting out here for hours."

At last she turned to face him. Her pain was palpable, a living, breathing thing that seemed to suck all the goodness right out of the garden. "This letter is from my sister-in-law," she said at last, her voice breaking. "She's written me all these lovely things about how much Christopher loved Orchard House, about how happy he was visiting his aunt Mathilde here, how glad she is that I'm here. She says...she says she hopes that I can feel his presence here, keeping me company, watching over me." Her voice tore on a sob. "But I haven't felt that at all, Jack. Not since you arrived, at least. What kind of woman am I, what kind of wife, to have forgotten him like that? To have moved on so quickly, so easily?"

He knelt before her, taking one of her trembling hands in his. "It's been a year, Emmaline. What kind of woman would sit here, day after day, pining away for a husband who's been gone so long? I'll tell you what kind—a lonely one," he answered when she said nothing. "The kind who buries herself right alongside her husband. You've every right to get on with your life."

Her eyes narrowed, and she snatched back her hand. "That's easy for you to say, considering you were engaged to marry someone else only a few short weeks ago. How easy it must seem to you."

"That's not fair," he protested. "You've no idea how hard it was for me, how much I hated hurting Claire like that. But this is different—Christopher's gone, Emmaline. He's gone, and he's not coming back. Your continued suffering doesn't change that."

"You think I don't know that?" she snapped.

"Then why punish yourself for moving on with your life? Do you honestly think if Chris were here with you in spirit, watching you, that he'd want to see you sad and lonely? Wouldn't he want you to be happy instead? To be loved?"

"Loved?" she choked out. "Who said anything about love?"

Jack took a deep, fortifying breath. "I am. I'm saying it now. I love you, Emmaline Gage."

Her eyes widened, her mouth forming an 'O' of surprise.

Jack continued on, needing to get it all out in the open. "I realize it seems rash, that I sound fickle and inconstant. And perhaps I am, but damn it all, I *do* love you. I'd planned to tell you so, right up until the moment I realized that you're still in love with your husband. Your *late* husband," he corrected.

"But...but you said you were still in love with your fiancée," Emmaline sputtered. "Just yesterday, you told me so."

"I said that perhaps I still loved her, not that I was still *in* love with her. There's an enormous difference, you know."

Emmaline shook her head. "No, I don't know. You either love someone, or you don't."

He raked a hand through his hair. "It's not that simple, Emmaline. I've known Claire for many years; we were friends long before we were lovers. I can't just turn off my feelings for her like a switch in my head."

"Of course not," Emmaline said with a shake of her head.

"It's just that...that...oh, never mind!" She rose, her gaze darting around wildly, as if she were looking for an escape.

Jack stood and reached for her wrist. "Just listen to—"

"If you'll excuse me," she interrupted, her voice cold and detached. She tried to tug her wrist from his grasp. "Tea will be ready shortly. I apologize for the delay."

Damn it. A sharp pain tore through his gut. He'd done this badly, and now he was going to lose her. He had to do something—*say* something—to make her understand, before it was too late. "Don't do this, Emmaline. Don't shut me out. I know I may seem like a man without much depth, but damn it, this cuts like a knife, straight through my heart."

A single tear slipped down her cheek. Still, she remained unmoved. "I can't do this right now, Jack. I can't have this conversation. Please release me—*now*."

It felt as if the air had been knocked from his lungs in a single blow. Stunned, he complied, flexing his hand as he released hers.

Without another word, Emmaline turned and briskly walked away from him. Jack didn't turn and watch her go— he simply stood motionless, staring at the spot where she'd stood only moments before, his hand now clenched into a fist.

As soon as the gate clattered shut, he cursed loudly. Almost as if on cue, the sky seemed to darken. The wind picked up, sounding eerily like a wail of despair as it blew through the garden's walls. One fat raindrop splashed onto Jack's bare head, then another. He knew he should hurry inside, knew that it was pure folly to remain outside in a downpour in his weakened state, but he didn't give a fuck.

Call it pride, call it stubborn foolishness, but if she wanted him to keep his distance from her, then he damn well would, whatever the cost.

With a groan, he sank to the stone bench and dropped his

head into his hands. When the rain came, it came hard, pounding Jack's shoulders with a ferocity that matched his frustration.

For the first time in nearly a fortnight, Emmaline slept in her own bed. After she'd cleaned up from tea, she'd climbed the stairs to her own bedroom without so much as telling Jack goodnight. She hadn't a choice—she could not face him, could not bear to see the hurt and betrayal there in his eyes.

He'd told her he loved her, and she'd entirely dismissed him. What else could she have done? She'd been overcome with guilt after reading Maria's letter, and not yet recovered from the shock of the news of Jack's recently ended engagement. It was all too much.

As it was, she was grappling with her own feelings for him, unable to believe that she could fall in love with Jack so quickly, even though she'd fallen for Christopher in an equally short space of time. Still, those had been war times, and everything moved at a quicker pace when life seemed so precarious.

And yet...she and Jack understood each other. She knew exactly why he got that haunted look on his face when he talked about Saint Quentin, and he understood why the sound of thunder could turn her dreams into nightmares. They seemed kindred spirits, two lost souls who were meant to find one another, somehow.

And they had, in the oddest of circumstances. Surely it was fate. At least, she wanted to believe that it was. But the rational part of her mind told her that it was nothing more than circumstance—two people from different worlds, thrown together at a time when both were vulnerable. After all, Jack was a baronet's son. She knew enough of England

and its social classes to realize that the heir to a baronetcy didn't usually consort with women like her—in fact, under normal circumstances they would not have ever crossed paths.

She was sure that his fiancée was a woman of good breeding, a socialite who would not do a day's work. The very idea of changing a dressing or bedpan would make her cringe in horror. She was a beauty, no doubt, her clothing and hair the height of fashion. How could she ever compete with that?

As it was, she'd been lucky enough to catch the eye of a man like Christopher Gage, who'd been handsome and charming and kind. He hadn't been titled, or even particularly rich, but he'd come from a good family, and truly, he'd been far more than she'd deserved.

That sort of luck only happened once in a lifetime, and she'd be a fool to think that anything could come from her affair with Jack, even if he did claim to love her.

Even if she loved him, too. And she *did* love him—oh, how she did. There was no sense in denying it. He was funny and gentle and kind and sweet, not to mention undeniably handsome. He set her blood afire, made her entire body ache with need.

She rolled over onto her back, staring up at the ceiling in the darkened room. Was he doing the same, downstairs in his own bed? She could barely stand it, being apart from him. However would she survive it, once he was gone?

Heaven help her, but just thinking about him made her damp between her legs, made her want to touch herself. Resisting the urge, she turned back to her side, clutching a pillow to her chest. She wanted to believe that Jack was right, that Christopher would want to see her happy and loved— that he'd want her to marry again, have children. Of course he would. Christopher had loved her, after all.

Unable to bear it a moment longer, she sat up in bed. Even if they weren't meant to be together, she couldn't bear to spend what time they had left away from his side. If that made her faithless and inconstant, then so be it. She was not perfect; she'd never claimed to be. But Jack deserved to know how she felt, even if she could not risk her heart by saying the words aloud.

Her resolve firmly in place, she threw off the bedclothes and slipped from the bed. Moving silently through the dark house, she made her way downstairs, tiptoeing across the hall toward the room where Jack slept. The door was ajar, and she paused just outside, listening for his soft snores, but she heard nothing. Reaching out, she pushed the door open, peering inside to where the moonlight cast silvery stripes across the narrow bed.

It was empty.

"Looking for me?" a voice called out behind her, and Emmaline gasped as she spun toward it.

"Good heavens, Jack! You nearly scared me half to death."

"Sorry about that." He took a step toward her, glass clinking. Peering more closely, she saw that he carried a tumbler in one hand, and a bottle in the other.

"Brandy," he said, holding out the bottle. "Found it in the study. Hope you don't mind." His voice was uneven, his speech slightly slurred, Emmaline realized.

"Are you drunk?" she asked, wrinkling her nose as the smell of liquor wafted toward her.

"Not even close," he answered, swaying toward her. With a *clunk*, he set the bottle down on the sideboard against the wall behind her. "Though I'd like to be."

He was clearly drunk, despite his protests. She glanced down at her nightdress, suddenly wishing she'd put on her robe.

"So, you must have a purpose. This little nighttime visit, I mean." He waved the hand carrying the glass, and Emmaline felt a slosh of liquid on her bare feet.

"Give me that," she snapped, taking it from him and setting it on the sideboard beside the bottle. "Just how much have you had to drink?"

"I say, not nearly enough." He reached for the glass, but Emmaline swatted away his hand.

"You're ill, you know. You shouldn't be drinking hard liquor—it's only going to set back your recovery." Which wasn't entirely truly, of course. It *was* just brandy, which was often considered medicinal.

"No, you wouldn't like that, would you?" he slurred. "The sooner I'm well and out of your hair, the better, right?"

She sighed heavily. "Just go to bed, Jack. It's late, and you're drunk."

"I'm not drunk," he bit out, sounding almost sober all of a sudden. "Not in the slightest. I can hold my liquor quite well, believe it or not."

"Come, now." She reached for his elbow. "You're going to regret this in the morning when your head is spinning and your stomach lurching."

"The only thing I'll regret in the morning is not doing this," he said, reaching behind her and pulling her against his chest. His mouth came down hard on hers, hot and demanding, tasting of brandy.

Caught entirely off balance, Emmaline clutched at his chest, trying to steady herself. His fingers bit into her shoulders as he pulled her closer still.

He kissed her deeply, and Emmaline realized she could not fight it; she had no desire to fight it. A soft moan escaped her lips as she opened her mouth against his.

And then, almost as suddenly as he'd grabbed her, he released her. "Why were you creeping around down here, looking for me? Tell me the truth," he demanded.

"I...I just wanted to check on you," she stammered, afraid to admit the truth. That she wanted him. Needed him. Couldn't go a single night without having him, not with him under the same roof.

"Liar," he spat. "You're a damned poor liar. You owe me the truth, at least. You wanted *this*, didn't you?" He turned her, pressing her back to the wall, grinding his pelvis into her. He caged her with his arms, his palms pressed against the wall behind her. She couldn't have escaped, had she wanted to. He was bigger and stronger than she was, even now. "You don't love me, won't have me, but you'll fuck me, all right, won't you?"

His mouth moved toward hers, and she turned her head, avoiding his kiss. She was trapped, cornered, and instinct took over. "Get away from me," she said coldly, tamping down the hysteria that rising in her breast. "You've no idea what I want. What I feel."

"Then tell me, Emmaline. Damn it, tell me what you feel. Tell me what you want from me."

Tears stung her eyes. She couldn't speak, couldn't possibly say the words she wanted to say.

"I laid my heart bare to you," he continued, his voice hard, "and you flayed it. And now you come down here, looking for a fuck. That's all it is to you, isn't it? Do you pretend I'm your husband while you—"

Her hand flew out and struck him hard across one cheek.

They stood there, glaring at one another for what felt like an eternity, not saying a single word. He rubbed his cheek with the palm of one hand, the other still pressed against the wall by her ear. There were no other sounds save their breathing, coming fast.

Finally, Jack broke the silence. "Goddamn it, Emmaline, I'm sorry. I—"

She silenced him with her mouth, rising up on tiptoe to

press her lips against his. Without breaking the kiss, she reached down, fumbling with his trousers, desperate to have him—*now*. Only, her hands were trembling so badly that she couldn't work the fastenings, and Jack grew impatient. Pushing aside her useless hands, he accomplished the task in a fraction of a second, then reached under her nightgown and dragged down her knickers, nearly ripping them in the process.

And then he was inside her, pressing her up against the wall as he buried himself in her, rocking his hips against hers. "Jack," she whimpered against his neck, her teeth scraping against his skin. "More."

Understanding her need, he reached down and lifted her off her feet, allowing her to wrap her legs around his waist, her back still pressed to the wall as he drove into her— harder and faster, till she was panting.

"Oh, God, Emma," he cried out, his voice ragged. "I can't...I won't last...come for me." He reached down to where their bodies were joined, pressing his thumb against her clit, stroking her hard while she cried out his name, over and over again.

In seconds, she climaxed, wave after wave of pleasure making her entire body vibrate. She felt him stiffen just as his head tipped back, the cords in his neck standing out in stark relief. Quickly, he pulled out of her, allowing her feet to return to the floor as his seed spurted hotly against her belly.

Emmaline leaned into his chest as she caught her breath, inhaling his scent, wanting to remember it forever.

"I think I need to lie down," he said at last.

*J*ack eyed Emmaline across the breakfast table, desperate to read something in her expression that would indicate how he should proceed where she was concerned. Her face had remained a polite mask throughout the interminable meal—she smiled as she passed him a plate of toast or poured his coffee, made small talk about the weather and her plans for the day. Indeed, she'd been pleasant enough, in a detached sort of way, ever since she'd woken up naked beside him.

But what did it mean? That she'd forgiven his brutish behavior? That she was willing to forget the fact that he'd all but taken her unwillingly, up against the wall? Or that she simply wanted to pretend that it hadn't happened? The last thing he wanted to do was misstep somehow, but damn it, he needed to know what was going on in that head of hers.

"I thought I might turn the beds in the far corner, over by the juniper bushes," she was saying as she smeared strawberry jam on her toast. "Those beds seem to get a fair amount of afternoon sun. Maybe I'll try to replant the bluebells over there, along with the lilacs. What do you think?"

"Perhaps," he replied, trying to catch her eye, but failing miserably. When she reached for the coffeepot, he caught her wrist, holding it firmly in his hand. "Emmaline, we need to talk. About last night…" He trailed off, hoping that she would say something first to lead him in the right direction.

She shook her head. "There's nothing to say, really."

"There's plenty to say," he countered. "If you'll just listen.

Her dark eyes filled with tears. "I'm sorry, Jack."

"*You're* sorry?" he asked. He could feel her hand trembling beneath his. "I'm the one who should be apologizing. I never should have been so rough, so violent—"

"Don't," she interrupted, meeting his gaze. The color had risen in her cheeks, staining them pink. "Please don't apologize. I acted foolishly yesterday, in the garden. You were right, and—"

The doorbell rang. Emmaline bolted from her seat, nearly spilling her juice in the process.

And what?

"Are you expecting someone?" he asked, rising from his seat and reaching for her shoulder to steady her.

She shook her head. "No, not at all. Dr. Hayward said he wasn't coming back till the end of the week. Perhaps it's Mrs. Talbot."

Again, the bell sounded. Emmaline glanced over her shoulder, toward the front hall. "I'd better go see who it is. You sit"—she gestured toward the chair he'd occupied only moments before—"and finish your breakfast."

But Jack remained standing, watching as Emmaline hurried out. Moments later, he heard the front door open.

"Hullo," came a crisp, feminine voice—far too familiar. "I'm looking for Jack Wainscott. They told me at the hotel that I might find him here. Are you Mrs. Gage?"

"I am," Emmaline answered. "I've been tending him since he took ill. You must be his sister Aisling."

No. Oh, no.

"I'm his fiancée," came the sharp reply. "Claire Lennox."

Without wasting another second, Jack strode off toward the front hall, hoping to salvage the situation as best as possible.

"What are you doing here?" he called out, stepping up beside Emmaline, who stood goggling at Claire. Why the hell had she called herself his fiancée?

"What do you mean, what am I doing here?" Claire asked, looking from Jack to Emmaline, and back to Jack again. "Your mother said you were only to be gone a few days. It's been more than a fortnight, and no one's heard a word from you. Everyone was worried."

"I fell ill with Influenza," he explained, slightly flummoxed. It wasn't like his mother to keep track of his whereabouts. "I was nearly unconscious for five days straight."

"And there isn't a hospital here you could be taken to? If you were so very ill, that is?" Claire's eyes were cold as she regarded him with unconcealed suspicion.

"It was a potentially lethal strain, Miss Lennox," Emmaline offered. "The doctor hoped to keep him under quarantine. Since I'm a trained nurse, it seemed best to leave him here."

"I see," Claire bit out. "Still, it seems as if you could have telephoned. Unless, of course, you've been otherwise occupied." Her look was accusing, and Jack's annoyance rose a pitch. What right did she have, barging in like this and making Emmaline uncomfortable? It wasn't any of Claire's business where he'd been, or what he'd been doing.

He took a protective step toward Emmaline, his arm brushing against her shoulder. "I think you should go—"

"Won't you come in?" Emmaline said at precisely the same time. "We were just finishing breakfast. I can offer you some coffee and toast, if you're hungry."

Claire swept inside, looking as regal and haughty as ever. "I breakfasted already, at the hotel. But thank you, I will come in."

For a moment, the three of them simply stood there awkwardly.

"Might I have a word with you in private, Jack?" Claire said at last. "If you don't mind, that is, Mrs. Gage." Claire offered Emmaline a tight smile, one that did not reach her eyes.

"Of course not." Emmaline's forehead was creased with a frown. "Here, use the front parlor. I'll go out to the garden for a bit and give you some privacy."

"Emmaline," Jack said, reaching for her elbow. "I'll only be a few minutes."

She wouldn't meet his eyes. "No," she murmured, looking at her shoes, the doorway—anywhere but at him. "Take all the time you need. If you'll both excuse me."

"Well, isn't this cozy," Claire said, as soon as Emmaline left them. "I suppose *this* is the real reason you broke off our engagement?"

"Whatever are you talking about, Claire? I only just met Emma—Mrs. Gage," he corrected.

She raised one perfectly arched blond brow. "And where, pray tell, is *Mr.* Gage?"

"Dead," he answered simply. "A casualty of the war."

Her mouth curved into an ugly smile. "Well, then. Aren't you two a match made in heaven?"

"Look, Claire," he said, clenching his hands into fists by his sides. "I have no idea what you're doing here, what game you're playing at. But I made it quite clear before I left Bedlington that we were done. You've no right to come here and start making accusations—"

"Are you denying that you're playing house with her, then? Your little war widow?"

"It's none of your damn business."

"I suppose that's my answer, then," she said with a sneer. "What's happened to you, Jack?" She shook her head. "Running off and abandoning Wainscott House in favor of your latest piece of ass is your father's style, not yours."

"Get out," he said, barely able to control his rage. If she didn't get out his face immediately, he would be sorely tempted to do or say something that he'd no doubt regret later on.

And then her face crumpled, tears filling her eyes. "I'm sorry, Jack. I shouldn't have said that. But you must understand, your mother was frantic. Something...something happened at Wainscott House—a burst pipe of some sort, I can't say, exactly. Some rooms were flooded, the carpet ruined. Your father's in London, of course, and you were nowhere to be found. You know how your mother is, and so I said I'd come and find you. And then when I heard that you were here, alone with some woman..." The tears ran freely down her cheeks now, and she wiped them away with the back of one hand. "Did I mean so very little to you, Jack? I gave you five years of my life—five years! And this is what I get for it?"

He raked a hand through his hair, his stomach lurching uncomfortably in his gut. "I'm sorry, Claire. Honestly. I don't what else to say."

"I waited for you. All those years, I waited," she continued on.

He shook his head. "I never asked you to wait. I was glad that you did, but I never expected that you would."

"And I didn't even care that you couldn't...well, you know, when you came home from the war. If you'd only given it time, perhaps tried a bit harder—"

"Tried harder?" God, talk about emasculating. He *had* tried. Perhaps he just hadn't wanted it enough, hadn't wanted *her* enough. But he'd never say that, not to her. It would be far too cruel.

"Have you been able to...you know...with *her?*" she asked, so well bred that she couldn't bear to say the words aloud.

He would not lie to her. "Yes," was all he said in reply.

Claire nodded. He saw her swallow hard as she straightened her spine, digesting the truth. And then she laid a hand on his sleeve. "Come home, Jack," she said, earnest now. "To Dorset. You've got responsibilities there, a life there." She glanced around, as if seeing her surroundings for the first time, and shuddered. "This...this isn't you. It near enough broke your mother's heart when Aisling married Will Cooper. How do you think she'll take it if you throw everything away for...well, for this woman, whoever she is? She's not like you, Jack. Like *us.*"

He held up one hand in warning. "Don't say another word."

"Don't run out on your responsibilities like your father does," she pushed, going for broke. "You're far better than that—I know you are."

Perhaps I'm not, after all. He shook his head, trying to clear it. "I don't owe anyone anything. My responsibility is to Wainscott House alone, and I will see to those responsibilities. You may tell my mother that I'll be home by the end of the week. Beyond that, where I go or what I do is no one's business but my own. I'm sorry that I've hurt you. Truly, I am. But we're done, Claire. *Done.* And now I must ask that you leave."

She raised her chin in the air, as proud as ever. "I'm staying at the hotel in town till the day after tomorrow. When you come to your senses, you can find me there."

"Goodbye, Claire," he said, hoping she understood the finality of his words.

"Goodbye, Jack," she answered, and then she was gone.

Jack slumped to the sofa with a groan. Devil take it, but he suddenly felt like the villain that Claire had made him out to be. How was he going to explain it all to Emmaline now? Claire was staying in Haverham, for fuck's sake. She was no longer the faceless ex-fiancée who Jack claimed to be done with, but the very real woman who was just up the road, waiting for him. Things had just gone from bad to worse, and there wasn't a damn thing he could do about it.

At once bone tired and weary, he rose and strode out, headed to the garden to learn his fate.

*E*mmaline heard the car drive away, knew that Jack would come looking for her any minute now. She continued turning the soil in the bed, digging into the rich, loamy earth with her spade. She knew what she had to do, and what she would tell him. It had become crystal clear, the moment she'd opened the door and seen Claire Lennox standing there.

The woman had been even more beautiful than she'd imagined, like a perfect little china doll. She exuded wealth and breeding and fashionable taste—everything that Emmaline so sorely lacked. Emmaline was a poor country girl from Pennsylvania, after all, one who'd spent the majority of her adult years on hospital wards. If there had ever been a youthful bloom to her cheeks, it was long gone now, taken from her by the war, by widowhood.

Jack belonged with a woman like Claire—she had been raised to marry a gentleman like him, to run his household and raise his children. She would entertain his guests with practiced ease, delighting everyone with her wit and charm.

She would be intimately acquainted with his family and friends, an integral part of his social circle.

Emmaline could do none of these things, could *be* none of those things. She would always be an outsider, awkward and unsure of herself when away from the wards. After all, the hospital was the one place where she felt competent and self-assured. She was a good nurse. An *excellent* nurse, she corrected.

Besides, working with a village doctor in his Cotswold office would be a far cry from the Army hospitals in which she'd toiled. Children with sniffles, women in childbirth, broken bones to be set—these were the concerns of a country nurse. There would be no wards, no nurses' dormitories, nothing to remind her of the life she'd left behind. She would take a room in the boarding house beside the grocery, perhaps even begin to attend services at the little stone church over which Mr. Talbot presided. Yes, Mrs. Talbot would like that, she thought with a smile.

A bead of perspiration ran down her forehead, and she swiped at it with the back of her forearm, hoping she hadn't trailed soil across her skin in the process. It was warm for May, the sun bright and strong against the clear blue sky.

The hinge on the gate creaked open, and Emmaline let out her breath in a rush. It was time—time to send Jack home, back where he belonged.

"There you are," he called out, striding over to where she knelt. He looked drawn, tired. But he was well, far more so than she'd been willing to admit. It might take him some time to regain his strength, but there was no real danger in sending him home with Claire.

Setting down her spade, she peeled off her gloves and tossed them to the cobbles. Standing, she reached for Jack's hand. "Come, let's sit."

Silently, he nodded, following her to the stone bench and taking a seat beside her.

"I *do* love you, Jack," she began tentatively. "I want you to know that, first and foremost. Perhaps it's rash, perhaps we've both lost our wits, perhaps this garden really is enchanted," she said, attempting to smile. "Who knows? But whatever the case, I love you."

Jack raked a hand through his hair, mussing it. There was a look of defeat, of resignation in his hazel eyes that made Emmaline's heart hurt. "Then Christ, Emma, why does it sound as if you're about to break my heart?"

She took a deep breath before answering. "Because I have to set things right. This time we've spent together—it's been wonderful, magical even. A healing time for us both. But don't you see? We've been shuttered away, removed from the rest of the world, living a dream. It can't go on like this forever."

"And you've decided this in the space of time that I was inside, talking to Claire? And I've no say in the matter?"

"Oh, Jack, you were so very ill. I'm not certain you realize how grave it was when you first collapsed. These were extraordinary circumstances—had we met some other, more ordinary way, there's no telling what might have happened. But this...this isn't real."

"I know what I felt when I first saw you there across the bonfire—the instant attraction, the desire to know you. Are you saying that wasn't real, either?"

"That hardly counts. We hadn't met, hadn't spoken a single word to each other."

"But I knew, even then—"

"Oh, Jack," she interrupted with a sigh. "That's easy for you to say now, but if your business hadn't brought you here to Orchard House, we never would have met at all."

"But my business *did* bring me here. To you," he added, squeezing her hand. "I see that as fate intervening."

She shook her head. "You may not realize it now, but you need to be with someone who doesn't hear mortar explosions in every crack of thunder, who doesn't share your memories of the stink of mustard gas, of flesh wounds left too long untreated. You need someone to bring light into your life, not sustain the dark memories of war. Someone like Claire, Jack. You used to love her—you said so yourself. You were going to marry her, and if not her, then someone just like her. You were thrown off your path, that's all. I'm just putting you back on that path. Someday, you'll thank me for it."

A muscle in his jaw twitched. "If you think that's true, then you don't know me at all."

"And there you have it, Jack. I *don't* know you. It's only been a fortnight, and none of it spent in the real world. This was a lovely interlude, but that's all it can ever be—a wonderful memory that I will treasure forever."

"And there's no changing your mind?" he asked. "Nothing I can say or do to convince you otherwise?"

She shook her head, her eyes damp now. He nearly groaned aloud—not one but *two* crying women in a single day. Lovely.

"You should go to her, Jack. Find her, before she leaves town, and allow her to see you home safely. You can come back later for your car—it'll be safe enough here. I'll have my things out of Orchard House by the end of the week. I've decided to rent a room in town and accept Dr. Hayward's offer of employment."

"You're not leaving Orchard House," he said, his voice flat. "This is your home now. I'll speak to my father and explain the situation—he won't turn you out. I damn well won't let him."

She was startled by his outburst. "It's rightfully his, Jack. You were quite clear on that when you arrived here. I have no legal claim besides Maria's word, and I'm sure she had no knowledge of the situation besides what it said in her aunt Mathilde's will."

"And I'm my father's heir, which means the property will rightfully be mine someday. And I'm saying that it's yours."

She swallowed hard. "You can't do that."

He rose, releasing her hand. "Of course I can. If you'd feel better about it, I'll talk to my solicitor and have some papers drawn up. An agreement of sorts, whereby you lease the property from me for a pound a year, or some such nonsense."

"It doesn't seem right," she said, though her heart swelled with hope. "What will your family say?"

"As if I give a damn what my family says," he sneered. "My father spends a small fortune to keep his mistress in style in London. Let him think whatever he wants. It's of no consequence to me."

"But...but what will Claire think? Your wife might not be so—"

"I'm not marrying Claire," he said coldly. "I decided so when I broke off our engagement last month, and nothing has changed on that count. If anything, her appearance here has only made it clear just how ill suited we were to begin with. Your doing this—forcing me from your life—accomplishes nothing, Emmaline. *Nothing*," he repeated. "Now if you'll excuse me, I'll go inside and pack my things."

With that, he turned and strode angrily away.

Emmaline just sat there, watching him go as her heart broke into a million little pieces.

❧

EMMALINE SAT BACK on her heels, staring at the flowerbeds in frustration. Why, there had been buds on these plantings a fortnight ago. And now...now they were a brown, withered mess, despite her efforts. Blast it!

Must she fail at everything? She'd poured her heart and soul into this garden, and yet it refused to flourish. Oh, things had begun well enough—before Jack had left it seemed as if she were going to succeed where no one else had, at least according to Mrs. Talbot. First the roses, then the lavender. Bit by bit, things had begun to show signs of life. She'd gotten ambitious, replanting beds based on color schemes—blues and lavenders in one bed, reds and pinks in another.

They'd seemed fine at first, the blooms just beginning to bud in several sunny spots. And then...nothing. She'd watered, she'd fertilized, she'd even spoken to them daily, trying to coax them to life. And still they refused to cooperate.

She let out a sigh of frustration. Perhaps she should take Mrs. Talbot's advice and give up. After all, giving up what was she did best. However had she let Jack walk out that door, convinced it was for the best? *I'm nothing but a coward,* she thought bitterly, wishing for the millionth time since he'd gone that she'd taken more time to consider her decision before acting so rashly.

It had been two full weeks since he'd gone, and Emmaline hadn't set foot once in the downstairs bedroom he'd occupied, not even to strip the bed and change the linens. She couldn't do it, couldn't bring herself to go inside and touch the things he'd touched, afraid the scent of him would linger, afraid the memories would be too much to bear.

But Mrs. Babbitt was set to return to her housekeeping duties in the morning—she would no doubt wonder why the room sat untouched. *I'm going to have to do it myself,* she realized. *Tonight.* Once and for all, she would enter the room and face the memories head on. There was no other way.

She rose, glancing toward the house in the distance. Orchard House was officially hers now, at least according to the letter that arrived in yesterday's post from Jack's solicitor in London. He certainly hadn't wasted any time. She knew she should be grateful—he'd provided her with a home, after all, when he had every right to take it away from her. But it all seemed so final, especially since he'd already sent someone to retrieve his sporty red roadster and drive it back to Dorset.

He wasn't coming back. She'd driven him away, and now he was gone forever. Her shoulders sagging, she picked her way across the flagstones and headed back inside, determined to tackle the downstairs bedroom now, while she still had the courage.

A quarter hour later, she pushed open the door and stepped inside the room in question. She inhaled deeply, expecting to smell his scent, but it was gone. The room smelled slightly stuffy, nothing more. An unexpected wave of disappointment washed over her, and she found herself moving toward the bed, reaching for the pillow on which he'd slept so many nights.

Picking it up, she pressed it against her nose, closing her eyes as she imagined him there, his golden head pressed to the soft cotton pillowcase. *Nothing.* There was nothing, no lingering scent.

Feeling almost frantic now, she dropped the pillow back to the bed and began to search the room, looking for something—anything—to prove that he had been there. A button, perhaps, or a misplaced sock. In his haste to leave, he must have forgotten some little thing, something worthless and yet priceless, all at once. She pulled back the bedclothes, nearly ripping them from the bed.

And then she found it. Tears stung her eyes as she reached for the crumpled undershirt. She remembered pulling it over his head the last night they'd spent together, right after he'd made love to her in the hallway, half drunk and a little wild.

Once they'd reached the bedroom, she'd removed his clothing, piece by piece, till he'd been entirely naked. And then she'd stood there in the light of moon and stripped off her own clothes, completely unabashed and unashamed before him. They'd made love twice more before the sun had come up, before they'd fallen into a deep, satisfied sleep.

And when she'd awakened, she'd allowed herself a measure of hope. It had been a glorious feeling, no matter how uncertain. Perhaps they *could* have a future together, despite the unorthodox way they'd met, despite their differences. She'd allowed herself to actually believe it possible.

Right up until Claire Lennox had shown up and shattered that illusion. Damn the woman! If not for her intrusion, they would have had several days more to figure it all out, to sort through the uncertainties and reassure themselves that fate *had* meant for them to find each other.

Crumpling the undershirt into a ball, she held it close as she sank to the bed. Still fully clothed, she lay down, her knees tucked into her chest, the shirt pressed to her face. If she breathed deeply enough, she could still make out his scent, however faint. She could almost imagine his warmth, curled up there beside her.

When the tears came, she did not hold them back. She let them flow freely, let the sobs tear from her throat unchecked.

"You sit, dear. I'll pour." Mrs. Talbot reached for the ceramic teapot. It was Emmaline's favorite—a pale rose-colored floral design that she'd found tucked away in a box in the attic. The petals had been hand-painted in raised enamel, the detail particularly impressive. Why it had been put away so unceremoniously would remain a mystery, considering its pristine condition.

"Thank you, Mrs. Talbot," she said, watching as the steaming, caramel-colored liquid filled her dainty cup. "But truly, I'm fine. You needn't trouble yourself on my account."

"It's no trouble at all." Mrs. Talbot set down the teapot and patted Emmaline gently on one cheek. "Besides, isn't it obvious that I'm buttering you up? I vow, I'm going to convince you to tell me what's troubling you before the day's out."

Emmaline spooned two lumps of sugar into her cup, avoiding the woman's prying gaze as she did so. "What makes you think something's troubling me?"

"Well, dear, it's as obvious as the nose on your face. You haven't been yourself for weeks now. At first, I assumed it was simply exhaustion from tending that man all on your own. But if that were the case, then you should be well recovered by now. He's been gone, what? Nearly two months now?"

"Nearly," Emmaline murmured, bringing the cup to her lips. It had been fifty-four days, to be precise. Each day just as bleak as the one before it.

"Then I can only assume it's something to do with your job. Is Dr. Hayward working you too hard? I can speak with him, if you'd like."

Emmaline set down her cup too hard, sloshing tea onto the saucer. "No, of course not. I'm enjoying my work with the doctor. It's quite rewarding, actually."

Which was the truth—particularly her work with the village's children. Perhaps she'd found her true calling in pediatrics.

Mrs. Talbot eyed her sharply. "Well, then, what is it that's taken the bloom from your cheeks? The light from your eyes? Don't get me wrong—you were a bit melancholy when you first arrived here in Haverham. But now..." She trailed off, shaking her head. "You should be getting better, not worse. Mrs. Babbitt says that when you're not working, you spend most of your time sitting in the garden—"

"She told you that?"

Mrs. Talbot waved one hand in dismissal. "Oh, don't be cross with her. She's worried about you, that's all."

"I *like* the garden," Emmaline said with a shrug.

Mrs. Talbot shook her head, her mouth pursed in disbelief. "It's a wasteland, Emmaline, in case you did not notice. I would have expected you to give up by now. I don't know what it is...bad soil, perhaps? Something to do with acidity or something like that. Whatever the case, Mathilde Collins couldn't make a go of it, and neither will you be able to. And then there's the rumors of it being haunted—"

"It's not haunted," she interrupted impatiently. She'd long since dismissed such notions.

Mrs. Talbot laid her hand atop Emmaline's. "I'm a good listener, you know. Whatever it is, you can tell me."

"I...I don't know what you mean," she stammered, the heat rising in her cheeks. Mrs. Talbot was far too perceptive. Perhaps it came from being a minister's wife?

Mrs. Talbot just smiled, patting her hand. "Of course you do, dear. And I'm not leaving here until you tell me."

Emmaline swallowed hard, feeling cornered.

"A burden is always best shared," Mrs. Talbot pushed.

"Is that from the gospels?" she hedged.

"Yes, the gospel according to Clara Talbot. Go on."

"Oh, very well." Emmaline let out her breath in a rush. Perhaps she *would* feel better if she unburdened herself. Either way, it was tell the truth, or come up with a convincing lie—and she'd never been a good liar. "If you must know, it's to do with Mr. Wainscott," she blurted out before she had time to think better of it.

Mrs. Talbot's eyes narrowed at once. "I knew it. Taking care of him has exhausted you, hasn't it? Are you ill? Have you spoken to Dr. Hayward about it?"

She sighed, dropping her gaze to the napkin in her lap. "I'm not ill, Mrs. Talbot. I'm...heartsick."

She chanced a glance up and saw Mrs. Talbot's faded eyes widen with surprise. "Ohhh," she murmured. "I see. You're suffering from a bit of...of unrequited feelings?"

"No." She cleared her throat uncomfortably. "My feelings...they were...requited." Good God, she'd never been so humiliated in all her life.

Mrs. Talbot's brows knitted. "I don't understand. Are you saying that you...that he..."

Emmaline nodded. "We fell in love. I know it was fast—I realize how utterly mad it must seem, considering how ill he was. Still, there's no denying what I felt. Some women are lucky to find a perfect love just once in their lives. I was lucky twice."

"Did you—that is to say, were you…"

"Yes, we were intimate." Emmaline's cheeks were burning now, her shame complete.

"And then he *left* you?" Mrs. Talbot sputtered indignantly. "But wait, wasn't that woman who came to town, the one he left with…wasn't that his fiancée?"

"His ex-fiancée," she corrected. "He'd broken off the engagement before he came here to Haverham. Apparently, she was having a hard time accepting it as fact."

Mrs. Talbot looked entirely flummoxed. "I still don't understand. If the two of you were in love, then why did he leave with her?"

How could she explain, when she barely understood it herself? "He left with her because I told him to; because I felt guilty and frightened and confused, all at once. I told him we could not have a future together. At the time, I believed it to be true. But now…now I'm not so sure."

"Oh, dear. There must be something you can do. Have you telephoned him?"

She shook her head, cupping her hands around her now-cold teacup. "It's not that simple."

"Of course it is," Mrs. Talbot said with a shrug. "You ended the relationship—so un-end it."

She sighed heavily. "I'm afraid there's no undoing it. I made my decision, and he readily accepted it. I cannot blame him—I was firm on the matter, and I left him no room for argument. Still…so much time has passed, and he has not made a single effort to contact me. I can only assume that that means he has moved on. Perhaps he's married Miss Lennox, after all. I told him that he should."

"I can't believe you would give up so easily. If you truly

love him, that is," Mrs. Talbot said. "And I would guess that you do, considering how miserable you've looked these past two months. Oh, dear God"—she clutched at Emmaline's wrist, her gaze drawn directly to Emmaline's midsection —"you're not...that's to say, he didn't...are you certain..."

"No, I'm not with child, if that's what you're asking." It was only after Jack left that she realized she very well might be. She'd actually cried when her menses came a week later, and to this day she wasn't sure if they were tears of relief or disappointment.

Mrs. Talbot let out a sigh of relief. "Thank heavens for that."

The sound of a car's motor in the drive drew their attention toward the front hall.

"Oh, that'll be Mr. Talbot," Mrs. Talbot cried, rising from her seat. "Bother that. What terrible timing the man has!How can I leave you now?"

"I'll be fine, Mrs. Talbot. Truly. And you were right—I do feel much better for having told you. How can I ever thank you for listening and not judging?"

Mrs. Talbot smiled weakly. "Just promise me that you won't give up, that you'll try to set things right with him. If you think he's deserving of your affection, that is."

"He's a lovely man," she said softly, realizing that she meant it with all her heart. "I only wish you'd had the chance to get to know him."

"Well, perhaps I will someday." A horn sounded, making Mrs. Talbot jump. "Oh, dear. I really must go. But don't fret, I have a feeling that this isn't quite over yet."

If only she were correct! The trouble was, Emmaline was nearly certain that she wasn't. She'd wasted too much time as it was waiting, hoping, biding her time. It was time to get on with her life, once and for all.

And that meant life *without* Jack Wainscott.

⌒

"Oh, don't laugh. I can try if I want." Emmaline filled the watering pail from the well, then carried it toward the roses —or, the barren rose bushes, as was the case.

This is what I'm reduced to, she thought to herself—talking to the image of the Green Man etched into the bench while she gardened. Anyone watching through the peephole in the garden gate, listening to her as she went about her business, would think that she'd lost her wits. And perhaps she had. She smiled to herself as she bent over the most promising of the bushes and doused it with water. This was the same bush that had produced the pink blooms in early May. Even now, she could see the beginnings of a few buds, though they never seemed to progress any more than that before withering away.

It was growing late in the season for roses, anyway. Perhaps she should turn her attention to something else, something that might bloom well into autumn. She knew she ought to give it up, that it was just an exercise in frustration, but she took pleasure in going through the motions. She'd come to enjoy the physical exertion. As long as she considered gardening a pleasant activity in which to indulge rather than a means to an end, there was no risk of disappointment.

Much like the letter she'd written to Jack just last week. She wasn't expecting a reply, but it had felt good to put the words on paper, to open up her heart and let the sentiments pour out. Mostly, she'd apologized—for doubting him, for pushing him away, for underestimating the strength of her feelings.

She'd managed to get his direction from the hotel. It had taken a bit of finagling on her part—she'd claimed that he'd left behind an expensive personal article that she'd only just found. And so she'd learned that he resided at Wainscott

House in Bedlington, Dorset. Apparently, that was all the direction needed. She'd gathered her courage and posted her letter with no expectations whatsoever of a reply.

At least, that's what she kept telling herself.

With a shrug, she set down the watering pail by the well and turned to survey the day's work. Beds were turned, dead stems were trimmed away, everything was watered and clipped and trimmed. Not that there was much to show for it.

She turned toward the Green Man's image. "I'm wasting my time, aren't I?" she asked with a laugh. "Go on and say it —I'm a stubborn, pig-headed woman who simply doesn't know when to give up."

"You're a stubborn, pig-headed woman who simply doesn't know when to give up," came a deep, decidedly male voice behind her.

It couldn't be...

With a gasp, Emmaline turned toward the voice, her heart beating so fast that she feared it might burst.

Dear God, it was him! Standing in front of the gate, his bowler hat in his hands, the late afternoon sun turning his fair hair to burnished gold. He looked like a vision, the most beautiful vision in all of England.

"Jack!" she called out, launching herself toward him. But she stopped short when she reached his side, suddenly afraid. What if she'd misinterpreted his presence there? What if he'd only come to deliver some papers regarding their lease agreement? Or worse, what if he'd changed his mind about allowing her to stay?

"I got your letter," he said, reaching inside his jacket and removing the folded page in question. He held it out, its edges frayed and worn. "I read it, over and over again."

She nodded, her mouth dry. "I see that."

"I hadn't allowed myself to hope, and yet your words...

well, I had to read them several times before I could believe them." He paused, staring down at the page, turning it over in his hands. "I hadn't expected this."

Oh, God, it was too late! He'd gone and married Claire Lennox. Her stomach clenched into a knot, and she feared that she might begin to retch.

He just continued to stare at the letter, saying nothing.

"Please, Jack," she whispered hoarsely, unable to bear it a moment more. "Don't torment me so. Just answer me this—is it too late? Did you...are you and Claire—"

"No!" he interjected, his hazel eyes widening. "Good God, no. Is that what you thought? I would have waited for you forever." His mouth curved into a smile, making her pulse leap.

Emmaline shook her head. "I should not have made you wait a single day. Will you ever forgive me?"

"There's nothing to forgive," he said. "If you'll have me, that is."

Her heart soared, her blood thrumming hotly through her veins. "How long were you planning to stay?"

He shrugged. "I was thinking perhaps forever. Unless, of course, you have other plans."

"But your home is in Dorset. However will we manage—"

"My father's home is in Dorset," he corrected. "Mine is wherever you are. I say, you've a spot of dirt, there on your nose."

Emmaline laughed, reaching up to swipe at her nose. Only Jack could finish off a romantic declaration in such a fashion! "There, is that better?"

"Come here," he said, voice breaking slightly on the last syllable.

She didn't waste a moment complying. Tears of relief flooded her eyes as he wrapped his arms around her. She could hear his heart hammering against his ribs, matching the rhythm of her own. She felt his lips against her hair, sending a shiver of delight down her spine.

"So, did he answer you?" Jack murmured against her ear.

Emmaline pulled away, looking up into Jack's amused eyes. Heavens, but she'd almost forgotten that such a lovely shade of hazel existed. "Did *who* answer me?"

"Why, the Green Man, I suppose. Isn't that who you were speaking with when I arrived?"

"Oh, *do* shut up!" she said, playfully punching his arm. "Besides, it's not polite to spy on someone unaware."

"Then why is there a peephole in the gate?"

"A fine question, indeed." The breeze stirred, warm and sultry against her cheek. Soon, it picked up momentum, making that odd sound it made when it blew through the garden's stone walls. Emmaline reached up to brush a stray lock of hair from her eyes.

"It almost sounds like laughter, doesn't it?" Jack asked, glancing around. "I think we've pleased him."

Emmaline rolled her eyes. "Pleased *who*? I vow, you speak in riddles!"

"Why, your Green Man, of course. I've an idea," he said, grinning now.

Emmaline decided to play along. "Oh?"

"Let's give him a show," Jack suggested. "One he won't soon forget. If he's to be imprisoned here forever, we might as well entertain him, don't you think?"

"He's not imprisoned forever," she corrected. "Just until three couples find true love in his enchanted garden. Wasn't that how the legend went?"

He shook his head. "I've forgotten. Maybe it was 'unleash their passion.' Something like that, I suppose."

"Perhaps *we're* the third," she said. "Wouldn't that be grand?"

Jack's grin grew wicked. "Let's show him, then."

"Here?" She glanced around, watching as the wind blew a twig across the flagstones behind him.

"I can't wait a moment more, Emmaline." His voice was hoarse, laced with desire.

She nodded. "Nor can I."

CHAPTER 12

*E*mmaline's fingers flew over her blouse's buttons. Jack stood back and watched, barely able to believe that this was happening—his wildest dream come true. He let out his breath in a rush as her blouse parted, revealing the creamy skin above her chemise.

"Come," she said, crooking one finger as she turned and led him farther into the garden, toward her favorite stone bench. He'd pictured her there so many times in the past two hellish months, the image of her burned into his brain. Now she looked like Eve herself, removing her clothing bit by bit as she made her way across the flagstones. By the time they reached the bench, nothing remained but her chemise and lacy knickers.

He quirked one brow. "My turn?" he asked, his fingers already hovering over his jacket's buttons, his cock hard and straining against his trousers.

"It's only fair, don't you think?" she asked, sitting on the bench and primly crossing her legs.

He turned and glanced back over his shoulder before

returning his attention to a near-naked Emmaline. In seconds, he'd doffed his coat and unbuttoned his shirt. "You're not expecting Mrs. Talbot, are you?" he asked, pulling his shirttails from the band of his trousers. "She does have a knack for arriving at inopportune moments. And there *is* a peephole, as we've discussed."

"Are you afraid of being caught in a compromising situation, Jack Wainscott?" A smile danced on her lips, lighting up her entire face.

He unbuttoned his trousers and stepped out of them, tossing them to the bench beside her. "Well, she *is* the vicar's wife. We would not want to shock her too horribly with our scandalous behavior. I haven't yet made an honest woman of you, after all."

"Oh, had you planned to?" she asked, reaching for the hem of her chemise and pulling it over her head, baring her breasts to his hungry gaze.

He stifled a groan, his hands nearly shaking with anticipation now. "Dear God, Emmaline," he groaned, barely able to keep his hands off her. "Just as soon as you'll let me. Tomorrow, if possible."

She laughed, rising to stand before him. Her fingers hooked into the waistband of her knickers, and he held his breath as she slowly slid them down, past her hips, to her ankles. Graceful as ever, she stepped out of them, entirely bare now.

His gaze skimmed down her body, from her face to her rose-tipped breasts, to the tantalizing dark triangle where her thighs joined, to her shapely calves down to her toes, and back up again. He saw her shiver in response, her skin flushed pink, her dark eyes burning with unconcealed desire.

"You are so very beautiful," he said in awe, amazed as ever that she was real, that she was there, that she was his.

"Tomorrow's a bit soon, don't you think?" she asked, taking two steps toward him. Her fingertips skimmed down his chest, drawing gooseflesh in their wake. "After all, I'm not going anywhere. And if you're here to stay..." Her fingers pushed past the band of his drawers, moving toward his cock.

"I'm here to stay," he answered breathlessly, watching incredulously as she lowered herself to the bench before him, her dark head bent toward him as she pushed down his drawers several more inches, till his erection sprang free. Devil take it, if she did what he thought she was going to—

A groan caught in the back of his throat as Emmaline's mouth closed over the tip of his cock. Slowly, she eased him deeper into her mouth, until the tip of him pressed against the back of her throat. Her lips tightened against his shaft, increasing the pressure as she drew him out again. Instinctively, he reached out to cup the back of her head, resisting the urge to close his eyes.

No, he wanted to see her. Holy hell and damnation, he wasn't going to last another second—he was going to come right then and there, before he'd even had the chance to pleasure *her*.

He tugged her to her feet, swinging her around so that she faced the bench now. In a matter of seconds, he'd managed to free himself of his drawers and pull her down atop him, straddling him, ready for her to ride him.

Their coupling was quick—hurried and frantic. With each stroke, he pulled her down harder, wanting to fill her entirely, wanting to make her writhe against him and cry out his name as she came.

Only when she began to do just that did he find his own release.

Emmaline laid her head against his shoulder, her

breathing slowing as they sat there, their bodies one as they listened to the songbirds calling gaily to one another, to the breeze ruffling the leaves, to an automobile horn off in the distance.

Jack could have sat like that forever, his heart thumping against hers, their bare skin warmed by the sun. A sense of peace filled him, and he bent to kiss her fragrant neck.

"That should do nicely," she murmured, sounding entirely sated.

He raised one brow. "Oh?"

"To convince the Green Man that we've found true love, I meant. Though if you'd like to try again—"

"Give me ten minutes," he said with a laugh.

She nodded, her tongue tracing lazy circles on his shoulder.

"I would say five, but I've been ill, remember?"

She sat up, her gaze meeting his. "Thank God for the Influenza. Otherwise, who's to say what might have happened?"

"Regardless, I would have preferred a more...well, *masculine* way of getting acquainted."

She brushed back a lock of his hair that had fallen across his forehead. "You were charming, even unconscious."

"How many days was I out again?"

"Nearly five. You talk, you know. In your sleep," she clarified, grinning at him. "Even when unconscious."

His brow furrowed. "Should I be worried?"

She shook her head. "You called out my name, more than once. Even though you'd only learned it moments before you collapsed."

He shifted her in his lap. "When I first awoke, I had no memory of you—of your name. Odd, isn't it?"

"Your subconscious must have remembered, that's all."

She shivered against him. "It's getting cool. We should go inside."

He rubbed his hands down her arms, trying to warm her. "I suppose we should. As much as I'd love to stay here, just like this, forever." Though in truth, the rough stones beneath him were starting to feel abrasive. Amazing how he hadn't even noticed before.

She disentangled herself and stood, reaching for her discarded clothing. "Let's go in and I'll give you a full examination, to make certain you've recovered fully," she offered, and he wasn't sure if she was teasing or not.

"No examinations! I'm no longer your patient." Dear God, the humiliation of it all.

"Well, then, perhaps you'd like to examine *me*, instead?" she teased.

"I say, now that's a fine idea." He nodded, excited by the possibilities.

She reached down and plucked his drawers from the stones, her eyes dancing with mischief. "Catch me, then," she called out, dashing toward the garden gate.

He wasted no time at all in complying.

As the gate latched shut behind the pair of lovers, a voice on the wind could be heard on the breeze, laughing in delight.

Then there were three, it seemed to say.

And now...I am free.

Two weeks later...

"But...but it's impossible," Emmaline stammered, turning in a slow circle.

Jack shrugged. "It would seem so. And yet...just look."

Emmaline could barely believe her eyes—she was standing amid a sea of color. Green, blue, purple, pink, yellow...color, everywhere.

The roses, well past their season, were in full bloom. Bluebells, violets, lilies, peonies, hollyhocks...they all blossomed in a lush profusion of color and scent, creating a multicolored palette that filled the entire walled-in space.

Emmaline blinked rapidly, thinking that perhaps her eyes were playing tricks on her, but the view remained the same.

The well still stood in the center, and the bench remained in the shady corner. That much hadn't changed.

Only, the garden had come to life around them.

"Amazing, isn't?" Mrs. Talbot asked. "I declare, I simply did not think it possible."

"Nor did I," said Jack, the fading sun turning his hair a dull copper.

Emmaline planted her hands on her hips. "I don't see how anyone could have thought it possible."

Mrs. Talbot nodded, her eyes shining brightly. "I should bring Mr. Talbot here to see this. It's almost like...like a miracle."

"Or something like that," Jack said, holding up the tattered leather book that he'd retrieved from the library just before they'd stepped outside.

"You don't think..." Emmaline trailed off, unwilling to voice her thoughts aloud in front of Mrs. Talbot.

Jack strode purposely toward the stone bench, tapping the Green Man's image while grinning at Emmaline. His look seemed to say, "I told you so."

Emmaline just grinned back at him.

"Shall we go inside for dinner?" Jack asked, reaching for Emmaline's hand.

"Indeed. I'm famished," said Mrs. Talbot.

Emmaline nodded, allowing Jack to thread his fingers through hers. She glanced up at him—her Beltane miracle—and smiled, saying a silent thanks to whomever had brought them together.

And then, no longer alone, she fell into step between them—Jack and Mrs. Talbot—and headed toward home.

EPILOGUE

Two years later...

"I'm so glad you were able to come for the christening," Emmaline said as she passed a steaming cup of tea to Aisling.

Aisling took it and set it on the wrought iron table between the two women, then glanced over at the small, pink-cheeked babe sleeping in the pram beneath a dipping branch of lush, fragrant peonies.

"I wouldn't have missed it for the world," Aisling said with a grin. "Damn, but Corinne is a beautiful baby. I still can't believe it...Jack, a father?" She shook her head. "Honestly, I never thought I'd see the day."

"He's wonderful with her," Emmaline said, beaming. "All he has to do is pick her up and she stops crying at once. I've never seen anything quite like it. He must have the magic touch with infants. It's truly a delight to watch them together."

"I've never seen him so happy, Emmaline. He's walking on air these days."

"Who's walking on air?" Jack called out as he opened the gate.

Aisling waved her brother away. "Oh, bugger off. Can't you leave us in peace for a moment? I thought you and Will were going into town?"

"We were, but look who we found instead." Jack moved aside, revealing a smartly dressed woman in a traveling dress and wide-brimmed straw hat.

Emmaline rose abruptly. "Madeline! I can't believe you're really here. And look at you! As beautiful as ever."

"Look at *you*," Madeline demurred. "I see that marriage and motherhood suit you well. You're positively radiant."

Emmaline took her arm and led her forward, into the garden. "Come, you must meet my sister-in-law, Aisling Cooper."

The two women greeted each other warmly before their attention turned to the sleeping babe.

"What a little beauty," Madeline said. "I'm so delighted for you, Emmaline." Tears shone in her eyes. "Truly, I am."

"Did Henry and Genevieve travel with you?" Emmaline asked, glancing over to where the men stood near the garden gate, conversing easily. She did not see Madeline's ginger-haired children in tow, but perhaps they'd been left at the hotel with a nursemaid. They were lovely children, both.

Madeline shook her head. "Lord, no. They're spending the week in London with Francis. The timing was perfect, really."

Emmaline was not acquainted with Madeline's husband Francis, and from what she'd heard about the man, she was glad—glad that the pair lived separately, that Madeline had taken a lover.

Emmaline had first met Madeline, Lady Briarton, on a holiday to Herefordshire the previous year. A chance meeting in the village had led to an immediate bond of friendship, one they'd continued via regular correspondence. After all, Emmaline was not one to discount chance encounters—it had seemed as if the two women were fated to meet, to become kindred spirits.

The twinkle in her friend's eyes and the blush in her cheeks meant that Madeline continued to find happiness with her lover—a happiness she much deserved, no matter the unconventional circumstances. Madeline had remained rather secretive about the man, claiming he'd been away from Herefordshire during Emmaline's visit, but she was sure there was more to the story than her friend was letting on.

"Is there any chance I'll finally get to meet the mysterious Simon McKenzie?" she asked in a hushed tone.

"After nightfall, perhaps," Madeline whispered back. "There's much to explain, though you may not believe it."

"This sounds very intriguing, indeed," Aisling added, rubbing her hands together conspiratorially.

Emmaline nodded. "Just beware, Madeline—Aisling here in a novelist, and anything you tell her might find its way into one of her scandalous stories."

"Oh, don't listen to her," Aisling said with a smirk. "Besides, she loves my stories."

Madeline glanced around in wide-eyed appreciation, as if she'd just taken notice of her surroundings. "Heavens, but this garden! It's a veritable Eden. I had no idea you had such a green thumb."

"Nor did I." Emmaline exchanged a secret smile with her husband.

"I've never seen peonies so large, or roses so full. I vow, that one's the size of a dinner plate." Madeline leaned toward a blush-colored bloom and inhaled deeply. "So fragrant, too."

Will joined them, nodding as he glanced around the outdoor space. "This garden is nothing short of amazing. I hope Emmaline will let me take some cuttings and soil samples back to Cambridge."

"And I hope you'll let me keep some of your sketches," Emmaline returned with a smile. Will had spent the past two mornings in the garden, painstakingly sketching each species in colored pencil, capturing incredible detail in his work. "I'd love to frame them to hang in the front parlor. You know, bring a bit of the garden into the room, since its windows only look out on the lane."

"It would be my pleasure," Will said, looking pleased. "You've really done remarkable things here."

"My husband is a botanist," Aisling said to Madeline in way of explanation. "This garden is like his every fantasy come true."

"No, love, *you're* my every fantasy come true," Will teased. "But you must admit, this garden is quite miraculous."

"My wife is a miracle worker." Jack moved to his wife's side and placed a gentle kiss on her cheek. "In more ways than one," he added with a grin.

"Will you two save it for the bedroom?" Aisling said snappily, though her twinkling eyes belied her amusement. Jack and Aisling always pretended to scrabble, but it was all for show. Emmaline had never seen such honest affection between siblings, and it never failed to warm her heart. She hoped to give Corinne a brother someday, and that they would be as close as Jack and Aisling were—as close as Aisling and Will's own children were, a boy and two girls, all as thick as thieves.

Emmaline shooed away her husband. "Now, off with you —into town as you promised, and bring us back some scones from the bakery. Us ladies have much to discuss before this wee one wakes up, demanding to be fed."

"Oh, very well," Jack said with mock indignation. "It was lovely to see you again, Lady Briarton."

"Likewise," Madeline said with a nod in Jack's direction.

"Sit," Emmaline said to Madeline, indicating the empty chair beside Aisling, "and let me pour you some tea."

As the gate clicked shut behind the departing men, Emmaline's gaze was drawn toward the carving of the Green Man, who seemed to be smiling at her—laughing, perhaps. She smiled back, then returned her attention to the women before her.

"I've much to tell you—both of you. But first...do you believe in magic?"

～

ABOUT THE AUTHOR

Kristina Cook (writing here as Kristi Astor) is the author of more than a dozen books for adults and teens, ranging from historical and NASCAR romance to paranormal and contemporary young adult fiction (also writing as Kristi Cook). Since the publication of her first novel in 2004, her books (with Kensington/Zebra Books, Harlequin Books, and Simon & Schuster) have hit national bestseller lists, landed on bookseller association lists, and won awards, including the National Reader's Choice Award.

Kristina lives in New York City with her husband and two daughters.

ALSO BY KRISTI ASTOR

Lover's Dawn (Celtic Heat Vol. 1)

Midnight Sins (Celtic Heat Vol. 2)

Rites of Passion (Celtic Heat Vol. 3)

Swept Away

A Midnight Clear

ALSO BY KRISTINA COOK

Unlaced

Unveiled

Undressed

To Love a Scoundrel

CPSIA information can be obtained
at www.ICGtesting.com
Printed in the USA
BVHW051704220622
640430BV00001B/9